Praise for R. J. Pineiro's *Retribution*

"A story as frighteningly real as tomorrow's headlines . . . extensively researched . . . introduces a potpourri of the latest high-tech military hardware . . . One has to look no further than this book to get the most probable scenario for World War III."

—Richard Henrick, bestselling author of
Crimson Tide and *Ice Wolf*

"Pineiro's *Retribution* is a tightly plotted, fast-paced thriller that reads like future history. Terrorism has come to our shores in many ways, but Pineiro's version of what might be evokes visceral fear. We should heed the warning in this work of fiction, lest we suffer the consequences of reality."

—Mark Berent, bestselling author of
Rolling Thunder and *Storm Flight*

"R. J. Pineiro has a superb command of the shadowy world of nuclear proliferation and the forces of Islamic extremism that could lead to a nuclear attack on the West. *Retribution* is a blueprint for nuclear terrorism in the twenty first century."

—Dick Couch, author of
Pressure Point and *Silent Descent*

Praise for R. J. Pineiro's *Ultimatum*

"Ultimately, the book has it all: current defense technology, well-crafted characters and an action-packed plot. Move over Tom Clancy, there us a new kid on the block."

—*Library Journal*

"*Ultimatum* is the purest technothriller I've seen in years. This book may define the genre."   —Stephen Coonts

"A realistic and timely scenario a la Desert Storm . . . the jet fighters are new, but the action has that dramatic, urgent flair that has entertained readers and audiences since the days of Errol Flynn . . . Get two and give one to a friend."   —*Austin Chronicle*

Praise for R. J. Pineiro's *Conspiracy.com*

"Pineiro writes with humor and flair . . . a mainstream adrenaline rush . . . an entertaining story."   —*Publishers Weekly*

"Pineiro's latest high-tech thriller should please his fans. This one is very detailed, very technical, and very intricate. The story here is smart."   —*Booklist*

Praise for R. J. Pineiro's *Exposure*

"A lickety-split new novel . . . keeps the action churning and the suspense on high." —*Publishers Weekly*

"Grisham fans will enjoy this well-written version of *The Pelican Brief* meets *The Net*." —*Austin American Statesman*

"Taut . . . gets off to a bang-up start . . . a fast-paced thriller that cuts to the chase often." —*Kirkus Reviews*

"Suspenseful . . . exciting." —*The Baton Rouge Morning Advocate*

Praise for R. J. Pineiro's *Breakthrough*

"A suspenseful, transnational thriller . . . rough-and-tumble entertainment with violent action and plot twists aplenty." —*Kirkus Reviews*

"Fast paced, suspenseful." —*Publishers Weekly*

BOOKS BY R. J. PINEIRO

SHUTDOWN

R. J. PINEIRO

FORGE®

A TOM DOHERTY ASSOCIATES BOOK
NEW YORK

NOTE: If you purchased this book without a cover you should be aware that this book is stolen property. It was reported as "unsold and destroyed" to the publisher, and neither the author nor the publisher has received any payment for this "stripped book."

This is a work of fiction. All the characters and events portrayed in this book are either products of the author's imagination or are used fictitiously.

SHUTDOWN

Copyright © 2000 by Rogelio J. Pineiro

All rights reserved, including the right to reproduce this book, or portions thereof, in any form.

A Forge Book
Published by Tom Doherty Associates, LLC
175 Fifth Avenue
New York, NY 10010

www.tor.com

Forge® is a registered trademark of Tom Doherty Associates, LLC.

ISBN: 0-812-57504-0
Library of Congress Catalog Card Number: 00-026434

First edition: May 2000
First mass market edition: January 2002

Printed in the United States of America

0 9 8 7 6 5 4 3 2 1

This book is dedicated to the most brilliant, innovative, passionate, and courageous man I know:

My father, Rogelio A. Pineiro. *El Ingeniero.*

And

For the victims of the September 11th terrorist strikes in New York City, Washington, D.C., and Pennsylvania.

AUTHOR'S NOTE AND ACKNOWLEDGMENTS

The terrorist strikes against America on September 11th changed our nation forever. As we mourned our dead and braced ourselves for a long war against terrorism at home and abroad, we also must realize that another kind of terrorist threat is looming over the horizon. I'm not talking about chemical, biological, or nuclear terrorism. I'm talking about the much overlooked cyberterrorism threat. While a traditional terrorist must first acquire or develop explosives, chemicals, germs, or other type of weapon, and then devise an effective means of delivering it to his target, a cyberterrorist can achieve the same objective far easier from anywhere on the planet as long as he has access to a cheap computer, a modem, and a phone line. Launching cyberterrorist strikes against America from halfway around the world is as attractive to a rogue group as it is deadly—and very real.

2001 was called in the high-tech community "The Year of the Worm." The *computer* worm, that is. *Code Red*, a worm that infected a half million sites and caused over a billion dollars in damages worldwide is but one example of what a determined criminal hacker, or a cyberterrorist, can do to our vulnerable Internet. Early in 2001, commercial sites like Yahoo and Amazon were shut down through well-orchestrated Denial-of-Services attacks. And there are many other virtual weapons beyond worms, viruses, and DOS strikes available to cyberterrorists. The Internet—and our high-tech society in general—is quite susceptible to such attacks. All it takes is a determined rogue group with the right skills, connections, and resources to pull it off. And it can all be done without ever setting foot on American soil.

This book, which explores the possibility of a very innovative and devastating cyberterrorism strike against America, came about with the help of many talented individuals who contributed in different but significant ways throughout the entire process. All errors that remain, or course, are my own.

The following have my gratitude: Saint Jude, saint of the impossible, for continuing to make it possible.

My father, Rogelio A. Pineiro, for setting the highest example of what a husband, a father, and an engineer should be. Your discipline, courage, guidance, patience, and love has made me the man I am today. I can only hope to be half as good a father to Cameron as you were to me.

My wife and best friend, Lory Anne. What can I say to someone who is spending the best years of her life by my side, supporting my endeavors, my projects, helping me fulfill my own dreams at the cost of putting hers on hold? Lory, you have my eternal gratitude, loyalty, and love. None of this would ever have happened without you.

My son, Cameron, for making me so proud with your good heart and accomplishments. You have already passed your old man in just about every aspect of your life, from schoolwork to martial arts. Keep up the good work, kid! Your dad loves you very much.

Many thanks go to Tom Doherty and Bob Gleason, for your continued support, encouragement, and guidance through the turbulent world of publishing. Thanks also go to the rest of the staff at Tor Books, including Linda Quinton, Karen Lovell, Jennifer Marcus, and Brian Callaghan. You're the best.

My agent at Trident Media, Matthew Bialer. All authors should be as lucky as I've been to find the right partner so early in their writing careers.

My good friend and coworker Dave. In addition to being one heck of an engineer, your vast knowledge of weapons, aviation, and intelligence tactics has helped *Shutdown* become a better story.

The rest of my family: Dora, Irene, Dorita, Mike, Linda, Bill, Maureen, and all the children, for always being there for me.

A month ago I celebrated the twelfth-year anniversary of my writing career. Never in my wildest dreams did I imagine it would have taken off this way. Thanks go to all of my readers for your support through the years. Please drop me a note if you get a chance. I always take the time to read them and also to reply.

God Bless,

R. J. Pineiro
Austin, Texas
October 2001

Visit the author at www.rjpineiro.com or send him an E-mail at author@rjpineiro.com

"This is our calling. This is the calling of the United States of America. Terrorists live in the shadows under the cover of darkness. We will shine the light of justice on them."

—President George W. Bush, speaking about the
    terrorists responsible for the September 11th attacks.

"The General Accounting Office concluded that the capabilities needed to protect the nation's critical infrastructure from cyber attacks have not yet been achieved."

—*Computerworld* Magazine article titled,
    "FBI Cybersecurity Unit Faulted, Again."

PROLOGUE

CIA officer Paul Maddox advanced silently, with practiced ease, under a crystalline sky in southern Japan, carefully checking his surroundings for sounds that didn't belong in the woods.

Beads of perspiration ran down his face, into his eyes, stinging them. His dark olive camouflage shirt, drenched with sweat, stuck to his back, bothering him. Maddox twisted his back in both directions to no avail; the soaked fabric remained glued to his skin.

He exhaled in frustration and checked his 9-mm Beretta pistol, safely tucked inside the Velcro-secured pocket of the black gear vest he wore over the cammies.

A pine resin fragrance filled his lungs as a light breeze caressed his face. Maddox momentarily closed his eyes, chin high, welcoming it.

He followed the narrow trail as it veered to the left, bordering knee-high bushes and opulent trees overlooking Osaka. The heat, humidity, and incessant buzzing of mosquitoes made the long hike all the more challenging, particularly when shouldering a nylon backpack that became heavier with every step he took up the slippery incline.

Exhausted, his lungs burning as much as his legs and shoulders, Maddox paused by a cluster of wiry trees flanked by moss-slick boulders, his tired eyes momentarily taking in the vast city expanding across the valley.

I'm too old for this job, he thought, wondering why he had not sent one of his young subordinates to do it. But the answer came a second later. This mission was too important to leave in the hands of a rookie, making the forty-five-year-old Tokyo CIA station chief regret the extra twenty pounds he had gained in the past five years.

The glow from the city diffused in the smog trapped by the surrounding mountains.

Osaka. Colorful and prosperous, polluted and overcrowded, one of Japan's top economic centers during the 1980s, second only to Tokyo. From a distance Maddox couldn't see the crime and corruption that had come with the old tidal wave of economic prosperity. But the corruption was there, in the boardrooms of shrewd businessmen manipulating the world's markets to suit their personal agendas, beneath the glowing lights of luxurious hotels built to resemble prototypes for future architecture, where the virgin daughters of unknown fishermen and street merchants were regularly used to close business deals, to win over the competition, to add a level of decadence to the capitalistic credo of economic proliferation, even in Japan's worst recession. With such greed also came a black market, controlled by organized crime, which had ties to the deadly Aum Shinrikyo, the Japanese terrorist organization responsible for the Sarin nerve-gas attack in a Tokyo subway many years ago. From women, alcohol, and drugs, to clothing, jewelry, and electronics, the underground markets of Asia belonged to the opportunists, the ruthless . . . the deceitful.

Maddox glared at the glass, marble, and steel structure of the Osaka Hilton International, in the heart of Osaka's business district, recalling the meeting the night before with a young courtesan, a beautiful child corrupted by the system. He remembered the offer he had made for information. The girl, no older than Maddox's own daughter at UCLA, often entertained local executives and visiting officials from Tokyo, some of them suspected by the CIA to have connections inside the Aum Shinrikyo.

Maddox wiped the perspiration accumulated on his brow and continued up the trail, just as he had been instructed the night before, reaching the edge of a leaf-littered plateau roughly halfway up the mountain, where the whistling wind channeling through the range swirled the canopy overhead, masking the noise from the city. The place was remote, secluded, safe, providing a perfect vantage point for his mission.

He dropped to a crouch, removed his backpack, and unzipped the top. He extracted a powerful camera lens with night-vision capability and attached it to the body of a 35-mm Nikon before pressing the rubber end against his left eye, disabling the automatic zoom to minimize noise. He adjusted the manual zoom by turning the front of the foot-long lens clockwise. The low-light intensifying hardware in the lens changed the night into palettes of green, providing Maddox with a view of the clearing where, according to the young courtesan, a secret meeting between high-ranking Japanese officials was supposed to take place this evening.

Maddox set up a small antenna dish connected to a listening device with a range of five hundred feet. He put on a pair of headphones, adjusted the settings to mask out background noise, and inserted a miniature tape into the recording unit. Checking his watch, he settled in between two trees and a clump of boulders, safely out of sight from the road, and covered himself and his equipment with a camouflage poncho that he had already sprayed with an herbal scent that matched the local flora.

Thirty minutes later a pair of headlights pierced the night, their yellowish glow forking through the trees. The van came to a stop next to the clearing and four figures got out, all bearing automatic weapons. A leashed Doberman leaped out of the van last, remaining close to one of the armed men.

Probes.

Maddox tensed when he saw the monstrous dog accompanying the probes, sent ahead to ensure the safety of the meeting. He silently prayed that the herbal spray would do its magical job.

The foursome performed a thorough sweep of the clearing, coming to within ten feet of Maddox, who kept his Beretta leveled at the closest figure, hoping that he would not have to use the pistol on this warm and breezy night. The Doberman sniffed the ground and momentarily looked in Maddox's direction. The CIA officer froze, holding his breath, his index finger softly rubbing the trigger. The dog was much bigger than he had originally estimated, mostly black with a few brown spots over its powerful hind legs. Not relishing the thought of what kind of damage such a beast could do to a man, Maddox decided he would take it first, then the sentries.

The monster dog kept going.

Maddox slowly let go of the breath he had been holding. *There's got to be an easier way to make a living.* He holstered the Beretta.

The probes returned to the van, one of them reaching for a radio strapped to his belt.

More lights came up the road a minute later. This time he spotted two Mercedes limousines. Maddox snapped pictures of the license plates and of the face of one of the men who got out of the first Mercedes, Konichi Tanaka, head of the Japanese Defense Agency, Japan's CIA. He shifted the camera to the second Mercedes and waited as three more armed men left the vehicle and quickly scanned the grounds with visible apprehension before assisting their passenger out of the rear door.

Swallowing hard, forcing his professional side to quench his growing excitement, Maddox silently thanked the young courtesan while snapping pictures of the short figure stepping out of the German car: Fuji Yokonawa, Japan's minister of industry and commerce.

Maddox's left index finger frantically pressed the Nikon's trigger as Minister Yokonawa approached Tanaka. He activated the recording device and listened intently to a language he had learned to master long ago. Still, he was glad the recorder was there, because they spoke with such alacrity that Maddox had trouble deciphering the entire conversation real time. He would use the recorder to perform a full transcription back at the American embassy in Tokyo.

Yokonawa:	Have you . . . the recruiting in America?
Tanaka:	We have . . . twenty-three engineers . . . Money can be a . . . motivator.
Yokonawa:	I need assurances that . . . secret will . . . The recruits must be . . .
Tanaka:	They are expendable. All links . . . eliminated by the Aum Shinrikyo . . .
Yokonawa:	. . . plans . . . activation date must be executed . . . without mistake . . . Timed with our . . . investments . . .
Tanaka:	The time . . . set for two years . . . Before the First . . . occurs.
Yokonawa:	Our . . . not be harmed, right?
Tanaka:	. . . companies safe from . . .

Aching from tension, Maddox was so caught up in the conversation, struggling to capture and comprehend every word, that he missed the fact that the driver of Minister Yokonawa's Mercedes began to turn the vehicle around for the trip downhill. In doing so, the driver inadvertently flashed the headlights directly at Maddox for a brief moment as he straightened the vehicle.

A few seconds later two guards raced to the minister and Tanaka, whispered something Maddox could not capture, and rapidly ushered them to the waiting vehicles while three guards began to run in Maddox's direction, their flashlights converging on him.

His skin crawled when he realized that the guards must have spotted the glint of glass reflecting off his camera lens when the headlights had flashed him.

Engines roared as the Mercedes fled.

Out of choices, Maddox crept back from the edge of the clearing, drawing his Beretta, leveling it at the chest of the center guard and firing twice, the reports thundering in the night.

The dark figure arched back on impact.

Maddox rolled to his right as bullets ripped through his equipment, the debris striking his torso, tearing his clothing, piercing his skin. The Beretta's muzzle flashes had given the surviving guards a clear target in the night.

His side ablaze, Maddox continued the roll as the rattle of machine guns whipped through the woods, creating multiple explosions of grass, dirt, leaves, and fragments of surveillance gear. His right shoulder crashed against a tree. The adrenaline rush deadening the pain, Maddox jumped to his feet, racing deep in the forest, searching for a new vantage point, spotting a wide tree stump beyond a bundle of ferns. The operative took three leaping steps through the waist-high ferns before diving behind the stump, landing on his side, next to the stump's fallen log, narrowed eyes looking for a new target.

Thirty feet away the two surviving guards reached his original vantage point as three others caught up with them, one of them accompanied by the Doberman on steroids. He could not possibly take them and the horse they called a dog all in a straight fight. He aimed the Beretta at the closest target and fired once. A man clutched his chest as the others whipped their weapons in his direction.

Pivoting, Maddox wriggled away from the stump, which exploded in a puff of rotted wood as he rose to a deep crouch and raced downhill, the wind hissing, his side burning, the firing momentarily stopping, replaced by the footsteps of his pursuers.

Branches scratched him, trees blurred as he scrambled down the trail, sweat sticking to his shirt. Or was it blood?

A bullet walloped into a tree to his left, bursting into a cloud of bark. Another round nipped the collar of his shirt.

Maddox cut left and zigzagged past several wide trunks, hiding behind one, pressing his back against the bark, Beretta clutched with both hands, muzzle pointed at the canopy overhead, through which moonlight filtered to induce a soft glow in the otherwise dark woods.

A burst of gunfire struck a tree a dozen feet away. His pursuers had momentarily lost him, providing him with the opportunity to fire again without the risk of getting shot first. Two down, four more to go. He had seven rounds in the Beretta and two more clips of ten in his vest. Confidence suddenly filled him. Perhaps he did have a chance.

Crouching while turning around and sidestepping, Maddox watched a dark shape sprint toward him at great speed. The Doberman's distorted face, crowned by a set of gleaming fangs that appeared to dislodge themselves from the jaw, rushed toward him like a biblical curse. The beast leaped the ten feet separating them in a single bound, knocking him back with great force before he could fire. Maddox landed hard on his back as the Doberman clamped its jaw on his groin.

The CIA officer screamed in agonizing pain as the Doberman shook its head vigorously while growling, lifting Maddox's lower body off the ground, tearing into him with incredible strength. Pain maddened, fighting the urge to vomit, his vision tunneling, Maddox invoked the last of his self-control, bringing the Beretta down, firing point-blank at the dog's head.

An explosion of bloody debris momentarily blinded him. Trembling hands reached down, freeing himself from the dog's snout, still clamped on him like a medieval torture device.

Moaning, swallowing hard, Maddox heard footsteps crushing the cushion of dry leaves to his left.

Clenching his teeth, remaining on his knees, he blinked rapidly to clear his vision and followed one of the nearing silhouettes with the Beretta, squeezing a single shot, the muzzle flash briefly illuminating the woods, like a bolt of lightning. The figure dropped and the others immediately turned in his direction.

Maddox had a second silhouette already aligned but

didn't get the chance to fire. A powerful blow to his abdomen lifted him off the ground and shoved him against a wide trunk with animal strength. Maddox tried to get up, but his legs would not obey him. He had lost sensation below the waist and suddenly felt cold, nauseated. In a way he felt lucky. He could no longer feel the pain in his maimed groin.

Maddox's vision failed as he fiddled at the edge of consciousness for another moment before expiring.

1

THE *SILVER COMET*

SOUTHERN FLORIDA, TWO YEARS LATER

A light fog lifted off the tranquil swamp, enveloping concrete piers supporting a double set of railroad tracks that disappeared in the darkness. Moonlight diffused through the rising haze, casting a grayish glow across the Everglades on this warm and clear evening. Birds squawked in the distance as they found a place to settle for the night. Nocturnal creatures began to stir, readying themselves to hunt for food while at the same time trying to avoid becoming food in this vast ecosystem. Hundreds of pairs of red-orange coals caught in the moonglow began to drift along the dark water, sometimes disappearing below the surface. Alligators, the top of the region's food chain, reaching lengths of up to eighteen feet and sporting jaws capable of ripping a man in half, hunted their natural prey, killifish, mullet, silversides, and menhaden, occasionally feasting on unsuspecting birds like grebes and bitterns. The bellows emitted by the cigar-shaped predators mixed with the whistling breeze and the incessant clicking of insects.

Beyond the edge of the swamp, another sound joined the natural noises of southern Florida. The sleek shape of Amtrak's flagship, the *Silver Comet*, raced down the tracks at eighty miles per hour on its way to Miami, its halogen headlights slicing through the fog. Six deluxe passenger carriages, four double-decker cars with glass tops for observation, three spacious dining cars, and six Pullman cars for sleeping made up the most luxurious passenger train in the United States. The *Comet* had provided travelers with a safer alternative to air travel after the terrorist strikes of 2001. Two diesel engines pulled the *Comet* and its two hundred passengers, some of whom dined on gourmet meals prepared by the experienced kitchen staff. Other passengers gazed at the stars in the double-deckers while the rest retired to the Pullmans. Most of them would die in minutes, their fate sealed five minutes before, when the *Silver Comet* passed a computer-controlled switching station west of Boca Raton, prior to entering the east edge of the Everglades. The fully automated station controlled railroad traffic flowing north and south by assigning tracks to specific trains at preprogrammed times. Up to that point the system had performed flawlessly since becoming operational two years ago, eliminating the need for operators at remote switching stations and the possibility of human error due to boredom and fatigue.

The *Comet* had traveled most of its way south from West Palm Beach on the right track of the railway system, passing a couple of freight trains traveling north on the left track. Southwest of Boca Raton, the computer-controlled system malfunctioned, switching the *Comet* to the left track, putting it in a collision course with a northbound train from Miami, before abruptly shutting down. Track monitors installed along the railway to prevent such collisions sent repeated distress signals to the computerized system, but the malfunctioning equipment did not relay the messages to the Orlando or Miami Amtrak stations, where operators on duty might have been able to alert the trains in time to avoid a disaster.

The shift engineer in the *Silver Comet*'s lead engine thought nothing of the change. Track switching was commonplace in the railways. The first hint of a problem didn't occur until a minute before the trains collided, when the freight train engineer noticed that the *Silver Comet* appeared to be running on the same track. He immediately applied the brakes while blowing the horn. But the phenomenal momentum of a two-mile-long freight train could not be stopped in such short distance. The engineer aboard the *Comet* reacted quickly, also slamming on the brakes as the two trains approached each other at a closing speed of over a hundred and twenty miles per hour. Passengers and crew members were hurled forward, thrown against the front sections of each cabin as the train decelerated.

Steel wheels skidded across the tracks with the sound of a million nails scratching a blackboard. Metal ground against metal, creating clouds of sparks that cascaded over the swamp. The impact came thirty seconds later, as thousands of tons of metal travelling in opposite directions collided head-on, compressing the lead engines to three quarters of their original length, applying incredible pressure to the fuel tanks, which exploded a fraction of a second later with metal-ripping force. The outburst of ignited diesel turned the night into day, blasting metallic debris in a radial pattern. The scorching shrapnel whistled through the air, piercing the fuel cells in the other engines in a chain reaction that lasted but two seconds, creating a roaring fist of orange and yellow-gold flames five hundred feet high.

The force of the impact and the shockwave from the blast propagated down the cars closest to the front of each train, lifting them off the tracks, tossing them in the air like toys. The *Comet*'s passenger carriages plunged into the swamp like harpoons, splashing sheets of water and mud over the twisted tracks. The dining and Pullman cars followed, colliding into each other, slicing through the hazy night like bullets, stabbing the swamp. The double-deckers in the rear derailed and jackknifed, their glass domes reflecting the scarlet glow of the billowing fire before shattering from the impact.

The freight train, many times longer than the *Comet*, continued to derail for another thirty seconds. Tank cars spilled toxic chemicals in the water on impact, some also exploding, creating stroboscopic bursts of crimson flames in the distance. Vehicles shot out the thin walls of auto carriers like pellets from a shotgun, crashing into the water. A dozen boxcars leaped off a broken section of the track, turning on their sides as they fell into the swamp, some spilling their contents while smashing into the darkness below. A group of lucky hoboes emerged from one of the few box cars that remained on the tracks, their bewildered eyes scanning the destruction around them. Train cars angled in every direction crowded the sides of the elevated tracks, some jammed into the swamp, others hanging halfway off the tracks, many resting on their sides in the dark waters.

Half of the *Comet*'s passengers perished in the initial seconds following the collision, incinerated by the expanding fireball or crushed by the wreckage. The rest found themselves trapped inside the carriages, water streaming through broken windows, through gashes in the floor and sides, along with the stench of burnt flesh mixed with the smoke billowing from the blaze. Women screamed. Children cried. The wounded moaned. A group of men in a double-decker turned on its side dragged survivors out of the carriage and waded away from the swelling flames spreading over the surface of the swamp. Many were bleeding from the wounds sustained during the collision or when the glass dome collapsed on them. Survivors from the other cars slowly surfaced and began gathering atop the silver islands of twisted metal that were the farthest from the flames and the intense heat. The spilled fuel continued to burn, its flames licking the night sky, illuminating the macabre sight, swallowing two additional passenger cars before all survivors could escape. Agonizing shrieks filled the night as the flames enveloped a dozen passengers trapped inside, their skin peeling away from the intense heat inside the ovenlike carriages.

Then the alligators came, their nostrils detecting blood in the water, sensing wounded prey. They closed in on the unsuspecting survivors as they struggled to leave the lashing flames and scorching heat, as they tried to climb up the wrecked cars to get out of the water. A woman holding an infant screamed as a reptile whipped its tail and leaped out of the darkness, clamping its jaws over her head and shoulders, dragging her beneath the surface. The baby fell into the water and another alligator jumped after it.

Havoc set in. People screamed in horror, shoving others aside to reach high ground. The first helicopter arrived almost thirty minutes after the accident, its rotor downwash blowing away the rising smoke. The craft's powerful halogens swept the wreckage, searching for survivors, finding them in tightly packed clusters atop a few derailed cars sprinkled on the swamp, away from the ravaging flames. Soon other rescue craft reached the scene, including a half dozen coast guard helicopters, which lowered harnesses to airlift survivors.

The following day the cleanup job began, the removal of tens of thousands of gallons of toxic chemicals ranging from sulfuric acid to ammonia. It took Amtrak officials, working in conjunction with the Florida Railway Commission and the U.S. Army Corps of Engineers, over a month to clean the area, including the sickening task of matching body parts. Out of the 247 passengers and staff only eighty-three survived. Many were never found.

A thorough investigation tracked the cause of the accident to a faulty computer board in the primary control system of the switching station. The old analog backup system had failed to come on line. Further analysis revealed that the board had failed due to a mysterious shutdown of the TI6500, a microcontroller chip manufactured by Texas Instruments. The computer giant began the immediate recall of tens of thousands of TI6500 microcontrollers from the field. The instant that the results of the Florida Railroad Commission were made public, a class-action suit was filed by the families of the victims against Texas Instruments, Inc.

2

ACCELERATION FACTOR

WASHINGTON, D.C.

Dusk in the nation's capital.

The midsummer sun's dying beams splashed the Washington Monument, the Capitol, the Lincoln Memorial, and the White House with majestic crimson hues before a blanket of stars rolled over the city. Streetlights flickered and came on, washing avenues and boulevards with grayish light.

The sight, however, was largely ignored by the commuters stuck in the congested traffic around Dupont Circle. Impatient and angered drivers lay on their horns, many shouting from open windows, kicking off a cacophonous concerto up Massachusetts, New Hampshire, and Connecticut avenues. Most were government employees, servants of the people, eager to leave their hundreds of thousands of bureaucratic desks, keyboards, phones, rubber stamps, staplers, and paper clips, to finally head home. Some of them had been elected to their jobs, others had been appointed, most everyone else had been hired through talent, connections, deception, extortion, or sexual favors.

One commuter, going in the opposite direction of the massive exodus, had been hired to work at the FBI headquarters in the J. Edgar Hoover Building not because of her master's degree in computer engineering, or because she happened to have been among the top ten graduates from the University of California at Berkeley almost four years ago, or because she had willingly chosen to work for Uncle Sam instead of Microsoft, DreamWorks, Oracle, Intel, or IBM. Erika Conklin wore an FBI badge because of a bet she had made with several classmates the week after their graduation.

Behind the wheel of a weathered Honda Accord, Erika shook her head at how fast time had passed since the night when she had released a password-snatching virus into the Internet, gaining access to several major corporations, banks, and even government institutions across the country, including the Central Intelligence Agency and the Federal Bureau of Investigation.

Just to show who was the best programmer.

Grimacing at her poor judgment, she turned onto M Street and cut left into the Bureau's parking garage, quite empty at this time of the day. In the rush of writing the code and beating her classmates to it, Erika had forgotten to add an origin scrambler routine into the virus. She didn't regret creating and releasing the code. In fact, that had not been the first time that the female hacker had acted mischievously—without really intending to cause any real harm to others. Erika regretted not having written the password-snatching code smartly enough to *not* get caught, like during her early college days, when she had broken into her school's administrative department and given herself an A in chemistry. Or the time when she had erased a speeding ticket with a simple fifteen-minute phantom penetration of the California Highway Patrol network. But botching Snatcher, the password-snatching virus, a piece of work that she had created after so much experience and training, had been inexcusable. The FBI's high-tech crime unit had isolated her elusive virus, decoded it, and traced it straight back to her.

Instead of prosecuting, the Bureau, eager to inject the cyber division with young and talented blood to bolster America's cyber defenses in the years following the terrorist stikes of 2001, had offered Erika a choice: six years of Bureau work as a technical analyst—at a nominal government salary—or ten years in a federal prison plus the possibility of not being able to get a job in the high-tech world after her release because of her criminal record. The offers from Bill Gates, Steven Spielberg, and others had suddenly lost their original appeal. Erika had declined them, hating the Bureau as much as herself for the unfortunate turn of events. She had regretted most having to turn down the software engineering position at Dream-Works, the company where she had co-oped for two terms developing DigiSoft, a custom digital video editing software package for enhanced special effects on films. Without looking back, Erika had said good-bye to her family— to whom she had lied regarding her sudden change of plans—and moved to the East Coast.

"Evening, Miss Conklin."

"Hi," Erika replied while flashing her ID at the stocky security guard in the parking garage, before driving to a spot next to the elevators and getting out, a red backpack hanging loosely from her left shoulder. Erika locked her car and took the elevator to the lobby, where she had to get past a second security point before gaining access to the interior of the building.

The high-tech crime unit of the FBI was located on the fourth floor. Erika reached it two minutes later and strolled past rows of empty cubicles, finally dropping her backpack on the working surface of her cube, located in a corner of a large office area with a terrific view of the Washington skyline. It had not taken her long to stick out among the second-tier analysts that the Bureau usually hired after the top-notch graduates got snatched by the private sector. Uncle Sam simply couldn't compete with Fortune 500 companies and their far more generous base salaries, sign-on bonuses, incentive plans, and stock options. Even though the high-tech industry was experiencing tough times, top-notch engineers were still enjoying handsome compensation packages—but not her.

Erika officially began her FBI career as a junior analyst. Within three years she was breaking viruses and tracking hackers in a fraction of the time of her more experienced colleagues, earning an early promotion to senior analyst. Erika now managed a team of junior analysts in cases ranging from viruses and pirated software and hardware, to clamping the rising wave of high-tech espionage and sabotage. And she did it all from the safety of her cubicle. Special agents, who acted on the information gathered by Bureau's analysts, handled the high-risk field jobs, involving anything from simple arrests to raids.

In the information age everyone spied on everyone else. American companies spied on each other. The Japanese kept a close watch on American technology. The Koreans were after the Japanese. The Germans after the British and the Americans. The Russians and the Chinese were after all of the above. Computer trade shows, particularly the ones held in Europe and Southeast Asia, were packed with high-tech spies, each looking out for his or her own company or country. That same information age gave Erika Conklin the freedom to carry out her assignments from home and only have to come in at night. Like many top-notch computer gurus, she enjoyed working odd hours, when the Bureau was quiet and she could concentrate and do her best work.

Programming is an art, she thought, settling down before her computer, a late-model system, and turning it on. *You can't rush art. You have to focus, take your time, and make the code taut.*

She kicked off her sneakers and rubbed her feet together while Windows came up, noticing the dozen yellow notes pasted around her monitor—her daily to-do list. In the information age, everyone in the division knew that yellow Post-it notes were the best way to bring issues to her attention.

Erika frowned while staring at her reflection on the nineteen-inch display as the screen momentarily went dark before her custom wallpaper—a photo of Erika and her dad riding horses at their northern California ranch—filled the screen. Short auburn hair framed a narrow, pale face, round hazel eyes, and lips that had not been covered with lipstick for the past two months, since her last date, which had been a disaster.

As her antivirus software went through its routine check during boot-up, Erika closed her eyes at the thought of the special agent from the operations division who had put a hand on her thigh and tried to move it below her skirt while en route to a restaurant. She had slapped him before leaping out of the car at a stoplight. And before that had been the data-entry jerk from technical services, who had repeatedly gone for her breasts while parked in front of her apartment following a movie. She had also dated for a very short time a nerd, a narcissist, and two workaholics. And on two separate occasions married men had made passes at her, one at the water fountain and the other in the elevator.

Feds had been permanently removed from her list of choices after the thigh incident. It was at times like this when, in spite of the enjoyment she got from her work—a joy she had never expected to get by working for the government—that Erika would check the calendar and see how much time she had left before her FBI contract expired and she could catch the next flight heading west. Born and raised on a farm north of Berkeley, Erika was used to living outdoors. She enjoyed the clean air and beautiful weather of one of the country's finest agricultural regions. She missed the smell of fresh grapes, the sound of horses at dawn, and the hot air balloons floating in the skies over the Napa and Sonoma valleys, which their land overlooked.

Her father had raised Erika and her older brothers after her mother, a frail, thin-blooded woman, had died from a rattlesnake bite the same year Erika was born. Erika drew her strength from her paternal grandmother, Karla Conklin, a brave and influential Irish immigrant who had built Rancho de las Vistas in the forties almost single-handedly after her husband, thirty years her senior, had passed away of old age and left her thirty acres of land northeast of Napa, fifteen head of cattle, and a twenty-thousand-dollar debt. Five years later the enterprising woman had turned the once-decaying ranch into a self-sustaining business of award-winning bulls and their profitable stud services. In addition, she had taken advantage of the mild California weather to plant grapes, starting a small winery a few years later.

Erika had some of her grandmother's looks. The light skin, hazel eyes, and long, firm legs had been Karla's trademark at every exhibition in the West, where the distinguished Irish lady would show her bulls and wines and walk away with the best awards. The thin build, full lips, auburn hair, and generous bosom, however, had been her mother's, the woman whom Erika Conklin only knew from the framed pictures above the fireplace and her father's bedtime stories, which on occasion included an incredible tale about Karla Conklin. In one such tale, Karla had protected her son, Erika's father, from a rattlesnake by throwing herself in front of it as it neared the playing youngster. Lacking a weapon, Karla had grabbed the rattler's tail with her left hand, before snagging the head with her right, and used her mouth to bite hard behind the snake's head, cracking its neck.

In addition to using her grandmother as a role model, growing up with boys in a ranch had given Erika Conklin a thick skin and a tough attitude, without causing her to lose her femininity. While her girlfriends in nearby Oakland went to the movies, Erika was out fishing at the large pond in the middle of the ranch, or quail hunting with the boys. She rode horses instead of bicycles, learned how to use a rope before the third grade, and became proficient with firearms by the time she reached ten. Her father started her in the winery business, teaching her everything he knew. She developed a taste for fine wines and over time grew to polish her palate, assisting her father in the development and manufacturing of the Vista Winery label.

But by the time she graduated from high school, however, Erika had grown tired of ranch life and longed for something better. She had surprised her family one day at breakfast, the most important meal of the day, by deciding to go to college at Berkeley. Her father had been shocked, her brothers angry, but she had gone anyway. At UC Berkeley she changed majors from agriculture to psychology, to preveterinarian, and back to agriculture, at the insistence of her father, who wanted her to get at the very least a practical degree. During her sophomore year, a guest speaker from Microsoft gave a talk about the future of the computer industry. Erika, still very much a farm girl at heart, had liked the idea of working with computers and decided to take an introductory course. Six months later she had changed her major for the final time, deciding that she would like to be a part of the high-tech revolution, to make a difference in the computer industry, to prevail in a world mostly dominated by men, just as her grandmother had thrived as the head of Rancho de las Vistas. Three years later she earned a B.S. in computer engineering and opted to pursue a master's, which she completed two years later. And just as she was about to unfold her wings and start a professional life in the place of her choosing, the FBI had come and snatched her away.

She made a face. Now she was stuck in a tiny efficiency apartment in overcrowded and crime-ridden Washington, D.C.

That'll teach you about being careless again.
She glanced at the screen.

VIRUS CHECK COMPLETE
NO KNOWN VIRUSES FOUND
32,560,000,543 BYTES FREE
PRESS ANY KEY TO CONTINUE

Erika nodded while checking the available space on her hard drive and comparing it to the number written on the desk calendar.

Thirty-two gigabytes and change.

The numbers matched, providing her with an extra level of safety on top of the scan performed by the antivirus software. Viruses proliferated by multiplying, taking up hard drive space. By jotting down her available disk space at the end of each working session and performing this simple comparison at the beginning of a new working session, Erika could indirectly monitor the possibility of viral activity in her system—like a new strain of a virus not checked by her antivirus software. Although an expert in computer viruses, she still feared them. Having the knowledge and the tools to write a virus, like the one she had used to snatch passwords, made her only too aware of the destructive power of one if it were to fall in the wrong hands.

But that, my dear Erika, is why the Bureau keeps you living in the lap of luxury.

She sighed at the thought. Luxury is what she had given up by not working at Microsoft. Had she gone to work for Bill Gates, she would be driving a Corvette in Seattle instead of a used Honda in D.C. *You might have prevented Bureau perverts from screwing you, but the FBI's still doing it to you in more ways than one.*

But there's an end to the madness, darling, she told herself while hitting the space bar and letting her system finish booting up. She had done almost four of her six obligatory years and still managed to remain technically current—quite a challenge in government jobs. After that she was home free to go work for the highest bidder—as long as that highest bidder was located on the West Coast.

"Okay," she mumbled. "Let's get down to business."

Peeling off a yellow note, she nodded. It was a message from Charlie Chang, one of the junior analysts under her supervision.

THE DETROIT VIRUS IS IN!

I'LL BE IN THE LAB TILL MIDNIGHT

C. C.

She launched her E-mail software and sent Chang a short message, reminding him not to do a thing with it. She would be there as soon as she checked her messages. Erika had been expecting a diskette with the highly toxic virus responsible for wiping out the computer network at a small bank in Detroit. The author of the virus, a renegade programmer who had gotten laid off a month before, had been killed in an auto accident while trying to escape from the police. The firm had formated their systems to eradicate the virus, but not before making a copy for the FBI—and not before losing thousands of files and millions of dollars.

Being at the other end of the virus wars had given Erika Conklin a perspective she'd never had as a hacker. Her boss had flown her to Detroit to see firsthand the real damage done by the virus, the harm done to families who had lost their investments, their bank accounts, their records, and who were now struggling to survive while waiting for FDIC assistance. It had definitely been a moving experience, which her boss had insisted on her witnessing for her own good.

She pouted. Although she would never admit it in public, a part of her wondered if this forced tour of duty was just what she had needed to keep her from using her skills for the wrong reasons.

She eyed the list of unread E-mails on her screen.

>>>	CCHANG@FBI.GOV	THE VIRUS IS HERE!
>>>	JWALKINGS@BERKELEY.EDU.COM	HI, STRANGER
>>>	HTALBOT@FBI.GOV	EXCEEDED LIMIT
>>>	MARKD@DREAMWORKS.COM⌐	NEW DIGISOFT BUG—HELP!
>>>	FRUSSO@FBI.GOV	REPORT DUE TOMORROW
>>>	JENKINGS@TI.COM	NEED IMMEDIATE ASSISTANCE

The list continued, filling the screen. There were thirty-six in all, the messages she had received since she had last logged in from home at three in the afternoon. Erika averaged a hundred E-mails a day, and on crunch days the number would go as high as a hundred and fifty.

Erika deleted Chang's E-mail, skipped the one from Joanne Walkings, a former schoolmate who went on to become a professor at Berkeley, as well as the one from the system administrator informing her that she had exceeded her allowed disk space quota. She browsed through the E-mail from Mark DeSilva, her former boss during her two co-op terms at DreamWorks. DeSilva needed help again debugging DigiSoft, the complex software package understood only by a handful of people, most of whom had left DreamWorks to work elsewhere. It seemed that in the past two years every time film editors used DigiSoft, they would push its features beyond their intended usage, breaking something.

And voilà, Mark sends me an E-mail for help, a description of the bug, and the latest version of the software.

Erika glanced at the open manila envelope icon following DeSilva's E-mail address. She would take a look at the version of DigiSoft in the E-mail attachment later. At the moment her eyes zeroed in on the E-mail from Texas Instruments requiring assistance. She clicked twice on it.

FROM: KEITH JENKINS—PRODUCT AND TEST ENGINEERING DIRECTOR,
　　　　 TEXAS INSTRUMENTS, INC., HOUSTON, TX.
TO: 　　ERIKA CONKLIN—TECHNICAL ANALYST, FBI HIGH-TECH CRIME UNIT,
　　　　 WASHINGTON, D.C.
DEAR MS. CONKLIN,
AS YOU MAY HAVE HEARD BY NOW, THE TRAIN ACCIDENT IN FLORIDA TWO
MONTHS AGO WAS TRACKED DOWN TO ONE OF OUR MICROPROCESSORS, THE
TI6500. SINCE THEN, MY ENGINEERING TEAM HAS BEEN WORKING AROUND
THE CLOCK PERFORMING FAILURE ANALYSIS OF THE FAULTY COMPUTER CHIP
TO FIND AN ASSIGNABLE CAUSE FOR THE FAILURE. WE NOW HAVE REASON TO
BELIEVE THAT THE CAUSE OF THE MALFUNCTION WAS DUE TO POTENTIAL
SABOTAGE BY AN EMPLOYEE WHO IS NO LONGER WITH OUR FIRM. PLEASE
CONTACT ME IMMEDIATELY FOR DETAILS.

Erika jotted down Jenkins's work phone number and checked her watch. Seven o'clock in Washington; six in

Houston. She dialed the number. A rough male voice in a sepulchral tone answered after the second ring.

"Jenkins."

"Mr. Jenkins, this is Erika Conklin from the Federal Bureau of Investigation. I've just read your E-mail. How can I be of service?"

The voice quickly lightened up. "Yes—hello. Hi. *Hi!* Thank you for calling so quickly. I got your name from the FBI Web page and thought you should know what we have just discovered."

He paused.

"Go on, sir."

"Well, as I said in my E-mail, my engineering team has been working round the clock to figure out what went wrong with our IC. Our records show that we performed all customary checks, including burn-in with an acceleration factor high enough to guarantee fifteen years of field life. This IC failed after only two years."

Erika nodded, familiar with the terminology.

During the development stage of an integrated circuit (IC), commonly known as a computer chip, prototype samples went through a series of stress tests to guarantee their long-term functionality in their commercial, industrial, or military applications. The industry standard for the life of an IC was a minimum of fifteen years, longer in some applications. In order to guarantee this minimum lifetime, semiconductor manufacturers aged ICs by putting them through a process called burn-in, where the ICs were electrically exercised in a chamber at a much higher temperature and voltage than what they would ever see inside a personal computer or other end-user applications. This delta in temperature and voltage of operation between the burn-in chamber and the field environment accelerated the life of the integrated circuits. A typical acceleration factor was around fifty, meaning that every hour in a chamber equated to fifty hours of field life. Therefore, it took roughly four months to age a chip the equivalent of fifteen years operating in the real world. If failures occurred before the fifteen-year minimum, the manufacturer would have to fix the design problem and go through the burn-in cycle again.

"What was the failure mechanism?" she asked.

"Metal migration."

"That's a typical IC burn-in failure, Mr. Jenkins, not sabotage," Erika replied. One of the most characteristic burn-in failures was called metal migration. The millions of transistors in an IC were hooked together by microtraces of metal, mostly aluminum or copper. Over time, the molecules in the metal migrated in the direction of the electrical current flowing through them, eventually narrowing the microtraces to the point that they opened, like a blown fuse, causing the IC to fail. Semiconductor manufacturers constantly monitored these burn-in tests very carefully to ensure that no fatal metal migration occurred for at least fifteen years, otherwise the faulty computer chips would become ticking bombs, waiting to fail at the worst possible moment, as had happened in Florida two months ago.

"It *is* a typical failure," Jenkins agreed. "But it was not the result of human error or a hole in our design methodology."

"Then?"

"Someone deliberately revised the design of the TI6500 to narrow a metal line in the reset logic such that the line would become the weak link in the design and open up after around seventeen thousand hours of operation, according to our calculations."

Erika grabbed her pocket calculator and quickly did the math. "That's just under two years," she said.

"Which matches the observed field failure in Florida," said Jenkins.

Erika leaned forward, fished her engineering notebook out of her backpack, and began to scribble notes. "How is it that you know for certain that a design engineer didn't make a mistake when calculating the amount of current that the metal line could handle and sized it incorrectly?"

"Because the logs indicate that the design was not modified *after* it had passed the electrical design rules check and the burn-in tests. No one is allowed to touch the design after it has been qualified. Otherwise we have to go through a requalification. We figured out that it had been changed by doing a comparison between the last approved version of the design and the version that went into production."

"Aren't those two versions supposed to be the same?"

"Yes, they are. But in this case there was one minor but critical difference."

"The narrowed metal trace."

"Right. The change was made without creating a new revision. The engineer who did it simply edited the design and saved it right on top of the production version. That's why we never knew it had been changed . . . until now."

"Do you know who made the illegal change?"

"It took us a while but eventually we figured it out. It was Gerome Pasdats, a senior design engineer. He left our firm two years ago, right after making the change."

Erika tapped her pencil on the notebook. "How do you know it was him?"

"Every IC design is made up of hundreds of thousands of smaller transistor circuits, or cells, connected together by a software tool that places the cells on the design at preprogrammed locations, as called by the design's functional specification, before hooking them up. Some cells are repeated many times, like memory cells. Other cells, like the ones making up custom logic, are placed only once. The reset logic is made up of such custom cells. Now, whenever a cell in the design is modified, the tool automatically updates its time stamp to indicate that a change was made. The tool also updates the time stamp of the entire design, also called the top level, to signal that a change was made to one of its cells. We normally monitor only top-level time stamps. If we notice a change at the top level, we run a program to find which of the individual cells was modified. Well, according to our archives, the time stamp of the reset cell was modified at eleven-thirty-two in the evening on April tenth two years ago. The modification was made by Gerome Pasdats."

Erika looked at her notes and then looked up, staring into the distance. "But the software tool was supposed to update the top-level time stamp when that change was done, alerting everyone of the modification."

"That's the way it's supposed to work. This time, however, several of the tool's features, including the one that automatically updates the top-level time stamp when an individual cell is modified, was disabled from eleven-twenty to eleven-forty-five that same evening."

"Disabled? Why?"

"To make software updates, which are routinely done at night, when the systems are least utilized."

"Doesn't the coincidence bother you?"

"It did. To make changes to this specific tool you need root privilege. Gerome Pasdats, who was the assistant system administrator, had such privilege. The log shows that Mr. Pasdats was performing a routine software update of the tool that evening, which required him to disable those specific features of the tool. No one suspected any wrongdoing when the system logs showed him using root privilege to work on it because that was his job. He was performing a legal software update. However, during that critical time period, Mr. Pasdats mortally wounded a cell in the reset logic of the TI6500 after qualification but prior to production. There was no way we could have caught this, and he knew it."

"Where is he now?"

"Nobody knows. He just stopped showing up for work one day. He was single and had no immediate relatives living in town. We tried to contact a sister living in Little Rock but she had a nonworking number. Failing to contact the next of kin, we filed a missing person report with the Houston Police Department and turned over his retirement savings plan funds and profit-sharing account to the state of Texas."

Erika stayed on the line for five additional minutes, jotting down more information on the case. She also requested the name and E-mail addresses of every engineer involved in the analysis of the failed computer chip, as well as the technical reports on the failure analysis and schematics of the reset logic of the TI6500. Jenkins told her that she would need a court order to contact the engineers because the attorneys representing the families of the victims of the train disaster were deposing them. All files pertinent to the case had also been archived in preparation for the trial in the fall. No one could access them without a court order.

After spending another ten minutes convincing Jenkins that he would not get in trouble by sending the documents that she had requested, and also assuring him that she would personally contact the judge in the morning to explain why the case now warranted the immediate involvement of the FBI's high-tech crime unit, Jenkins finally agreed to send her names, E-mail addresses, and key technical reports, including a failure analysis report and schematics, in an E-mail attachment within the hour.

While she waited for the reports to arrive, she dialed into a special Web page of the Internal Revenue Service, where she used an FBI access password to search for the personal records of Gerome Arnold Pasdats. The computer came up with a single listing. The IRS wanted Mr. Pasdats for failing to file his taxes for the past two years. All of his personal assets had been frozen by the federal agency, including a retirement savings account and a profit-sharing account under the control of the state of Texas.

Leaning back on her swivel chair and yawning, Erika placed both hands behind her back. The case smelled like a dead end. Pasdats had apparently done a very thorough job of covering his tracks following the illegal design change, which resulted in one of the worst train accidents in the history of this country. The act of sabotage, however, lacked a motive. Was Mr. Pasdats a discontented employee? Jenkins had indicated that Pasdats's annual reviews showed above-average performance, no reports of misconduct from his supervisor, and his salary was quite competitive.

Why then, she thought. *Why do something like that for no apparent gain? For the hell of it? To prove that it could be done? Like I did at Berkeley?*

Erika put her feet up on her desk, staring at the overheads. *What if a competitive firm paid him to do it? What if they promised him a lot of money, enough to change identities and start a new life? But then what would be that other company's motive? Market share?*

Erika made a note in her notebook to think through that angle after reviewing the E-mail from Jenkins. As she did so, another thought entered her mind.

What if this is just a cover-up on the part of Texas Instruments to avoid the class-action suit filed by the families of the victims by making itself look like the victim of sabotage?

Erika pondered on that as she left the cubicle area and headed for the vending machines down the hall, where she inserted a few coins and punched the button for a soda before walking to the systems lab on the next floor to check on Charlie Chang.

She decided to reserve judgment until she had gotten the opportunity to review the technical reports and obtain statements from the engineers involved. Perhaps she would ask the magistrate permission to review the transcripts of the depositions of the engineers involved in the class-action suit.

Erika reached the lab and inserted her access card, which she kept clipped to her badge, into the reader by the double glass doors. The red light above the doors turned green and the thick glass slid into the wall. Erika walked into the systems lab, her eyes scanning the huge rectangular room filled with equipment. Walls of bookcases packed with software overlooked rows of tables cluttered with the latest and greatest computer hardware, most of it purchased at Erika's request. It was bad enough that the Bureau went cheap when hiring computer science or computer engineering graduates. At least she had managed to compensate some of that by kicking and screaming until her boss had agreed to a healthy equipment budget, which Erika had used wisely to purchase the right mix of software and hardware to give the FBI a competitive edge when fighting hackers, who were usually armed with the best of the best.

This is a battle, she had argued. *Just like the fight against conventional terrorism. You can't go cheap or you will certainly lose.*

Her hazel eyes zeroed in on the desktop PC that she had set up as an electronic "petri dish" to dissect and diagnose prescriptions for new viruses. Charlie Chang, dressed in a regulation white lab coat, sat behind the keyboard. She saw no one else in the lab.

Erika had spent nearly six months of her FBI career developing the virus-breaking tool. Her subordinates were now tasked with upkeeping it. It was the finest piece of software she had ever written, and the FBI, in recognition of her hard work, had given her a cheap plaque and a two-hundred-dollar check.

Erika sighed. Mark DeSilva at DreamWorks would have given her a thousand shares of stock as a bonus for coming up with this piece of work.

"All right, Charlie. Where is it?"

Chang, a short and slim second-generation Chinese hired straight out of UCLA, blinked twice, typed a few extra commands, sniffled once, and stepped back while pushing thick glasses up the bridge of his nose, alert eyes staring at a floppy next to the system as if it were a vial of Ebola. "There it is."

"When did it come in?"

"A couple of hours ago," he said while sniffling from what seemed to be an eternal case of the flu, which annoyed Erika as much as Chang's habit of trying to learn everything he could from everyone without reciprocating. Erika knew that Chang was after her job, and therefore was trying to learn as much as he could from her.

If he only knew how much I'd love to give him my job and get the hell out of here!

Chang looking over her left shoulder, Erika sat on the stool in front of the desktop system, which large hard drive had been partitioned to process several viruses at once.

A virus needed a host in order to survive. In the case of a computer virus, that host could be a legal computer program, like the accounting software of the bank in Detroit. The Detroit virus, however, was special in the way that it made itself look invisible to its host system. The moment the infected program was run in a clean hard drive, a snippet of computer code attached to the beginning of the legal software was executed. The short computer code, no longer than a few bytes in length, was the activation signal for a much larger program that had been broken up into dozens of sections woven through the accounting software. As the program ran, the hidden virus released an electronic homing torpedo that searched for the directory containing the resident antivirus software in the system's hard drive. The torpedo found the target directory and opened up the signature file of the antivirus software, where the John Hancock of every known virus, plus educated guesses of possible future mutations, resided. Virus signatures were typically quite short, five to fifteen bytes out of the many thousands that made up a complete virus. During a virus scan check, the antivirus software compared tens of thousands of virus signatures with the code in every file in the system, just like biological immune receptors bound to short sequences of amino acids out of the thousands that made up a viral protein. A match indicated the strong possibility of a virus, alerting the user to perform further tests on the suspect file. The homing torpedo then released its payload, a program that searched the signature file and deleted every instance that remotely resembled its own code. Future antivirus checks would not detect the virus.

She copied the first infected virus into a special directory in the desktop system, which operated as a stand-alone computer, without any modem or Ethernet connections to the outside world. If a virus ever broke the system, it would remain contained.

In the closed directory, the infected file was placed with six other "decoy" files. The petri-dish software then ran the files to lure the virus in the infected file to replicate in the decoy files. The program was set up such that the instant the first decoy became infected, the original infected file would be deleted. That way, the new source, the infected decoy—which original composition was known by the program—could be used as a baseline for the subsequent infections. The process took less than a tenth of a second of real time. The extremely hot virus quickly spread across the decoy files.

The custom petri-dish software performed a comparison of the infected decoys with uninfected replicas kept in a different directory, and ten seconds later Erika read the differences on the screen.

PETRI-DISH SOFTWARE
FEDERAL BUREAU OF INVESTIGATION
©2004 BY ERIKA J. CONKLIN
NUMBER OF DECOYS: 6
ORDER OF INFECTION: 1,2,4,3,6,5
NUMBER OF STRAINS: 6
SIGNATURE LENGTH: 7 BYTES
ST101011010.10101010.01011001.01110100.10111010.01000110.11010101
ST201111011.00101000.01011001.01110110.01111010.01000110.11010101
ST401001010.11101010.01011111.01101100.10111011.01000110.11010101
ST301101011.10101010.01111001.01110100.00100010.01000110.11010101
ST601110010.10101100.01001001.01111100.11111001.01000110.01010101
ST501111110.11101010.01111000.01110100.10111010.01000110.01010101

She inspected the viral sequences in silence for several minutes, the extreme complexity of the virus making her hold her breath. The lines under specific bits within a byte highlighted the differences between the baseline strain in the first decoy file and the subsequently infected decoys.

"That's what I was afraid of," she said, lightly tapping the edge of the keyboard with her thumb.

"Looks like it mutates every time it replicates itself into another file," Chang offered while sniffling right behind her.

"Yep," she said. A virus that mutated in between replications was nearly impossible to catch, especially with such a long signature, because the possible combinations were nearly astronomical. But the hacker in her knew of a simpler way to break it.

"What about writing a prescription to handle all possible permutations?" He sniffled again.

"There's too many . . . Please blow your nose."

"Ah . . . yes, sure. Sorry." He reached for a tissue next to the computer while Erika wrote down some numbers on a piece of paper.

"This is why we can't use the brute-force method of just writing a potion to handle all possible combinations," she said, deciding to teach him a little. She pointed to the paper.

$$1 \text{ strain byte} = 8 \text{ bits}$$
$$7 \text{ bytes} = 56 \text{ bits}$$
$$\text{possible combinations} = 2^{56} \text{ or } 7.2 \times 10^{16}$$

"Astronomical number of combinations," she said. "There are . . . how big is this number . . . one trillion repeated seventy-two billion times?"

"Like, real big," Chang said, rubbing his nose with a tissue, his eyes alive with greedy interest.

"As close to infinity as we're ever going to get. I can certainly write an antivirus to kill these six specific strains, but there's no way to kill every strain if it ever got out, unless . . ."

"Unless what?"

"Unless we can come up with the formula that controls the sequence. Then we can predict the future mutations and write an antidote that will seek out and eliminate *just* the combinations of interest, not every *possible* combination."

They loaded the sequence in a set of five networked workstations and waited ten minutes for the answer, which came in the form of a long formula.

"That's it," she said, a bit disappointed at the relative easiness with which she had broken it. Now Chang could write the antidote and post it on the Internet, where virus-scan software houses would include it in their next release of their software.

Erika smiled, the hacker in her coming alive. "Now, if the author of this virus would have been *really* smart, he would have done this just a little different, making it much more difficult—if not impossible—to break."

"How?" he asked, filled with anticipation.

Erika checked her watch, deciding that she had shown the selfish little bastard enough for one evening. Besides, the information from Texas Instruments should have arrived by now. "That's a lesson for another day, Charlie. Let's walk before we try to run. For now concentrate on writing the potion to kill this one."

"*Man . . .*" Chang said, drawing out the word before exhaling heavily.

Erika smiled and walked away.

3

FALLEN STAR

The commander of Space Shuttle *Endeavour* waited patiently as the digital display of the mission timer showed T minus three minutes. The veteran astronaut, commander of four previous shuttle missions, didn't show an ounce of concern, not even to the flight surgeon, who continued to monitor his heartbeat at a steady eighty beats per minute while everyone else aboard had already rocketed past one hundred. The commander had neither the sweaty palms, dry mouth, nor wide-eyed stare of the rookie mission pilot next to him or the payload specialists sitting in the row behind him.

Breathing in the oxygen-and-nitrogen air mixture inside the flight deck, the commander checked the mission timer as the NASA launch room controller's voice crackled through the orbiter's speakers.

"T minus thirty-seven seconds and counting; switching control of the launch to the computer sequence. The countdown is being controlled by the computer sequence aboard *Endeavour*."

Launch countdown control switched from KSC's launch processing system to *Endeavour*'s five general purpose computers, four working in parallel, the fifth checking the output from the other four.

"T minus twenty seconds; SRB hydraulic power unit

started, the SRB nozzles have been moved to the start position. Coming up on fifteen. Switching to redundant start sequence. T minus twelve . . . eleven . . . ten . . . nine."

The commander closed his eyes and visualized the sound-suppression water system nozzles popping up from the mobile launch platform base, like lawn sprinklers, spraying water onto the base of the MLP at the rate of 900,000 gallons per minute in anticipation of main engine start.

"Seven . . . six . . . we're going for main engine start!"

The soul-numbing rumble that followed reverberated through the entire orbiter as each of the three SSMEs kicked into life and automatically throttled up to the 90 percent level.

"We've got main engine start . . . three . . . two!"

The microprocessors in the five general-purpose computers ran at maximum speed, processing hundreds of thousands of instructions in the blink of an eye as they computed inputs from a large number of sensors to verify that all three engines had maintained the required thrust level, before firing the pyrotechnic device in each of the two solid rocket boosters. The resulting blast echoed through the commander's soul as the astounding uproar of 7.5 million pounds of thrust thundered across the warm and humid evening. The brightness from *Endeavour*'s engines illuminated the night sky, casting a yellowish glow for miles around.

"Liftoff! We have achieved liftoff!"

The 4.5-million-pound shuttle rose vertically in attitude hold until the solid rocket booster nozzles cleared the tower by forty feet.

"Houston, *Endeavour*. Starting roll maneuver," commented the commander in a monotone and controlled voice.

Endeavour began a combined roll, pitch, and yaw maneuver to position it head down, with the wings leveled and aligned with the launch pad.

"Roll maneuver completed."

"*Endeavour*, Houston. Got a visual from the ground. You're looking good. Mark twenty seconds," the CapCom said from the Johnson Space Center in Houston, Texas.

"Roger, Houston."

The commander glanced at CRT number 1, where an ascent trajectory graph showed the desired ascent route and *Endeavour*'s current position as the GPCs issued millions of commands every second to the gimbal-mounted SSMEs and the SRBs to keep the orbiter on track. With this part of the mission totally automated, the commander and the pilot limited themselves to monitoring equipment and instruments as the shuttle rose higher and higher, leaving behind a billowing trail of steam and smoke.

"Houston, *Endeavour*. Mark thirty seconds. Throttling down for Max Q."

"Roger, *Endeavour*. Throttling down."

Endeavour's main engines throttled down to reduce the aerodynamic stress on the 21,000 thermal protection tiles glued to the orbiter's all-aluminum skin as the vehicle approached the speed of sound.

"Passed Max Q. Engines back up to one hundred four percent," reported the commander as ice broke off from the external tank and crashed against the front windowpanes, their minute explosions washing away in the slipstream. At 1.3 Mach *Endeavour* had gone supersonic.

"Houston, *Endeavour*. Mark one minute ten seconds," reported the mission pilot. "Five nautical miles high, three nautical miles downrange, velocity reads at twenty-three hundred feet per second."

The commander's eyes drifted to CRT number 1. *Right on track*, he thought. The new microprocessors in the GPCs and their complex ascent phase algorithms performed beautifully. Right next to CRT number 1 were the master alarm warning lights. All looked nominal.

"Mark one minute twenty seconds, Houston," the commander read out. "Nine nautical miles high, six nautical miles downrange. . . . Houston, we have a problem. Mark one minute thirty-five seconds." Two of the general-purpose computers abruptly went into shutdown mode. The last set of parameters of their processing of the ascent algorithms were locked at their outputs. The main system automatically shut off the two malfunctioning GPCs, overriding the incorrect outputs, but not before the bad data had made its way to the space shuttle main engines for two and a half seconds, ordering their gimbal control system to position them incorrectly for that portion of the ascent. At that speed, the computer error threw the shuttle off course by over two miles.

The commander felt the pressure on his chest, as if he were pulling Gs in a fighter jet, as the shuttle suddenly changed course, putting enormous stress on the external tank and the solid rocket boosters, before the correct set of commands arrived, turning the SSMEs in the opposite direction.

Warning lights filled the control panel. Two of the latching mechanisms holding the left solid rocket booster had broken loose from the pressure. Amazingly enough, the remaining locks were keeping the shuttle assembly intact, momentarily avoiding a repeat of the *Challenger* disaster.

"Roger, *Endeavour*. We copy you at one minute forty-five seconds. GPC malfunction on number three and five. Return to launch site."

"Roger, RTLS abort sequence following SRB sep," responded the commander, initiating solid rocket booster separation before the abort sequence could begin.

The commander watched the pyrotechnic display as *Endeavour*, still mated on top of the external tank, rocketed at nearly five thousand feet per second while both solid rocket boosters arced down toward the ocean almost ten miles below.

"*Endeavour*, Houston. Confirm SRB sep."

"Confirmed," he said, relieved to see the volatile boosters away from the shuttle. "Mark two minutes twenty-five seconds. Starting RTLS abort sequence"

"Roger, *Endeavour*."

The commander placed the abort rotary switch in the

RTLS position and depressed the abort button. The remaining general-purpose computers began to run the abort-sequence algorithms, turning the vehicle around to head back to the cape.

The commander monitored the readings from the CRTs for the next minute as *Endeavour* dropped speed and altitude while depleting the propellant and heavy oxidizer in the external tank, at which point he ejected the tank and began the glide phase to the long runway at Kennedy Space Center. From there on, the commander executed a textbook approach, landing the shuttle safely four minutes later.

In the two weeks following the near miss, NASA and all of its GPC subcontractors performed a thorough check of the malfunctioning computers, narrowing down the problem to the IBM12000 super scalar microprocessors, both of which would not come out of reset following their unexpected shutdowns.

4

FAILURE ANALYSIS

Erika Conklin grew tired of having to repeat the same story over and over again. First she had spent an hour bringing her boss, Frank Russo, up to date. Then her boss had called his boss, the deputy director of the FBI, and Erika had explained the situation to him as well. Then the deputy director had called his boss, the director of the FBI, who had arrived just thirty minutes ago followed by his caravan of bodyguards and aides.

Erika now sat across from FBI director Roman Palenski in his office. She had never been up here before. The director's suite occupied an entire corner of the building's eighth floor. Dark wood paneling and heavily ornate furniture gave the place the grave look that matched Palenski's stare as he understood the seriousness of the situation.

Completely bald at fifty-five, Palenski was a tall and plump man who wore suspenders instead of belts, and sucked on lollipops to control his urge to smoke. During really stressful times he would gnaw on unlit cigars. The director removed a pair of spectacles, rubbed his eyes, and carefully balanced them on the tip of his nose, inspecting Erika over their wire frame while sucking on a lollipop he had gotten out of a jar at the corner of his desk.

Setting his elbows on the table and pointing at her with the candy, he asked, "So, Miss Conklin, are these the malfunctioning parts of the Texas Instruments's chip?"

Erika fought a yawn, her eyelids feeling heavy. She was exhausted, having worked almost round-the-clock for the past few weeks. She just wanted to go home and get in bed, but there was something about Palenski's armor-piercing stare that had the same effect on her as a shot of caffeine. She leaned forward, using a pencil to point at a scanning electron microscope (SEM) photo of a section of the TI6500, magnified over five thousand times. "If you notice, sir, this aluminum microtrace connects power to the logic of the reset circuit of the TI6500." She ran the tip of the pencil along a narrow light gray line on a black-and-white photo that resembled a metropolitan area from two thousand feet high. "And this is where it opened up, halting the flow of current to the reset logic, inducing the failure that triggered a shutdown in the integrated circuit."

"Integrated circuit?" Palenski asked.

"That's what we call computer chips in the industry, sir."

"I see."

She stopped the pencil at a tiny break in the line before providing the same explanation on a SEM image of the IBM12000 chip, which she had gotten as an E-mail attachment last night from the IBM engineers in Raleigh, North Carolina, and which she had then printed on a high-resolution color printer. "The failure modes are identical between the two companies."

"You also mentioned that the circumstances surrounding both incidents were also similar?"

Erika nodded. "Yes, sir. In both cases, the changes to narrow the metal lines feeding the reset logic were made after the designs were qualified through burn-in but before ramping production. And the individuals making the illegal design modifications have both disappeared. See here?" She pointed the pencil at a printout of a section of the layout database of the TI6500 that matched the SEM photo of the actual IC. The aluminum microtraces on the layout were drawn in blue; the transistors in red and green. She pointed to a blue line that was noticeably narrower half way between the reset logic and the integrated circuit's main power feed. "That's the actual change, as found by Texas Instruments's engineers about a month ago. Then we have a problem on the shuttle, which is tracked to an IBM microprocessor, and the exact same illegal modification is found. I strongly suspect that someone out there is sabotaging chips. Last night I got a call from Motorola. It seems that a faulty computer chip may have also caused the blackout in Denver last week. I'm expecting a detail E-mail and attachments from Motorola this evening."

Palenski briefly shifted his gaze to the two men flanking Erika, her boss and the deputy director, both of whom had remained silent since she had begun explaining the problem to the director, who returned his attention to her.

"What's our exposure at this time?"

Erika crossed her legs and inspected her short and unpainted fingernails. "None for the TI and IBM ICs. Both companies have already gone through a massive recall while they ramp production on fixed versions. A little from Motorola until all of the ICs are pulled back from the field. The exposure problem is with other ICs that may have been sabotaged and are just waiting to fail."

"Beyond these three?"

"Yes, sir. I think we need to assume there are more ICs sabotaged out there."

"So, what can we do to prevent future failures?"

"We need to find a pattern, sir, something that might assist us in figuring out which ICs have been sabotaged. That's when a motive would be quite valuable."

The director nodded, his intelligent eyes studying Erika. "If we knew why these chips, or ICs, as you call them, are being sabotaged, then we could come up with ways to track down possible leads that might get us to the source of the sabotage scheme."

"Exactly. At this moment, however, the situation looks pretty bleak. There are literally trillions of integrated circuits out there. So far two types have malfunctioned, and look at what happened. A train derailment claimed many of lives plus millions in damages. Then we almost lost *billions* in the NASA near miss. And if the Denver blackout is also the result of a sabotage, we will have to add another thirty deaths, hundreds of wounded, and tens of millions in damages from the overnight riots and looting. That's with three sabotaged chips, sir. If these . . . cyberterrorists have deployed a dozen or more of these ticking bombs out there . . ." She let her words trail off.

"What's your opinion on how bad the situation can get?" Palenski asked after a few moments.

Erika looked in the distance for a moment before leveling her gaze with Palenski's. "My professional opinion, sir, is that absolutely nothing in this country works without a computer being involved in some fashion. Everything you see, or touch, or hear, or wear, or eat has been made, or said, or tailored, or prepared with the use of software and hardware at some point in the process. Without this high-tech monster that we have created and learned to depend on for our daily lives, we're all regressing very quickly to a kind of technological Stone Age. A simple malfunction in Florida caused the worst train accident in the history of this country. Two malfunctioning microprocessors almost destroyed a multibillion-dollar space shuttle. And I think that's just the tip of the iceberg. If a malfunctioning chip caused the Denver blackout, that city should consider itself lucky that the problem was fixed by morning thanks to electricity piped in by the adjacent states. Say the malfunction hits several places at once, like the power companies lighting up Virginia, Maryland, and the District of Columbia. The computers controlling the careful balance of electrical distribution among thousands of sectors of land in all three states is suddenly corrupted. The systems hang and shut down. Normally other systems in the surrounding states would kick in to avoid a blackout, but say those systems are also malfunctioning due to computer shutdowns, or maybe they try to help but are quickly overloaded by the sudden demand. So there is a blackout.

No electricity means no heating or cooling. Means no communications. Means no gas at the pumps or lights at the operating table. Means America doesn't get the morning paper and supermarkets don't get their produce. Means people go hungry. Means riots, havoc, anarchy. Means Denver all over the place, for more than just one night. Lack of communications will also affect the military, which could be also having its own logistical problems because of ICs shutting down. Simply nothing works. Can't pick up the phone and touch someone because the computer-controlled relay systems of AT&T are down. Can't get money from the ATM because the banks have shut down. Can't drive down the street because the computer-controlled traffic light systems—in places that somehow still have electricity—are malfunctioning, causing thousands of wrecks in minutes. Of course, there is no dialing nine one one to get an ambulance because communications are down. Any way you look at it you can come up with some pretty terrifying scenarios. It could turn out to be a serious mess, sir. A mess of unprecedented proportions certainly well beyond the repercussions from the terrorist strikes of 2001. That was just four jetliners causing havoc. Imagine a whole fleet of jets falling from the sky because of malfunctioning chips. We have dug ourselves into this technological hole, and the cyberterrorists behind this are capitalizing on this inherent weakness in our society."

Palenski frowned, his eyes filmed with disbelief. "Will it really be *that* bad, Miss Conklin?"

Erika smiled at the skepticism displayed by those who did not really know or understand the true power that computers had over today's society. "I'm a computer engineer, sir, and I just gave you a very, *very* plausible scenario based on my scientific assessment of the situation with the data I have seen to date. Look at what happened several years ago. A malfunctioning nozzle in a Hughes communications satellite misfired, misaligning the satellite, and voilà, over twenty million pagers and a hundred thousand cellular phones were disabled for a couple of days in North America, causing millions in damages. Doctors didn't get emergency pages. Business deals failed due to poor communications. I guess the only good thing that came out of it was that many drug dealers were caught because their pagers failed. Here's another one. A number of years ago, malfunctioning software on the navigation system of Airbus's newest jetliner sent it crashing over southern Germany, killing dozens of people, setting back the airline manufacturer for months while they scrambled to find the cause of the accident, which actually worked to Boeing's advantage. And what about all of the viruses and worms plaguing the Internet in recent years? That alone has caused businesses in this country hundreds of millions in damages. Should I go on?"

The room fell silent.

Palenski stood and tucked his thumbs under his suspenders as he said, "If we're indeed facing such scenario, why can't we contact every semiconductor manufacturer and request them to run checks on their current designs, especially those that went into production about two years ago?"

Toying with an earring, she said, "I've already sent confidential E-mails to every semiconductor manufacturer operating in the United States, but I'm not holding much hope for that tactic."

"Why?"

Erika exhaled heavily while extending her lower lip, ruffling her bangs. Crossing her arms while staring at her sneakers, she said, "You need to understand the way semiconductor manufacturers operate, sir. Archives of two-year-old designs are not as easily retrievable as one might think. Many of the backup tapes have been stored at off-site locations to make room for current designs. In many cases, the designers who worked on that particular chip have already switched jobs. Also, the software and tools utilized in a design created two years ago are fairly obsolete and oftentimes incompatible with current tools. Remember that this industry moves at a pace that's many times faster than any other industry, which explains why a computer purchased this year becomes obsolete in less than two years, forcing consumers to keep visiting their local computer stores. That neck-breaking pace has the associated price of poor documentation and archive procedures for old designs. Once a design has been ramped into production, the engineering resources assigned to the development of that design are quickly shifted to a new design, leaving the old design running on autopilot, with little documentation. Within a year everyone has forgotten about the design, and it takes something of the enormity of the TI6500 or IBM12000 fiascoes to get management in a corporation to pull valuable resources from profit-generating projects to go figure out what went wrong with a two-year-old design. That's why I'm not holding much hope that any company, aside from TI, IBM, and probably Motorola, has taken the warning seriously. Right now corporations are worried about making this quarter's sales numbers, not about retrieving a two-year-old design and assigning expensive engineering and equipment resources to find a problem that may not be there at all just to please the FBI. Corporations care only about pleasing their paying customers and their stockholders, sir. Corporations are quarter-to-quarter entities that pride themselves in making the right decisions to keep their stocks as high as possible at the cost of everything else. It takes a slap in the face of the magnitude of a class-action suit to get them to pry resources from profit-generating projects."

Palenski stared in the distance. "I still intend to follow up your E-mails with personal phone calls to the CEOs of the lead American high-tech companies and remind them that they have been officially warned by the FBI to put in a serious effort to check their previous designs. I will make sure that they all understand the severity of the trouble that they will be in if an accident occurs.

Erika nodded thoughtfully, not convinced if that would do any good. She said, "It certainly won't hurt to do that, sir. But I think we should also try to approach this problem from another angle."

"What's that?"

"Looking at the *motive* side of this problem. The only reason that makes sense to me is that someone has targeted certain corporations, two of which we know for certain, in order to profit from their loss of market share."

Palenski replaced the lollipop with an unlit cigar and began to chew the end. "Do you have anyone in mind?"

Erika frowned. "Not yet, sir."

Palenski solemnly nodded. "All right, what do you need, Miss Conklin?"

"Time to do some digging before I can come up with a theory worth pursuing."

"And the clock is ticking," said the director, gnawing on the cigar, thumbs back under the suspenders. "Rich?"

Deputy Director Richard Quinn stood. He was a well-built African American man in his late forties.

"Yes, sir?" Quinn crossed his arms. He was dressed in a suit, just like Palenski and Frank Russo, Erika's boss, making Erika feel a bit out of place with her faded blue jeans, polo shirt, and sneakers when she had first stepped inside the plush office. Right now, however, her casual apparel was the least of her worries.

"How are we handling this with the press? The last thing I want to do is trigger a general panic because of this apparent trend of sabotaged chips."

Quinn adjusted the knot of his tie. "Due to the litigation battle, the problem at Texas Instruments got a lot of press. TI lawyers used the sabotage angle to minimize punitive damages. The IBM chip, fortunately, didn't cause a disaster that involved loss of life, therefore IBM has been quite willing to work with us. Also, IBM's customer, NASA, is a federal agency, which, at our request, has asked IBM's upper management to keep the origin of the malfunction confidential. IBM has recalled all of their faulty chips and has already replaced them with a corrected design. Now, the problem at Motorola might be tricky to keep under wraps for the same reasons that Texas Instruments couldn't. If a company finds that someone sabotaged them, they will likely use that in a court of law to fight off class-action suits. Also don't forget that, as Miss Conklin has already stated, we sent confidential requests to the heads of thirty different semiconductor corporations in North America to check their two-year-old designs."

Palenski nodded. "My feeling here's that soon, *very soon*, word's going to get out."

Quinn said, "I think you're right, sir."

"All right, Rich. I want every available resource in my organization made available to Miss Conklin. I need to get to the bottom of this one right away. There is nothing, *absolutely nothing*, more important than finding the cyberterrorists responsible for the sabotages. I want agents tracking down the whereabouts of these missing engineers. I want to interview their families, their friends, their coworkers. And I want every piece of data relayed back to this office. Understood?"

"Yes, sir." Quinn took off.

"Russo?"

"Sir?"

"I want to make sure that Miss Conklin's other job responsibilities are temporarily transferred to someone else. I need her focused on this problem."

"Yes, sir."

Palenski nodded. "Now, I would like a brief word in private with her."

Russo left.

Palenski turned to face the skies over Washington and said, "Miss Conklin?"

"Yes, sir?" Erika stood.

"Russo briefed me on the circumstances of your hiring at the FBI."

Erika dropped her gaze and crossed her arms while frowning. "It definitely wasn't one of my finest moments, sir."

"How much time you have to go?"

"Two years, one month, and three days, sir . . . give or take a few hours."

Palenski faced her again, a grin breaking up his stern mask. "If you pull this off, the balance of your time will be eliminated."

Erika opened her mouth to say something but nothing came out.

"Now if you'll excuse me, I think I need to brief the president."

5

HOME, SWEET HOME

Hauling a bag of groceries and her backpack, Erika reached the ninth floor of her apartment complex nearly out of breath, her shoulders and thighs burning. For the third time this month the elevator was out of service. Sighing in exasperation, she fumbled with her keys as she stepped away from the stairs and walked toward her unit, located halfway down the worn-out carpet. Walls of peeling paint under a long line of fluorescent lights flanked her.

She was beyond exhaustion, having to work most of the day before Russo allowed her to go home. She had informed her team that she would not be going in to work this evening.

Erika went inside the apartment and flipped the switch by the entryway, frowning when several roaches raced for cover on the brown linoleum floor. Dropping her backpack next to a computer system on the breakfast table of an efficiency apartment that cost her over fifteen hundred dollars per month, she walked to the kitchen and shoved the bag into the refrigerator. She would unpack it later. Right now she needed a shower. She pushed the power and play buttons of her small stereo, and Aaron Neville's rendition of "White Christmas" began to flow out of the small speakers. Erika loved Christmas music and she listened to it all year long, especially when she became depressed, which lately had occurred more often than she would have liked. She also listened to it while working through complex code. The familiar melodies relaxed her, allowing her to do her best work.

An old Oriental screen divided the bedroom from the living area. Erika kicked off her sneakers and tossed her jeans and T-shirt on the bed. She wore no bra. She walked into the bathroom wearing just socks and panties, taking a glimpse at her reflection in the mirror over the sink, noticing the pale skin of her thin limbs, the results of too many hours indoors working at the computer She also noticed the slight sag of her breasts—the result of spending a little too much time on the treadmill during her UC Berkeley days.

Erika finished undressing and showered quickly, listening to the music. She towel dried her short hair, wrapping the towel around her and returning to the breakfast table, where she turned on the computer. Erika put on an oversized San Francisco 49ers T-shirt while the system booted up, and fished a soda, a pack of baby carrots, and fat-free dressing out of the grocery bag, which rested on a refrigerator shelf next to an unopened bottle of wine.

Erika paused, setting everything on the counter and grabbing the wine. She smiled, reading the label, which showed a small drawing of mountains and a hot-air balloon. Beneath the drawing were the words:

BLANC SAUVIGNON 1999
VISTA WINERY
SAM CONKLIN & FAMILY
SONOMA VALLEY, CALIFORNIA

She had been saving it for a special occasion, perhaps for the last day of her FBI prison term, which according to Palenski could be just around the corner.

If I do this right.

For now, she couldn't afford to drink it because she was

out of practice. The last time she had gone out drinking with a couple of co-workers she had been surprised at how easily it had gone to her head. During her years at the ranch she could sip wine all day long.

Now all it takes is just a couple of glasses.

She frowned, remembering her freshmen year at Berkeley when she had gotten drunk after drinking a single glass of wine at a fraternity party. It had turned out that someone had slipped her a mickey. The episode had taught Erika to be cautious about public drinking.

She put the wine back in the refrigerator, squirted dressing into a cup, and brought her dinner to the table as Aaron Neville went on to sing "O Holy Night," one of Erika's favorites.

A cockroach emerged from under the curtains in the living room. Erika ignored it, the holiday music helping her concentrate, keeping her mind focused on a way to find the origin of the sabotaged chips—her ticket out of this dump and into profit-sharing checks and stock options at Microsoft or DreamWorks. On her hour-long commute from D.C. she had thought of a lead, which she intended to pursue for a little while before going to bed. She launched her Web browser and accessed an address given to her by her contact at Motorola in Austin, Texas.

Erika frowned. The information she had received from Motorola had matched the failure analysis results from TI and IBM. Revision E of the M98000, one of Motorola's microprocessors, had been sabotaged. Palenski had immediately ordered the special agents resident in Austin to search for the missing design engineer responsible for the illegal change. Agents from the Houston and San Antonio offices were also working the case.

"Let's see what we can find," she mumbled, fighting a yawn while ripping open the pack of carrots and dipping one in the dressing before taking a bite. The screen changed to:

MOTOROLA, INC.
MICROPROCESSORS PRODUCTS DIVISION

```
GENERAL DATABASE
>>>>>ENTER PASSWORD
```

Erika typed in ALPHA567, the password she had jotted down in her notebook after her last phone conversation with the engineering director at Motorola, and pressed EN-TER.

```
MPD GENERAL DATABASE
>>ENTER SELECTION
1. ENGINEERING
2. MARKETING
3. SALES
4. QUALITY AND RELIABILITY
5. SYSTEMS ENGINEERING
6. LEGAL
```

She selected option three and the display showed:

```
MPD SALES DATABASE
>>ENTER SELECTION
1. 2006 SALES PLAN
2. 2005 SALES
3. 2004 SALES
4. 2003 SALES
5. 2002 SALES
6. ARCHIVES PRE-2001
7. RETURN TO PREVIOUS MENU
8. RETURN TO HOME PAGE
```

She selected option number four, the year before the M98000 was sabotaged.

```
MPD 2003 SALES DATABASE
>>ENTER SELECTION
1. PROFIT & LOSSES REPORT BY QUARTER
2. AVERAGE SELLING PRICE BY PRODUCT
3. SALES BY REGION
```

4. SALES OFFICES

5. CUSTOMER LIST BY PRODUCT

6. RETURN TO PREVIOUS MENU

7. RETURN TO HOME PAGE

After selecting option number five, the system prompted her for a product name. She typed M98000.

MPD 2003 SALES DATABASE

CUSTOMER DATABASE FOR M98000—ALL REVISIONS

>>ENTER SELECTION

1. ADVANCED CONTROLLERS, INC.

2. AKITA ELECTRONICS

3. ATX CORPORATION

4. COMPUTADORAS NACIONALES

5. EUROTECH, LTD.

6. GURZENICH TECHNOLOGIE

7. LINK TECHNOLOGIES

8. MITSUI SYSTEMS

9. OLIVETTI, LTD.

10. RÉPUBLIQUE TÉLÉCOMMUNICATIONS

11. SAKATA ELECTRONICS

12. SAMSUNG ELECTRONICS

13. TELNET SYSTEMS

14. VOBIS SYSTEMS

15. RETURN TO PREVIOUS MENU

16. RETURN TO HOME PAGE

Erika studied the list. Fourteen customers. The blackout in Denver had been caused by multiple malfunctions of ATX-7000 control systems, driven by M98000 chips that abruptly had gone into shutdown due to metal migration. She clicked on the ATX option.

CUSTOMER:	ATX CORPORATION			
PRODUCT:	M98000 REV D			
SALES RECORD:	QUARTER	QTY	ASP	SALES
	Q103	3500	$340.00	$1.19M

Q203	2700	$310.00	$.837M
Q303	4500	$270.00	$1.215M
Q403	3000	$210.00	$.63M

>>>>PRESS ENTER TO RETURN TO PREVIOUS MENU

Erika ate another carrot while reviewing the information on the screen, rubbing her feet together under the table.

She saw nothing unexpected, except that the version of the M98000 purchased during 2003 by ATX was Revision D. Revision E was the one that had caused the problem. The data looked like a typical sales record between a semiconductor manufacturer and an OEM—original equipment manufacturer—even down to the average selling price (ASP) attrition typical of leading-edge microprocessors as new designs and higher speeds rolled into the market, displacing older designs.

She selected another corporation.

CUSTOMER:	AKITA ELECTRONICS			
PRODUCT:	M98000 REV D			
SALES RECORD:	QUARTER	QTY	ASP	SALES
	Q103	29,000	$210.00	$6.09M
	Q203	35,000	$175.00	$6.125M
	Q303	17,900	$120.00	$2.148M
	Q403	34,000	$95.00	$3.23M

>>>>PRESS ENTER TO RETURN TO PREVIOUS MENU

Erika ate another carrot while raising an eyebrow and mumbling, "Pretty big customer." Akita had certainly placed quite the number of orders of the M98000 Rev D during 2003. The higher volume also carried along lower prices, just as she would have expected.

She continued to browse through other customers in 2003, noticing their volumes, their ASPs, and the revision of the chip. Rev D dominated 2003, the year that the ill-fated Rev E was in development. Volume production of Rev E, however, did not begin until early 2004. Erika navigated through the menus and reached the customer database for 2004, which looked similar to the 2003 list, plus a few additions.

```
MPD 2004 SALES DATABASE
CUSTOMER DATABASE FOR M98000—ALL REVISIONS
>>ENTER SELECTION
  1. ADVANCED CONTROLLERS, INC.
  2. AKITA ELECTRONICS
  3. ATX CORPORATION
  4. COMPUTADORAS NACIONALES
  5. EUROTECH, LTD.
  6. FARADAY SYSTEMS
  7. GURZENICH TECHNOLOGIE
  8. LINK TECHNOLOGIES
  9. MITSUI SYSTEMS
 10. OLIVETTI, LTD.
 11. RÉPUBLIQUE TÉLÉCOMMUNICATIONS
 12. SAKATA ELECTRONICS
 13. SAMSUNG ELECTRONICS
 14. TANDEM COMPUTERS, INC
 15. TELNET SYSTEMS
 16. VOBIS SYSTEMS
 17. ZEBRA COMMUNICATIONS
 18. RETURN TO PREVIOUS MENU
 19. RETURN TO HOME PAGE
```

Again, she clicked on ATX.

COMPANY:	ATX CORPORATION			
PRODUCT:	M98000 REV D			
SALES RECORD:	QUARTER	QTY	ASP	SALES
	Q104	1000	$170.00	$.170M
	Q204	540	$150.00	$81.0K
	Q304	0	$0	$0
	Q404	0	$0	$0
PRODUCT:	M98000 REV E			
SALES RECORD:	QUARTER	QTY	ASP	SALES
	Q104	2500	$450.00	$1.125M

Q204	3500	$390.00	$1.365M
Q304	4600	$300.00	$1.380M
Q404	3900	$270.00	$1.530M

>>>>PRESS ENTER TO RETURN TO PREVIOUS MENU

Erika noticed the typical ramp down of Rev D as Motorola phased the older revision out and rolled in its new and improved Rev E, which also carried along a higher price tag due to its innovations in performance.

"New, improved, fast, high performance . . . and very, *very* deadly," she said, sipping soda, recalling the images on TV the other night about the nightmarish hours in Denver during the blackout. Dozens dead and hundred wounded, plus tens of millions in damages. "And that's just in a few hours without electricity." She shook her head. The entire country could fall into anarchy in a matter of hours if something like that were to happen at the national level.

She checked the next customer on the list.

COMPANY:	AKITA ELECTRONICS			
PRODUCT:	M98000 REV D			
SALES RECORD:	QUARTER	QTY	ASP	SALES
	Q104	16,000	$80.00	$1.28M
	Q204	8,000	$65.00	$.520M
	Q304	1,000	$30.00	$30.00K
	Q404	0	$0	$0
PRODUCT:	M98000 REV E			

ALL ORDERS CANCELLED

>>>>PRESS ENTER TO RETURN TO PREVIOUS MENU

"Now, there's one lucky customer," she said, tapping a finger against the side of the can of soda. The Japanese conglomerate had ramped down orders of the Rev D, just like ATX, but had not replaced its volume with Rev E. It had simply cancelled its future orders.

I wonder why?

She made a note and moved on, checking the next customer on the list, *Computadoras Nacionales*, a large OEM house in Madrid, Spain. Its 2004 sales record looked similar to ATX's, ramping down Rev D and ramping up Rev E. Next came Eurotech, Ltd., the European electronics giant based in Munich, which had purchased over ten thousand Rev Ds and twice as many Rev Es in 2004.

Erika leaned back and yawned, clicking her way through the entire list, reaching the sales records for Mitsui Systems, another Japanese corporation.

COMPANY:	MITSUI SYSTEMS			
PRODUCT:	M98000 REV D			
SALES RECORD:	QUARTER	QTY	ASP	SALES
	Q104	13.000	$95.00	$1.235M
	Q204	6,500	$50.00	$.325M
	Q304	0	$0	$0
	Q404	0	$0	$0
PRODUCT:	M98000 REV E			

ALL ORDERS CANCELLED

>>>>PRESS ENTER TO RETURN TO PREVIOUS MENU

"All orders cancelled . . . just like Akita. . . ."
Erika frowned. Something smelled here. She checked the next Japanese customer on the list, Sakata Electronics.

COMPANY:	SAKATA ELECTRONICS			
PRODUCT:	M98000 REV D			
SALES RECORD:	QUARTER	QTY	ASP	SALES
	Q104	6,500	$87.00	$.435M
	Q204	1,300	$50.00	$65.0K
	Q304	540	$45.00	$24.3K
	Q404	0	$0	$0
PRODUCT:	M98000 REV E			

ALL ORDERS CANCELLED

>>>>PRESS ENTER TO RETURN TO PREVIOUS MENU

"Son of a . . ."
As the Christmas CD played "Jingle Bells," Erika quickly browsed through the rest of the customer list for

2004. All other customers had ordered the Rev E version of the M98000, except for the three Japanese companies, which had timely stopped ordering the sabotaged version.

A coincidence?

The little FBI classroom training that Erika received during her first year in the Bureau had taught her to question coincidences, and this one was pretty incriminating.

Why did all three companies stop ordering the sabotaged version, particularly when the year before they had ordered huge volumes?

She stood, stretched, and headed for the bathroom to relieve herself, scaring off a couple of roaches that ventured out from underneath the sofa in the living room. On her way back, she grabbed a second can of soda from the rumbling refrigerator, settled behind the off-white keyboard, and explored 2005. She found that the three Japanese corporations had dropped off from the Motorola customer list for the M98000. They were also missing in 2006.

Erika popped the soda, took a sip, logged out of the Motorola network, and logged onto the Texas Instruments Web page, going through a similar search, taking just over thirty minutes to find the same pattern: Japanese corporations had abruptly stopped orders when the sabotaged version of the TI6500 was rolled into production. An hour later she logged off from the IBM network, her mind racing as she made a short list of the Japanese companies involved: Akita, Sakata, and Mitsui. There could be others, of course, but those three were the ones flagged by her search at all three American manufacturers.

American manufacturers.

The thought made her blink twice.

Japanese corporations canceling orders from American semiconductor manufacturers whose ICs have been sabotaged.

"If this is true . . ."

She checked her watch. Just past eleven o'clock in the evening, but she doubted she would be able to sleep, not after finding the first good lead on this case. Was it possible that someone had tipped Japanese corporations about the sabotaged ICs, and those companies had then complied by canceling their orders to avoid the mess plaguing IBM, Motorola, and Texas Instruments?

But what's the motive? Is someone trying to sink American corporations?

Erika checked the stock history for IBM, TI, and Motorola in the past months, since the incidents. IBM's stock had dropped almost 30 percent, putting Big Blue's shares at their lowest point in years. She found similar results on TI and Motorola. The NASDAQ, which was driven by high-tech companies, had dropped by almost 20% since the initial incident.

Before logging off she decided to check the Nikkei, Japan's version of the DJIA. In the same timeframe, the Nikkei index had climbed 10%, apparently as a direct result of high stock prices from the high-tech sector of the Japanese economy. A few more clicks of the mouse revealed the top twenty stocks driving the Nikkei Index. It included semiconductor companies like NEC, Sony, Akita, Fujitsu, Hitachi, Mitsui, Toshiba, and Sakata.

Erika leaned back, finishing off the second soda. Going through sales records of every American semiconductor corporation to look for similar patterns might be easier to accomplish than Palenski's suggestion of having those companies go back and check every two-year-old design. But that was still quite a significant and time-consuming effort, and it was not a sure bet. So far all three sabotaged chips fell in the same time frame, give or take a few months. But there could be other ICs that had been sabotaged before or after that, making the search all the more challenging. In addition, there could also be sabotaged ICs that were never purchased by Japanese corporations before or after the sabotage, further complicating the task.

Erika went to the bathroom again. "You better stop drinking those sodas," she said to the walls while thinking of a more direct approach to tracking down the origin of the sabotages, which, as she sat on the toilet and glanced at an inch-long roach crawling up the wall next to the tub, also meant an early release from her federal prison term.

By midnight she couldn't keep her eyes open. After sending a detailed E-mail with her suspicions to her boss, Erika turned off the computer and the overheads, letting the Christmas CD replay. She crawled in bed, propping herself up with a couple of pillows and grabbing the remote on the wicker nightstand. A matching wicker dresser by the foot of the bed served as a stand for a twenty-seven-inch TV. She put on CNN's *Headline News*. Erika couldn't fall asleep without the TV on, and as she did, she also took the opportunity to catch the news.

Billowing flames gushing out of a window filled the screen as the anchorwoman in an insert on the top left-hand corner of the screen spoke about the intense fire in Chicago, the result of a midair collision between two jetliners an hour ago. Erica sat up in bed, bewildered at the vast destruction of several city blocks. Streams of water fought flickering flames as firefighters worked to contain the blaze. An American Airlines plane on final approach had collided with a Delta flight moments after takeoff. Three hundred sixty-two passengers and crew members had perished instantly. The scorching debris had fallen over a suburb in southwest Chicago, killing an estimated fifty residents and sending hundreds to emergency rooms across the city. Initial reports from three air traffic controllers at Chicago O'Hare International airport suggested that the disaster might have been the result of a computer error in the tower. FAA investigators were already at the scene.

Erika remained still, her eyes taking in the images, the destruction, the deaths. Firefighters wearing bright yellow coats and face masks raced through the billowing smoke, one of them cradling an infant, bringing back memories of the 2001 terrorist strikes against the World Trade Center and the Pentagon. Several men held back a woman screaming with her arms stretched toward a burning house. Ambulances and fire trucks dashed across the city, sirens wailing, horns blaring. A boy smeared in black cried on the front lawn of another burning house as firefighters rushed by hauling the scorched bodies of two adults.

And CNN displayed it all in vivid color.

Erika gasped.

A computer error. A computer error. A computer error.

The words from the anchorwoman echoed in Erika's mind over and over, again and again, as she hugged her knees, as she inhaled deeply through her nostrils and exhaled slowly through her mouth. Somehow she knew, and the knowledge chilled her. Technical phrases like *burn-in*, *acceleration factor,* and *metal migration* took on a menacing tone. She closed her eyes, visualizing the flow of current through the narrowed metal line, picturing the slow erosion of the microtrace as charge rushing across it at the speed of light hauled off a few molecules of metal at a time, slowly but systematically thinning the line, shaving it, stripping it of its ability to carry the vital information that would have kept the airliners from colliding. Erika imagined the computerized system in the control tower, storing the location, altitude, heading, and speed of hundreds of jetliners in the airport traffic area, providing the air traffic controllers with the vital statistics of each flight, tracking their progress on the large color displays crowding the control tower. Erika imagined the Delta flight rolling off the tarmac, retracting its landing gear, gaining altitude. She could see the American flight descending, its passengers tired from the trip, eager to land, to get home. And the microtrace continued to erode, to thin, the current flowing through it stripping it from its ability to transfer information to the microprocessor's reset logic, until it snapped, bursting into millions of molecular-size globules of scorched metal that erupted through the layers of silicon that made up the integrated circuit, like a miniature volcano, forcing a hard shutdown in the central processing unit.

Erika muted the TV, no longer wanting to hear the cries,

the sirens, the screams. But the Christmas music still played, transposing the scenes flashing on the screen to a new dimension of terror.

"Let It Snow, Let It Snow, Let It Snow," with lyrics by the great Sammy Cahn, was playing. The music played on while apocalyptic images came and went, each more dreadful than the next. Erika watched them all, absorbed them all, ingrained them in her mind. Fists tight, knuckles white, Erika Conklin knew then that she had to put a stop to this madness, and not because of the prospect of a shortened federal sentence. She had to do it because people— innocent people—had died tonight, had died in Denver, in southern Florida, and would surely die in the future unless the sabotaged computer chips could be identified and removed from the field before more lives were lost.

Before the next shutdown.

6

OLD HABITS

SANTA CLARA COUNTY, CALIFORNIA

The noon sun shone bright over Silicon Valley, bringing along a pleasant seventy-two degrees, its luminous beams reflecting off the glass-and-steel structures of the corporate headquarters of America's high-tech industry. Names like Intel, IBM, Hewlett-Packard, United Technologies, AMD, and Applied Materials—companies with yearly sales larger than the gross national products of many small countries—dominated this cyberworld, where fortunes were made and lost overnight, where today's hottest products were tomorrow's relics, where the mere hint of a breakthrough or a failure would send Wall Street into a spin. On this terribly expensive real estate, wedged between two mountain ranges, corporate executives gathered in opulent boardrooms to plan the future of the computer industry, to decide which products would make it to market and which would not go beyond design concepts, to map out strategies that would maximize profits at any cost, that would win over the competition. In this neck-breaking race, where many lost and few prevailed, where the difference between obscene profits and huge losses was defined by terms like frequency of operation, memory capacity, manufacturing margin, customer acceptance, and time to market, a shadowy entity had emerged over the years, gathering strength as the high-tech industry accrued momentum and established itself as America's largest manufacturing employer, as the single largest industry in the United States measured in sales, blasting past textile and auto manufacturing. Like remoras on a shark, this underground organization fed on the efforts of the corporations whose buildings rose high up in the skies of northern California. This high-tech mafia, powerful and obscure, ruthless and widespread, with tentacles reaching the heart of Southeast Asia, monitored the flow of computer goods from manufacturers to wholesale distributors and retailers, siphoning profits along the way—and willing to go to any extreme to protect their operation, including open attacks against federal agents attempting to interfere with their shadowy but thriving business. The FBI had lost many good street agents over the years, both in the United States and abroad, particularly in South Korea, Hong Kong, and Taiwan. These men and women had simply vanished while working undercover or during ill-fated raids, when agents had found themselves outnumbered and outgunned. Sometimes their bodies would be found at the scene of the raid, the lucky ones dead from bullet wounds, the rest showing signs of torture. Other times agents would just disappear, presumably captured alive and tortured. On occasion a body would emerge maimed, mutilated, bearing the marks of barbaric torture, allowed to surface to send the feds a clear message about the impending fate of those who dared meddle in their affairs. Only once had a federal agent been captured by the high-tech mafia and survived. It happened in Seoul, Korea, where the FBI kept an office to work with local law enforcement to fight international computer crime and most recently, cyberterrorism. The unfortunate agent, victim of North Korean terrorists with strong ties to Japan's infamous Aum Shinrikyo terrorist group, now lived in a hospital in New England, emasculated and unable to communicate from the loss of his hands, eyes, tongue, and hearing—another message to strike fear in the hearts of federal agents, a reminder of the storm cloud hovering in the otherwise clear skies of Silicon Valley.

A passing cumulus momentarily blocked the sun, allowing Brent MacClaine to stop squinting as he moved through the downtown lunch crowd with relative ease, inspecting the people around him without looking at anyone, averting eye contact, avoiding attention. Beneath the jacket of his business suit, MacClaine carried a Smith & Wesson model 659 pistol, along with a badge that identified him as a special agent of the FBI.

Halfway down the block, MacClaine paused to check his watch. He overheard two elderly men in business suits discussing an article about cyberterrorism in *Electronic Engineering Times,* the industry's newspaper for engineering and technical management. Past them, a few young men in tuxedos worked the valet service of a luxurious restaurant. Two of the kids argued for the right to park a red Ferrari while a patron drove up in a Porsche. A woman in a business suit walked by, her ear pegged to a cellular phone while blabbering technojargon. Two kids in jeans and untucked flannel shirts walked in the opposite direction hauling laptop computers and pocket calculators. Behind them a plump woman munched a taco purchased from a nearby vendor selling them out of the side of his van. Two men leaned on the van's small side counter while exchanging cash for foil-wrapped tacos. They had laptops tucked under their armpits.

MacClaine exhaled. As one of the few surviving members of the old school of espionage and counterespionage, he knew little about computers and in some cases considered them a threat, especially when they caused trains to derail and jetliners to collide. He found it ironic that in spite of his contempt for high technology, the Internet, and everything Bill Gates and his kind stood for, he had wound up working in this town, especially when the Bureau had trained so many new agents to handle this type of work. And not only did he work in this area, but he also assisted technical FBI agents in Seoul, Taiwan, Hong Kong, and Japan working to preven cyberterrorism in America.

Technical agents.

He grunted at the thought, not understanding when exactly the Bureau had started recruiting soft college kids instead of real agents—the reason why so many of them had been killed in recent years in the United States and Southeast Asia, and also the reason he was here. MacClaine knew how to fight crime *and* stay alive, skills his superiors wanted him to instill in the junior agents fighting technocrime.

MacClaine sighed, remembering the old days, when agents would be recruited from the police force, the various branches of the armed forces, and even from the CIA and the NSA. Before a candidate even got near the FBI training academy at Quantico he would have already experienced combat, have already been shot at, and most importantly, have become proficient with a number of weapons and some degree of hand-to-hand combat. That type of candidate made up less than half of today's FBI force. The rest were arrogant college kids with guns, badges, attitudes, and cemetery plots in their not-so-distant futures. Most of them considered MacClaine an old dinosaur with nothing to teach them beyond what they had already learned at Quantico.

The hell with it, MacClaine thought. Next month would be his twentieth year with the Bureau. Five more and he could retire with a full pension. *Then it's adios, California and hello, Texas, home, sweet home.*

MacClaine peered over the heads of the eclectic mob rushing to grab a bite to eat before returning to their desk jobs. He sighed again, not understanding how someone could spend his or her life sitting behind a computer terminal, slowly going blind from the screen's glare while clicking their way into advanced tendonitis.

His gaze landed on a two-story building across the street, the Kyoto Club, an exclusive Japanese restaurant, the favorite lunch place of Mr. Nakamura, senior vice president of sales for Akita Electronics in North America. Word of the possible connection between the recent computer-triggered disasters and certain Japanese companies had reached the San Jose FBI office this morning.

The lead's thin but worth pursuing, he thought, remembering the flash report he had read this morning. The theory of Senior Analyst Conklin was weak, but it was the best lead in the investigation, enough for Brent MacClaine to take a break from a case he had been working in conjunction with the FBI office in Seoul, South Korea, on cyberterrorism—the same case that resulted in the emasculation of the junior agent now living in New England.

The message from Washington had also indicated that Conklin was en route aboard a commercial flight and due to arrive later in the afternoon. Washington had requested that he work the lead with the technical assistance of Conklin, who had a computer engineering degree and should be able to provide MacClaine with added insight into the case.

He shook his head. *Technical assistance, my ass.* Still, he had been ordered to pick up the analyst at the airport later that afternoon and kick off the investigation. Between now and then, MacClaine figured he might as well get a head start.

Obeying professional habits, MacClaine walked to the end of the block, paused to check his watch, and abruptly doubled back, scanning the crowd for a pair of eyes suddenly looking away, for a newspaper shielding a face, for someone turning hastily, reacting to his trick. Finding no signs of compromise, he momentarily relaxed.

So far, so good.

The two businessmen were still discussing the *EE Times* article. A bare-chested kid in shorts and high-tops walked past him unwrapping a steaming taco, the smell of grilled beef and onions making his stomach rumble. MacClaine kept his back to the businessmen while studying the restaurant, two stories of redbrick and glass. Patrons, all Japanese men, some accompanied by tall and beautiful Caucasian women, walked through a revolving door. Behind tall windowpanes people sat under dimmed red paper lanterns while Asian waiters move about them with grace.

Brent MacClaine groaned, not familiar with that particular restaurant, but recognizing the type of place, a *ryotei,* an exclusive Japanese eatery, like the ones in Los Angeles, Miami, Houston, and New York, charging an exorbitant amount of money just to walk in the door. But more than money was required to get past the two corpulent Asians in business suits guarding the entrance. One had to be invited by a regular patron, who was himself introduced years before by another regular patron who had vouched for his reputation with his own. American females were also accepted if accompanied by a patron. The exclusive restaurant, along with the private clubs, golf courses, and resorts, were part of a parallel world that most people in America did not know existed, where Japanese nationals enjoyed the benefits of their wealth and the best America had to offer, particularly its women. MacClaine believed that many Japanese men enjoyed looking up to tall and slim American models.

MacClaine despised Japanese executives for trying to buy America one block at a time, and he had been first in line cheering when the Nikkei collapsed a few years back, the result of losing first place to the Americans in the race for high technology. The land of the rising sun had seen its first sunset since the war. Now America had the lead in the computer industry, and although MacClaine knew little about this cyberworld, he knew enough to know that it was a major economical advantage, one America had to protect at all cost.

Which is why Uncle Sam pays you the big bucks.

MacClaine frowned. *Big bucks, my ass.* Besides, whatever bucks he had managed to save over the years, his wife's slick lawyers had taken away during a heated divorce five years ago. She had taken the BMW, the house in a Houston suburb, the furniture, the savings, and even the damned cat, leaving MacClaine with a used Nissan and a handful of legal bills.

I knew I was in deep shit when the judge turned out to be a woman.

Soon after the divorce, whose only bright spot was that there hadn't been any kids, MacClaine had requested a transfer to El Paso, his hometown. He simply couldn't stomach the thought of being in the same city with Jessica, whom he still loved despite everything. The Bureau had sent him instead to sunny California, where he'd picked up thirty pounds and begun to drink more heavily than ever before, perhaps to forget a failed marriage, or to heal his scars; perhaps to remember how things had gone wrong, or maybe because he simply didn't give a damn anymore. Whatever the reason, it had nearly destroyed what life he had left in him—along with his FBI career. Eight months ago he had checked himself into a clinic and had also joined a local AA group. He had not fallen off the wagon since.

Another street vendor sold hot dogs and hamburgers to pedestrians. To his right, a man with an unkempt beard, long hair, and dressed in a stained grayish overcoat and sneakers drank from a bottle inside a paper bag. He seemed unaware of the stares shot by an elegantly dressed couple walking by. A Federal Express truck pulled up by the building next to the restaurant, a law office. The driver double-parked, put on the flashing lights, and got out hauling a package, disappearing behind smoked-glass doors.

MacClaine crossed the street, pondering his strategy. Two hours ago he had contacted Nakamura's office to request an appointment. A pleasant and apologetic female voice had informed him that the earliest opening in Mr. Nakamura's schedule would be in two weeks. When MacClaine had insisted that he meet with the executive immediately regarding an investigation related to the disasters in Florida and Texas, the line had gone silent for a moment before another female voice came on. This one was firm and tinged with a Japanese accent, informing him that Nakamura-san would be available during lunch today. She had given MacClaine the name of the downtown club, as well as instructions on exactly what to say to the doormen to gain admission.

The FedEx driver returned to the truck and drove off. The transient downed the bottle, left it by the wall he'd been leaning against, belched loudly while patting his protruding stomach, and, hands shoved in the pockets of the overcoat, walked toward the street.

MacClaine tightened the knot of his tie to make himself presentable. Appearances meant a lot to the Japanese, as did hand gestures and tone of voice. He had learned that much while assisting the San Jose Police Department on a murder case two years ago at the headquarters of Hitachi-America.

He made a mental note to control his mannerisms and not raise his voice, as well as avoid being too confrontational—something he found particularly difficult because twenty years in the Bureau, plus getting royally screwed by his ex-wife's attorneys, plus not having had a drink in nearly eight months, had turned Brent MacClaine into one mean and sarcastic son of a bitch.

He reached into a side pocket to make sure he had a business card, very important in their culture. Checking his watch again and verifying that it was just past noon, he started to go inside and—

MacClaine felt a gun pressed against his back.

"Don't turn around," said a heavily accented voice, pronouncing it more like "Don tun awound."

MacClaine remained still, regretting having come alone, but he was not supposed to be working the case until the afternoon, after picking up Conklin and mapping out a strategy. He had chosen to do this one solo. "What are you going to do, buddy? Shoot me in public?"

A van pulled up to the curb, its side door opening just a few feet away from MacClaine. Two husky Asians wearing business suits stretched their powerful arms at the fed, grabbing him, pulling him inside, throwing him in the large space behind the front seats. MacClaine moaned while landing on the metallic floor, tearing the left shoulder of his suit. He lifted his gaze, spotting the wino, who pulled off a beard and a wig, revealing a bold and wiry Asian with a pillow wrapped around his waistline. He grinned at the fed as he dropped the pillow. He wore jeans and a black shirt underneath.

"Hello, Agent MacClaine. My name Hashimoto."

One of the husky Asians sat in front but kept a weapon pointed at MacClaine. The driver never turned around. The engine was gunned and MacClaine sensed movement, wondering where they were taking him. The other Asian, sporting a bleached-blond crew cut and a large gold earring, grabbed the fed's wrist and twisted his arm, shoving it against MacClaine's back, almost in unison with Hashimoto, who did the same to his other arm. The swift move finished with the sound of clicking handcuffs, which nearly cut off the circulation to his hands.

Hashimoto searched MacClaine, finding not just the model 659 but also the fed's backup weapon, a snub-nosed .38 Special in his ankle holster. He passed both weapons to the Asian in the front seat.

"You guys are making a big mist—"

The lean Asian kicked him hard in the solar plexus.

His breath exploding through his mouth, Brent MacClaine bent over and collapsed on the van's floor, his ribs on fire. A second kick to his abdomen forced bile to his gorge.

"What is your interest in Mr. Nakamura?"

The words, barely discernible as he lay there twitching, rattling gasps escaping his cramped throat, told MacClaine that he would certainly follow the footsteps of so many missing agents unless he could figure a way out of this predicament. None of the men wore masks, which meant he would be killed after they forced a confession out of him. The worst part was that he was not supposed to be working this case yet. If he disappeared, the FBI probably wouldn't associate his vanishing with his meeting with Nakamura because he had told no one about it.

MacClaine's only hope was to follow FBI procedures

when captured. First he had to make the enemy feel at ease with him by letting them beat him, creating the illusion that cuffed and whipped he no longer posed a threat to them. That would make them relax to the point of becoming just careless enough to give MacClaine the opportunity to strike back. He could only hope that in the process of relaxing them, they would not break something that he might need to escape, like a leg.

Through the agonizing pain, MacClaine forced himself to say, "Go to hell."

The knuckle punch to his left cheek almost jerked his head one hundred eighty degrees. The skinny bastard surely knew how to throw a punch. The side of his face burned for a moment and then began to throb. It would look lovely in a couple of hours—if he lived that long. Before he could recover, a second blow struck him straight in the nose, bringing tears to his eyes.

His torso and face ablaze, MacClaine felt light-headed and began to collapse but the firm grip of the blond Asian kept him facing Hashimoto.

"You are making this very difficult on yourself, Agent MacClaine. Just tell us what we need to know and we will kill you quickly."

"All right," MacClaine said after a long pause, nodding. "I'll . . . I'll tell you."

The Asian smiled broadly. MacClaine leaned forward. Hashimoto did likewise. MacClaine gathered his phlegm and scored a direct hit on the Asian's left eye.

Two more blows to his abdomen and one to his groin left Brent MacClaine wishing that he had never joined the FBI. The pain streaking up his testicles made him lose control of his bladder for a couple of seconds.

While the blond Asian held him down by the shoulders, Hashimoto asked, "Why do you think Akita Electronics might have been involved in the recent accidents?"

"I came here . . . to ask questions . . . not to answer them . . . asshole."

Hashimoto flashed MacClaine a grin of yellow, crooked

teeth. "A noble and brave gesture, Brent—may I call you Brent?" The grin turned into a frown. "But a very *stupid* one." Hashimoto snapped his fingers. The sumo wrestler in the front seat put away the gun, reached down in between his feet, and picked up a wire cage, slightly larger than a shoebox. A pair of blazing, red eyes above two small rows of shiny, ivory teeth stared back at MacClaine from behind the twisted wire. He handed the cage to Hashimoto, who set it down in front of MacClaine.

Hashimoto removed a pencil from his pocket and began poking the large rat through the small holes in between the wire. The angered rodent, the fur along its back bristling in waves, snapped the pencil while sneering.

MacClaine's heart began to race. This didn't look good.

Grabbing a heavy-duty laundry bag by his feet, Hashimoto opened it and covered the cage's small trap door while the husky Asian tilted the cage toward the white bag and pulled up the door. The rodent fell into the bag, which became alive as the crazed animal struggled to get out.

"One last chance, Brent," Hashimoto said while keeping the top of the bag closed. "Why do you want to talk to Nakamura-san? Why is the FBI interested in Akita Electronics? Tell me or I'll slip this bag over your head."

The blows he had endured suddenly taking second place to the convulsing bag, MacClaine felt his gut filling with molten lead. Instead of panicking, however, he stuck to his plan. Phase one was complete. He had made his captors feel at ease by letting them beat him up. He now felt the relaxed pressure the Asian applied to his shoulders. He also noticed the Asian in front no longer looking in his direction or holding a weapon. They were growing confident of their position.

MacClaine reached for a small pin he kept stuck in the inside lining of his jacket's sleeve. Handcuffs were easily picked if one happened to have the right tool at hand. While the blond Asian kept both hands on his shoulders, MacClaine, hands cuffed behind his back, grabbed the end of the pin in his left sleeve with the thumb and index fingers of his right hand, pulling it out and immediately going to work on the lock. He had done this many times at his apartment in total darkness in under thirty seconds.

"In Japan, I saw men go as long as twenty minutes," the Asian said. "But in America, most won't last but five. The screaming, however, usually stops after the first minute, turning into groaning. You see . . . rats love tongues . . . and eyeballs."

MacClaine freed his left arm, wasting no time, striking the brute behind him with an elbow to the midchest area. Bones cracked. The man screamed, collapsing while holding his torso.

Before Hashimoto could react, MacClaine brought his left hand forward, striking Hashimoto's sternum with the heel of his right palm. Hashimoto let go of the laundry bag and fell back clutching his chest.

As the Asian in the passenger seat began to turn around, weapon in hand, MacClaine grabbed the bag and threw it at the driver. The rodent scurried through the opening and jumped on the driver, who screamed while slamming on the brakes, letting go of the wheel. The van swerved into oncoming traffic, shoving MacClaine against Hashimoto, crashing the side of MacClaine's head on the side door. He caught a glimpse of a city bus coming straight for them while the Asian in the passenger seat reached over to grab the wheel.

The diversion having achieved the desired effect, MacClaine yanked open the side door and jumped out shortly before the van came to a complete stop.

He fell on the asphalt, skinning both knees, rolling, crashing against the front wheel of a parked sedan, staggering to his feet, racing away, his ribs protesting his brusque movements. Ignoring the pain, sidestepping to avoid hitting two pedestrians, the federal agent focused on the upcoming intersection, ignoring the stares and complaints of the people he shoved aside, struggling to reach the corner before the men in the van recovered and went after him. He had seen their faces, heard their questions. He knew they could not let him get away.

The crack of a gunshot echoed down the crowded avenue like a whip, shattering the headlight of a sedan to his immediate right. People screamed. Havoc set in. Mac-Claine used the stampeding crowd to his advantage, hiding in it while rushing toward the end of the block.

A second bullet walloped a palm tree by the corner. MacClaine cut left at the intersection, getting out of the line of fire, rushing down the street, turning right at the next corner, left at the following corner, and running for two more blocks before slowing to a fast walk when noticing that no one was following him. He heard sirens in the distance, spotted three taxicabs parked in front of the Fairmont Hotel. Ignoring the curious stares of the uniformed bellboys, MacClaine climbed into the rear seat of the first cab.

"Where to, mister?" the driver said, placing an elbow over the back of the seat while turning around, a Hispanic in his midthirties with a trimmed mustache and short dark hair. His brown eyes widened. "Are you okay? Would you like me to take you to a hospital?"

MacClaine shook his head, giving the driver the address of the San Jose FBI office.

"Look, mister, if you're in trouble with—"

MacClaine flashed his badge at him. "Drive."

The driver complied.

Exhaling as the vehicle left the hotel, MacClaine realized he was now a target. His apartment was no longer safe, and neither was his car, still parked at the office. The people who'd sent those men would be very disappointed. Not only had their hired guns failed to extract any information from him but they had allowed him to escape after letting him know through the kidnapping and the questioning that they had obviously been involved in the chip-sabotage scheme. Their only choice now was to eliminate MacClaine as quickly and quietly as possible.

In spite of the pain, MacClaine managed a thin smile. *That's exactly what I want them do to,* he thought, his operative's mind already coming up with a plan to turn the tables.

7

NEW FACES

The driver got on Highway 101 heading north. MacClaine just stared out the window while breathing slowly. His ribs had been bruised but not broken. After twenty years in the force he could tell the difference. The road cruised through the heart of Silicon Valley. In the distance he could see the large blue buildings of Intel. Closer to the highway was NEC and Lucent Technologies.

They exited 101 at Lawrence Expressway and headed south, passing AMD's opulent headquarters, turning right on El Camino Real, a wide boulevard packed with restaurants, shopping centers, hotels, and office buildings. The FBI office was located on the third floor of a flashy steel-and-glass building a few blocks down from Lawrence.

MacClaine paid the fare and walked slowly up the steps to the small lobby, going in, stabbing the elevator button, reaching his floor seconds later.

The FBI office occupied the entire floor. It was composed of three conference rooms, two of them connected by a one-way mirror; a cubicle area for clerical workers and junior agents, mostly former college kids; and a few offices for the senior agents. As special agent in charge, MacClaine had the only corner office.

"Good heavens, Mr. MacClaine. What in the world—?"

MacClaine held up a palm at Margaret Crawford, his

assistant. Once a pretty California blond, the fifty-one-year-old woman was now paying the price of living on the beach for so many years. Her skin was leathery and wrinkled, and lately she had put on some weight. But as far as her job was concerned, MacClaine considered her top notch. "Maggie, just get me some peroxide, cotton, and bandages from the first-aid kit."

"Yes—yes, sir. Right away, Mr. MacClaine. By the way, sir, you've gotten a dozens different calls from—"

"Later, Maggie."

"But, sir, they're regarding—"

"Not now."

"Also the analyst from—"

"Also, Maggie," he said, cutting her off while turning the doorknob to go in his office, "get me a clean shirt and a pair of jeans from the cabinet, and send one of the rookies to pick up that nerd analyst from Washington, would you?" MacClaine oftentimes had to spend the night at the office working on a case. He always kept a few changes of clothes handy.

"The nerd took an earlier flight and grabbed a cab at the airport. Thank you," said a crisp female voice from inside his office.

Maggie shrugged while opening the medicine cabinet. "I tried to warn you."

"Just get me the stuff I asked for," he said, going inside, momentarily taken aback by the naturally attractive woman silhouetted by the sunshine streaming through the windows behind her. She wore faded jeans, a white T-shirt under a light cotton jacket, and sneakers. A red backpack rested by her feet. Short auburn hair framed a pair of hazel eyes and a provocative mouth that awakened something in Brent MacClaine. Externally, however, he didn't flinch, professionally hiding not only his surprise that Conklin was a skirt—a Bureau term for a female—but also that she was quite a *lovely* skirt. Instead he asked in a tired tone of voice, "What do you want to do?"

"I'm Erika Conklin, technical analyst from the Wash—"

"I *know* who you are. You're the one who's blaming the Japs," he interrupted, removing his jacket and holding it to the light, grimacing at the torn fabric. He had paid three hundred bucks for this one. "I asked you what do you want to do?"

"Didn't you get the message?" she asked, placing fine hands on a small waist while dropping one shoulder, her breasts thrusting forward.

MacClaine sighed heavily, removed his empty holster, and began to unbutton his shirt. After getting beat up so badly he didn't feel like talking to anyone, much less a Washington nerd who also happened to be a skirt.

"Shouldn't we get properly introduced before you start taking your clothes off?"

MacClaine grinned ever so slightly. "Bad morning, Conklin. Pleasure to meet you." He extended a hand and shook hers, pleasantly surprised at her firm grip, even with such delicate hands, unlike the fishy handshakes he usually got from women.

"What happened to you?" she asked while MacClaine removed his shirt, exposing not just a healthy love handle but also a huge purple blotch running the length of his torso.

"Fans. Couldn't keep their hands off me."

At that moment Margaret Crawford entered the room, dropping the change of clothes on the desk and handing MacClaine a bottle of peroxide and a bag of cotton balls. She also gave him a wet towel.

"Would you mind, Maggie?" he asked, pointing at his skinned shoulder.

"I'm your assistant, not your nurse or your mother." She turned around and briskly walked out of the room, leaving MacClaine staring at the items in his hands.

He gave Erika a pleading look while holding the peroxide and the cotton in front of him like a peace offering.

"I don't think so," she replied, crossing her arms while frowning.

"Figures," MacClaine said under his breath, ripping

open the plastic bag, soaking a couple of cotton balls with peroxide, and going to work on his left shoulder. "All right, Conklin. What's the plan?"

Erika sat on one of two chairs across his desk. Mac-Claine remained standing by the windows rubbing the dirt off his shoulder while making faces.

"First thing we need to do is contact someone from Akita's sales department. I was thinking of pret—"

"I'm afraid that won't be necessary," MacClaine interrupted. "That's what I tried to do this morning and all I got were these beauty marks."

She jumped to her feet. "You've already contacted Akita Electronics?" Her voice carried an edge.

"This morning."

She placed a hand on her waist and shook the other at him, her index finger cocked. "How . . . how *dare* you? Who gave you authorization to start this investigation without me?"

"Easy, easy," MacClaine said without looking at her, throwing the used cotton balls in the wastebasket, snagging a couple more, and soaking them.

"Don't you dare *easy* me, mister, or I'm calling Washington."

"Look. I just wanted to get a head start. I think I've already paid plenty for that mistake."

She remained still for a few moments, measuring him. Slowly, she calmed down, took a deep breath, and approached him, pointing at the purplish skin over his ribs. "Does that hurt?"

He nodded. "You have no idea."

She stabbed him with a finger.

"Son of a bitch!" he screamed while jumping away from her. "That *really* hurt, dammit!"

"Good," she replied, "because I want you to remember something, Agent MacClaine. I may be just the analyst working this case—the *nerd* from Washington—but I do have a say, at least according to Palenski. Remember that all of the leads that you and the rest of the FBI supermen were tracking down have led to nowhere. There are no theories left except for mine, and that means that we make the calls together. This case is very dear to me and I'm not going to let you screw it up. Got it? Now tell me, *exactly*, what is it that you did this morning?"

MacClaine stood, grimacing at the bloody cotton ball in his hand. She folded her arms, hazel eyes shooting laser beams.

He grabbed the wet towel and calmly wiped his face.

"This is ridiculous," she said, reaching for the phone. "I'm getting Palenski on the line."

"Calm down," he said, leaning against the windowsill. "No need to get your panties all tied up in a knot. I'll tell you what has happened so far."

"You've got five minutes. If I'm not satisfied with what I hear, I'm dialing."

MacClaine actually took ten minutes, careful not to leave out any details from the moment he received the flash report to the instant he walked into the office. By the time he was finished, Erika's contempt was tinged with compassion and admiration for this reckless and crude yet brave and ingenious stranger.

"They just kidnapped you? Just because of a phone call to set up a meeting?"

"Don't forget that I mentioned to them that I needed to see Nakamura regarding the accidents."

"Still," she said, biting her lower lip, exposing shiny white teeth. "Why would they take such a risk? In doing so they have gone from just a company who happened to stop purchasing a certain type of computer chip to a real suspect."

"Well, they didn't really expect me to escape. I was supposed to be interrogated and terminated. Instead, now I'm a walking target."

"Sorry to hear that."

"It's better this way, actually," he replied, securing a nonstick pad with medical tape over his shoulder. He put on a clean shirt. "Now we definitely know what kind of people we're dealing with."

"Well, I hope you don't take offense at my comment, but I would have used a little less frontal approach." She paused.

"Go on."

"I was considering the angle of calling Akita's purchasing department as a sales representative from a European semiconductor company." She fished out a few business cards form her backpack and handed one to MacClaine.

MELISSA ACKMANN
REGIONAL ACCOUNT MANAGER
SIEMENS ELECTRONICS, LTD.

"What were you going to tell them?"

"I was going to offer them an IC equivalent to the TI6500 but faster and cheaper. Siemens even happens to make one. I've contacted Siemens already and a couple of execs were ready to back me up. Once I got to chatting with the purchasing department, I figure I would be able to learn enough to pick up other leads."

MacClaine nodded, holding the card in both hands, realizing his mistake. Frontal approaches had worked well many times in the past, but it was obvious that he had blown it this time around.

She took the card from him and shoved it in the backpack. "That's out now, though, thanks to your little stunt. If I were to try this now I'll probably be walking into a setup, just like you did."

Technical analyst or not, MacClaine had to give her credit. There was a brain behind the pretty face.

"One thing we now know for certain is that they're definitely involved in this. Now we need to find out just how much they know." MacClaine looked away. "If we can just figure a way to get close to Nakamura . . ."

"MacClaine?"

"Yeah?"

"Did they really try to put a bag with a rat over your head?"

He nodded solemnly. "Conklin, in my twenty years with the Bureau I've been kicked, shot, stabbed, punched, bitten, scratched, burned, and nearly drowned, but the rat thing was a first."

Erika exhaled heavily while extending her lower lip, ruffling her bangs in a way that made MacClaine briefly inspect the rest of her before facing the windows, hands on the windowsill.

"This was our last lead. Following up on the missing engineers has led us nowhere. Whoever did this covered his tracks quite well."

MacClaine closed his eyes. He was out of choices. "I'm a target now," he said, walking to a tall safe in the corner of the room and dialing the combination. "I think I know how to turn that to our advantage."

"How's that?"

He opened the door and pulled out a Beretta 92F, a 9-mm pistol with the same fifteen-shot capacity as his model 659. He also snatched a small Walther PPK and shoved it into his ankle holster. "FBI analysts carry weapons?"

Erika shook her head.

He made a face. *"Nothing?"*

"I'm an analyst, a computer engineer with some investigative training. I'm not a cop or agent."

"Wait," he said, reaching into a drawer and handing her a small can of pepper spray. "Just point and shoot. It's good up to ten feet. After you spray, kick him in the balls and run like hell. Got that?"

"Why would I ever need something like—"

"Insurance, Conklin. You can even take it home as a souvenir from sunny California."

Erika inspected the small metallic cylinder, which she shoved in a pocket.

"Now you're armed and dangerous." MacClaine grinned.

She smiled without humor.

He reached for the jeans on the desk, motioning her to turn around. "Unless you want to watch."

She turned to face the wall, arms folded. "So, how is it that you plan to force a break in the investigation?"

MacClaine inspected her from behind, disappointed that the cotton jacket broke up what he knew would be a beautiful ass. Too bad he was too old and too fat. "I'll explain it to you on the way."

As they walked in front of his assistant's desk, she said, "Mr. MacClaine?"

"We need to get going, Maggie. What is it?"

She handed him a dozen pink notes. "Here. Read them on the way."

"What's this?"

"We've gotten many calls this afternoon, including two from the mayor's office, two from Senator Horton, one from the mayor of San Francisco, and three from the governor's mansion. They're all very concerned about the FBI harassing Japanese corporations doing business in the state of California."

He stopped cold. "What? Why didn't you tell me before?"

Margaret Crawford rolled up her eyes.

"Harassment? What kind of crap is that?"

Erika nodded. "Sounds like pressure."

"What?"

"Pressure. They're applying pressure, indirectly, that is."

MacClaine nodded, remembering the case in which he had assisted a few years ago. Some Japanese businessmen, particularly those well connected in America, had a way of indirectly screwing with you. He recalled how the two lead detectives from the San Jose tech-crime unit were featured in the local paper as racists. Then bad things began happening to them. Car loans were not approved, credit cards were not renewed, one of them lost custody of his child. MacClaine suddenly got a really bad feeling about this investigation. After making one simple phone call he had been kidnapped, beaten, and nearly disfigured by a rat. Then he'd managed to escape and now it turned out that he was the one harassing them.

"That's why I was opting for the less confrontational approach," Erika said.

"Let's go, Conklin. And Maggie, if anyone calls to bitch about me being anti-Japanese, just forward the calls to my mobile phone."

"*If* they call again, sir."

"What do you mean?"

"At least Senator Horton and the governor informed me that that they will be registering their complaints directly with Washington."

"Great," said MacClaine, rubbing his sore nose while heading for the door, the lump on his cheek throbbing. "Just fucking great."

8

THE JDA

Oruku "Willie" Matsubara slid a shoji screen back, crossing into the living room of one of his *bettakus*, residences he maintained for his mistresses, most of them American. He was naked and carried two flute glasses filled with chilled Dom Perignom, which he set on a black lacquer cocktail table, next to three gardenia-scented candles, a mobile phone, and a small cup of soy sauce. A beautiful woman lay on her back on several *daiwan* cushions spread over tatami mats, her silky skin glistening in the flickering candlelight.

Armed with a set of chopsticks, he sat next to her and picked up off her belly a nigiri sushi, rice formed into a bite-size cake topped with chopped sea urchin. A dozen cakes extended from her blond pubic hair to the middle of her perfectly shaped breasts, the result of ten thousand dollars he had paid at a cosmetic surgery clinic in Beverly Hills. Willie Matsubara dipped the sea urchin side of the cake in the soy sauce and ate it, breathing deeply while chewing with his eyes closed. He picked up one of the glasses and spilled several drops of Champagne on her left thigh, which he then kissed. She smiled, squirming over the cushions as a cold droplet ran in between her legs.

A handsome Asian, Willie Matsubara also smiled while

picking up another rice cake. He'd already had this woman twenty minutes ago, and after finishing his meal he would have her again.

The mobile phone ran. Matsubara picked it up.

"Hai?" he said into the tiny unit.

"Matsubara-san?"

It was Hashimoto. He sounded agitated.

"Hai."

"There has been a . . . complication."

Matsubara knew exactly what his subordinate meant. He set the chopsticks on the table and spoke rapid Japanese. "Meet me in twenty minutes. Usual place."

"Arigato gozaimasu, Matsubara-san."

He hung up.

"I'm afraid we will have to finish this some other time, my dear," he said, having one last cake and a sip of Champagne before getting up and putting on the clothes he had tossed over a black leather sofa thirty minutes ago.

"Oh, Willie," she said, pouting like a little girl, picking up the rest of the cakes and placing them back in a small plastic box under the cocktail table. "Now I'm going to be depressed all afternoon." She stood, her breasts defying gravity.

Slipping into his designer slacks, Matsubara reached in his back pocket and pulled out five crisp one-hundred-dollar bills, which he set on the table. "Go buy yourself something pretty, *hai?"*

"Boy, you sure are slick, Willie."

Matsubara's hard-edged features softened. His American girlfriends had nicknamed him 'Slick Willie' because of the way he handled himself, always knowing the right thing to say or do, never losing his posture, and always appearing to be in control—something that his mistresses found incredibly appealing, in addition, of course, to the fact that he spent a fortune pampering them. Matsubara liked the former presidential nickname, which made him feel important, just as he had felt all of his life.

Oruku Matsubara had been born to wealth in Sendai, the

largest city between Tokyo and Sapporo. The only son of the multibillionaire industrialist Harachi Matsubara, Oruku was given all of the privileges of a royal prince. He was educated in Tokyo's finest schools before attending the prestigious Tohoku University in Sendai, where he earned a double degree in business and criminal law. He followed with a master's degree in international law from Stanford University in Palo Alto, California. Upon his return home, his father set him up to work as liaison between Japan's private industry and the government. The young Matsubara spent five years in conference rooms attacking the many difficult issues facing his country's once almighty high-tech industry, now demoted to second place by the thriving American semiconductor conglomerates. During those turbulent times, when the Japanese economy witnessed its first recession, Matsubara's family lost millions, nearing bankruptcy and the shame that it would have brought to his family name. It was during those struggling months that that Oruku Matsubara met Konichi Tanaka, head of the Japanese Defense Agency. The two of them, under the leadership of Fuji Yokonawa, Japan's minister of industry and commerce, plotted a plan to ensure Japan's victory in the race for high technology. In return, Matsubara would get the financial assistance that his family's businesses in Sendai needed to return to profitability. Determined to turn his father's company around, Oruku Matsubara had moved to Silicon Valley three years ago, under a cover provided by the JDA and certain Japanese companies doing business in America, to execute this plan with the assistance of Tanaka's agents, some of whom were members of the Aum Shinrikyo. The JDA had recruited the assistance of the rogue terrorist organization in order to minimize the actual number of JDA agents involved. Both the JDA and the Aum Shinrikyo, which had ties to Osama bin Laden's al Qaeda, hated America, thus making them temporary allies against a common enemy.

For Slick Willie Matsubara, America offered many opportunities absent in his homeland, like the ability to get away with crime. In Japan, 99 percent of all crimes were solved and resulted in convictions. In America the number dropped to less than 15 percent. That alone had provided Matsubara's clandestine operation with the opportunity to execute his plan with little risk of exposure.

As he dressed with the help of his American mistress, Matsubara felt he was losing control for the first time and wasn't certain how to proceed. So far everything he had done, or had commanded his team to do, had followed a carefully detailed agenda, and any deviations were handled according to a preestablished set of rules, all based on precedence.

Matsubara kissed the woman and left, walking down the main hallway of Ocean Breeze Apartments, a building that blended all too well with its surrounding middle-class neighborhood. Only this was no ordinary building. The entire complex belonged to the Tohoku Exports, Ltd., a wholly owned subsidiary of Matsubara Industries, which was now under the financial assistance and management of Japan's Ministry of Economy and Industry until Oruku Matsubara completed his assignment in America, at which time the conglomerate's reins would be his once again. The apartment building had been thoroughly renovated after its acquisition, but only on the inside. The exterior still kept the same worn-down appearance required to avoid drawing unwanted attention. The entire building, lavishly furnished and protected by state-of-the-art surveillance equipment and highly trusted security guards, was used exclusively and discreetly by Japanese businessmen to keep their mistresses.

He reached the lobby of the one-story structure and bowed slightly to the two doormen sitting behind the security counter immediately to the right of the only entrance to the building. Both Japanese men, experts in judo and karate, stood.

"*Konichiwa*, Matsubara-san," one of them said while bowing.

Willie Matsubara returned the bow but did not reply as

he pushed the bulletproof glass door and walked into a radiant afternoon, his Armani suit hanging gracefully from his thin but athletic frame. He put on a pair of designer sunglasses and pressed a button on his Acura NSX's remote keyless entry system. A series of short beeps and the driver-side door unlocked. He gave the Lexus sedan parked behind him a brief glance, verifying that his bodyguards were awake.

Sweat began to develop above his upper lip as he drove off. Fumbling with the climate control unit, Slick Willie sighed. He lacked guidelines on how to proceed. There was no contingency plan for this morning's complication, when he had dispatched four of Tanaka's agents to handle a curious FBI agent.

Precedence.

Everything Matsubara had done to carry out his mission had been based on either the master plan or on a set of precedence-based responses to situations that may have deviated from the plan.

But this?

How was he supposed to handle such complication when from the onset no complications of this type had been expected because the plan developed by the JDA and the Aum Shinrikyo had been designed to eliminate all possibility of error?

The plan.

Matsubara went through the plan, remembering the multiple briefings with JDA and Aum operatives before they went out recruiting candidates from American firms. The targets fit a specific profile, outlined by Tokyo's foremost experts in American psychological behavior. The team sought American engineers in considerable debt, single, resentful because someone else got the promotion, and wishing for a break, for a better life, in a way contemplating how to get even with their employers. A series of meetings followed initial contacts at diverse locations, like malls, restaurants, and health clubs. Agreements were reached, down payments issued, debts canceled, promises made for further financial incentives after completion of their assignments. The design changes had been minor, easily implemented in minutes, even more easily covered up, buried in imperfect revision systems, beyond the reach of standard verification routines.

Matsubara tightened his grip on the leather-wrapped steering wheel as he got on Highway 101 and headed north, toward Mountain View, noticing the sun reflecting off the gold ring he wore on his left hand, which marked him as a member of the Yamato Ichizotu, a secret network within the JDA, which he had joined in order to save his family's conglomerate from the shame of bankruptcy. The emblem of the Ichizotu, or clan, a curved cross with a circle on top, was etched in onyx on top of the ring, covering a tiny cyanide capsule. A millennium-old tradition called for members of the Yamato Ichizotu to bite into the ring and swallow the pill if captured alive in order to preserve the group's secrecy. The Yamato Ichizotu took its name from the legendary warriors from the early centuries, who emerged from northern Kyushu and fought their way eastward, across the Japanese islands, conquering many small kingdoms in the region, unifying the country and asserting their right to rule all of Japan. In the process, the Yamato leaders built some of Japan's greatest cities, including Osaka, Nara, and Kyoto. Some of Yamato's elite samurais protected their clan by spying on enemy forces or sometimes by carrying out clandestine assassination missions against enemy leaders. Yamato samurais were the secret force that maintained order and dispensed justice for many centuries in Japan, preempting attacks from foreign and domestic enemies of the government by eliminating potential threats before they became threats.

Oruku Matsubara considered himself a Yamato samurai, a modern-day warrior, secretly fighting for Japan's right for dominance of the high-tech world, of the future.

In a society that did not tolerate error, where trains and airplanes arrived and departed on time, where everything from home appliances and automobiles to industrial equipment worked reliably, where the individual worked not to better himself but to better his society, falling in second place in the high-tech race to the imperfect Americans had shaken the Japanese society with a force greater than the earthquake that had struck Kobe in 1995. Refusing to accept failure, to admit that their perfect economic machine had indeed been beaten by the Americans and their semiconductor technology, brave visionaries within the government of Japan had called upon its bravest technological, financial, and intelligence warriors to find a solution to their dilemma. The Yamato Ichizotu had quickly sprung into action for the glory of Japan, making a secret alliance with the Aum Shinrikyo in order to join forces against America.

Matsubara accelerated and switched lanes, frowning at the bad news. Everything had gone according to plan, just as his superiors had predicted. The small army of engineering recruits had done their job and returned to get the balance of their payments. Hashimoto's men, all members of the Aum network, had handled the termination phase and disposal of bodies. There had been no trace left behind for America's less-than-perfect police system to follow, and once again his superiors had been correct. None of the missing cases were ever solved.

Everything has gone just as we had planned it, he thought, getting off the highway and heading toward an affluent residential neighborhood up the mountains west of Silicon Valley. Now Matsubara found himself faced with the difficult task of doing what Americans referred to as damage control, something seldom heard of in Japan.

He passed the least expensive residences of the neighborhood, which increased in price as he drove up the hill, starting in the half-million-dollar range at the bottom and ending in the multimillion-dollar estates overlooking Silicon Valley. His house occupied an acre of land that protruded like a lookout point over the valley. Priced at over $10 million—half of it spent on the land, the foundation, and its dozens of steel beams driven deep into the mountain side to protect the structure against mudslides—the fenced estate provided housing for Matsubara, his close associates, and the detachment of Aum operatives at his disposal. No outsiders were ever allowed inside the wrought-iron gates, guarded around the clock.

The heavy gate slid to the side and Matsubara drove onto the cobblestone driveway, flanked by a manicured garden. The Lexus followed him, but stopped just past the gate, by the guard house.

The road curved to the left, toward the two-story structure, a Victorian mansion once belonging to the CEO of a long-forgotten American corporation that went bankrupt in the mid-eighties, when Japanese companies had dumped DRAM memory chips into the world's market at below-cost prices, swallowing market share while driving the competition into the ground. Matsubara, through Sakata Electronics, had acquired the estate three years ago and had it thoroughly renovated using his discretionary fund, including the installation of state-of-the-art surveillance equipment, dedicated data, video, and audio satellite links with Tokyo, and even a *rotemburo*, an open-air heated pool that resembled a large pond surrounded by maple and cypress trees. Hot water ran along bamboo gutters and poured into the pool, creating the gurgling sound that replaced the NSX's light droning as Matsubara shut off the engine.

Perhaps a short bath in the steaming water to experience *yudedako*, the degree of sublimity achieved by immersing naked in the steaming water for a few minutes, was just what Matsubara needed. But the thought vanished as he spotted Aum Shinrikyo local leader Hioki Hashimoto, leaning against one of the front columns, arms crossed. Matsubara considered his methods medieval, in sharp contrast with the modern JDA. But Hashimoto and his associates were a necessary evil in this most critical mission to return his country to the front of the high-tech race, and in the process humiliate the American semiconductor industry.

"*Konichiwa*, Matsubara-san." Hashimoto bowed his head slightly.

Matsubara didn't return the salute, something he would have never done only three years ago. But living in America for so long had stripped him of some of his traditional values, particularly when problems arose, replacing them with crude American behavior. "Let's do away with the formalities, *hai*? Tell me what happened."

Dressed in blue jeans and a plain shirt, Hashimoto, one of the terrorists behind the 1995 Sarin gas attack in Tokyo, rubbed his chest with his left hand and grimaced, obviously in pain. His crooked teeth and unkempt hair made the patrician businessman wonder why Tanaka ever picked such character to work with the JDA in this mission.

"The American agent . . . we underestimated him," Hashimoto began, taking ten minutes to explain what had taken place.

Getting progressively angrier as he listened to the terrorist, Matsubara restrained himself from losing his temper, which was considered extreme bad form in his culture. He had been against this approach from the moment Hashimoto had made his recommendation this morning, and he had reluctantly agreed to proceed after Tanaka himself had sanctioned the strike. At the time it had seemed like a risky but somewhat reasonable move to just make the FBI agent disappear, particularly given that agency's terrible track record solving cases that involved missing agents. On the other hand, a simple meeting between a well-briefed Fuji Nakamura and the FBI agent might have been a simpler approach, but Matsubara didn't know what kind of questions the Akita executive might be facing. As corporate liaison, it was his job to protect the reputation of the Japanese companies. In order to avoid such risky confrontation, he had agreed to shelter Nakamura and support the kidnapping approach, which had the potential of gathering information by using interrogation methods that Matsubara preferred not to know. In the end that approach had backfired.

Matsubara frowned, calculating the magnitude of the problem. This morning, following their meeting with Tanaka, he had contacted his associates in politics and the press to put pressure on the FBI to halt the investigation of Akita Electronics on the grounds of racial discrimination, a tactic that usually worked quite well for Japanese corporations doing business in America. Through the years, Matsubara, through Akita and Sakata Electronics, had contributed heavily to the campaigns of city mayors, U.S. senators and congressmen, and even the governor of California. He had made several calls this morning to put some pressure on the FBI, an effort that now seemed meaningless because MacClaine would probably be unwilling to stop the investigation after having been nearly killed.

This is all Tanaka's fault! he thought, realizing that his reaction was being influenced by his years in America. He was focusing on *who*, the American way, instead of *how*, the Japanese way. Matsubara forced himself to remember that the best way to solve a problem was by concentrating on how to solve the problem instead of finding who should be blamed for the problem. Americans spent too much time assigning blame, worrying about whose heads were going to roll, instead of solving problems. But it was particularly difficult for Oruku Matsubara because his entire family estate was at stake. Failure in this mission would be considered *hangyaku*, treason, disloyalty to his country, which had saved him from the shame of bankruptcy. It would mean the loss of his father's conglomerate in Sendai, the loss of his family's honor. His younger brothers and sisters, his cousins, his uncles, every Matsubara in Sendai would become *burakumin*, undesirable, untouchable, shamed for generations to come. His sisters would be unable to marry decent men. His brothers would be unable to find brides. No one would employ them, give them shelter. His family name would be eradicated.

"Ima kono gotagota o katazukete okanai to, watakushitachi wa ato de taihen na me ni au desho!" blasted Mat-

subara after Hashimoto finished, telling the JDA agent that if this mess wasn't cleaned up right away there would be hell to pay.

"Koko de akiramenaide tsuzukenasai!" said Hashimoto, blinking rapidly.

"I'm *not* giving up! But it is very critical that we resolve this quickly, otherwise our mission will fail!"

"Rirakussu suru! I have people observing the FBI office. We'll get another chance soon enough."

"Kono shigoto wa taisetsu dakara!" said Matsubara, shaking his head.

"I know this mission is important," Hashimoto replied, palms open, obviously trying to calm him down. *"Hema o shite koto o dainashi ni shiani yo ni shimasho!"*

"Let's not do anything to screw things up? I think it's too late for that! What do you think the FBI is going to do now that they know that Akita Electronics is definitely involved?"

Hashimoto shrugged. "They have no proof of that. The *gaijin* never actually met with Nakamura. As far as he's concerned no one showed up for the meeting. The FBI has *kuzu*, garbage." *Gaijin* was the term used by the Japanese to reference someone non-Japanese, not one of their own.

Matsubara considered that. He had nothing to fear and neither did Akita Electronics. All the FBI had were bruises. The agent had no proof of their wrongdoing, only *kuzu*. "All right. I'll make sure that Nakamura is clear on the official position of Akita. But how do we discourage further FBI probing?"

"We do it the Aum Shinrikyo way. We will make them vanish while also embarrassing their families."

Matsubara frowned.

Hashimoto pressed on. "I've already contacted Tanaka-san. All of my men have been deployed and we are getting more in the next twenty-four hours."

Matsubara didn't like it, but didn't see much of a choice either. They had to protect Japan, which meant protecting the Japanese corporations at all cost. They had to buy time until the other sabotaged chips malfunctioned, triggering more disasters, achieving the critical mass required to irreversibly cripple the American semiconductor industry, to deliver a blow from which it might never recover. The Nikkei index had already climbed over twenty percent while the Dow and the NASDAQ continued to drop. The world was beginning to lose confidence in American high technology, just as it had written off American auto makers in the early eighties. And once a nation fell behind, as America's big three had learned two decades before, it took more than just technical innovation to get back on top, particularly when the competition continued to move forward at a relentless pace, refusing to let the gap close.

But the gap is closing, thought Slick Willie Matsubara, standing in front of his luxurious estate overlooking Silicon Valley. *A death valley after we kick them back to a dark hole from which they shall never recover.*

• • •

COMPUTER ERROR CAUSES EXPLOSION AT OIL REFINERY. PASADENA, TEXAS (CNN)—OVER THREE HUNDRED WORKERS PERISHED AND THOUSANDS WERE INJURED IN THE EARLY MORNING HOURS WHEN LIQUEFIED PETROLEUM GAS WAS LEAKED TO THE ATMOSPHERE BY A MALFUNCTIONING COMPUTERIZED SAFETY VALVE, TRIGGERING A HUGE EXPLOSION FOLLOWED BY A SERIES OF OTHERS AND A RAGING FIRE. THE ACCIDENT WAS THE FIRST IN PASADENA SINCE THE 1989 EXPLOSION AT A PLASTICS MANUFACTURING PLANT OWNED BY PHILLIPS PETROLEUM CO., WHICH KILLED 22 AND INJURED MORE THAN 80 PERSONS.

BY NOONTIME, THE FIRE HAD SPREAD TO NEARBY PASADENA, FORCING THOUSANDS OUT OF THEIR HOMES AND TRIGGERING THE WORST FIRE IN THE HISTORY OF THAT SOUTHERN TEXAS CITY. THE GOVERNOR OF TEXAS DECLARED PASADENA A DISASTER AREA AND HAS ALREADY REQUESTED FEDERAL ASSISTANCE. "I WILL GET FEDERAL HELP WITHIN THE NEXT TWENTY-FOUR HOURS," A SPOKESMAN QUOTED THE GOVERNOR AS SAYING DURING A SHORT MEETING FOLLOWING A HELICOPTER FLIGHT OVER THE REGION. "IN THE MEANTIME," THE GOVERNOR ADDED, "EMERGENCY CREWS WILL WORK DAY AND NIGHT TO GET THE INJURED TO SAFETY AND TO CONTROL THE FIRE. I WILL ALSO APPOINT AN INVESTIGATIVE PANEL IN THE MORNING TO GET TO

THE BOTTOM OF THIS DISASTER AND MAKE SURE THAT IT NEVER HAPPENS
AGAIN."

A WHITE HOUSE SPOKESMAN ISSUED A PRESS RELEASE JUST AN HOUR
AGO, STATING THAT THE PRESIDENT HAS BEEN IN CONTACT WITH THE TEXAS
GOVERNOR TO DISCUSS FEDERAL ASSISTANCE.

9

EXECUTIVE DECISIONS

President Lester Williams sat behind his desk holding a football and a remote control for the television set he kept in the Oval Office. He had just hung up the phone after a short conversation with the Texas governor, and he now watched scenes from the disaster in Pasadena with some of his top advisors: the secretary of state, the secretary of defense, the national security advisor, and the director of the FBI.

He muted the television set when CNN cut to a commercial and set the remote control on the desk. The sudden quietness in the room descended on all of them as heavily as the severity of the situation. Since the railroad collision in southern Florida, four other computer-triggered disasters had shaken the nation, including the airliner mid air collision over Chicago and now the inferno in Pasadena, which continued to burn despite the brave efforts of an army of firefighters from all over the lone star state. The images brought back memories from the terrorist strikes of 2001.

President Williams dug his fingers into the leather of a football from his Naval Academy days. Etched on the pigskin read Navy 21, Army 20. Williams had rushed this very football into the army's end zone with just five seconds remaining in the fourth quarter. Whenever the pressure began to mount, he would automatically reach for this lucky charm on the marble stand on the corner of his desk and toy with it. To this day he wondered if he could run the nation without it.

"The fire's still out of control," President Williams said out loud while absently inspecting the dark stitches on the football, the remark not directed at anyone in particular. "There is a chemical plant less than a half mile from the blaze and the winds are blowing the flames in its direction. When is that army team going to get down there, Jim?" he asked Defense Secretary James T. Vuono, also a former naval officer.

The stocky secretary, who still maintained the crew cut of his Navy days, replied, "Our finest demolition team will be there within the hour, Mr. President. They're some of the folks that helped clean up New York City in 2001."

Williams nodded and closed his eyes. "Since the computer chips began to shut down, over a thousand people have died and tens of thousands have been injured or left homeless. The last tally I saw estimated the financial damage at over fifty billion dollars. Of course, that doesn't take into consideration the damage done to date to Wall Street. And there is no apparent end in sight." The chief executive glanced at the images on the silent TV. "And now the press has also learned that the accidents might all be linked together to a madman who is sabotaging chips." Despite the FBI's best efforts to keep it contained, the secret of the sabotaged chips had leaked at IBM. Two reporters from the *Washington Post* had made the connection between the IBM12000 and the TI6500. CNN broke the news to the world three days ago. Within a day word arrived at the *Post* from an anonymous engineer at Motorola, who was part of the team performing the failure analysis on the malfunctioning chip that had triggered the Denver blackout. The description of the sabotage fit the others. The news had shocked the nation. Then someone at the FAA leaked information to the press that the computer malfunction at the Midway control tower in Chicago had been tracked to another American-made chip. Domestic flights were down by almost 40 percent since the *Post* article, a situation which was also very reminiscent of several years back. High-tech stocks had dropped an average of twenty points, even if the corporations had not experienced a malfunctioning chip.

And it's only going to get worse.

President Williams turned to the FBI director. "Roman, what's the situation on your front?" Williams conducted his Oval Office affairs in the same manner with which he'd successfully commanded an aircraft carrier for fifteen years. During a crisis, he always pulled in his closest advisors, men whose judgment he trusted, and carefully listened to their opinions before formulating his own strategy.

Palenski shifted his weight on the chair, obviously uncomfortable at being in the hot seat. "All of our initial theories have led us to dead ends. The investigations on the missing engineers have proved fruitless. Right now we're pursuing a theory that the Japanese might be behind this, Mr. President. I have one of my best technical analysts working in conjunction with special agents from the San Jose field office."

Williams set the football on the table and leaned forward. This was the first time that Palenski had mentioned a possible origin for the sabotages.

"The Japanese?"

"Yes, sir."

"Why?"

Palenski cleared his throat and leaned forward to answer, but Secretary of State Christopher Milley, a veteran diplomat and former economist cut in, "Economic superiority, Mr. President. It makes sense." Impeccably dressed in a pinstriped suit, Milley adjusted the wire-frame glasses perched on the bridge of his nose, and added, "Our high-tech industry knocked Japan down to second place many years ago and they have been falling behind since, particularly with the emergence of South Korea, Taiwan, and most recently China in the high-tech world. Up to a couple of months ago, American semiconductor manufacturers topped the world in technological innovation, sales, and profits. It would have taken a crucial mistake in strategy and execution on the part of American corporations to lose this lead. That someone in Japan resorted to such measures to get back on top is a true indication of the state of their industry and their level of desperation."

The president pressed his palms against the football. "Roman? Is that in sync with your theory?"

Palenski nodded. "Yes, sir. In recent years, Japanese corporations have suffered a number of technological set backs, some at our hands, others at the hands of South Korea, Taiwan, and China—nations that have invested heavily in research and development over the past decade to create the correct infrastructure from which to launch their products, oftentimes manufactured at a fraction of the cost of the more expensive Japanese products. That, in my opinion, has opened the door for a rogue faction cyberter-rorists within Japanese corporations—probably working in conjunction with a handful of corrupt government offi-cials—with no choice but to resort to industrial sabotage in order to slow down the competition and give its own industries a chance to catch up."

Williams toyed with the football. "What evidence do you have that it is the Japanese?"

Palenski told them about the sales records of all of the American companies with sabotaged semiconductors. In every case, Japanese customers had stopped ordering com-ponents just before the sabotaged chips went into produc-tion. "When one of my agents approached a corporate executive from Akita Electronics to question him regarding this possible link, he was kidnapped by what looked to him like Japanese terrorists. Fortunately, he managed to escape. That basically confirmed our theory."

Williams pressed one end of the football against his chin as he considered Palenski's explanation. "All right. Let's assume for the time being that it is a group of cyberter-rorists in Japan. What should be our next move? Should I go with this to the Japanese ambassador or maybe even the prime minister himself?"

Milley, Vuono, and Palenski all shook their heads at the same time. Milley spoke first.

"The Japanese are a very closed society when it comes to protecting their own industry, sir, particularly if the disasters seem to be giving them the upper hand in the high-tech world. Without proper motivation, I don't believe anyone in the Japanese government will be inclined to help. I'm quite certain that they will be sympathetic and promise to assist in any way they can, but absolutely nothing will happen."

"I agree, Mr. President," said Defense Secretary Vuono, leaning forward, his booming voice reminding the president of their Navy days, when Commander Vuono, back then Rear Admiral Lester William's executive officer, would convey his commanding officer's orders to the carrier's crew. "My experience dealing with the Japanese is that they will not budge unless we show them that we have a bigger hammer. Right now we don't. Our bargaining position is weak."

"We need to find the list, gentlemen," said Palenski.

All heads turned to him.

"The list?" asked the president.

"That's correct, Mr. President. "If our theory is true, then we also believe that the leader of these cyberterrorists is in possession of the master list of sabotaged components."

"What makes you think that?" asked Vuono.

"Sabotaging components the way it has been done at Texas Instruments, IBM, and Motorola requires a lot of planning ahead, a lot of strategizing about the right engineers to recruit, as well as plenty of central coordination to pull it off as cleanly as they have. Whoever is at the heart of this scheme must possess a list of targeted companies. That someone, through a number of buffers, has obviously alerted Japanese corporations regarding the further purchase of certain American semiconductors."

"Makes sense," said Milley.

"Go on, Roman," said the president.

"Our best course of action is to use covert tactics to find this master list and pull the sabotaged components off the market before more lives are lost." He went on to explain Brent MacClaine's current plan, which carried a high degree of risk, but also the potential for new leads.

"Where do you think this list might be?" asked Vuono.

"I'm hoping to learn that by following our current lead."

"The problem," said Secretary Milley, pausing to consider his comment for a moment before adding, "is that the location of this master list might not be in America but in Japan. *Then* what do we do?"

"We go in and grab it," said Vuono without hesitation.

"Grab it?" asked Secretary Milley while adjusting the knot of his tie.

"What choice do we have? Look at the state of the nation." He pointed at the images on the color screen. Flames ravaged a building. "This is far worse than what happened in 2001. We must go in, grab this list and in the process punish those responsible."

"How do you propose to do that?" asked Milley.

"Are you thinking about CIA or FBI personnel, Jim?" asked Palenski.

"No," replied Vuono. "If the feds and maybe even the CIA can find the location of the cyberterrorists responsible for this with a high degree of confidence, then send in the SEALs. Japan is not Afghanistan, Mr. President. We can't just go in and launch open strikes. We have to utilize our covert forces."

President Williams's eyes gravitated to a framed photo of his stepson's graduation picture from the Naval Academy over twenty years ago. Lieutenant Commander Derek Ray had joined the SEALs shortly after Annapolis, just in time for Panama and Desert Storm, where he participated in the critical mission off the coast of Kuwait that served as a decoy to fool the Iraqis into thinking that the coalition's invasion would come from the sea instead of the

Saudi border. Later, he also led a number of covert terrorist-purging strikes in the Middle-East following the September 11, 2001 attack. He now commanded SEAL Team Five, stationed in San Diego, California, until his Pentagon appointment came through in a couple of months. Ray had married a girl from San Diego a few years ago and there was a baby on the way in five months. At the insistence of his young wife and his mother—the First Lady—Ray had agreed to retire from the SEALs and accept a Navy strategist job at the Pentagon. President Williams loved Derek Ray as his own and had adopted him soon after marrying the boy's mother a few years after the father died in Vietnam.

President Williams stood, football in hand, the conflict of interest burning a hole in his stomach. The chief executive in him knew that Commander Ray's SEAL Team Five was by far the most qualified for this job. The father, and future grandfather in him, however, hoped that the navy would assign the mission to another team. But as commander in chief, Williams refrained from making such suggestion. Ray was, above all, a naval officer serving his country, and his country was now in time of need. "All right, Jim. Let's get a SEAL team ready. And send nothing but the *best* we have."

"Yes, Mr. President."

Williams turned to Palenski. "Roman, how long before your men have everything set up?"

"It's happening real time, sir. We're setting up the trap now, and we're using a bait that they simply will not be able to refuse."

"Very well. Anything else, gentlemen?" asked the president.

"What should we do about the complaints from the Japanese community about FBI discrimination against them?" asked Palenski. "Everyone from the governor of California to the mayors of San Jose and San Francisco have registered complaints against the FBI for harassment."

"Do what they do," said Secretary Milley. "Issue apologies and assurances that we will look into the situation with the utmost urgency. The fact that someone's complaining is actually good news. It tells me that you're on the right path."

The president nodded, his eyes gravitating to the images flickering on the silent television unit. Streams of water rose up to battle fists of flames gushing out of the windows of an apartment complex in Pasadena. Billowing smoke curled up into the skies of south Texas. Men, women, and children wearing robes and blankets huddled across the street. Ambulances rushed past, lights flashing. Paramedics hauling equipment raced toward a circle of bystanders, shoving their way through the wall of people. Chaos, destruction, anguish, death.

A new kind of terrorism had been launched against America, and unfortunately, the perpetrators were even more elusive than Osama bin Laden and his kind. The deadly beauty of their approach had left a large number of ticking bombs across this country, making the situation much more worse than in 2001.

"Get to work, gentlemen," he commanded without taking his eyes off the screen, which flashed image after image in vivid color, with unparalleled clarity. A suburban neighborhood burned next to the oil refinery. Houses collapsed, dust, smoke, and flaming debris boiled skyward, caking firefighters with shades of black and gray.

President Lester Williams watched it in silence.

10

REVERSAL OF FORTUNE

SANTA CLARA COUNTY

Erika Conklin was alone in her seventh-floor Milpitas
Sheraton suite overlooking the waterfall-fed pond surrounding the north side of the pool. Beyond the hotel
grounds, past the palm trees and trimmed landscape, extended Silicon Valley and the mountains leading to San
Francisco. Wearing an old pair of jean shorts and an extralarge T-shirt that reached the middle of her thighs, she lay
in bed on her side hugging a pillow between her legs, her
eyes watching the moonlight reflecting off the water, a
dozen thoughts cruising through her mind. She had the TV
tuned to CNN and had just spent five minutes watching
the latest report from Pasadena. The fire had finally been
controlled, sparing most of the city, but not the fifteen
blocks adjacent to the refinery.

She exhaled. *Crazy day.*

It had actually been a disappointing day. MacClaine's
plan so far had proved fruitless. The fed had set himself
up as bait by staying at his apartment alone while twenty
agents covered him from around and inside the building.
The Japanese had either decided to stay low or had smelled
a trap and chosen to wait for a better opportunity. Whatever the reason, she had wound up spending the entire day
in the rear of a van across from the apartment building.
To show himself, MacClaine had come out twice, once to

buy a newspaper from a machine in front of the apartment complex, and once more to walk across the street and get a cup of coffee. No one had attacked him. At the end of the day, MacClaine had sent Erika to her hotel, along with an armed agent for protection. That agent now guarded the hallway.

The full moon's wan light diffused through the glass doors leading to a small balcony, colliding with the pulsating glow from the television.

Erika looked at the mountains to the north, running past San Francisco, beyond Oakland. She thought of the fertile Napa and Sonoma valleys. She thought of home.

She had been tempted to call her dad and let him know that she was in town but FBI regulations prohibited her from making personal calls during field operations. Instead she had settled for the pleasure of just being in California, the delight of seeing mountains, of breathing the fresh and cool air.

A dark cloud, however, shaded that joy. Innocent people were dying at the hands of Japanese cyberterrorists.

Erika sat up in bed and absently watched the images of destruction flickering on the TV screen.

There's got to be a way . . . somehow.

Taking a deep breath and reaching for the remote on the nightstand, she turned off the TV, walked to the desk in the living area of her suite, and switched on her notebook computer, fitted with a wireless modem preprogrammed for a dedicated satellite link to the FBI headquarters in Washington. The system booted up, but before Windows came up, it paused for twenty seconds.

Erika typed a password to deactivate a virus that she had created two years ago for FBI-owned laptops as a security device in case a mobile computer carrying sensitive FBI information in its hard drive was ever stolen or misplaced. A thief would have failed to enter the password, unknowingly releasing the virus, which would then allow the system to continue its normal boot-up routine while secretly dialing a special FBI number in Washington, ordering the immediate satellite trace of the call using Remote Determination Satellite Service (RDSS), a technology that worked on the same principle as the well-known Global Positioning System but in reverse. Erika's wireless modem served as a ground transmitter, sending a signal that would be then received by two or more satellites in the system. By measuring the different arrival times of the signal, RDSS used tridimensional geometry to calculate the location of the terrestrial transmission. RDSS would then provide FBI analysts in Washington with the exact coordinates of the stolen laptop to an accuracy of around ten meters, or thirty feet. The closest agents would be sent to retrieve the system and arrest the thief. As an additional safety feature, the virus would also hide all classified information from the unauthorized user, protecting sensitive data until federal agents arrived to retrieve the stolen laptop.

Erika had received another cheap plaque and two hundred dollars for the nifty virus, along with a nondisclosure letter that she had to sign pledging never to discuss this safety feature with anyone not associated with the Bureau.

She slipped a Christmas CD into the tray that slid out of the side of the laptop and listened to Bing Crosby's rendition of "White Christmas" through the system's built-in speakers while waiting for the virus scan software to check her system. She had removed the signature of her own security virus from the scan software's signature file to keep it from flagging it every time she booted the machine.

She glanced at the front door, next to the minibar, and verified that she had bolted it, before returning her attention to the screen.

VIRUS CHECK COMPLETE
NO KNOWN VIRUSES FOUND
21,235,190,345 BYTES FREE
PRESS ANY KEY TO CONTINUE

She dialed in to the FBI and was about to check her E-mails to get updates on the tasks she had assigned to her subordinates before leaving Washington but instead she decided to check her department's chat line. This late at night only one showed active on her private address list: Charles Chang. She clicked the log-in icon and the system rewarded her with an empty window for her chat session.

Erika: Hi, Charlie. How're things?

Chang: Boss! How was your flight? How's California?

Erika: Flight uneventful. California's great. Miss this place a lot and there's no roaches in my room! How're you doing? How're things at the office? Any breakthrough?

Chang: Good news from Motorola.

Erika: Yeah?

Chang: They found a sabotaged design by going through their archives. The M32050, a microcontroller sold exclusively to the military market had a narrowed microtrace.

Erika made a fist while tucking her elbow. *Yes!*

She had held little hope that corporations would be willing to spend valuable resources on this task, particularly those not yet affected by the sabotages. But apparently Motorola, hit hard by their malfunctioning M98000, had taken the verification job seriously enough to find another sabotaged design, a very difficult task, particularly when the standard checks might not catch the sabotage, like top-level verification routines, forcing designers to perform their checks at the cell-library level, which multiplied the effort by several orders of magnitude.

Erika: Hey, that's terrific!

Chang: Yep. One down. Hopefully more companies will find them.

Erika: Will keep my fingers crossed.

Chang: This blows the theory that comparing purchasing records to find which chips the Japs had stopped buying would lead to all of the sabotaged chips. This one was never sold to anyone but the Pentagon, yet it was sabotaged like the others.

Erika: You're right. But the comparisons might still find additional
           chips. It's just not our complete solution.
Chang: We'll keep looking.
Erika: Speaking of looking. How're you coming along on the search?

In her absence, Erika had instructed Chang to gather a
list of all American semiconductor manufacturers and perform extensive searches on their sales databases to look
for patterns of Japanese customers canceling orders.

Chang: So far nothing. But like I said, we'll keep looking. We've gone
           through seven companies and so far no luck.
Erika: How are you doing on the passwords?
Chang: Got three roots for Akita and two for Sakata. No luck on Mitsui.
           It's all in my E-mail. Passwords should be good for twenty-four
           hours from three o'clock Pacific time today.
Erika: Good job.

Chang had extracted the key passwords to penetrate the
Japanese conglomerates by using an enhanced version of
the password-snatching virus that had gotten her in trouble
with the FBI. She smiled at the irony. The improved version included an origin scrambler to prevent companies
from tracing the call back to the FBI.

Chang: Good job to you. It's your piece of work, just like Detroit II.

Erika smiled. In the past month she had spent some of
her free time improving the original version of the Detroit
virus.

Erika: You like my new puppy?
Chang: New puppy has big teeth.

Erika had created multiple versions of the virus, each
with a different mutating sequence, and each nested within
the others. This simple change made the resulting virus
mutate in quite unpredictable ways, impossible to break

with current technology. She had learned this trick from a professor at Berkeley. Of course, the trick only worked if the initial virus was very complex, like the Detroit virus. Adding multiple levels of complexity with the nesting scheme turned an already dangerous virus into an unbreakable monster.

Erika:	Keep up the good work and keep Detroit II in an off-line system. Don't want this puppy anywhere near a network connection.
Chang:	Mind if I try to break it?
Erika:	Go for it. If you do I'll buy you lunch.
Chang:	You've got yourself a deal.
Erika:	Got to go. 'Bye.
Chang:	'Bye, Boss.

Erika logged off chat and launched her E-mail software, frowning at the one hundred twenty unread E-mails since last night. She yawned and glanced at the time on the bottom right corner of the screen.

Just past nine in the evening.

It was going to be a long night.

11

BAIT

In his San Jose apartment, Brent MacClaine glanced at his watch, frowning.

The bastards ain't going for it.

He got up slowly from an old leather couch in the living room, one of the few possessions his wife had let him keep, along with the bar stools by the counter separating this room from the small kitchen, where a pile of dirty dishes in the sink challenged the laws of physics while angling up toward the ceiling.

His ribs throbbing and his mouth dry and pasty, MacClaine headed for the refrigerator and grabbed a can of diet soda, his only attempt at weight control. He had already given up on the bicycle he had purchased soon after moving to California with the hope of getting in shape. He had used it twice and now it was a permanent fixture of the living room decor, right next to an old color TV, another item that he had been allowed to keep during the divorce settlement.

He drank the soda in seconds, partly suppressed a belch, and walked into the bathroom to relieve himself, wincing at the pain in his groin while urinating a yellow-red liquid, bringing back memories of his days recovering from a beating by a Houston gang many years ago.

Afterward he inspected his face in the mirror over the

sink. His once-square face had turned slightly bottom
heavy thanks to his sagging fat cheeks. A saffron hue surrounded a deep purple band under his left eye, which had
grown bloodshot as the day went on. At least that wound
seemed cosmetic, unlike his nose and ribs, which hurt
every time he breathed. He peered at the bloody tissues in
the waste basket next to the sink. He'd had three nose
bleeds in the past four hours.

MacClaine coughed, spitting bloody phlegm into the
sink.

*Pissing blood, coughing blood, and sneezing blood.
Bastards are gonna pay for this.*

MacClaine swore to get even with them, and he had
hoped to have accomplished that by now, but no one had
made a move against him since arriving at his apartment
shortly after convincing Erika Conklin that it was their best
tactic at the moment. Now he began to wonder if perhaps
the cyberterrorists had anticipated this move and chosen to
remain out of sight.

"But you know sooner or later they're gonna try. They
simply can't let you live. You've seen their faces."

"Talking to yourself, sir?"

MacClaine tapped his lapel microphone, connected to a
tiny unit strapped to his chest, also linked to an earpiece.
"Mind your own business and stay crisp!"

"Ye-yes, sir."

Damned rookies, MacClaine thought, walking to his
window and inspecting the street below, spotting two unmarked sedans at each end of the block and a sniper atop
the building across the street. Plenty of fishermen and bait
but no sign of the fish.

He thought about calling Erika to think through their
options, but decided to give this idea a little more time.
Perhaps the Japanese were just being cautious, afraid of
rushing into anything before having inspected the place
from a safe distance.

MacClaine snagged a cleaning kit from a cabinet in the
kitchen and sat on a bar stool, unholstering the small

Walther, his back-up piece, which he began to clean to pass the time.

At one o'clock in the morning a figure in black made his way up the emergency stairs, reaching the landing of the target floor, slowly inching the heavy door forward while extending an oral surgeon's mirror through the opening, spotting a man in a business suit standing next to the elevator. A closer inspection revealed a bulk beneath his coat's left breast.

While abruptly pushing the door, the figure lunged in and threw a knife with great force at the man guarding the floor. The blade found its mark, stabbing the neck, slicing through the larynx. The man collapsed.

The hallway cleared, the figure dragged the body into the stairway before proceeding toward the target room.

Brent MacClaine jumped off the sofa when he heard a noise in the hallway, his right hand already clutching the Beretta, muzzle pointed at the ceiling.

"Movement outside my door," he whispered into his lapel microphone.

"A couple's heading for their unit. Area's clear," came the immediate reply from one of his young subordinates guarding the hallway.

Erika Conklin jumped out of bed at the sound of splintering wood. Trembling, she looked all around her before checking her watch. Just past one o'clock in the morning. She had been sleeping for about an hour.

Confused, scared, she listened to hastening footsteps on the ceramic tile of the suite's living room, their clicking echoing in the bedroom. Erika stopped breathing, her mind racing, her stomach knotting. Someone had broken in, and that someone would reach the bedroom in a matter of seconds.

How did someone get past that agent outside?

No time to analyze! Just do!

But what? I'm trapped!

A weapon, Erika! You need a weapon!

She grabbed the can of pepper spray and glanced at the open bedroom door. The TV rested on a stand to the left of the door. On the right side another door led to the bathroom.

Nearly hysterical, Erika shoved two pillows under the sheets and dove for the space between the TV and the corner of the room, temporarily out of sight from anyone going through the doorway. Her thumb fumbled with the safety cap of the small spray can, finally popping it, index finger resting over the dispensing button as she held it in front of her at eye level.

The footsteps dashed down the hallway, the vibration on the floor reaching Erika as she remained hiding behind the TV unit, her left eye peeking at the doorway through the space between the rear of the television set and the wall.

A shadow entered the room, a large man clutching a bulky pistol in his gloved hand. He leveled the weapon at her bed and fired twice. Small darts stabbed the mattress seconds before he yanked the sheets off, stepping back in surprise when exposing pillows.

Terrified, Erika took a shallow breath, her trembling hand keeping the tip of the spray can aligned with the man's hood while the intruder swept the room with the dart gun.

The man's eyes landed on her before the weapon made it around. Asian eyes flickered recognition through the large holes in the black hood.

Erika pressed the spray button as hard as she could and was rewarded with the hissing sound of the pepper mist dashing across the space separating them.

"Aghh . . . *Chikuso!*"

Dropping the weapon, the intruder brought both hands to his eyes, screaming in Japanese.

Uncertain of what to do next, Erika opted to stand, the advice from Brent MacClaine suddenly echoing in her mind.

Kick him in the balls and run like hell.

While the man screamed in agonizing pain, Erika kicked him in between his legs as hard as she could with her bare foot. The assassin doubled over, landing on his side in a fetal position. "Hoooo . . . *kogan* . . . hoooo, hoooo," he groaned in a deep voice while holding his groin, eyes closed, tears wetting the dark fabric around his eyes.

Her instep throbbing, the can of pepper spray still in her hand, she looked at the weapon and thought about picking it up. Her heart hammered as she briefly inspected the strange-looking pistol with the bulky silencer, remembering the darts it had shot at the bed. This man didn't want to kill her but kidnap her. She considering taking the gun.

Who do you think you are? Get the gun away from him and call MacClaine!

She kicked the pistol under the bed and slipped into her jean shorts and penny loafers before rushing to the living room, the muffled sounds of the assassin streaming out of the room.

Feeling a shot of adrenaline in her bloodstream, keeping a watchful eye toward the bedroom, Erika reached for the phone. The black unit rested on the small desk, next to her soft computer case.

The phone rang before she could get it.

The sound made her jerk back her hand.

Who's calling this late? MacClaine?

The phone rang a second time.

Should I—?

The phone rang a third time.

She glanced at the bedroom door, as if needing permission from the wounded intruder, and then decided to answer it. "Hello?"

Pause.

Click.

She dropped the phone on the sofa, feeling the urge to vomit but controlling the convulsion. She sensed motion from the room, the intruder was on his feet and staggering into the hallway, a hand on his face, the other on his groin.

She screamed in terror while spraying him once more, the mist enveloping his face. He cursed in Japanese, falling to his knees.

Erika grabbed her purse and ran out of the door, tripping, falling headfirst, skinning her left cheek, getting up and running again, racing toward the elevators at the end of the hallway, the can of pepper spray still in her right hand. She had to get away, find a place to hide, call MacClaine for help. Taking in lungfuls of air, her legs beginning to burn, she kicked harder against the carpeted floor.

Before she could press the elevator button, she noticed the number displayed above the doors increasing. Someone was coming up from the building's lobby.

What if—?

Erika darted to her left, toward the stairs, just as a single bell announced that the elevator would stop at her floor. She pushed down on the heavy door's handle, opening it, squeezing in, closing it before the elevator doors opened, nearly tripping over the body of the FBI agent MacClaine had sent to guard her room.

Erika felt light-headed at finding the agent's dead eyes in the murky stairways. Everything was happening too fast. She felt about to faint.

Focus! You must focus! Find out what you can!

Feeling a lump in her throat, she inched open the door, creating a small crack, spotting four men rushing out of the elevator.

"Why in the hell is she answering the phone?" asked a bald and skinny Asian in a deep, raspy voice with a heavy accent as they ran toward her apartment.

"I don't know. . . . Police! Get back in your room!" shouted a bulky Asian with bleached-blond hair in unaccented English while flashing a laminated badge as someone stuck his head out.

Erika gently closed the door and was about to head down when she heard multiple steps charging up from below. Someone was coming up the emergency stairs in a hurry.

Out of options, she tiptoed up one floor, reaching the concrete landing, slowly pushing down the handle and peeking down the hallway, seeing no one.

Cautiously, she approached the elevator and pressed the down button, her only clear choice. They had the stairs covered, and right now the wounded man's associates were probably reaching her apartment, finding their disabled colleague, about to double back to the elevators. She could continue moving up until reaching the top floor, at which point she would be trapped, or she could risk taking the elevator down before the intruder and his associates returned.

The bell rang. Apprehensively, Erika stood to the side, can in hand, ready to spray and run back for the stairs if she spotted someone inside.

Empty.

She rushed in and pressed the button for the basement, theorizing that the men after her might have left someone covering the lobby.

The doors closed. A light rumble and the elevator headed down. Holding her breath while staring at the digital display over the control panel, Erika placed her thumb over the red emergency stop button in case the elevator slowed down as it approached the floor below.

It didn't.

She sighed in relief and leaned back, crossing her arms as she descended to the basement, reaching for the mobile phone in her purse, silently cursing when the unit failed to give her a signal while in the elevator.

She caught her reflection on the polished metal door of the emergency phone, grimacing at the patch of red skin on her left cheek.

You're lucky that's all you've got.

The elevator reached the basement. Again, she held her breath, spray can pointed at the doors, waiting for them to open, which they did a moment later, exposing a huge room filled with machinery. Pipes, ventilation ducts, and cables lined the ceiling, many of them connecting to rumbling hardware, hissing water heaters, and humming fans. The high humidity and warm temperature struck Erika as she stepped away from the air-conditioned elevator, doors closing behind her.

She took off toward the back of the room, disappearing in the array of weathered equipment, toward the red exit sign over a metallic door.

Already breaking a sweat, Erika moved as fast as she could through the narrow spaces between the ocean of equipment, careful not to touch any surfaces for fear of getting burnt. She could feel the heat radiating from some of the overhead pipes and could only guess that they carried hot water or steam. The heat stung the open wound on her cheek, making her wince in pain.

It took over a minute to reach the back, just as someone burst into the front of the room. Hard-soled shoes stomping over concrete mixed with the noisy equipment.

Erika hesitated for a moment before rushing toward the exit in a deep crouch, her ears detecting the elevator bell through the distant footsteps and reverberating machinery.

"Is she down here?" Asked a voice with an Asian accent.

"Doesn't look like it," answered a man without an accent.

"*Chikuso*! Seal the building!"

"*Hai!*"

Erika waited, feeling out of breath, the heat from a nearby hissing pipe making her dizzy. She fought it, inhaling deeply, keeping quiet until they had left the basement. Drenched in sweat, she sneaked out of the rear door and into an alley that led her to a flight of stairs, which went up to the street level on the side of the building.

Heaving, the cool sweat on her face and chest making her shiver, Erika checked the signal strength of her mobile phone, which increased while rushing into the trees beyond the parking lot adjacent to the hotel. She dialed MacClaine.

Hiding behind a thick oak, the lights from the hotel casting a yellowish glow across the parking lot and the woods that led to the access road for Highway 880, Erika pressed the send button.

"Yeah?" came MacClaine's grumpy voice after two rings. Erika felt relieved at hearing it.

"MacClaine! They came after me."

"Conklin? Shit! Where?"

"My room at the Sheraton. Your man is dead. I managed to escape!"

"Dammit! Where are you?"

"Across the . . . the parking lot from the hotel."

"How long ago did they attack you?"

She checked her watch. Ten minutes had elapsed since the intruder had kicked in her door.

"About—around ten minutes ago."

"All right. Now try to keep your cool and not panic."

"I'm not panicking!"

"All right, all right. I'm sending a car to pick you up."

Mosquitoes buzzed in her ears. Her skinned cheek burned from the sweat filming her face.

Two men ran out of the same exit she had just used. Erika froze.

"Conklin? You still there?"

"They're onto me," she whispered. "They're searching the parking lot." As she said this, two vans drove up to the middle of the lot, half-filled with vehicles. Four men got out of each van. "There's about ten of them."

"All right. Slowly back away from there while avoiding any open areas. Whatever you do, don't hang up. I'm getting a GPS fix on your mobile phone. In another minute we're going to be tracking you."

Trying to remain calm, Erika Conklin retreated into the woods, shoving branches aside, keeping them off her face,

the underbrush scratching her exposed calves. She reached
the opposite edge moments later, where the lawn sloped
down toward the access road of Highway 880.

"Where are you now?"

She told him.

"Can you see them?"

"Not anymore."

"Good. That probably means they can't see you either."

Erika began to think, her engineering mind slowly
emerging through the madness of having become a target.
As she moved parallel to the access road, remaining a few
feet away from the woods, her fear slowly faded as her
logical side realized that she had been able to fool at least
a dozen men sent after her. Without telling MacClaine,
Erika doubled back, returning to the edge of the parking
lot, spotting figures hastily walking in between cars,
searching for her, two of them quite close to the edge of
the parking lot.

Kneeling behind a row of thick bushes, cradling the
phone with both hands against her right ear, she whispered,
"MacClaine?"

"Yeah?"

"I'm back at the edge of the lot. The men are still here,
looking for me."

"What—are you *crazy*? Dammit, Conklin! You're going
to get yourself killed! Get the hell out of there. You have
no idea who you're dealing with!"

"Listen to me, MacClaine," Erika said, a surge of confidence sweeping through her. "By the time your people
get here these guys will be long gone. We still have time
to track them. That's what you wanted to do, right?"

"No way, Conklin. You're an analyst, not a field operative. You wouldn't last a minute."

"So far, I've lasted—"

A stabbing pain on her side made Erika drop the phone
and cringe in unbelievable agony as the blow lifted her
light frame off the ground, sending her crashing against a
trunk, bark ripping the side of her shirt, tearing a gash into

her torso. She landed on her stomach, the pain inducing uncontrollable spasms, bile reaching her gorge, her bladder muscles weakening.

A figure grabbed her by the hair and the waist of her jeans, snatching her out of the underbrush with incredible ease, hurling her toward the edge of the parking lot with animal strength. She tried to put her hands in front but failed, smashing through the line of waist-high bushes, crash landing on the other side, the manicured lawn bordering the lot cushioning the impact.

Gasping for air, scourged, her ribs ablaze, her face numb, tears blinding her, Erika Conklin saw a blurry image approach her, saw a leg swinging back, braced herself for—

The powerful kick connected right below the sternum, her bladder muscles loosening on impact, her lids twitching, her mind blanking out from the inconceivable pain. A brew of blood and bile rose up her throat. Everything began to spin around her as she grew dizzy, light-headed.

She heard a distant voice in heavily accented English. "Hello, Erika Conklin. My name is Hashimoto." Then she fainted.

"Son of a bitch!" Brent MacClaine shouted while racing out of the apartment complex and jumping into the back of a sedan, which fishtailed as it accelerated down the street. "Hurry up, dammit!" he screamed while stabbing the mobile phone to dial the men in the car he had sent five minutes ago to the Sheraton.

"You guys there yet?"

"Almost, sir."

He exhaled in frustration as they got on 101 and headed south, exiting at Montague, rushing past dozens of apartment complexes and hotels stuffed in between high-tech corporations. MacClaine made a tight fist and pressed it against his chin. He had just lost one of his best agents and now maybe Erika Conklin. His experience told him that what his men were now doing was just a futile exercise to attempt a rescue. MacClaine confirmed his suspicions when the sedan turned left on McCarthy and right on Barber Lane, passing the front of the Sheraton, where two police patrols were already parked, and pulling up in the parking lot behind the hotel. The place was devoid of people, save for three figures walking by the woods outlining the lot. His men. Two police officers were coming out of the rear of the hotel holding flashlights.

As the sedan stopped at the edge of the asphalt, he saw one of his agents walking out of the woods holding a small black object. MacClaine inspected it, a sinking feeling descending over him. For a moment he had hoped that Erika might have been kidnapped along with the phone, which, if kept on, would had given him a way to track her and possibly intervene before her interrogation and certain execution. But that hope vanished as he stared at the smashed unit in his hands.

The agent saw the police officers approaching him and pulled out his FBI ID. They were going to be here for a while.

12

CONFLICT OF INTEREST

President Williams untied the knot in his robe and got in bed wearing a pair of cotton pajamas. The First Lady, Elizabeth Williams, sat up reading a magazine.

The president put on a pair of glasses and pretended to read a report on Pentagon procurement plans for the next year but in reality was struggling on how to break the news to her that there was a chance that Derek Ray and his SEAL team could get deployed to Japan.

"What's wrong, honey?" Elizabeth asked, her blond hair falling gracefully over her exposed shoulders, reminding the president of the first time that he had seen her in Saigon, during the summer of 1969, the year after her husband was killed. She was the head nurse at a local GI hospital.

Williams smiled warmly, pulling her over, kissing her on the forehead. "Why is it that even though I'm supposed to be the most powerful man in the world, you always have a way of knowing what's on my mind?"

She narrowed her blue eyes, just as she had done the first time he saw her, assisting a doctor giving polio vaccines to South Vietnamese children. "Les, after almost forty years I know your every mood. I can tell there's something on your mind. What's bothering you?"

He put down the glasses and rubbed the bridge of his nose. "We have a situation that may require SEAL intervention. There's a chance that Derek may have to go."

She shook her head. "But—but I thought that he was being reassigned, what with the baby on the way and all. How can the Navy do this to him now?"

"His Pentagon assignment doesn't start for at least two months."

She clutched the magazine with both hands and rolled it tight. For a moment he wondered if she was going to hit him with it. "He's already served in combat enough times, Les, and we almost lost him in Panama and Kuwait."

"Beth, try to understand. The SEALs are going through a lot of changes. There's too many rookies. He's the most experienced member at Coronado."

"Nobody's indispensable, Les. You yourself told me that on more than one occasion. I'm sure there's plenty of testosterone-filled men in the SEALs starving for action. Why him? Why?" Tears welled in her eyes.

President Williams remained quiet.

"How risky is the operation?" she asked.

He shrugged. "Hard to tell at this point. We're not even sure if they'll have to go in at all, but we're deploying them just in case. And I still don't know if it will be his team."

"Level with me, Les. If the SEAL team has to go in, will he be in that team?"

President Williams gave her a short nod. "I think so."

A tear rolled down her cheek. She brushed it off with a finger, kissed him good night, and rolled over. The president switched off the light and scooted over, hugging her from behind.

"Derek's always been quite independent," she said. "I begged him to get out after the Afghan missions in 2002, but he would not. He's as hardheaded as his father *and* stepfather. But I tell you this, I don't know if I can bear the thought of losing him like I lost John, Les. I just don't think I can."

"I know," he whispered in her ear as she sobbed. "I

know. Let's just pray it doesn't get to that."

And in the darkness of the presidential suite, hugging the woman he loved, resolved to do whatever it took to stop the accidents slowly sinking his nation, but torn by his feelings for his family, the president of the United States silently prayed for wisdom and strength.

13

CORPORATE ENTERTAINMENT

Slick Willie Matsubara sang along in a private room in a karaoke bar in San Jose together with two visiting executives from Sony Corporation and three stunning blonds from southern California. The Japanese trio stood in the middle of a circle while Matsubara held the mike in between them. The model-thin women surrounded them while clapping and giggling at their appalling rendition of Rod Stewart's "Do You Think I'm Sexy?"

Matsubara had picked up the executives at San Jose International four hours ago and had already wined and dined them, as requested by Tokyo. The girls he had called at the last moment. They all held modeling jobs in the Bay Area thanks not just to Matsubara for coming up with the bucks for nose and chin jobs, breast implants, and liposuction at a San Francisco clinic, but also for hooking them up with the Bay Area Modeling Agency, owned by Sakata Electronics.

Matsubara leaned over while the two Sony executives sang the lines on the screen. He whispered something at two of the blonds, who nodded and hugged the Japanese executives from behind, kissing their grayish heads. One of the men, almost a foot shorter that the model, turned around and hugged his escort, burying his face in her breasts, squeezing her buttocks, and laughing loudly. She also laughed, leaning down and kissing his neck, loosening his tie. The other sat down and put the woman on his lap, running his hand beneath her black miniskirt.

Matsubara put away the mike and sat across from them, smiling, whistling the old tune. His escort joined him while he poured a glass of wine, sharing it with her, smiling cordially. The girl, a former prom queen at her L.A. high school, took a sip of wine before reaching for his groin under the table. He shook his head while moving her hand away.

"Why not, Willie?" she whispered in his ear, before tickling it with her tongue.

"Later," he said, nicely but firmly, a smile on his face. "Maybe later."

The mobile phone rang and he picked it up.

"Hai?"

"Our associates have obtained the photos, Matsubara-san. They're being delivered to the newspaper. The article should be out in the morning."

"Good," he said.

"We also have the woman. Come to the warehouse."

Matsubara checked his watch before glancing at the two executives, who were practically ready to start undressing the models. It was time to call the limousine and get them all to the Fairmont. "I'll be there in an hour." He hung up.

"What about me, Willie?" the girl asked.

Matsubara turned to her. She was incredibly gorgeous. "You will go with Hakashita-san in the limo to the hotel." He pointed to the higher-ranking of the two Japanese men. "I want them to remember this night for a long time. Understand?" He winked and gave her a charming smile.

"Sure, Willie."

"Then you and I can have some fun together, maybe go to Tahoe for the weekend, *hai*? You like that?"

She nodded, said, "That sounds great," and proceeded to join them.

Matsubara reached into his pocket, extracted a small plastic container, took one round pill, and shoved it in the hand of the Sony senior executive while whispering in his ear, "Viagra, Hakashita-san. Take it now so that you can best enjoy the evening."

The senior executive, already engaged with both women, his face smeared with red lipstick, pulled out of a lip lock with one of the blonds, and patted Matsubara on the back while bowing slightly.

Slick Willie bowed back and then used his cell phone to call the limo.

14

RODENTS

Erika Conklin shivered as she slowly came around. Freezing water soaked her shirt and shorts. She heard voices around her and tried to open her eyes to look at her captors, but even *that* hurt, although not as badly as the invisible claw that raked her rib cage every time she breathed.

Erika knew how to take a punch. She had received the first one during a brawl at the ranch with one of her brothers over the right to ride a pony. Erika had won the short fight, but it had also cost her and her sibling a month cleaning the stables. She had since survived a rattlesnake bite and getting stomped by a wild horse. But she had *never* been beaten.

"Wake up, Conklin!"

Trembling, Erika opened one eye and stared at an Asian man. Two larger Asians, one with a bleached-blond crew cut, flanked him while holding silvery water buckets. She tried to move but found herself strapped to a chair. She was in some sort of equipment warehouse. To her right, aisles stacked with boxed computer equipment rose to meet the exposed rafters supporting twenty-foot-tall corrugated metal ceilings. To her left, wide garage doors provided access to the street. Three forklifts were parked by one of the doors, next to a black sports car and the same two vans she had spotted at the Sheraton.

"She still stinks," said the smaller Asian to one of his muscular companions before crinkling his nose and turning to Erika. "You pissed on yourself."

"Maybe's not the piss," said the blond bucket holder with contempt. "Maybe that's just how FBI pigs stink."

Erika remembered now. The beating at the Sheraton had caused her to—

A slight nod of the head by the wiry Asian, and Erika got another bucket of chilled water.

She sneezed, the agonizing pain of her bruised ribs magnifying the headache pounding her temples. A brief downward glance showed her a pair of shorts still on her. These animals had beaten her, but at least they had not raped her . . . yet.

"Hello, Agent Conklin. My name is Hashimoto," said the short and bald Japanese as he bowed and grinned, exposing yellow teeth.

Erika didn't reply, her lips quivering from the cold, her skin prickling with goosebumps. She remained quiet but sensed that this wasn't going to end well. Behind the trio she spotted a table, noticed her opened laptop softcase. The system was next to the case . . . *turned on!*

Of course!

They had powered it up to try to learn anything they could about the ongoing investigation while she was unconscious. Fortunately, the vital directories in her hard drive were hidden by the same virus that should have linked up to Washington by now using Remote Determination Satellite Service. Erika filled with hope.

Hashimoto turned serious. "What is your interest in Akita Electronics?"

"I don't know what . . . what you're talking about," she said, sneezing again, her ribs on fire. She fought to control the pain, to stay focused, hoping to buy herself as much time as possible, praying that RDSS had already alerted the Bureau. For the first time in her life she actually looked forward to seeing special agents.

"Who is leading the investigation?"

"In—investigation?"

"We were following MacClaine and saw you working with him. We went through your personal belongings. You are from Washington. Why is the FBI interested in Akita? Why did Brent MacClaine contact Mr. Nakamura?"

Erika tilted her head, water still dripping from her soaked hair and into her eyes, forcing her to blink rapidly. "Look . . . I'm just an analyst . . . at the FBI. I don't even own a gun. I'm here on . . . on holiday. I grew up in California."

"I'm going to give you one more chance, Agent Conklin."

"Please . . . I'm not . . . an agent, I'm an analyst."

A well-dressed Asian joined them. Hashimoto and the two brutes moved to the side.

"Such a terrible tragedy, Erika," the handsome Asian said in flawless English while leaning down. His breath smelled like scotch. "My name is Willie Matsubara. I look after the interests of Japanese companies doing business in your country."

The stranger gently cupped her chin, steering her face up. "I can tell there is a beautiful face behind the scratches and bruises. Please understand we wish you no harm. We just want to know why the FBI is interested in talking to Nakamura-san. You can help us by just being honest. If you do, I give you my word that you will not be harmed any further."

Erika couldn't believe this character. Did he really expect her to think that if she confessed they were just going to let her walk out of here?

Before Erika could reply, Hashimoto blasted a few sentences in Japanese and handed him what looked like an ID card.

Matsubara glanced at it before asking Erika, "My associate says that if you are here on holiday, why was there an armed agent guarding your floor at the Sheraton?"

"An armed agent?"

Matsubara frowned, showing her the ID card for the special agent who had escorted her to the Sheraton. "I'm afraid I won't be able to help you if you don't help me."

Erika remained silent.

"I see." He nodded at Hashimoto before walking toward his sports car.

"Wait . . . wait a moment . . . please," she whispered.

Matsubara turned around.

"I do work for the FBI . . . and I am working on a case linking certain Japanese corporations . . . to the computer . . . triggered accidents."

Matsubara smiled. "Good, Erika. Very good."

"Why . . . what is your motive?" she asked. "Economic superiority?"

Matsubara continued to smile. "Very good again, Erika. Now, how is it that you figured out the link to Japan?"

Erika slowly regained her focus. She considered the question, wondering just how much information to reveal while also trying to gather information herself. If the laptop was indeed broadcasting her location, then it would just be a matter of time before the FBI had this place surrounded, which meant that anything that she released would remain contained. But everything that she learned, information her captors felt would not go beyond this place, she could later use to get closer to the source of the sabotages. On the other hand, she didn't really want to give up her only ace by revealing that the link had been established through sales records.

"All right," she said, breathing shallowly to avoid expanding her rib cage. She decided to take a chance. "We figured it out by tracking down the girlfriend of . . . of one of the engineers that you . . . bribed to sabotage a design at Texas Instruments."

Matsubara's hard-edged features sharpened as he narrowed his eyes. "Who?"

Erika closed her eyes for a moment, feeling dizzy but

trying to make the story tight. "I think the name was . . . Pasdats? Yes, Gerome Pasdats. He lived in Houston. We couldn't find a sister that supposedly lived in Little Rock . . . but found his girlfriend."

Matsubara was obviously upset. "I see. And what did she tell you?"

"I didn't . . . didn't work that part of the investigation. I'm an engineer . . . worked with the engineers from the sabotaged corporations to track down the cause of the failures. I just—just know that out of that investigation Akita Electronics became a prime suspect."

"Were there any other companies?"

She slowly shook her head without hesitation. "Akita's the only suspect. That's . . . that's why we contacted Nakamura."

"Well, Nakamura-san was recalled to corporate headquarters in Osaka."

She sighed. "Who . . . who are you . . . really?"

"I told you, Erika. I'm Oruku Matsubara. I help protect Japanese corporations in this country."

"Cover . . . that's just a cover."

Matsubara smiled. "It's really a shame that the FBI is going to lose such fine agent."

"Analyst."

"Analyst. I guess there is no harm now in you knowing that we're in a way colleagues. I work for the Japanese Defense Agency. My associates belong to the Aum Shinrikyo."

Erika closed her eyes again. The room was beginning to spin around her. A splash of cold water brought her back.

Did he say that he worked for the JDA? And the animals with him are Aum Shinrikyo terrorists?

When she came around Matsubara was walking to his car.

"How . . . how many . . . how many more ICs? . . ." she asked.

Matsubara stopped and turned around, still smiling,

hands shoved in the slacks of his suit. "That's for your agency to find out. All I can tell you is that there will be many, many more surprises before it's over. In the end, my country will once again rise as the dominant nation in high technology." He turned to Hashimoto. "Make sure she has told the truth."

Hashimoto gave him a slight bow. "*Hai*, Matsubara-san."

One of the garage doors rose just enough to let him drive off before lowering again, slamming against the concrete floor.

Hashimoto turned to the corpulent Asian with the blond hair and said, "Bring me my pet."

Swallowing a lump in her throat, Erika felt quite certain what kind of animal the Asian had for a pet.

15

THE PROFESSIONAL

In spite of his extra weight, Brent MacClaine still knew how to move swiftly, silently, with expert ease, his senses tuned to his environment. The distant traffic on 101 echoing down the alley, MacClaine stopped to inspect the one-story structure occupying an entire city block across the street.

MacClaine read the sign for West Coast Distributors under the floodlights installed all around the warehouse, casting a dim glow in every direction, making it difficult to approach the brick-and-metal structure unannounced.

He checked his watch. Three in the morning. Erika had been kidnapped at little past one, and the FBI had received a beacon from her laptop an hour ago. Washington had called him right away, while his team worked with the San Jose Police Department looking for clues in and around Erika's room at the Sheraton. MacClaine had chosen a silent approach to the building, which was now surrounded by a small army of FBI and police officers. A few minutes ago he had seen an Acura NSX leave, followed by a Lexus sedan parked outside the building. He had both cars followed.

MacClaine approached the building alone, bringing not only the Beretta, which he carried tucked in his jeans at his spine, but a silenced Heckler & Koch submachine gun.

He also carried the Walther PPK in an ankle hoster.

He moved diagonally across the street, his dark figure hidden in the long shadow of one of many posts supporting the array of electrical cables used by the San Jose public transportation system. The shadow ended at the base of the post, where a manhole provided access to the city's drain system.

MacClaine had come prepared, having spent ten minutes going over the building's blueprints brought over by the SJPD. He used a pair of heavy-duty pliers to pull up the metal handles of the round cover. Anchoring his sneakers on each side of the hole, he leaned down and painfully pulled up the heavy cover just enough to slide it over the edge by a few inches.

He released it and exhaled, his back muscles tingling.

Quietly, he sat on the sidewalk, pressed both feet against the edge of the cover, and slowly pushed it aside enough to squeeze through.

Feet groping for the ladder built into the side of the vertical tunnel, MacClaine detected the foul stench rising from the stationary water at the bottom of the manhole. Fortunately, he only had to descend halfway down the hole, where a horizontal tunnel ran straight into the warehouse.

Huge roaches crawled on the concrete walls, just inches from his face. A few of them took flight and cruised through the opening above, disappearing into the night.

In near darkness, the operative climbed down the ladder to the connecting tunnel eight feet below, where he crawled forward until the drainpipe made a right angle up to the floor of the warehouse.

MacClaine stood, his head barely touching a metallic floor grid. He heard noises in the distance and recognized a heavily accented voice. He had heard it the day before.

Hashimoto.

He hurried, taking just under three minutes to crawl out of the drain pipe and disable the first guard, an Asian who'd stood guard behind the television monitors in the rear of the building, amid mountains of boxes sporting pictures of PCs, printers, scanners, monitors, software packages, and other computer gear he readily recognized. The guard never saw the karate chop coming, which rendered him unconscious. MacClaine could have killed him, but he had decided against it because he wanted to capture some of these characters alive. In addition to rescuing Erika Conklin, MacClaine was on a mission to capture prisoners. The FBI needed leads.

He now cruised down one of many alleys created by the mountains of computer gear stacked in a gridlike pattern.

Under the glow of sporadic fluorescents dangling at the end of long black cords, Brent MacClaine walked sideways down one alley, his back against wooden crates, right hand clutching the MP5. His left fist held the twelve-inch stainless-steel pipe he'd picked up next to the fallen guard. The pipe protruded from the top of his fist, as taught by his FBI training, giving him the option to deliver a variety of nonlethal blows from waist level.

MacClaine sensed movement around the next corner and dropped to a crouch, adrenaline heightening his perception. Nearing footsteps made him increase his grip on the pipe. He wanted to avoid any noise that might endanger Erika Conklin's life. The MP5, albeit silenced, was still loud enough to telegraph his presence. .

A shadow projected over the floor across his field of view, followed by a large Asian, whom MacClaine recognized as one of the brutes who had assisted Hashimoto in the van.

MacClaine lunged while spinning to amplify the power of his strikes, driving his left elbow into the man's left flank with locomotive strength. In the same fluid turn his right hand swung the pipe up and around, striking the larynx with enough force to keep him from screaming, but without breaking it.

The combination of blows had the desired effect. The operative fell to his knees, both hands on his bruised windpipe, his eyes rolling to the back of his head as he struggled to breathe.

MacClaine completed the spin by bringing his left knee up and forward, crashing it against the man's face, breaking his nose. The Asian collapsed.

MacClaine used the man's socks to secure his wrists and ankles, also shoving a rag in his mouth. He hid him in between two wooden crates, before returning to the aisle, resuming his hunt.

Erika Conklin's stomach turned over when she spotted the furry creature inside the wire cage, a pair of red eyes and sneering fangs staring back at her.

Hashimoto grinned as he held a pillowcase in his hands.

"Sick bastard," Erika hissed, anger suddenly replacing the fear, something that surprised her. Perhaps her grandmother's strength lived in her after all. "I've already told you everything I know."

Hashimoto stared at her for a moment, and then he grinned. "That's what we're about to find out. We'll do thirty seconds at a time."

The Asian began to poke the rat with a stick. The rodent went crazy, its fur bristling as it began to snap at the stick.

Erika felt a knot forming deep in her gut. She had been bitten by snakes and stung by spiders and scorpions. But the mere sight of that rat unleashed a wave of fear through her.

Hashimoto turned to her, his bald head glistening under the fluorescent overheads. "Is there anything different you wish to tell us?"

"No," Erika said.

Hashimoto opened the pillowcase and fit the open end over the cage while the blond Asian opened it. A second later the bag came alive in frantic agitation.

* * *

Brent MacClaine surged from beneath a workbench just as another guard walked by. He thrust the end of the pipe into his opponent's abdomen, right below the sternum.

Air exploded through the vigilante's open mouth as he fell on his side gasping, giving MacClaine the precious seconds he needed to deliver a karate chop to the side of the neck, knocking him out.

Three down.

He reached the front of the building, an open area roughly the size of two basketball courts back-to-back. Two vans and a couple of forklifts took up a small portion of the available space.

MacClaine's eyes landed on the trio standing in front of Erika Conklin, currently strapped to a chair. He breathed in relief. She was still alive.

It took him another second to realize what was going on. Hashimoto was approaching Erika while holding the pillowcase with the rat.

His professional side told him there could be more than six guns in the building and that he should spend more time scouting. But he could not.

Erika Conklin was out of time. He whispered into his lapel microphone.

For Erika Conklin, the end of the line had never looked so close. It was obvious to her that regardless of what she said, these characters were going to give her the treatment that Brent MacClaine had so narrowly escaped.

Erika controlled her feelings, staring at her soaked shorts while the blond Asian pushed her head toward her thighs. It was at that moment that the image of Karla Conklin, entered her mind. Her grandmother would have fought back.

But how?

The bag swallowed her and she found herself staring at the glistening fangs of the rodent. For the first time in many years, Erika realized that she was truly afraid. But with the feeling of raw terror also came an idea, a thought. Erika remembered her father's bedside stories.

Then the large rat lunged.

From a distance of fifty feet, Brent MacClaine took aim and fired repeatedly, keeping the MP5 in single-shot mode, cursing under his breath at his backup team for taking so long to storm the warehouse. The Asian to the left of Hashimoto arched back, his chest exploding from the silent fusillade of 9-mm Parabellum rounds. The blond Asian and Hashimoto dove for cover behind Erika, who jerked and struggled against the rope binding her to the chair.

MacClaine went into a roll, leaving the protection of the towering hardware and fired twice at floor level, under the chair. One of the rounds found its mark.

Hashimoto screamed and fell back, crawling toward a stack of spare tires, leaving a trail of blood from a wounded calf.

Running out of time to save her, MacClaine fired again at the Asian but the MP5 was empty.

Dropping the submachine gun and reaching for the Beretta, MacClaine jumped to his feet and went after the woman twisting in pain. She jerked so violently that the chair tipped to the side and she crashed against the stained floor, the bag convulsing, turning red.

Five Asians reached the front of the warehouse, all bearing automatic weapons. MacClaine took aim and squeezed the trigger multiple times, the reports deafening. One of the men clutched his chest and fell. A second jerked back as a round struck his face, falling to the floor. The other three swung their weapons toward MacClaine, muzzles alive with gunfire.

MacClaine dove for the cover of a yellow forklift as silenced bullets ricocheted off the floor with the sound of a dozen hammer blows. He crashed against the wall behind the forklift, his shoulder burning from the impact, his bruised ribs scourging him. Clenching his teeth, he ignored it, scrambling forward, sneakers scraping against the floor as he stooped behind the rear wheel, just a few feet from one of the vans.

Gunfire ceased, followed by hastening footsteps. The men were separating, hoping to sandwich him.

Where is the damned backup team?

His back pressed against the vehicle, MacClaine waited a few seconds before jumping toward the van, crawling under it, rolling to the center, aiming the Beretta in the direction of the nearest footsteps. He saw an operative's legs dash by a dozen feet away. They had not seen him get under the van.

An edge.

But one he would lose the moment he opened fire, which he did, squeezing the trigger once, the hollow-point round echoing loudly inside the warehouse, hitting the operative's right knee.

Agonizing screams filled the cavernous room. The Asian fell, hands on his wounded limb. MacClaine sought a new target and fired twice more from under the van, this time missing the running legs.

MacClaine heard a commotion outside. Someone was banging against one of the garage doors.

It's about time!

He spotted another set of legs running in the opposite direction and squeezed the trigger but nothing happened. The Beretta was empty. He reached for the Walther PPK in his ankle holster, but by the time he clutched it, the target had vanished.

MacClaine gave Erika Conklin an apologetic glance. The analyst was still convulsing on the floor.

The footsteps returned. One set from behind and another from the front.

MacClaine had seconds to react before both men swept the van's underside with bullets.

Priorities.

Clear in his mind, the closest enemy ranked the highest

in his target list. MacClaine swung the small pistol toward an Asian clutching an Uzi.

As he aimed the PPK, two shots cracked and his target fell, the Uzi skittering toward Erika Conklin, who had ceased moving.

The last man also fell victim to another unexpected gun report.

"FBI. Put your weapons down!" one of his men shouted from the equipment shelves.

MacClaine heard an engine gunning, tires screeching, a loud collision of metal against metal. One of the garage doors burst open. Agents in blue and police officers rushed inside.

Rolling from under the van and rising to his feet, he spotted Hashimoto dragging himself away from the incoming officers while popping a pill in his mouth. The Asian suddenly went into seizures as two agents reached him, struggling to hold him down. Movement ceased seconds later.

"Cyanide, sir!" one of the agents screamed after leaning over him.

Engine fumes mixed with the smell of gunpowder. He tucked the Walther in his jeans and raced toward the limp FBI analyst, dreading what he would find. Erika Conklin had had that hood on for at least three minutes.

His men checked for survivors. Two other terrorists had also taken the cyanide and were now trembling on the concrete floor.

"There's some terrorists in the back!" MacClaine shouted. "I want them alive!"

While two agents sat Erika back up, MacClaine worked the knot quickly, noticing there was no movement inside the bag. The moment he removed it he understood why.

One of the agents stepped back in terror. The other remained silent. Brent MacClaine, in all his years of field work, had never seen *anything* like this. His eyes locked with the wild gaze of Erika Conklin, who'd managed to snag the rat's neck with her teeth and broken it. And to make certain it was dead, she had not let go of it, until now, when she spat it at MacClaine, taking a deep breath, lips and chin smeared with blood, her fine features contorted in animal rage. She looked like a predator who'd just been caught consuming its prey.

"We came as soon as we got the—" MacClaine began to say.

"Oh, go to hell. All of you!" she barked.

"Don't rush me, lady," MacClaine said while cutting her loose. "I'm heading down there soon enough, but hopefully not today."

"Bastard," she said, getting up on her own and wiping her mouth with the sleeve of her T-shirt. "What took you so long?"

MacClaine regarded her with respect. "I think you're going to be all right, Conklin. I think you're going to be just fine."

16

CITY LIGHTS

The angular shape of an F-117A stealth fighter left the tarmac at Nellis Air Force Base in Nevada and climbed into the indigo sky at two hundred knots. The jet's jagged edges, optimized to minimize radar returns, bit into the night air as the pilot turned the nose northwest, toward the practice area, where he would join two other F-117As.

Fully fueled and housing two live Paveway II laser-guided bombs in its ordnance compartment, the F-117A reached an altitude of two thousand feet as it flew on the outskirts of Las Vegas, just two miles northeast of the Strip, bustling with activity at this time of the night.

The pilot gave the city a brief glance before focusing on the large central CRT display, the place where most of the fighter's vital statistics were constantly displayed.

The pilot noticed a flicker on the screen right before alarms filled his cockpit. The CRT flashed once more and went black.

His eyes shifting to the backup analog instrumentation, the pilot suddenly realized the jet was losing altitude while its nose turned southwest, directly toward the city.

Pulling on the control stick had little effect. The fly-by-wire system, which read the movements of the control stick, enhanced them to compensate for the jet's natural instability, and then converted them to electric current to drive the servomotors governing the control surfaces, was not responding. He had lost control of the aircraft.

"Mayday, Mayday. Nellis, Ghost Rider Eight Two Eight. Lost the flight computer. Going down. Mayday, Mayday," the pilot said into his headset.

No response.

Before the pilot could say another word, the fighter flipped and dove. A brief glance at the artificial horizon told him he was outside the ejection envelope.

Dropping below one thousand feet, one hand on the throttle controls and the other on the center stick, he struggled to turn the jet back up, but the flight computer did not relay his commands to the ailerons. The stealth fighter remained inverted as the Sahara Hotel filled his windscreen.

Plummeting out of control, unable to eject, and unable to chose his crash site, the pilot tried at least to do a fuel dump. His hand reached for a switch on the control panel, but it never got there.

The empennage section was the first to hit the hotel's roof.

Hard.

Flames swallowed him as a bright explosion stabbed the night. Flaming debris enveloped not only a corner of the hotel but also the street below, packed with tourists. Like a scorching chastisement from the heavens, the ignited fuel descended over the terrified crowd just as the main fuselage cracked in half, exposing its deadly cargo.

Both Paveway IIs went off with thundering, concrete-ripping force. The shockwave blasted through three floors, turning the luxurious interior into an inferno, bathing the crowd with molten steel, shards of glass, and crumbling concrete.

It all happened within thirty seconds. Over seven hundred people turned into blazing objects or perished crushed under mounds of smoldering rubble. Men, women, and children, alive with bluish flames, ran, screamed, and fell, dozens of them finally going limp as the fire consumed them.

The first ambulances got to the scene minutes after the explosion, but the number of wounded quickly overwhelmed the medics. Many victims remained untreated for as long as an hour, over half of them dying without receiving medical attention.

The Las Vegas Fire Department did all it could to minimize the damage to the rest of the hotel, showering undamaged sections with water and foam. But the fire continued to spread, weakening the structure, which finally collapsed just like the twin towers in New York City in 2001.

Ambulances crowded the streets, hauling victims to nearby hospitals as the police department set up barricades to isolate the disaster zone and give medics and doctors the room they needed to treat survivors.

Billowing smoke, alive with flashes of orange and yellow from the burning inferno, rose high above the Nevada desert, above the cries and screams, above the sirens and horns, until it lost itself in the night sky.

17

REGROUP

Two hours later, Erika Conklin sat across from Brent MacClaine in his office sipping coffee while comparing notes. He had driven her to an emergency room to get her wounds treated.

Only three Asians had been captured alive and were now under federal custody at the SJPD headquarters. The rest had either died in the gunfight or had killed themselves. Two of the Asians were claiming diplomatic immunity. One of them, however, was not a Japanese national but an American citizen. He wanted a lawyer.

"Do you believe these people?" fumed MacClaine, holding one of the cappuccinos he'd purchased at a nearby shop on their way over. "They kidnap you, kill one of my men, and now think they can walk out of jail just because they have diplomatic passports."

"And under diplomatic status they are protected," said Erika, who had used the small shower in MacClaine's office and now wore one of his white shirts over a clean pair of denim shorts. SJPD had just dropped over her suitcase from the hotel. Erika had replaced her soiled shorts with clean ones, keeping the agent's shirt on. MacClaine, who felt Erika looked quite lovely in anything she wore, but looked particularly great wearing one of his shirts, didn't mind at all. And the events of the past few hours had only served to increase his attraction for the brunette with the captivating hazel eyes and provocative mouth.

"Are we dealing with fanatics here? They said they were from the JDA and also the Aum Shinrikyo." Erika asked.

"I'm having our people check into it."

"What about the Asian American? Any chance of him confessing?"

MacClaine checked his watch. "He's under questioning right now by our people. They're due to call me any moment."

"And Matsubara? The guy in the sports car? He's the one who claimed to be working for the JDA."

MacClaine looked at one of the loose sheets of paper layering his messy desk. "Acura NSX registered to Oruku Matsubara, liaison for the Japanese consulate and senior vice president of Sakata Electronics. Also under diplomatic status. I guess liaisons get paid quite well these days, especially those also working for the JDA."

She brought her cup of coffee to her lips, took a sip, and grimaced. "Bastards," she said, setting it down. "It hurts to drink."

"Have you gone to the bathroom since?"

She nodded. "I'll get over the blood. Where's Matsubara now? Are you bringing him in?"

MacClaine shook his head. "We've passed his surveillance to the CIA."

"The CIA? I thought they weren't allowed to operate inside the United States?"

MacClaine grinned. "They can if the threat's foreign. This one certainly qualifies. There's supposed to be a high-ranking meeting going on in Washington right now to decide how to act on both the JDA and Aum Shinrikyo leads that you gave us."

Erika sipped coffee and closed her eyes while frowning. "I think I got Matsubara convinced that we figured out their scheme thanks to the girlfriend of one of the engineers."

MacClaine held up his cup of coffee. "Gotta hand it to you, Conklin. That was quick thinking."

Erika stood and slowly stretched. The white shirt looked huge on her, coming down to the middle of her thighs. MacClaine enjoyed the sight as she walked to the window and stared at a dawning sky splashed with streaks of yellow and orange, which backlit her figure beneath the white cotton. She turned around and caught him looking at her legs.

He searched for something to say to hide his embarrassment. "So, where are you from?"

"Northern California," she replied turning back to face the sunrise. "I grew up just east of Napa and went to school at Berkeley."

"What were you doing back East? Got tired of the sun and clear skies?"

She laughed and immediately braced herself, moaning lightly. "Damn. It even hurts to laugh." She slowly leaned forward and placed both hands on the windowsill. "I got busted by the FBI for writing a virus to steal passwords and break into government agencies. It happened right after graduating from Berkeley. I was given two options: ten years in a federal prison without the possibility of parole, or six without vacation working at the Bureau as an analyst for slave wages." She turned to face him. "Pretty easy call."

"Man, and I thought *I* was getting screwed by Uncle Sam."

"Join the club," she replied, returning to her chair across from his desk and yawning.

"What're they really paying you?"

Erika shook her head. "Peanuts compared to what I could be making at Microsoft. But, hey, look at the bright side, at least I'm not in jail. My record's clean and they've even given me a couple of bonuses for some pieces of code I wrote for them, like the handy virus that told you where I was being held captive."

"Who knows about your past?"

"Just a few HBOs," she said, referring to her boss and a few other high bureau officials. "And now you. None of my co-workers or staff knows the truth. I guess the HBOs didn't want to humiliate me all the way."

By now he was feeling pretty sorry for her.

"So, MacClaine. What's your story?"

He leaned back and grinned. "Mine's less complicated. I was born and raised in El Paso, Texas. Went to school at Texas A&M with an Army scholarship. Graduated, did my four years stationed at Fort Hood, south of Dallas, and then got recruited by the FBI. I've been a fed since."

"Any family?"

"Only child. Both parents are dead."

"I'm sorry."

"It was a long time ago."

"No wife or kids?"

He rubbed his chin while looking at an empty picture frame on the corner of his cluttered desk. During his first few months after his transfer to California, MacClaine had kept a picture of Jessica. In those days he had been hopeful that they might get back together again, but after a failed attempt, he had ripped the photo to shreds and started drinking heavily. "Just an ex-wife."

She tilted her head in what seemed to be an act of compassion. "Sorry to hear that."

"I'm sorry too, but the ex ain't. She got everything but a used Nissan, an old sofa, a TV, and a pair of barstools. What about you? Any family around these areas?"

"Dad still runs the Rancho de las Vistas. He raises prize bulls and also operates a small winery in the mountains overlooking Napa. I also have a bunch of brothers."

"What's a bunch?"

"Five."

"That's a bunch."

She didn't reply.

"Do they know about your arrangement with the FBI?"

She shook her head. "They think I decided to take a job on the East Coast."

"How do you explain the lack of vacations?"

She shrugged while sitting down across his desk. "It's expensive to fly across the country and my salary is okay but not great for living around Washington. I was able to visit them a few days for Christmas last year."

"Has your father offered to fly you in?"

"Can't afford to."

"Why? I would have thought that your family's pretty wealthy . . . you know with the bulls and the wines."

She shook her head. "Sales numbers are high, but margins are really low. Overhead is big. Most of the money from sales goes right back into the farm to cover expenses and improvements to remain competitive. It's a tough market. Some years my dad did make significant profits, but he had to stash the money in the bank to cover expenses for the bad years, when excessive rain or a long drought ruined the crops. Cattle ranches and wineries of the size of Rancho de las Vistas are more prestige than wealth. I had to work my way through college."

They remained silent for a few moments, and then both spoke at the same time. They laughed.

"You first," she said.

"That's all right. You go first."

"I've been thinking about our next move."

"And?"

The phone rang. MacClaine picked it up. "Yeah?" He listened for a few minutes. "A what? . . . Who are you? Hello? Hello?"

Erika leaned forward as MacClaine slammed the phone down. "What was that all about?"

"Apparently there's a story in this morning's paper that I should read."

"Who was that?"

He shrugged. "Wouldn't give a name, but he had an Asian accent. Somehow I get the feeling I'm not going to like what's printed."

"Pressure is being applied," she said. "I don't believe we're going to learn much from those Asians. In fact, I'm willing to bet that in a few hours the State Department is going to get a lot of pressure from politicians, lobbyist, and special-interest groups requesting the release of those men."

"I get the same feeling, Conklin."

She held up a palm. "Erika, please. I think we've both been through enough to use first names."

MacClaine liked that. He grinned. "Sure, Erika."

She smiled while getting up and reaching for her laptop's softcase, unzipping it, extracting the unit, and setting it on the desk. She opened the system and waited for it to go through its boot-up sequence, entering the password to disable the autodialing virus.

"What are you doing?"

"We need to go about this a different way, a less confrontational way, which is the *only* way to defeat the Japanese. I told Matsubara that we only had one suspect, Akita Electronics, which means that security there should be pretty tight, but let's try something anyway."

Erika tried to log on using the root passwords that Charlie Chang had extracted, but just as she had suspected, they were now invalid.

"Fortunately, I also have roots for Sakata," she mumbled to herself.

"Roots?"

She ran an index finger on the small soft pad below the keyboard to click her way through a wireless penetration attempt into the computer backbone of Sakata Electronics. "It's the computer equivalent of a set of master keys to a building. With a root password I can access any directory in the system."

"How did you get that?"

She snickered. "One of my subordinates got them by using an enhanced version of the same password-snatching virus that got me in trouble with the FBI. Palenski didn't mind using it when it benefited the FBI. Kind of ironic when you think about it."

"What are we looking for?" He rolled his chair around

the desk, sitting next to her shoulder to shoulder as he leaned over to see the small color screen.

"I'm not sure. I just want to probe around a little. See where things might lead."

Erika tried one of the root passwords.

"Yes! I'm in!"

```
SAKATA ELECTRONICS, INC.
TOP-LEVEL MENU
  1. ENGINEERING
  2. PURCHASING
  3. SALES
  4. LEGAL
  5. MARKETING
  6. SECURITY
  7. PRODUCTION
  8. ADMINISTRATION
  9. RETURN TO PREVIOUS PAGE
 10. RETURN TO TOP LEVEL
```

"What do you feel like trying?" she said while looking at the screen.

MacClaine shrugged. "What about security?"

"We'll look at that in a moment. Let's try purchasing first."

She clicked on it and the screen changed to:

```
SAKATA ELECTRONICS, INC.
PURCHASING DEPARTMENT
  1. FOREIGN
  2. DOMESTIC
  3. RETURN TO PREVIOUS MENU
```

She selected the second option.

```
SAKATA ELECTRONICS, INC.
PURCHASING DEPARTMENT—DOMESTIC OPERATIONS
  1. EQUIPMENT
```

2. SERVICES

3. COMPONENTS

4. ADMINISTRATIVE

5. RETURN TO PREVIOUS MENU

6. RETURN TO TOP LEVEL

"Let's take a look at the components," she said to herself while MacClaine looked on.

SAKATA ELECTRONICS, INC.

PURCHASING DEPARTMENT—DOMESTIC OPERATIONS

ELECTRONIC COMPONENTS BY SUPPLIER

1. NEC

2. TOSHIBA

3. HITACHI

4. SONY ELECTRONICS

5. FUJITSU

6. NIKON

7. SEIKO-EPSON

8. MITSUBISHI

The list went on. Erika blinked twice. "*What?* I thought that . . . Oh, I get it." She clicked to go back two menus.

MacClaine was confused. "What's going on?"

"I selected the domestic menu intending to find the domestic companies from which Sakata purchases electronic components, microchips. My intention was to find the American semiconductor companies that supplied integrated circuits to Sakata. But being a Japanese company things are reversed. Domestic for Sakata means Japanese companies. She clicked on Foreign and then on Components.

SAKATA ELECTRONICS, INC.

PURCHASING DEPARTMENT—FOREIGN OPERATIONS

ELECTRONIC COMPONENTS BY SUPPLIER

1. IBM

2. INTEL

   3. MOTOROLA

   4. AMD

   5. VLSI LOGIC

   6. TEXAS INSTRUMENTS

   7. NATIONAL SEMICONDUCTOR

   8. FAIRCHILD

   9. ZILOG

   10. ANALOG DEVICES

   11. DALLAS SEMICONDUCTOR

   12. MICRON

   13. CYPRESS

   14. RETURN TO PREVIOUS MENU

   15. RETURN TO TOP LEVEL

"That's more like it," she said, selecting Motorola.

SAKATA ELECTRONICS, INC.

PURCHASING DEPARTMENT—FOREIGN OPERATIONS

ELECTRONIC COMPONENTS FROM:

MOTOROLA, INC.

1. 2002 PURCHASES

2. 2003 PURCHASES

3. 2004 PURCHASES

4. 2005 PURCHASES

5. 2006 PURCHASES

6. RETURN TO PREVIOUS MENU

7. RETURN TO TOP LEVEL

Erika smiled and clicked on the purchases made by Sakata from Texas Instruments in 2003, the year before the sabotages were made. "We could be onto something, Brent."

"I'm lost."

She glanced at him while smiling. "See, all of the sabotages to date were done during 2004, which is also the year when certain Japanese companies halted purchases of those ICs. I figured this out by comparing the sales records of TI, IBM, and Motorola between the year before the sabotages, 2003, and the year when the sabotaged ICs began shipping, 2004. It turned out that most companies bought sabotaged ICs, except for Japanese corporations, which mysteriously stopped placing orders. Using that method to figure out which of the millions of American semiconductor components were sabotaged is doable—and in fact we're doing that—but extremely time-consuming because there are hundreds of American suppliers, and some of them make hundreds of new ICs, or versions of new ICs, every year. In addition, that method is not an exact science. We already know of one IC from Motorola that was found by checking design revisions. That IC was never sold to the Japanese, so we would never have found it through sales records alone. But we can still identify some of the ICs this way. Now I'm also about to try this the opposite way. I'm inside a Japanese corporation, and I'm going to check which American components Sakata Electronics stopped acquiring between 2003 and 2004."

> SAKATA ELECTRONICS, INC.
> PURCHASING DEPARTMENT—FOREIGN OPERATIONS
> ELECTRONIC COMPONENTS FROM:
> MOTOROLA, INC.—2003 PURCHASES
> ***RECORDS NOT ON-LINE***

"Damn!" She leaned back on the chair and crossed her arms.

"What?"

"Stupid records are not on-line."

"What does that mean?"

"Due to disk space limitations, many companies remove old records from their primary drives and archive them in either magnetic tapes or Zip disks."

"Even I know what's a magnetic tape, but what's a Zip disk?"

"Looks just like a regular diskette but about four times thicker and can hold a lot of information, enough to make it a viable backup medium."

"How do you access them after they've been archived?"

"You need to know which tape or Zip disk it is. Usually companies have automatic backup systems to preserve the integrity of files currently in use. Once a year, more or less, companies take the last set of backups and archive them in cabinets in the archive room. Someone needs to physically pull them from the cabinet and download them into a server."

"What's a server?"

"That's the large disks that are on-line and can be accessed directly by the network. They represent the virtual working space for a corporation."

"I see," said MacClaine, rubbing his chin. "So someone inside Sakata has to actually go to one of these cabinets and physically load a tape or Zip disk into this server?"

"Right. Then I can browse through the data. Problem is I don't know which backup it is."

MacClaine frowned. "Sounds difficult."

"It is, and it means that we can't get that information unless we have someone on the inside loading the archives on-line for us."

She tried 2004 and got the same results. "Well, at least I can E-mail the list of companies to Charlie."

"Who's Charlie?"

"One of my subordinates in Washington. He's running things for me while I'm on holiday in California." She elbowed him lightly.

"Hey, you gotta find out how the other half lives."

She smiled before quickly becoming serious again. "I have a dozen analysts working with American semiconductor companies running checks in their designs to find other sabotaged chips. So far we have found one before it caused an accident. That's the Motorola microcontroller sold exclusively to the Pentagon. With some luck we'll nail others soon enough. In addition, we're working the sales-purchasing angle, but that approach has some holes."

"At least you got partial luck with Sakata. Sounds like the list of companies might get you somewhere."

She nodded. "Akita seems impregnable, though, and Chang had zero luck getting root passwords from anyone else."

"Sounds like the word's spreading among all Japanese corporations. They're all tightening security."

"Speaking of security," she said. "Did you say you wanted to check their security system?"

He shrugged. "Sure."

She pulled it up on the screen.

```
SAKATA ELECTRONICS, INC.
SECURITY DEPARTMENT
1. BUILDING
2. PERSONNEL
3. ADMINISTRATIVE
4. POLICIES
5. SCHEDULES
6. RETURN TO PREVIOUS MENU
7. RETURN TO TOP LEVEL
```

"Check out the building," MacClaine said.

She made the selection and the screen changed to a top view of one of three buildings making up the Sakata Electronics complex in Santa Clara, next door to Intel. To the right of the drawing were several categories to choose from:

```
BUILDING SECURITY
1. ALARM ZONES
2. MAGNETIC DOORS
3. VIDEO SURVEILLANCE
4. MOTION SENSORS
5. GUARD STATIONS
6. SECURITY ROUNDS
7. RETURN TO PREVIOUS MENU
8. RETURN TO TOP LEVEL
```

She clicked on the first one and the floor was divided by a dozen different color schemes, representing each alarm zone. To the left of the drawing were the icons for building selections and floor selections within a building. She clicked on option four and dozens of black diamonds peppered the drawing, marking the locations of the floor's motion sensors. The same happened when she selected the video cameras. The guard stations were marked as green boxes. The entire floor could be physically isolated in sections by activating the twenty or so magnetic doors, shown on the drawing as thick lines across hallways. A green line meant the door was open. A red line indicated a closed door.

"Let me try something," she said, running her finger over the soft pad and tapping it twice when positioning the cursor over a red line. A few seconds later the line turned green.

"I just opened a door." She quickly clicked it again, closing it. "Pretty cool, huh?"

"You can do all of that from your little computer?"

"As long as I have the right passwords. Do you now understand why the FBI punished me for writing a virus that snatches passwords? Think of the damage a hacker can—"

The phone rang. MacClaine picked it up. "Yeah?"

"Sir, Mr. Kojata refuses to cooperate. He claims that we're being racists, that we're violating his rights, that we're harassing him by refusing to let him get in touch with his attorney."

"I'm on my way." He hung up and stared at Erika for a moment.

"Who was that?" she asked, making another attempt to drink her coffee, grimacing, and setting it back on the desk.

He stood and snatched a thick manila envelope from his cluttered desk. "Let's go for a little ride."

"What's in there?"

He grinned. "You'll find out."

18

CONFESSIONS

Erika Conklin followed Brent MacClaine inside a holding cell at the SJPD headquarters. She braced herself not just because of the cold temperature inside the room but also because sitting behind a small table in the middle of the room was the Asian man with the bleached-blond hair who had forced her head down while Hashimoto put the bag with the rat over her head. The Asian sat quietly at a small table with his hands cuffed behind his back. He kept his eyes fixed on the wall in front of him, ignoring them. To their left was a one-way mirror, behind which a half dozen FBI agents and just as many detectives from the San Jose high-tech crime unit huddled to watch MacClaine take his turn with the suspect.

"Bad news, Freddie. Looks like your pals have abandoned you."

The well-built Asian in his late twenties didn't flinch, staring straight ahead.

"Remember her, Freddie? That's your name, right? Iko Kojata, also known as *Freddie*? Well, Freddie, meet Erika Conklin . . . again," MacClaine said, pointing to Erika, who kept bracing herself, not particularly enjoying the moment.

Kojata lifted his dark eyes and momentarily blinked in recognition before resuming his poker stare.

"In case you didn't know, blondie, she's a federal officer. And you put a bag with a rat over her head. You're looking at a minimum of twenty years."

Kojata ignored him.

"And of course you surely remember this pretty face," MacClaine stuck his face right in front of Kojata, who glared at him with contempt. "How are those ribs feeling today, *pal*?" He jabbed Kojata's torso with a finger and watched him wince in pain.

"This is police brutality," protested Kojata. "My attorney will be all over you guys for this. I'm a minority and you're discriminating against me."

"Yeah, right. Whatever you say. But you know what's the worst part of it?" MacClaine asked, slapping the table with the thick manila envelope, momentarily startling him. "That you're protecting the bastards who are causing so much destruction in your own country—the country that you served for five years while in the U.S. Army." MacClaine had reviewed the FBI background check done on Kojata shortly after his arrest. He was a third-generation Japanese American.

Kojata raised his gaze. "The country that wouldn't give me a job after my discharge from the Army." He resumed his pose.

"The country that gave your grandparents a home when they left Japan in the thirties and settled in Los Angeles, asshole. The same country that's kept you nice and warm since. And *this* is how you're paying it back. Take a look."

MacClaine opened the envelope and set a color eight-by-ten photo in front of him. Erika gasped, covering her mouth with her hand, abruptly looking away after seeing a child's shrunken face the color of gunmetal staring at her with puffy, milky eyes. Black hair combed straight back revealed an inch deep gash traversing the child's forehead, reminding MacClaine of Herman Munster. The head was still connected to a section of torso that had not been eaten by alligators. Puss oozed from his ears and mouth.

Several inches of the spinal cord extended down from the torso.

"Know what this is? Take a good look."

Freddie Kojata glanced at the picture, swallowed once, and closed his eyes.

"These are the mortal remains of an eleven-year-old boy eaten alive by alligators after the *Silver Comet* was derailed in the Everglades because of a sabotaged computer chip— sabotaged by the people that you're protecting."

MacClaine browsed through the file. "Now, this one's a beauty." He set another photo in front of him.

Erika felt her stomach churning while staring at a face that looked like fried bacon, lacking hair, ears, and eyelids. Bloated lips were melted shut under a scorched nose without nostrils. The corpse's seared neck displayed the hole of an emergency tracheotomy.

"The rescue crew found this woman alive, Freddie. *Alive.* Can you just for a moment think about the agony she must have felt? About what was going through her mind while she was burned alive inside one of the *Comet*'s carriages?"

Kojata swallowed hard again.

"And you know what?"

Kojata closed his eyes, slowly shaking his head.

"Her name was Yoko Sakamoto. She and her husband were celebrating part of their honeymoon by taking the *Comet* from New York to Miami to catch a Caribbean cruise. They're from Osaka, Freddie. Isn't *that* ironic?"

The young Asian American began to breath heavily, obviously upset.

"What would your parents back in L.A. say?"

Kojata briskly turned to MacClaine, eyes narrowed.

"I know, I know. They think their son is in the private security business in the valley. And that's just how it started, right, Freddie? Your army background got you a job as a security guard at Sakata Electronics. Then somewhere along the line someone approached you with an opportunity to make more dough, probably by doing nothing more than following certain people and reporting on their whereabouts. Perhaps protecting Japanese nationals while they went around screwing hot blonds. But something happened after that. Maybe you got used to the extra money. Maybe you wanted *more*. But you got involved with Hashimoto, who was a terrorist with the Aum Shinrikyo, and essentially became a hired gun, which makes you a collaborator for a terrorist network. In this country we call people like you traitors. But what the hell, you now find yourself making some serious bucks, driving around in a convertible BMW, cute chicks suddenly digging you, and all you have to do is assist in the handling of a few problems, like my abduction and the abduction of Erika Conklin. Now you're caught and essentially deeply screwed because your Japanese friends are bailing out on you, because in the end, you might *look* like them, you might party like them, and you might want to spend money like them, but you're really not one of them. You're an *American*. You're one of *us*. You don't get to claim diplomatic immunity and go home. You're a terrorist, the lowest of the lowest of criminals. You go to jail, where you'll become somebody's girlfriend and get butt fucked till your eyeballs pop out of your head."

MacClaine calmly pulled out a third picture from the envelope and set it in front of Kojata, whose eyes had softened, glistening with genuine concern.

Erika saw a grossly burnt and disfigured man. The skin over the cheeks, mouth, and chin had vaporized, leaving soot-filmed jawbones and teeth exposed in a permanent, macabre leer. The same had happened to the throat and neck, letting her stare straight through to the man's spine. She shook her head and took a step back, momentarily closing her eyes, fighting a spasm, angry at herself for not being able to handle this.

"You okay?" MacClaine asked.

"I'm . . . I'm fine," she finally whispered, barely unable to repress a shudder.

"Of course you are," whispered MacClaine. "But just in

case concrete gray isn't your normal color, feel free to use the rest rooms down the hallway."

Erika burned him with her stare.

MacClaine turned back to his prisoner. "This one's from the airline crash over Houston. The poor bastard was taking a crap at home while reading the paper when the sky fell over his ass, again thanks to a computer chip sabotaged by your Japanese friends. In all, thousands of Americans, like you and me, have died and many, many more have been injured."

By now MacClaine had his prisoner nervously looking at all three photos.

"Do you want to see more?" asked MacClaine, waving the stack at the Asian American. "I've got all ages, races, religions, and sexual inclinations in here."

Kojata shook his head.

"You're not one of them, Freddie. You're one of us. You had cyanide with you but, you didn't take it. Why?"

Freddie didn't reply but continued to breath heavily.

"They ordered you to kill yourself if captured, right?"

Kojata nodded.

"And why didn't you, Freddie? My people tell me that you were conscious when they found you in the warehouse. Why didn't you crack the capsule?"

He remained silent.

MacClaine leaned down, his face again only inches from Kojata's. "I'll tell you why, Freddie. Because you're *not* like them. You're an *American*, and whether you like it or not, you *think* like an American, and we don't believe in that shit. Now, you have two choices. The first one's to cooperate with us and I promise you that the Bureau will put in a good word with the judge to get you a reduced sentence at a minimum security prison. You'll be out in less than five years. Or . . . you can continue your charade and get life in a place that's worse than hell itself. Now I'll ask you one final time. Are you ready to cooperate with us?"

Freddie Kojata closed his eyes and gave him a slight nod.

19

PRESSURE

Twenty minutes later MacClaine bought a paper from a kid stocking the vending machine outside the SJPD headquarters. He quickly flipped through the pages while Erika looked on. Right there, on the third page of the San Jose *Mercury News,* he stared at two photos. The first was of himself holding a bottle of Jack Daniel's at a bus stop. The second was of Erika dancing half-naked on a tabletop. Both photos appeared under the headline, "Federal Agents Facing Disciplinary Board."

Erika went pale. MacClaine cursed and read on. The article, which according to the *Mercury News* was contributed by UPI reporter R. Hooks, stated that the internal affairs division of the Federal Bureau of Investigation was considering the suspension and possible prosecution of Special Agent Brent MacClaine and Analyst Erika Conklin in connection with multiple acts of harassment against the Japanese community in northern California. The article stated that this wasn't MacClaine's first incident involving Japanese nationals in America, citing an incident two years ago at Hitachi-America, where the agent had insulted and harassed several Japanese businessmen. The article then took a personal turn against MacClaine, claiming that his marriage had ended in divorce because of his abusive behavior against his wife. It also commented on his alcoholism and how he was now resorting to blackmail and harassment against the hardworking Japanese community for the purposes of personal profit and career advancement. Then the article focused on Erika Conklin, a former stripper and alleged prostitute who had apparently seduced a number of professors at UC Berkeley to get her degree and was now employed at the FBI, where she had had a number of alleged affairs with high-ranking officials. One source, who preferred to remain anonymous, had indicated that at least on one occasion, Erika Conklin had been alone with Director Roman Palenski in his suite in the middle of the night. The article stated that her family, who owned a ranch in northern California, had been contacted for comment but so far no one had returned the phone calls from the media.

Erika put a hand to her face, tears welling in her eyes. "Oh, my God . . . bastards!"

"The pressure is being applied," MacClaine said, hugging her. "The pressure is *definitely* being applied."

20

YUDEDAKO

Slick Willie Matsubara stepped into the changing room connected to the side of his Victorian mansion overlooking Silicon Valley, feeling the cold flagstone floor with his naked feet, the simplicity of the place contrasted sharply with the lavishly furnished estate.

He hung a *yukata*—a cotton dressing gown—on an iron hook on one of the stripped-oak walls and reached for a bar of soap on a wooden box next to a large bamboo dipper. Using a hand pump, which he had imported from a hot springs bathhouse in eastern Kyushu, Matsubara filled the dipper and submerged a *furoshiki*—a square of tie-dyed cloth—in the water before rubbing it against the bar of soap, working a bluish lather. Sitting naked on a wooden stool, he began to pummel himself ruthlessly with the *furoshiki*, scrubbing and scraping every square inch of his body, until his skin tingled when he rinsed it with the warm water in the dipper.

Taking a deep breath, he forced himself to relax. The message that had arrived just an hour ago told him that Hashimoto had broken the FBI analyst, forcing her to confess the names and addresses of three key agents involved in the case, including Brent MacClaine. Her body was now at the bottom of the San Francisco Bay wrapped with fifty pounds of chains.

Leaving the soap and the *furoshiki* in the rustic bath-house, Matsubara walked down the short flagstone path, flanked by tall bamboo and pine trees, to the *rotemburo*, the open-air pool heated to a perfect one hundred five degrees by natural-gas heaters hidden behind the woods. Steam rose from the surface, hovering a dozen feet over the pool like morning fog. Streams of gurgling water rushed from the heaters to the *rotemburo* along bamboo gutters. Matsubara had poured over a hundred thousand dollars into the artificial hot-springs bath to create the right environment, the right effect for his men and him to carry on the tradition of their fellow countrymen, who would journey for many miles to immerse themselves in a hot-springs bath and achieve *yudedako*, the triumphal step on the road to perfect physical health.

Matsubara dipped his left foot into the steaming bath, gasping at the slight shock, grinning in pleasure as he went farther, stepping onto a granite slab, and from there to a deeper slab, until he had immersed himself completely, enveloped by the invigorating temperature of the water.

Soon, he thought. *Soon it will be contained.*

Matsubara inhaled deeply, the heated water doing its magical work, purging his mind from all anxiety and stress. He closed his eyes and listened to the clicking of insects and the chirping of birds, sounds that mixed with splashing water.

The article in the *Mercury News* against the lead FBI agents working the case had been perfect, done in traditional Japanese style. When you want to ruin someone, just make a public claim against him. Whether the claim turns out to be real or not is beside the point, because human nature only remembers the claim. Even if the person is later exonerated, everyone will still wonder if the person was guilty. Erika Conklin, although already dead, would have her name, and her family's name, forever smeared. The same applied to Brent MacClaine.

Matsubara breathed in the steaming air rising off the water, letting his stress evaporate. There was so much at stake. So much. His family's reputation, his family's very future, rested on his ability to carry on this mission flawlessly. Only then would the Japanese government release his company back to him. Failure meant dishonor, a fate worse than death itself.

Matsubara purged thoughts of failure from his mind, focusing on success, on life in Sendai after his mission, on perhaps finding himself a good Japanese wife, a woman above the American whores he indulged in but secretly despised because they represented the vulgarism, the barbarism that he hated so much about America.

Ten minutes later, the scalding temperature having turned his skin a light pink, Matsubara grinned with the satisfaction of having achieved *yudedako*, the sublime state of ecstasy that also filled him with the confidence that the Yamato Ichizotu would continue its millennium-long tradition of secret and holy missions for the glory of his ancestors, for the glory of Japan.

21

WORTHY ADVERSARY

President Lester Williams sat behind his desk clutching his
football while silently considering the recommendations of
the three men sitting across from him. The most recent
break in the case involved the Japanese Defense Agency
and the Aum Shinrikyo, which added a new dimension to
the problem.

He shifted his gaze to Donald Bane, director of central
intelligence, sitting between FBI director Roman Palenski
and Defense Secretary James T. Vuono.

"Talk to me, Don."

Bane, a man as large as Palenski but with a full head
of salt-and-pepper hair and a rugged face, set one of the
brown manila folders he held in his hands in front of the
president. The words Tanaka—CIA Top Secret were written in red across the bottom.

"The JDA is headed by Kenichi Tanaka, Mr. President,"
Bane began. "He's a legend in the intelligence world, one
of many young operatives we trained for the Japanese government in the late fifties and early sixties. His father was
a key member of the Tokko, Japan's chief counterintelli-
gence organization during World War Two. Because of his
father's connections, particularly with Hoichi Yamasaki,
who led the JDA for many years, Tanaka was able to rise
fast within the Japanese intelligence community, holding

various posts as a member of the diplomatic staff. Berlin in '59, Seoul in '62, Manila two years later, Taiwan in '69, Beijing in '72, Madrid in '75, and Washington in the early eighties until a promotion returned him to Tokyo in '87. He became the deputy chief of the JDA in '89 and stepped up to chief a year later when Yamasaki retired. He has very close ties with the military and the industrial community. In fact, we believe that over half of the JDA's resources are dedicated to industrial espionage. Some of its agents pose as college students in this country, landing summer intern jobs at all major American corporations. Last year we caught a dozen of them and got them deported, but not before they were able to steal secrets from their employers and send them home via various routes, including E-mail. Tanaka runs a tight ship. He makes a worthy adversary in the industrial espionage and counterespionage world. He has been able to stop a number of our operations overseas, just as we have nailed a lot of his work in this country. Now it appears as if the JDA has associated itself with the Aum movement."

Williams nodded, setting the football next to the dossier, opening the file, and browsing through the myriad of photos, covert reports, and newspaper clips. "Do you feel he's devious and skilled enough to pull this sabotage scheme? Or is it possible that this might be going on at one or more levels below him without his knowledge?"

Donald Bane stared into the distance while running a finger over a depression next to his left eye, where an Iraqi soldier had kicked him during an operation in the gulf several years ago. He crossed his legs and slowly shook his head. "That agency doesn't move an inch without Tanaka's personal blessing. He had to be in on it from the onset."

"Which means that Tanaka is probably the one individual who would have full knowledge of this operation," commented Palenski while running his thumbs beneath his suspenders.

Bane nodded. "It's simply his style. He's a micromanager. He trusts very few people in his organization, mostly a handful of men that he recruited and personally trained to handle key sections of his operation."

"Like Matsubara," said Palenski, pointing to the other dossier in Bane's hands.

"That's correct," Bane said, handing the document to the president, who opened it right over Tanaka's. Bane added, "Oruku Matsubara is one of Tanaka's lieutenants. He's been in California for a few years. The man's well educated, son of a wealthy Japanese industrialist, now a liaison between the industrial sector and the JDA. He's under diplomatic immunity. We think he's the one who executed the operation that Tanaka masterminded.

"Where is he now?"

"Still in this country. We're tailing him, to see where he leads us."

Williams sat back and placed both hands on his lap. "What do you gentlemen propose we do next? And before you answer, I want to go on the record as saying that I will approve any sensible plan that results in information to stop the computer-triggered disasters. If Japan is indeed at the heart of this sabotage scheme, and you seem to have enough evidence to believe so, I consider this an act of war against the United States and I'll expect you to utilize every resource and skill available to you to stop the madness."

After a moment of silence, Bane spoke first. "I need presidential sanction to bring Matsubara in, Mr. President."

Williams liked Donald Bane, a straight shooter who would rather be up-front about his intentions rather than do anything clandestinely, like so many DCIs before him. The president nodded, granting the CIA permission to abduct a Japanese diplomat for reasons of national security.

"One of the risks, of course," said Secretary Vuono, "is that Matsubara's only a hired gun who carried out certain aspects of the operation but has no knowledge of the big picture."

"In which case," said Palenski, "bringing him in might telegraph our intentions to the big fish."

"Which brings me to my request, Mr. President," said Vuono. "I want to abduct Konichi Tanaka. Based on everything I've heard, he is the one individual that might have the master list of sabotaged computer chips in his possession."

Williams picked up his football, rubbing his fingertips against the pigskin. "What do you have in mind, Jim? The SEALs?"

Vuono nodded. "SEAL Team Five is already aboard the *Polk* in the Sea of Japan getting ready for a possible mission in the area, per our last conversation. The intelligence gathered by both the CIA and the DIA on Tanaka indicates that he spends most weekends at Cape Muroto, in the Japanese island of Shikoku, where he owns a house on the cliffs overlooking the Pacific Ocean. We're working through some scenarios to take him there."

"What's your confidence level on this intelligence?" asked the president.

Vuono turned to Bane, who crossed his legs, and said, "About sixty percent."

"Which means," said Vuono, returning his attention back to the president, "that it may take more than one attempt to get him."

"Is there a way to increase your confidence?"

"We're working on it, sir," said Vuono. "In the meantime SEAL Team Five is ready for multiple attempts."

Lester Williams shifted his gaze to the silver-framed picture of his stepson. Vuono and Bane were giving it to him straight. At least they had chosen wisely regarding SEAL Team Five, and not because the elite force happened to be led by the president's stepson. Williams didn't cherish the thought of Derek Ray going into action, but when wearing his presidential hat, he had to push those emotions aside and do the right thing for his country, even if that meant putting Ray's life on the line.

Williams nodded. "If we go with this option, how soon before it can be carried out?"

"Within the next seventy-two hours, when we estimate that Tanaka will visit his beach home."

"All right. Do it."

"Yes, Mr. President."

"We'll be needing technical support after Tanaka is brought in," said Palenski, rubbing his bald head.

Vuono and Bane turned to him. "Technical support?"

The FBI director nodded. "This is a case involving high-tech sabotage. It requires the on-site support of at least one of my technical analysts."

"Do you have someone in mind, Roman?" asked the president.

"The same analyst who came up with the theory on Japan and who then provided us with the JDA and Aum Shinrikyo intel after her brief kidnapping."

The president nodded. "Yes, yes. I did read about her in your report. Pretty amazing lady."

Palenski sighed. "That she is, sir."

"How did you manage to get your hands on such a fine analyst, Roman? My perception is that most hot-shot engineers go after the big bonuses and stock options offered by the private sector," said Lester Williams.

"Mr. President," Palenski said after a brief moment of hesitation, "you don't really want to know."

Williams smiled thinly before saying, "All right, Roman. You and Jim work this out to have technical assistance on site to minimize the delay on our intelligence gathering. Anything else?"

Vuono nodded. "Does it still make sense to move on Matsubara?"

Williams turned to Bane.

"Absolutely, Mr. President," said Bane. "Matsubara might have very key knowledge not just about the list but also regarding the whereabouts of Tanaka, which would improve the odds in the success of the SEAL mission."

Vuono turned to Bane while narrowing his eyes, contemplating the DCI's perspective, finally saying, "That's definitely an interesting possibility."

Bane said, "Anything we can learn about Tanaka is worth the risk, as long as it's done right. The last thing we want is Tanaka being warned that we're after him."

"There's another reason why we should move on Matsubara, and right away," said Palenski. "Tanaka already knows the FBI is investigating his operation. I'm sure that Matsubara has already contacted him. If I were in Tanaka's shoes, I would be trying to find ways to break the link in the investigation."

"Which can be accomplished easily by eliminating the people who can point their finger at Tanaka," said Vuono almost to himself. "Like Oruku Matsubara . . . We definitely need to grab this guy, Mr. President, before we find him floating facedown in a canal."

"So my initial decision remains," said Williams. "Anything else?"

"Yes, sir," said Palenski, crossing his legs while thumbing his suspenders. "There's a newspaper article floating around about harassment of Japanese nationals by my agency. The article really bashes my lead agents, Erika Conklin and Brent MacClaine."

Williams leaned forward. "Continue."

"Someone is trying to ruin their lives, sir, and even my own. The article says that I may have had an affair with Conklin."

"Did you?"

"Of course not, sir."

The president nodded. "Who printed it?"

"Several newspapers, including the *Post*. They all claim that they got it from a UPI reporter named Hooks, but when my office called UPI, they claimed no one works there by that name and they also have no idea how the article got published."

"Typical tactics by extreme factions within the Japanese business community," said Bane. "Bastards do that in Japan all the time. This was also common practice in the old

KGB, planting journalistic misinformation. Scandal is now used in Japan by ruthless businessmen as a weapon against an enemy firm. Once it makes it to the papers, it's all over, even if it turns out to be false. By that time resignations have taken place and new management has taken over. They also tried to pull that crap on my men working the Tokyo and Osaka stations, and we never knew where it originated, though we always suspected it had to be some rogue CEO trying to cover his tracks. It's always a dead end. You'll never find out who gave the order to publish the article. No one will be accountable and the most you'll get if you complain enough is a back-page paragraph apologizing for the mistake, but the damage is already done. I've seen many lives destroyed that way. Last week I had to bring one of my men home because of an article in the local paper that claimed he had sexually abused a number of children at a Tokyo day-care center. In reality he had been close to cracking a cyberterrorist ring in that country. The Japanese government tried to help us with damage control, but in the end, the article set us back months."

"Well, we can't afford to take MacClaine and Conklin off the case," Palenski replied. "The fact that we're being attacked by the them tells me we're definitely on the right track, confirming Conklin's theory. Now more than ever we need to continue pushing, but at the same time I'd like to put some pressure on the papers to scrutinize what they print before it goes through. Kind of like playing their game, only in reverse."

"I'll have my staff work with the press to fix this."

"Thank you, sir."

"Anything else?"

"Yes, Mr. President," said Palenski. "This leads to my next request. My agency wants to take a more indirect approach in the case. I believe we will be more successful if we are less confrontational and more subtle. Give them a taste of their own medicine."

"All right. What do you need?"

"Sanction to approve the clandestine penetration of a Japanese corporation in California."

"Explain."

Palenski went over the plan that he had received just a few hours ago from Special Agent Brent MacClaine. It took advantage of the confession from a captured Asian American, who had agreed to cooperate after realizing that all of his Japanese colleagues in captivity would be put on the next flight to Tokyo while he was left behind to face criminal charges.

"It sounds risky," said Bane. "But I like it. Again, I'll make the same argument for this proposal as I did for the kidnapping of Matsubara. We need to obtain as much information as possible before the SEAL strike, and in the process we might just get lucky and find this master list of components."

Williams nodded while standing, which also prompted all three of his guests to stand. "All right, gentlemen. Attack this problem on all fronts and take as much risk as you deem necessary. Just make sure to deliver the list of sabotaged components to this office as soon as humanly possible. If Palenski is correct in his assessment, we may have only seen the very beginning of a cyberterrorism attack that could very easily send this nation into a technological Stone Age."

22

DIRTY LAUNDRY

Erika and MacClaine sat in the front seat of his sedan sipping coffee while looking at the evening sky over Silicon Valley from the edge of a deserted parking lot in Mountain View. MacClaine had spent the day pushing paper while Erika worked with Charlie Chang and the rest of her team through a modem. Neither had discussed the article much, choosing instead to pass the time by performing their daily tasks while waiting for presidential sanction to carry out their plan. An hour ago they'd decided to grab a bite and get some coffee.

"It happened during my second year at Berkeley," said Erika, holding the cup with both hands while staring at the vast expanse of buildings covering the entire valley. "My roommate and I got invited to a party hosted by a couple of fraternities. All I got was a glass of wine, I swear, and then I just remember waking up the next morning half-naked in my dorm. Some bastard must have slipped me a mickey."

"What happened?"

"Nothing, thank God. Had it not been for my roommate, who dragged me out of the frat house kicking and screaming, I probably would have been . . ."

"And the picture?"

She shrugged. "Someone must have taken it before my

roommate got me out of there. Like I said, I don't remember." She glanced at the folded newspaper resting on the dashboard. "But it sure looks bad, doesn't it?"

MacClaine frowned. "I'm sorry you got dragged into this. I got word from Palenski that he's using all of the Bureau's powers to get our names cleared. He also assured me that there is no such internal affairs investigation. Right now the FBI, and the entire White House administration for that matter, is right behind us on this case."

"I know, but I still have a lot of explaining to do to my dad and my brothers. I was already lying to them about my work back East. I guess I'm going to have to confront them sooner or later with the truth."

MacClaine raised his cup. "And the truth shall set you free."

"Or disinherited." She shook her head. "Damn."

They remained silent for a few moments.

"You know, I never touched her," MacClaine said. "I may have neglected her during long FBI cases. I may have drunk heavily at times. I may have not been there during the times that she may have needed me for support. But I never, *ever* raised my hand against her. Not once. I never cheated on her. I never gambled. I never did drugs. And I always treated her fairly, with respect, even as she was sucking me dry in divorce court. Now those bastards pull this crap."

More silence.

"Well," she said, "if they were trying to discourage us from continuing the investigation, they're in for a big surprise, because all of this just proves one thing: that we're getting very close. In trying to make us stop investigating them, they in fact accomplished the exact opposite."

"And they've also made it quite personal," said MacClaine. "Maybe these Mickey Mouse tactics work in Japan and executives go and jump off buildings when their names are smeared in shit by defaming articles such as this one. But all they accomplished today's pissing me off, and they will be sorry they did that, because I will nail these bastards if it's the last thing I do."

"I'll drink to that," she said.

He checked his watch. "We better get going. There's someone waiting for us at the office."

"Who?"

He grinned. "It's a surprise."

23

PLEASANT SURPRISES

They arrived at their building at nine o'clock in the evening. MacClaine kept his hand under his jacket, clutching his weapon as they left the sedan and headed for the main entrance, taking the elevator to the third floor, where his office was located.

As he felt the gentle upward acceleration MacClaine checked his watch again. "He should be here by now."

"Who, Brent? Who is supposed to be here?"

He grinned. "I told you. It's a surprise."

She brushed back her short hair with her hands while sighing. "I don't think I can take any more surprises today."

"This one you should be able to handle. Trust me."

Erika Conklin stepped into the reception area of the FBI office. MacClaine walked right behind her.

She froze. There, sitting on one of the sofas, flanked by two FBI agents, was her father.

"Dad!" She ran to him just as he stood up, looking bigger than life, his tanned face cracking into a crooked smile under a full head of hair.

"How are you, princess?" he said, closing his eyes and embracing her. He was almost a foot taller, with muscular arms.

"I've definitely been better," she said, wiping her tears

as they sat down. MacClaine snapped his fingers and the two agents vanished. "But . . . but how did you get here?"

"Agent MacClaine and I chatted for a little while this afternoon. He was kind enough to send a helicopter to pick me up. I can't stay long, though. You know we're always short-handed at the ranch."

Erika turned to MacClaine, giving him a slow wink while saying "Thank you."

MacClaine smiled and went into his office.

"How's everybody? How's Terry, Lee, Doug, John, and Jerry? Oh, God, I miss you guys so much!" They sat down holding hands.

He smiled thinly. "Your brothers are doing fine, just really busy. Lots and lots of work, if you remember how it was."

Erika nodded, nostalgia filling her. "I do remember, and I do miss it."

"We'll love to have you back. We miss our wine-tasting expert."

She threw her arms around his neck and hugged him again, and began to cry. "God, I've missed you so much."

He patted her back. "Now, now, tell me, princess. What's going on? You never told me you worked for the FBI. And how did you get those nasty bruises? You look like you got stomped by a horse. Are you in trouble?"

Erika lowered her gaze. "I don't even know where to begin."

He lifted her chin. "Why don't you start at the beginning?"

She did, taking almost twenty minutes to tell him everything, her problem with the FBI, her agreement with them, the years living in Washington, her struggle to come out and tell him what was really happening, and then the accidents and her involvement in the case. She skipped the incident with the rat and made no comment on the photo in the newspaper.

"So you're working the case that's all over the news?

The one about the cyberterrorists sabotaging our computer chips?"

She nodded. "I'm right in the middle of it, actually, which is why that article got published. I came up with this theory that explains the reasoning for the sabotages, and also its originator. The newspaper article confirms our suspicions. They're trying to discourage us from investigating them."

"When I saw the picture and read those lies, I . . ." Sam Conklin's voice trailed off. "I just wanted to kill someone . . . because I know my girl. I know I raised you better than that."

She took a minute to explain how the picture was probably taken.

"What are you going to do now?" he asked.

"Keep going after them. All they've done is reinforce my belief that we're on the right track. I'm not about to stop now, Dad. They can print whatever they want about me. I will not stop. We must put an end to the disasters."

He smiled. "That's the princess I remember. You go and get those bastards, whoever they are. And you don't worry about a thing at Rancho de las Vistas. We're all rooting for you over there."

"Thanks, Dad."

24

RISKY BUSINESS

The president tiptoed inside their suite, trying not to wake up the First Lady. Quietly, he went straight to the bathroom and into his walk-in closet, where he changed into a pair of pajamas, washed his face, and brushed his teeth. Slowly, walking in the dark, he crawled in bed and closed his eyes.

"They're going in, aren't they?" Elizabeth Williams whispered.

President Williams turned to her. "There's a pretty good chance of that right now."

She didn't reply. Instead, she simply turned over to face him, resting the side of her head on his shoulder and placing a leg over his.

"No mission is ever easy, Beth, but this one's far less dangerous than Panama, Kuwait, or Afghanistan. It's in and out, with minimum resistance expected at the site. And we're out of options. Too many innocent people have died because of this, and many more stand to die before it's over unless we put a stop to it."

She hugged him. "I know, but I can't help worrying. And now he is going to be a father. I spoke to Melissa on the phone today. She's due in a month, Les, and it's a boy. Oh, God, I hope nothing goes wrong. I was so relieved when he got the Pentagon assignment, and I'm looking forward to their moving to this area. I'm going to be close to my boy and my grandson."

"And all of that is still happening, Beth. You'll have your son and grandson right here with you in no time."

"I don't think I can take another Panama, all the sleepless nights while he recovered from his wounds. And then Kuwait and Afghanistan, the weeks when I didn't know if he was dead or alive."

"I told you, sweetheart. This isn't Panama or Kuwait. This one's easy. In and out in less than a couple of hours with minimal resistance at the site."

"I'm just not sure what I'll do if I lose my baby boy."

"Your baby boy's forty-two and the most experienced SEAL commander in the Navy, Beth. He can take care of himself better than any other man I know."

"He's my baby boy, and he will continue to be my baby boy for the rest of his life."

Williams hugged her tight and closed his eyes, slowly falling asleep, but not without a short prayer for the well-being of his stepson and the SEAL team he led.

25

QUIET PROFESSIONALS

Commander Derek "Sting" Ray sat alone in the mess room of the Sturgeon-class submarine. It was just past three o'clock in the morning and the steel fish that would deliver SEAL Team Five to within four miles of the east coast of southern Japan cruised undetected at fifteen knots while maintaining a depth of three hundred feet.

Silenced reigned aboard the vessel, providing Ray with the focus he required to absorb the latest version of the insertion plan, which he had worked out with his SEAL commander back at Coronado, California, just outside San Diego, home of the Naval Special Warfare Group One.

Under the fluorescent light, Ray shifted his weight on the aluminum chair bolted to the floor of the vessel and yawned, rubbing his bloodshot eyes.

"Damn. I'm tired," he mumbled, reaching for a glass of water on the table and taking a couple of sips. Across the mess room, two sailors on kitchen detail, dressed in blue coveralls and wearing gas masks, chopped onions. Next to them another sailor, also fitted with a gas mask, worked on a sack of potatoes.

Setting the glass down, he pinched the bridge of his nose and momentarily closed his eyes to alleviate the discomfort from the peeled onions, which stung him in spite of the submarine's superb air recirculation system. The smell probably contributed to the redness in his eyes. But the real reason for his exhaustion had to do with the activities that had taken place in the past forty-eight hours, since the decision was made to deploy SEAL Team Five to the region. Ray had been right in the middle of a Lamaze class with Melissa to get ready for the birth of their first child

He frowned. She had not been happy. According to the Navy his Pentagon assignment had already gone through. He was wrapping up his instructor responsibilities at Coronado and assisting his superiors in selecting a new leader for his SEAL team prior to his transfer in two months. Yet, the order had come from high above directing that Commander Derek Ray's SEAL Team Five be deployed immediately.

And Derek Ray, like his father before him, had kissed his wife good-bye and headed off to the base, where a squad of eight hand-picked SEALs plus a half squad for beach recon, and twenty thousand pounds of gear, had boarded a military transport from Coronado to South Korea, where they'd transferred to three MH-53 Pavelow helicopters, which delivered them and their gear to the *Polk* twenty-four hours ago.

"Sting?"

Ray turned around. Master Chief Petty Officer Dan Bishop stood in the passageway leading to the forward torpedo room. Bishop was Ray's tall and corpulent right-hand man, second in command of SEAL Team Five. Unlike all other services in the U.S. armed forces, the SEALs didn't address their superior officers by rank during a mission.

"You should be catching Zs, Chief," said Ray.

Wearing a pair of jungle camouflage pants and a plain white T-shirt, Bishop walked to the table and sat down. The master chief was so bulked up that his mere presence qualified as psychological warfare. He always reminded Ray of the Hulk.

"Can't sleep until I know that the plan's finalized." He set his arms on the table and regarded his commanding officer while rubbing a large scar across his left forearm. "Don't need another Panama."

The SEAL commander ran a hand through his short black hair, fingering the hairless track right above his left temple, carved by an enemy round that had grazed his skull almost two decades before. That wound, plus the shrapnel that had turned his chin into scar tissue, reminded him of Panama and of the men he had lost there while taking over Paitilla Airport and disabling General Manuel Noriega's Learjet. He remembered with bitterness the last-minute request from central command during the middle of the mission to pull in the execution timetable by fifteen minutes, forcing the SEALs to rush into position—a move that had exposed their presence to Panamanian soldiers guarding the hangar. Noriega's forces had opened fire on the incoming SEAL team. Ray called in air support to handle the Panamanian soldiers, but a circling air force gunship never got the request. Radio malfunction was later blamed for the miscommunication. Even without air support, the SEALs were able to shoot their way through and disable the plane with a 40-mm grenade, but at the cost of four dead and nine wounded, including Ray and Bishop.

"Don't feel like picking up any more beauty marks," Ray said, pointing at the master plan.

"Are we clear for the SDV?" asked Bishop, referring to the MK VIII SEAL delivery vehicle, a minisubmarine mounted on the hull of the *Polk*.

"Just for recon. We're using a rubber duck for the insertion," he said, referring to the Zodiac inflatable boat that would be launched from the *Polk*'s deck after completing the recon phase of the mission using the minisub. Ray pointed to a rocky beach four miles south of Muroto on a color surveillance photo of the Japanese island of Shikoku taken twenty hours before by a spy plane. "This area is not guarded because of these cliffs. There's no way to get from the beach to the top of the cliffs except through a nice little climb."

"Lock and load. Just the way I like it," said Bishop, the

right end of his mouth curving up a notch. Lock and load was a term used in the military meaning get ready to fire. Among the SEALs, however, the term meant much more than that. It represented their credo, their state of mind, locked and loaded, *always* ready, living in a constant state of total preparedness for whatever task their superior officers threw at them.

"We'll go up right here. Looks like a two-hundred-foot vertical climb."

"Couple of ropes should do it."

"Yep. The mansion seems lightly guarded," Ray said, pointing to another photo. "I only see five guards. Two by the pool and three others by the front steps. All carrying automatic weapons."

"There might be more in the woods surrounding the mansion." He pointed at the forest encircling the estate and its well-trimmed lawns and manicured gardens.

Ray nodded. "That might explain the lack of a fence also. We'll have to go around the perimeter of the forest and disable all guards before going in."

"And then we'll be exposed for . . ." He pointed at the clearing between the house and the forest. "Looks like a hundred feet or so."

Ray just inspected the photo.

"How much time're we being given?" Bishop asked.

"One hour from beach insertion to the top of the cliff, thirty minutes to disable the guards and find Tanaka before a chopper from the *Blue Ridge*, a missile cruiser sailing just outside their waters, arrives to get us the hell out of Dodge."

"What's this?" Bishop asked, going back to a satellite photo and pointing at a facility three miles north of the target."

Ray shook his head. "You don't want to know. I couldn't believe it myself when the spooks in Washington told me. It's a Japanese army base."

Bishop made a face.

"But not just *any* army base."

Bishop didn't say anything.

"It's one of the training camps for Japan's Special Warfare Command, which trains counterinsurgency units as well as their First Airborne Brigade."

"Those are some tough hombres," said Bishop. "I'd rather not get tangled up with them."

Ray patted his large subordinate on the back. "Remember that only a handful of them would make it through Hell Week at Coronado. This mission's just a walk in the park for us compared to Iraq and Afghanistan. And besides, guess who trained their trainers?"

"We did?"

"Well, not exactly. We don't let any other nation know how we train SEALs, in case we have to do something like this. That's our edge. Their training is modeled after the Rangers, and you know how easy it is for us to whip them."

The master chief nodded before returning his attention to the map. "Just how much do you know about our target?"

"The Pentagon believes that this guy is the mastermind behind the cyberterrorism strikes. He is supposed to possess the list of the sabotaged computer chips."

"In that case I'll be more than happy to force the list out of the bastard myself. My brother's auto parts store in Denver was looted during the blackout."

"You never told me that."

Bishop shrugged. "There was nothing I could do about it then. Now it looks like I can."

Ray flipped to an enhanced satellite shot of the army base. "Due to its proximity to target, the base obviously presents certain dangers."

Bishop pointed to long and dark shapes lined up on one side of the base. "Are those what I think they are?"

"Yep. Black Hawk helicopters, still one of the best combat assault helicopters. There's twenty of them, at least that we can see. There could be more hidden in the hangars."

"How old is the intel on this target?" the paranoid master chief asked.

Ray fished out a one-page fax from under the color photos. "Twelve hours. The DIA spooks say the target's solid. The CIA backs them up."

"Spooks *always* back each other up." Bishop read the Defense Intelligence Agency report, including confirmation from the Central Intelligence Agency. "One of these days we should bring a couple of these spooks along. Let them feel what it's like to get stuck out there with bad intel."

Ray grinned. "C'mon, Chief. Give them some credit. They did a good job in the gulf."

Bishop rubbed his eyes and made a face. "Good job, my ass. They just got lucky. And even if it wasn't luck, I still don't trust them, just like I don't trust politicians, no offense intended."

Ray shrugged. A week never went by without somebody bringing up the fact, however subtly, that he was the president's stepson. In many ways he preferred that things went back to the way they were before the election, when people knew him because of his reputation as one of the finest SEALs in the Navy. Ray still remembered when three Secret Service agents had showed up at Coronado and insisted on following him wherever he went. Ray had given each agent a Basic Underwater Demolition/SEAL (BUD/S) candidate uniform and put them through Hell Week along with the rest of the volunteers for the SEAL program under way, arguing that if they indeed wanted to protect his life, they would have to follow him wherever he went. As a SEAL, Ray went to dangerous places via the least comfortable routes under the worst possible conditions. Anyone protecting his life would have to do the same. Two of the Secret Service agents collapsed from exhaustion on day three. The last one made it through day four before he had to be taken away on a stretcher. The Secret Service never bothered him again.

"There's something else," Ray said.

"Surprise me."

"Two civilians will be aboard the rescue chopper from the *Ridge*."

Bishop frowned. *"Civilians?"*

"FBI. The ones working this case back home. Given the critical timing of this problem, Washington wants them on site to find any hardware or software that might help the investigation. They also want to start debriefing our hostage as soon as possible in the hope of identifying the bad components right away. They don't even want to wait for the hour that it'll take the chopper to return to the *Ridge*."

"Why do we need them there? Why can't we just grab any hardware we find and also extract the info from Tanaka and pass it on to them while they wait at the *Ridge*?"

"Apparently, these folks will be able to tell pretty quickly what's the right hardware to take and also if the information Tanaka's providing is real or not."

Bishop leaned closer, and whispered, "Like I said, I don't trust spooks, just like I don't trust these overfed submariners."

Ray glanced at the sailors on kitchen detail. "Why?"

"I overheard the captain today. He's scared shitless about getting so close to shore to drop us off."

"That's his problem. His orders are crystal. We're his cargo and he'll deliver us precisely *where* we tell him, *when* we tell him." He checked his wristwatch. "Which, by the way, is in less than twelve hours."

"So it looks like we're going."

"So far it's a go. The minisub launches in eight hours. We follow four hours later, after we get the green light from the security team, and the final confirmation from Coronado. We have approval for recon but not for infiltration. But unless the spooks find this master list somewhere else in the next twelve hours, I think it's a safe bet to assume that we're going in."

Bishop's face hardened, his eyes narrowing. "Rookies better not fuck up . . . or they'll have to deal with Dan Bishop."

Commander Derek Ray looked at the array of wires and pipes running along the ceiling and walls of the submarine. Five rookies had replaced veterans, who had recently retired. Although the grueling six months of extreme physical and mental hell that BUD/S trainees went through before becoming SEALs did a fantastic job at weeding out weaklings, nothing could ever replace field experience. "Relax, Chief. They've got the training. They'll do just fine. Besides, we also have Loca Mendez to keep them in line."

That brought a smile to Bishop's stone face. Petty Officer First Class Norma Mendez, known among the SEALs simply as Loca, or crazy one, was among the toughest trainers at Naval Special Warfare Command. Norma Mendez had been one of the few SEALs to escape unscathed from the Panama fiasco, playing an instrumental role in the team's retrieval, especially after Ray and Bishop had been disabled by enemy fire. She had again saved Ray's hide during Desert Storm, when sand had jammed the bolt of his MP5 and he had almost bought the farm when facing two Iraqi soldiers armed with AK-47s during a Scud rocket hunt in southern Iraq. Mendez had taken out both Iraqis before they could open fire on Ray. Mendez had an innate ability not only to be at the right place at the right time, but also to escape unharmed from the toughest situations. Because of her small size, she was also quite adept at rock climbing, a skill that would be paramount to the success of this mission. Ray always made certain that she got plenty of face time with BUD/S candidates at Coronado in the hope of passing on some of her lifesaving instincts to the recruits.

Ray would certainly miss this life after his Pentagon transfer, but with Melissa carrying his child the seasoned SEAL felt it was time to take on a less dangerous assignment. Besides, he had seen enough action during his twenty-some years in the SEALs to last him many lifetimes. Most of the men that had gone through BUD/S training with him had retired or transferred out, some of them recently, which was the reason why SEAL Team Five had so many rookies today. Ray was one of the last ones hanging in there. The time had definitely come for the younger crowd to run this show.

"I don't know about you, Chief," Ray said, stretching, "but I'm going to have a chat with the skipper about the final details of the mission, and then I'm going to sleep until it's time."

Twenty minutes later, Ray walked into the aft torpedo room, feeling as though he could sleep for two straight days. He passed Bishop, already snoring in a lower bunk, and spotted Petty Officer Norma Mendez in the rear of the room, next to a pair of MK-42 torpedoes strapped to the left bulkhead. She was doing one-handed pull-ups using an overhead pipe.

"Better catch some Zs, Loca. You've got a little climb ahead of you."

Mendez, a Cuban who had escaped Castro's regime a-board a raft made of inner tubes, turned to Ray, the wiry muscles of her right arm throbbing under a glistening, honey-colored skin, tanned to near perfection from years of daily exposure at Coronado turning BUD/S candidates into SEALs. "I've slept long enough, Sting," she said, letting go of the pipe, landing silently on the floor. She faced her superior officer. "How big a climb?"

"About two hundred feet. Vertical."

She smiled. "No problem. Lock and load. When are we going in?"

Rivulets of sweat ran from the sides of her narrow face down her neck and into her white T-shirt, already soaked in perspiration.

"In twelve. Right after the recon's done. Just as we planned it on the way over."

She checked her black watch, which looked too large for her thin wrist. "That's plenty of time. I'll get the children up in another ten. Get them warmed up." She winked.

Ray grinned, his blue eyes focusing on a woman whose past was as intriguing as her accent, which sounded Hispanic at times and European at others. "Don't be too hard on them," he said, leaning down and getting into an empty bunk. "Don't want them too tired for their first mission."

"Don't worry. They'll be the toughest hombres you've ever seen by the time we get on the rubber duck."

Ray nodded while resting his head on a small pillow, setting the alarm of his watch to go off in seven hours, and closing his eyes. He fell asleep in seconds.

Norma Mendez worked out for another twenty minutes to the point of near exhaustion before collapsing on an empty bunk next to Bishop, the giant from Colorado whom Norma had been dating regularly for the past year. But unlike Bishop and Ray, who snored peacefully, Norma remained awake, her mind wondering as she stared at the wire mesh supporting the overhead bunk. She had difficulty falling asleep, but not because of her labored breathing, as she calmed down from the extreme exercise. Demons from her past crowded her mind. Norma Mendez remembered the warm surf as she helped push the crowded raft past the waves at Varadero Beach in Havana, always keeping a vigilant eye on Daniel, her two-year-old son. Norma had had no choice but to take the toddler with her on this dangerous journey. As family of a deserter from Castro's militia, Norma's son would have been executed by her former military colleagues when word of her escape reached the Palacio Nacional. The Cuban government was particularly ruthless when dealing with the children of traitors, especially if those traitors were from its own militia.

She placed both hands behind her head as she remembered the journey, the slapping waves, the blistering Caribbean sun, the pitch-black nights, the fifteen men and women with whom she shared the raft. She remembered their hostile stares because of her former affiliation with Castro's military. Those stares had turned to verbal threats when Norma had gotten her period on the third day. The blood dripping down her legs and into the sea would surely attract sharks. They voted unanimously to cut loose one inner tube and leave her adrift with a bottle of water and a broken oar for protection. Norma then had to decide if she would take her son with her on the inner tube or leave him aboard the raft with the hostile strangers and their dwindling supplies.

A tear escaped her eye. Every single decision in her life after that one had been easy.

26

DIFFICULT DECISIONS

Willie Matsubara sat in a fifth-storey office at the San Jose Police Department headquarters with his hands cuffed behind his back. Somehow the Americans had known about the Yamato Ichizotu's suicide pill because they had removed it from his pocket seconds after his seizure outside a restaurant in San Francisco.

Across from the small interview table in the center of the room sat one of the men who had shoved him into a blue van. His bodyguards, who normally waited outside the restaurant in the Lexus, had disappeared.

Perhaps they were also captured.

Matsubara tried to gather his thoughts. For the past hour he had been questioned by three men who had identified themselves as government officials but who had ignored his claim of diplomatic immunity and refused to let him use the phone to contact his lawyer, who could warn Hashimoto and his men, and also warn Tokyo. He also wanted to get his American allies in politics and the press to apply more pressure to stop the investigation against the Japanese corporations. Even though he had been caught, Matsubara was still hopeful that as long as he kept the list of sabotaged chips secret—while at the same time kindling the fire under the FBI for harassing Japanese nationals—that the JDA still had a chance of pulling this off. However, that might require him to perform the ultimate sacrifice for his country.

Matsubara glanced at the large mirror dominating the left wall of the room, feeling as certain that he was being observed through a one-way mirror as the probability of their using chemicals next to extract information. During his JDA training he had been warned of all methods of interrogation used by the world's intelligence services. The Americans and the British were among the most civilized. Israel's Mossad and Iraq's Mukhabarat ranked among the most brutal. Still, Matsubara knew he could not underestimate the skills of the Americans when it came to intelligence-gathering methods. If they got the list of sabotaged components out of him, all would be lost, and not just for Japan but for his family, who would become *burakumin*, outcasts among their people.

"Is there anything else you wish to tell us?" the large police detective asked, his prominent muscles wedged inside a brown sports coat. He unbuttoned the top button of his white shirt and loosened his tie.

Matsubara shook his head. "I just want to talk to my attorney, please."

"All in good time. First you need to help us so that we can in turn help you."

Matsubara exhaled and turned to face the windows opposite the large mirror. From this floor he could see the traffic on 101 flowing by the airport.

"You think about it," the detective said before getting up. "You think about it very carefully, because the people talking to you after me are not very nice." He left the room.

Matsubara now regretted not going for his suicide pill when spotting the large men approaching him. At the time he had hoped that his bodyguards would spring into action, but they had vanished. Now it was too late. He was at the mercy of the Americans, who were going down the right path to find the origin of the sabotages. And his confession would provide them with far more detail than they had ever expected to extract. Matsubara had memorized many aspects of the operation, including the names of engineers, their companies, the sabotaged computer chips, and their respective activation dates in the field. On top of that, he knew details of JDA and Aum Shinrikyo activities around the world, including the names of many agents, collaborators, and also people who owed Japan "favors." Many of those in debt were Americans, most of them politicians, lobbyists, businessmen, law enforcement officers, and members of the press. Finally, Matsubara knew the key members of the Yamato Ichizotu.

This is why you carry a suicide pill!

His eyes returned to the large windowpanes. He didn't have a choice. He had to protect the honor of his family, of his clan, of his agency, of his people, of his land. An honorable death was his only choice.

He looked at the large mirror one last time, smiled, and abruptly got up, hands cuffed behind his back. He raced across the small room, throwing himself against the glass panel, breaking it with his head and shoulders, shattering it, going through. His head felt on fire as shards of glass shredded his scalp, turning everything red. He heard shouts from above as he fell to the street. Matsubara closed his eyes, filling his lungs for the last time, the wind whipping his face. A woman screamed. A car blew its horn. His last thought before he struck the concrete sidewalk was the regret of not living long enough to see his sabotage scheme sink America's high-tech industry.

27

JET FUEL

American Airlines flight 1907 with service to Dallas-Fort Worth left the tarmac at Dulles International and began to climb to a cruising altitude of 31,000 feet over the West Virginia countryside. As it did, the Boeing 757's computerized fuel pumps feeding the starboard engine malfunctioned, spilling fuel into an array of electrical wires controlling the wing's de-icing system. The volatile fuel ignited on contact with the coils of the distributed heating system beneath the wing's aluminum skin. In an instant, clouds of flames covered the wing, reaching the engine. The turbine, spinning at thousands of revolutions per minute, disintegrated a second later, bursting into millions of metallic fragments. The shrapnel from the disintegrating jet stabbed wings and fuselage with metal-ripping force. Inside the Boeing, dozens of people perished in the first seconds following the explosion as the metallic fragments punched through the craft's aluminum skin, fusillading them.

Havoc broke out inside the main cabin. A flight attendant fell over screaming passengers, a metallic rod embedded in her chest. A mother shouted in agony while holding her bleeding son. A teenager screamed in fear as he fumbled with his seat-belt buckle after a large metal fragment decapitated the man sitting next to him, blood jetting from severed arteries. Screams, cries, and shouts filled the falling jetliner as the surviving flight attendants rushed down the aisles after the pilot, using the PA system, ordered them to prepare the main cabin for an emergency landing.

The engine broke off in a cloud of sparks, taking with it a section of the wing.

Crippled, only the port engine providing unbalanced thrust, the Boeing banked left and dropped its nose. Inside the cockpit, the pilot fought to regain control of his vessel as alarms blared and the copilot sent out a distress signal. The pilot cut back power to his surviving engines in an effort to level off the craft. The maneuver succeeded, but now the 757 lacked the power to remain airborne and began to lose altitude over the vast expanse of mountains, rivers, and valleys of West Virginia.

An ocean of green rushed up to meet them as flight 1907 continued to descend at a steep angle, dropping below five hundred feet. At that moment the pilot spotted a wide river snaking its way down the side of a mountain. He revved up the port engine. The plane responded by banking to the left, toward the river.

At just one hundred feet over the forest, the pilot, unable to pull out of the turn without cutting back power, partially made it to the river before the towering trees struck the underfuselage.

"Brace for impact!" the pilot announced as water burst through the cockpit's Plexiglas panels.

The tail section broke off from the main fuselage, which crash-landed over the river while maintaining a forward velocity of a hundred sixty miles per hour. The wings sliced through a hundred feet of forest on both banks of the river before also ripping off from the fuselage. The fuel stored in the wings detonated from the impact and the shockwave cracked the fuselage in three sections. The front of the 757 shot straight into the woods as the river turned, disappearing behind a sheet of flames. The rear section caught fire from the exploding wings and broke up into a cloud of debris. Only the center section remained in one piece, skimming the water for a few hundred feet before coming to a stop just as the river turned, close to where the front section had shaved a large area of forest by the river's left bank.

A handful of survivors slowly made their way out of the wreck and waded across the river to the south bank, where rescue crews would find them an hour later.

28

HIGH-TECH BREACH

Brent MacClaine moved through the deserted parking lot of Sakata Electronics swiftly, furtive eyes scanning the large building ahead, seeing no sign of trouble. His bulky figure, dressed in black to blend with the darkness, might have been picked up by one of the building's external surveillance cameras mounted along the roofline except that Erika had disabled them sixty seconds earlier.

MacClaine reached the south side of the building, adjacent to a large service entrance, probably reserved for equipment deliveries. A magnetic lock secured the large double doors, almost ten feet high and constructed of metal. He pressed his back against the brick wall next to the doors and spoke into his lapel microphone.

"I'm out of camera range."

From the rear of an unmarked FBI van parked two blocks from the complex, Erika said, "Got it," and quickly reactivated the rooftop cameras. Security guards who might have been alarmed by the momentary video shutdown on that side of the building would probably relax when the cameras came back on. The minor incident would get entered in their security log for a technician to check in the morning.

Fingering the laptop's touch pad, she placed the pointer on the locked delivery door in the diagram on her screen and clicked on it. The red line turned green.

"Door's unlocked. I'm going in," MacClaine said.

Erika took a deep breath, hoping that she had not underestimated the Japanese security system. But so far the stolen root passwords were doing their magical work.

"All right, Brent. Let's hope this works," she said moments before clicking the security-alert icon on the top-left section of the screen, automatically lowering all of the security gates in the building's hallways, isolating the building from the security guards on duty. The gates on her screen switched from green to red. At the same time, she shut down the control panels at the four security stations located at each corner of the building, preventing the guards from countering her commands. She also disabled the phone system, preventing any calls for help.

"Go straight ahead," Erika said, reading the blueprints on her screen. "There's a set of stairs coming up to your left, beyond the gate. Take them." She moved the pointer to a security gate and clicked on it, turning it green. She glanced at the other gates and made certain they remained red, particularly the ones blocking the security personnel. "They will lead you to the second floor. Take a right when you reach it and go through the set of glass doors to your left. That's the executive area."

Wearing skin-tight gloves and holding a stun gun, his Beretta shoved in his black jeans by his spine, Brent MacClaine rolled under the gate the moment it began to lift. "Got through," he said while rushing down the hallway, the light thudding of his sneakers blending with the humming of the motor lowering the door behind him. He reached the stairs and scrambled up, ignoring his bruised ribs, which throbbed as he inhaled deeply. Sweat had already formed above his lips. He had to get back in shape, perhaps pick up bike riding again. Or maybe—

Focus! Concentrate!

The stairs led to another carpeted hallway. A gate blocked the path. The metallic door began to lift. He went under and continued for another fifty feet, reaching the glass doors, which magically unlocked.

MacClaine walked over the hunter green carpet, stopping at the center of Sakata's executive area, inspecting the semicircular reception room surrounded by glass-walled offices, which allowed him to see through to the parking lot below and the downtown San Jose night skyline in the background. A secretary's glass desk on gray marble pedestals stood in front of each office. MacClaine walked past the gray leather sofas and chairs of the waiting area in the center of the half rotunda, reading the gray-and-gold nameplates by each office. "I'm inside. Lock the doors."

"They're already locked," she replied. "Did you find the office?"

"Looking, looking . . . There it is."

MacClaine stopped in front of a mahogany door. "Freddie was right. Looks like Matsubara does have an office in this building." Kojata's information seemed to be accurate so far. According to Kojata, Matsubara kept an office at Sakata Electronics, where Kojata saw him working two to three days every week, especially late at night, when the executive would use his private video conferencing equipment, custom installed in his PC, to contact Tokyo. On specific days of the week Kojata had spotted Matsubara in his glass office talking to an old man, who appeared on the top-left corner of the screen. After showing Kojata photos of key JDA officials, courtesy of the CIA, he had identified the old man as Konichi Tanaka.

The system, a Japanese PC monopolizing the left side of the large glass-and-marble desk, was off, just as Erika had predicted. It was the safest way to protect the contents of a networked system when the owner was away.

"You were right. It's off?"

"Turn it on."

MacClaine switched it on but the system didn't respond. "It's not turning on."

"Check the power cord. Make sure's it's plugged in to an AC outlet."

MacClaine leaned over to see the back of the PC and followed a black cable from the rear of the system to an outlet on the side of the wall next to the desk.

"It's plugged in."

"All right, then. Is there a keyhole somewhere along the front of the system?"

He looked and found one next to the CD-ROM drive.

"Got it. Now what?"

"Now open the small case I gave you."

He reached behind his back and removed his small backpack, extracting a soft-sided case, Erika's computer tool kit.

"All right."

"Okay. There's a silver tool shaped like a screw driver but its end looks more like a corrugated cylinder. That's a master key for personal computer locks. Try it on the lock."

He located the tool and inserted the end into the hole, turning it clockwise. "It turned. . . . Wait, the system's coming on now."

"Good. Now put the tool back in the case and relax," Erika said while opening a new window on her screen and using it to navigate her way through Sakata's directories until she found Matsubara's networked system, which continued to show as unavailable, just as it had earlier in the day, when she had first attempted to penetrate it.

"Relax? Talk to me. What are you going to do?"

"I'm going to browse through his personal files. See what I can find."

"I don't like being here. I'm too exposed. This place is like a fishbowl."

While waiting for Matsubara's system to boot, Erika

pulled up the window containing the building's status. All gates showed red. Phones and video cameras were disabled.

"No one can get anywhere near you. Just stay away from the windows."

"That's the problem. This place is *all* windows."

Erika smiled when hearing a heavy sigh through the speakers in the back of the van. An FBI agent sat in the driver's seat while two more sat in the rear with Erika. MacClaine had ordered these three to shadow her around the clock.

A minute later Matsubara's system became visible to the network. She minimized the building's status window to make room on her screen to view Matsubara's system. Using her root privilege to access Matsubara's local disk— the hard drive in his PC—Erika began to browse through his Windows directories, finding his E-mail directory, which contained only a dozen messages, none of them over a day old. The rest had been either deleted or possibly archived by the automatic daily backups that most companies have to protect their data in case of a system crash. She checked the networked directory and found that Matsubara's was one of thousands of hard drives that got automatically downloaded every day into one of a dozen disk servers, each of which was backed up once a week into Zip drives in the server room.

Pretty typical procedure, Erika thought. The small local hard drives all got copied to larger disk servers, providing immediate access to data not older than twenty-four hours in case a local hard drive crashed. As an added safety feature, the data in the servers was archived once a week, ensuring that in a worst-case situation, if a local hard drive and a server both crashed on the same day, the unfortunate user would not lose more than a week's worth of work. She traced his backups to ABSS67-24, automatic backup system server number sixty-seven, Zip disk number twenty-four.

Erika shook her head. Japanese companies in America

just didn't know how to have fun. American high-tech companies liked to personalize servers, as well as other types of large manufacturing or supporting equipment, using names from *Star Trek*, famous outlaws, dinosaurs, and predators to characters from *M*A*S*H*, *Cheers*, and *Seinfeld*.

She checked Matsubara's E-mails, mostly courtesy copies of benign communication E-mails sent to most employees of the firm. One described the day's menu at the building's cafeteria. Another reminded everyone to turn in their RSVPs for the upcoming company picnic at Great America Theme Park in Sunnyvale the following month. Another outlined a new travel policy.

Pretty useless stuff.

She clicked back up to the top level and scanned the names of the directories, finding the one housing the video conferencing software. She launched the software and opened the address book, finding two sections, one for company numbers and another for private numbers.

"Let's see what we find," she muttered.

"What was that?" asked MacClaine.

"Just talking to myself."

"Is the building still secured?"

"Oh, let me check." She clicked on the building status icon to pull up the blueprint and do a quick check before diving into Matsubara's private address book. "I found a video-conference phone book for—oh, rats!"

"What? What?"

"The gates! Several are green again!"

"Green? How in the *hell* did that happen? I thought you had the building under control!"

"I—I'm . . . I'm not sure how it happened! Maybe they have a manual override, or perhaps someone—"

"Never mind that! Close them again!"

"I am! I am!"

"And get me out of here! Find me a route that's still secured."

"But I need you to go to the archive room."

"What?"

"The archive room. It's on your way out."

Still clutching the stun gun, Brent MacClaine let go a string of profanities as he rushed out of the executive area. Security teams were rapidly converging on him and this woman wanted him to make a pit stop on the way out to pick up a damned archive disk!

"Which way?" he finally asked.

"To your right. Head straight for the stairs. I'll close the gates behind you."

"What about the gates in front of me? Aren't guards coming from different directions?"

"Just go! I'll navigate!"

He cursed again and raced toward the stairs, his black sneakers thumping loudly, his ribs once more protesting the strain. A steel gate at the end of the hallway began to rise. MacClaine rolled under it.

"Okay, I got through the first gate."

"Go up the stairs and take a right when you get to the third floor."

The gate behind him made a light rumble as it began to lower again. "The third floor? But I thought I was heading—"

"Minor detour. I'm trying to avoid the sections that are unsecured."

He scrambled up the stairs, breathing heavily again, one hand holding the stun gun, the other pressed against the left side of his torso. Reaching the landing in between floors, MacClaine froze, detecting movement from above. People were coming down the stairs!

He raced back down again, nostrils flaring as he took in lungfuls of air, his heart hammering his chest, rivulets of sweat running down the sides of his face.

Back in the same hallway, he faced one of many steel-and-glass doors. He turned the knob. Locked.

He spotted a number above it, 257.

"Open door two five seven."

"What?"

"Dammit! Open door number two five seven! Hurry!"

"Okay. Okay."

He glanced anxiously toward the stairs, waiting for security men to appear. He heard the door's magnetic lock clicking and shoved his left shoulder against it while turning the knob, going inside and quickly closing it behind him, dropping to a crouch while pressing his back against the wall next to the door.

He exhaled, relieved to hear multiple footsteps reaching the hallway, momentarily stopping, before continuing down the corridor.

He looked around him. He was in a conference room. A long table flanked by a dozen chairs. He turned around, peering through the rectangle of glass in the door at chest level, spotting three men bearing sidearms and walkie-talkies.

"Shit." Security guards at high-tech firms didn't carry weapons. Those guys did. MacClaine looked at the little stun gun in his hand and frowned. He reached for his Beretta while shoving the electric toy in a pocket of his jeans after carefully turning it off, not relishing the thought of zapping himself.

"What happened?"

"Three armed men. Almost ran into them in the stairs. I thought you were taking me through secured hallways."

"I did—I mean, I thought I did. The hallways on the third floor are still showing red for all of the gates."

"Then how in the hell could guards that were locked away on the first floor get to the third floor so quickly?"

Erika checked the blueprints for the second and third floors, quickly realizing her mistake. The gates were closed, but she had not disabled the elevators. A security team had taken an elevator from a hallway on the first floor to the third. She had been operating in two dimensions,

forgetting about elevators, which created a third set of hallways between floors.

"The elevators, Brent. That's how they got up there."

"Is that first-floor hallway clear after the guards took the
elevator to the third floor?"

As Erika checked her blueprints again, gates turned
green. She tried to click them back to red but they remained green. Someone was indeed overriding the automatic security system, slowly opening the building back
up. MacClaine was running out of time.

She looked for the route that MacClaine had recom-
mended. It seemed clean.

"Go for it," she said, praying that she had not overlooked anything. "And be careful. I'm rapidly losing control of the building." As she said this Matsubara's PC shut
down. Either Matsubara's system had malfunctioned or
someone had locked her out.

Brent MacClaine, Beretta clutched in his left hand, slowly
inched the conference room door open and inspected both
ends of the hallway.

Empty.

He doubled back to the stairs, this time pausing at the
bottom before rushing upstairs. Hearing nothing, he scrambled up to the third floor, sweat forming on his upper lip.
The elevator was just a quarter of the way down the hallway. He reached it, finding it curious that the doors were
open. An elevator, even if parked on a floor, always has
its doors closed.

Cautiously, the 92F leading the way, he stepped in,
quickly realizing the reason. The security team had pulled
out the emergency stop button, locking the elevator and
doors to prevent the intruder on the second floor from using it.

Understanding their tactic, MacClaine unlocked the elevator and selected the first floor. The door closed and he
felt the downward acceleration while the number above

the door changed from three to two to one. A woman's voice announced the first floor, first in English and then in Japanese as the doors began to slide into the wall.

MacClaine stood to one side, the 9-mm pistol pointed at the widening crack. He took a deep breath and tiptoed out when the gap was wide enough.

"Brent? Where are you?"

"First floor. There's an exit sign at the far side of the hallway."

"That's the south entrance. It leads to the opposite side of the parking lot that you used to go in."

"Looks clear. I'm heading that way."

"Wait."

MacClaine stopped in midstride. "What?"

"The archive room."

"What about it?" He resumed his motion, walking sideways, constantly shifting the weapon to cover both flanks.

"It's just off to the left halfway down the hallway."

"Forget it. You're losing control of the building. I better get out while I can."

"I got kicked out of Matsubara's system. I really need the backup to his hard drive, otherwise this whole deal would be useless. I think I can get you inside. Let me see. . . ."

Frowning, MacClaine picked up his pace, getting anxious, uncomfortable about his level of exposure while in the middle of this long corridor. If a team showed up at either end he would have no place to seek cover.

He reached the door to the archive room but it was locked.

"I can't get in."

"Hold on," she replied.

He swung the weapon toward the elevator, pausing long enough to verify no one was in sight before turning back toward the exit, finding—

Two guards, their white uniforms contrasting sharply with their shiny black belts, boots, and caps, blocked the exit. One spoke on a small radio, the other held a pistol, which he leveled at MacClaine.

"Stay where you are!" he shouted in a heavy Asian accent.

MacClaine turned back to the elevator, only to find three more guards, two clutching weapons, the third holding a radio close to his face while pointing at him.

"Got it!" Erika said just as the heavy door in front of him unlocked. He leaped toward it, shoving a shoulder against its metallic surface, pushing it open, rushing inside a very cold room, tripping on a chair, falling on the raised floor, slamming his forehead against the side of a machine.

He sat up, cursing, stunned, a hand pressed against his throbbing head. "Lock—lock it! Lock it now . . . quick!" He shouted while pushing it closed.

The magnetic lock engaged.

The guards started banging on the door a moment later.

"They're outside. I'm screwed," he said, breathing slowly, positioning his head in the path of the stream of cold air rising through the small holes in the white tiles layering the cavernous room. He momentarily enjoyed it.

"Do you see the archives?"

Staggering up with the help of the chair that had tripped him, MacClaine gazed around him. Dozens of floor-to-ceiling racks of Zip disks, thicker than regular diskettes, stood next to freezer-size equipment. MacClaine walked in between these large computer servers, shifting his gaze between the hammering outside and the robot arms protruding from the servers to grab disks from adjacent racks and shove them into the multiple slots in the units with incredible precision and speed while LEDs blinked all over without an apparent pattern.

"What is this place?" he asked, already feeling a lump on his forehead. Silvery arms jerked around him to the rhythm of their high-speed servomotors.

"The archive room. There should be large disk servers and lots of tapes or Zip disks for backups. Very expensive and critical area."

"No tapes. Only those Zip disks and lots of servers. The place looks more like a techno-grave to me. And those guys out there, their guns are bigger than mine. They'll break through any moment. I'm trapped." The commotion outside intensified.

"Archive rooms are usually built like fireproof vaults. That should buy you a little time."

"A little time for what? To bend over and kiss my ass good-bye?" MacClaine continued to stare at the computerized activity that reminded him of the movie *Terminator*. A robot arm replaced a Zip disk in a top rack and grabbed another disk from a middle rack at lightning speed. "There's no way out but through the front door."

"There might be a way out," she said, taking a minute to explain. "But first you need to find a couple of Zip disks for me."

Following Erika's instructions, his heart pounding, MacClaine inhaled a lungful of chilled air and searched for a server named ABSS67, spotting it at the far end of the sea of humming equipment. The banging and shouting outside became louder by the second.

"All right. I've found it."

"Great. Now get disk number twenty-four. That's the one that has the backup of the info in Matsubara's hard drive."

Cool sweat filming his cheeks, MacClaine regarded the rapidly moving robot arm servicing the Zip disk rack with respect. The collection of alloy rods, cables, and motors moved at a deathly speed. He couldn't possibly reach over the server and grab an archive disk without risking getting impaled by the arm's grappling hook.

"Is there a way to turn this thing off?"

"There should be a power switch somewhere around it."

He found it. A large red button that reminded him of the one in the elevators. He pushed it and the robot arm abruptly stopped while reaching for a disk in the lower rack. Inside the server the level of noise decreased as the spinning disks slowed down to a halt with the sound of a decelerating turbine as heard from inside a commercial jet.

Leaping over the server, grabbing on to the frozen arm to balance himself, he snatched the Zip disk, clutching it against his chest.

"I've got it."

"Good. Now, look around. Do you see any cabinets or racks of Zip disks away from the servers?"

He turned briskly to the door when he heard an object rammed against it, the muffled smash echoing above the whirling equipment. "Yes," he replied spotting what looked like a couple dozen racks of disks.

"Look at the labels on the racks. Find the ones for the purchasing department."

MacClaine spent thirty seconds fast-walking down the narrow aisle flanked by Zip disk racks on one side and servers on the other. He walked past racks of engineering databases, reaching the archives for the marketing division, followed by sales and purchasing. He remembered the way the purchasing division had been divided into foreign and domestic when looking over Erika's shoulder at the computer screen. That helped him narrow his search to one rack, containing the foreign purchasing records for the years 1985 through 2004. The years were further subdivided by the type of purchases. There were four categories, matching the choices in the menu he had seen with Erika the day before: equipment, services, components, and administrative.

"I've got the archive disks for the foreign component purchases for the years 2003 and 2004," he said, shoving them into his small nylon backpack.

"You're awesome, Brent."

"Tell me that after I get out of here with the loot."

"Just get that mask on—like I told you."

He glanced at the door, momentarily listening to the commotion outside before he moved quickly to the opposite side of the room, reaching the glass cover of the emergency equipment. "If this works I'll be your slave for life."

"I'm recording this."

Leaning back, he put the safety on the Beretta, grabbed the weapon by the muzzle, and used the handle to break the glass, which shattered on impact and landed by his feet.

"All right," he said. "I've got the mask."

"Put it on."

MacClaine did, strapping the black mask over his face, covering his eyes, mouth, and nose. Lifting it just a dash to speak, he said, "It's on."

"Now hide and wait."

He did, tensely, flipping the weapon's safety, ducking beneath the emergency station, out of sight from the door, which he heard opening, followed by footsteps.

"You are trapped!" someone screamed.

"Come out and you will not be shot!" another voice warned.

MacClaine remained in a deep crouch, standing over the broken glass, scanning his visual range with the Beretta. Multiple footsteps hastily walked around the servers.

Japanese phrases, briskly spoken, mixed with the clicking footsteps and whirling equipment.

He waited a few more seconds, eyes narrowed like a predator luring its prey deeper into the trap. More men entered the cavernous room, their shadows projecting on the ceiling, crisscrossing as they searched for him.

MacClaine depressed a button on the side of the mask, enabling the flow of oxygen from a pen-size canister attached to the side of the breathing apparatus.

He filled his lungs before reaching for a handle inside the emergency station and pulling it down hard.

A blaring siren went off inside the archive room with deafening strength, accompanied by flashing red and yellow lights. The Japanese phrases became agitated, shouted instead of spoken.

A bluish gas suddenly burst out of dozens of nozzles on the room's tiled ceiling, descending over men and machines.

MacClaine ran in a crouch toward the exit, past two

guards already on their hands and knees coughing loudly while crawling to the hallway, gasping for the oxygen rapidly displaced by the halox gas.

The fire extinguishing system, meant to save equipment in case of a fire without using water—which could damage the high-tech gear as much as fire—performed just as Erika had predicted, disabling the guards long enough for MacClaine to rush out of the room.

Yanking off the small mask and throwing it aside as he reached the hallway, the experienced Fed, his Beretta leading the way, dashed toward the exit, reaching it seconds later. Kicking the waist-high handle running across the metallic door, feeling the cool night air caressing his cheeks, Brent MacClaine disappeared in the darkness, the nylon backpack safely slung over his shoulders.

29

THE RISING SUN

TOKYO

The night sky gave way to wan streaks of magenta, slowly turning sapphire as another day loomed in the largest metropolis in the world. Beams of light brought to life the manicured gardens and centuries-old moats surrounding the Imperial Palace, occupying the grounds of the legendary Edo Castle, home to many generations of the Tokugawa shogunate, which came to power in 1590 and remained in control until its abolishment in 1868, when Emperor Meiji was restored to power. Very little remained of that glorious era, most of its castles and temples destroyed in the turmoil of the Meiji restoration.

Joggers stretched and warmed up in the little courtyard between portals at Sakuradamon, one of the many gates that accessed the Imperial Palace grounds from the traffic-congested streets surrounding it. The early-morning light revealed many joggers already running the three-mile course around the palace, a rituated that started every day at dawn and continued until dusk regardless of the weather.

East of the palace grounds stood the heart of Japan's economic center. Major banks, investment houses, insurance corporations, and trading companies flanked the wide avenue connecting the palace to the old Tokyo Station, designed after the railway station in Amsterdam. At this early hour the economic district already bustled with activity as a river of humanity flowed out of the many exits of Tokyo Station. Horns blared; drivers shouted; buses, cabs, and private vehicles fought against the relentless wave of pedestrians for the right of way.

The cacophony could be heard across the economic district, bordered to the southwest by less glamorous government buildings crowding Sakura-dori, the avenue running south from the Sakuradamon Gate through the center of official Japan, home to the ministries that comprised the central government, including defense, education, foreign affairs, communications, international trade, labor, energy, and industry.

Down Sakura-dori an elderly man dressed in a business suit stood by the windows of his top-floor corner suit, which provided him with a panoramic view of the entire economic district and the Imperial Palace. He sipped hot tea from a small porcelain cup while inspecting the morning crowd. In the distance, the Shinkansen decelerated as it approached Tokyo Station. The world-famous bullet train constituted one of several major forms of transportation to access the large metropolis, which housed 28 million people.

Fuji Yokonawa, minister of industry and commerce, savored his morning tea while waiting for the arrival of Konichi Tanaka, chief of the Japan Defense Agency, for their weekly one-on-one meeting to discuss the progress of their secret operation in America. Spread on the black-lacquer desk next to him was yesterday's international edition of *The New York Times*. The airline disaster had not yet been pinned to a computer chip, but it was just a matter of time before another American corporation suffered a severe setback, yielding a portion of its market to a Japanese competitor. This most recent disaster, however, had prompted the FAA to halt all commercial air travel in the United States, a move that was very reminiscent of the aftermath of September 11, 2001. The economic report released last week indicated that America was very quickly losing its status as world leader of high-tech goods. Massive layoffs continued across the United States as a result of the disasters. Both the Dow and the NASDAQ continued to drop threatening to send that country into a depression. Thousands of engineers from IBM, Intel, AMD, Cypress, and other major semiconductor manufacturers had attended a large job fair at San Francisco's Moscone Center, hosted by the Bay Area Job Finder Corporation, a wholly owned subsidiary of Sony America, Ltd.

His intercom line rang. Yokonawa snapped his fingers, activating the phone line. *"Hai?"*

"Yokonawa-san, Tanaka-san is here to see you."

"Very well," he replied, setting the cup of tea on his desk and facing the skies over Tokyo once more. "Tell him to come in."

The automatic door opposite his desk slid into the wall. Tanaka, also dressed in a dark business suit, stood in the doorway holding a briefcase.

"Ohayo gozaimasu, Yokonawa-san," said Tanaka with a slight bow, walking in the office.

"Good morning," replied the minister, returning the bow. "Would you like some tea?"

Tanaka shook his head. *"Kekko desu.* I've already had breakfast."

Yokonawa pointed to a chair across from his desk. Tanaka took it, setting the briefcase next to him and adjusting the knot of his tie before crossing his legs.

"What news do you bring, my friend?"

The elder intelligence officer said, "I received a brief report from Matsubara-san yesterday regarding the kidnapping of FBI analyst Erika Conklin. We had a successful interrogation and have obtained the names of three FBI agents involved in the investigation. One of them is MacClaine-san."

"Where is the woman now?"

Tanaka told him.

"What do you plan to do next?"

"Hashimoto-san has deployed his men to go after the three agents. I have also sent an additional ten men to assist him. They should arrive in the morning."

Yokonawa stood and faced the windows, watching a group of joggers disappear in the woods of the Imperial Palace's East Garden. He had been disappointed at Tanaka's judgment call a few days ago, when he had sanctioned the abduction of FBI agent Brent MacClaine, especially when all the *gaijin* had wanted to do was ask Nakamura a few questions. That initial attack had only kindled the FBI's suspicion that Japan was behind the multitude of computer-triggered accidents. Now they had been forced into a game of damage control, one which could also backfire if not handled properly.

"How many target chips have been expended?"

Tanaka reached for his briefcase and pulled out a manila folder, extracting a sheet of paper with a list of sabotaged components. Yokonawa had a similar list locked in the safe behind his desk, beneath a colorful landscape painting. It contained the list of all forty-seven sabotaged computer chips, done by twenty-three engineers at seventeen American semiconductor corporations.

"Seven, including the airliner in West Virginia. The others should reach the end of life in the next two to eight weeks, give or take a week."

"When are you getting your next update from Matsubara-san?"

"Tomorrow morning. We have a video conference in the morning."

Yokonawa nodded, his eyes surveying the vast grounds of the Imperial Palace, where Ieyasu Tokugawa, lord of Kanto, the richest fief in Japan, had built his castle in 1590. Tokugawa, well aware of the feudal wars of the time, opted to fortify his kingdom by devising a triple system of moats and canals, incorporating the Sumida River into a vast maze of waterways that protected the castles, palaces, and villas of his court, which extended to over 450 acres of land and encircling water. In addition, Tokugawa gave the land surrounding his inner city to his allies and most trusted subordinates, who turned them into outposts that formed a perimeter defense of the lowlands surrounding the inner city and its nearly impenetrable defenses. Beyond these outposts, Tokugawa kept the barons he trusted the least, providing them with estates and men to form an even wider defense perimeter. To maintain the barons' loyalty, Tokugawa insisted that their wives and children live in palaces within the inner city, in effect keeping them hostage to force the barons to fight for the shogun. Ieyasu Tokugawa's precautions worked well, his shogunate enjoying over 250 years of peace.

Minister Yokonawa continued to inspect the lush gardens of the Imperial Palace while considering the multiple precautions Japan's most famous shogun had taken to ensure the success of his dynasty. Tokugawa had surrounded himself with buffers, safety zones that would delay enemy forces long enough to give him the opportunity to counterattack. If the barons' garrisons came under attack, they would fight back and either repel the enemy or at least reduce their numbers. Then the thousands of men in the lowlands surrounding the castle and its huge network of waterways would come into action, further decimating the advancing force. In the event that the enemy managed to make it through this second layer of defenses, the multiple layers of moats and walls beyond the lowlands would certainly discourage all but the most determined—or foolish— of armies. Behind those walls waited the shogun's finest forces, fresh and armed with the latest weaponry, many of them warriors of the Yamato Ichizotu, prepared to die while protecting their shogun.

Yokonawa had set up this operation in similar fashion, using the American engineers as the first line of defense, eliminating them after they completed their assignments, thus preventing the enemy from finding who had originated the attack. Matsubara and Hashimoto constituted a second line of defense, ordered to protect the mission's secrecy at all cost, even with their lives. Tanaka and the entire JDA formed a third line of defense, along with the Aum Shinrikyo. Should the enemy manage to get this far,

Tanaka would take the fall, thus protecting the ministry, which formed a fourth line of defense to protect the prime minister himself, the man who had indirectly sanctioned this mission by ordering Minister Yokonawa to find a way—*any way*—to get Japan back at the head of the race for high technology, which would in turn bootstrap the economy. Just two months ago, unemployment had reached a postwar record high of 5.3 percent. Inventories also rose to a new record high even as manufacturing showed an overall decline of 1.1 percent for the closing fiscal year. Even the planned devaluation of the yen against the dollar, a move that lowered prices of Japanese goods overseas, had failed to eat into the huge inventory stockpiled in warehouses across Japan and around the world. Retail sales had fallen by a half percentage point compared with the year before, which indicated an even steeper decline in industrial output as manufacturers struggled to manage their growing inventories. The result would be more layoffs, which would result in larger unemployment figures as the country spiraled down into a deep recession.

While Tanaka remained seated, Minister Yokonawa picked up his teacup and once more faced the window-panes, glaring at the tall buildings housing Japan's largest banks. Despite a government low-interest-rate policy, most banks had increased interest rates to protect themselves against a flurry of credit risks, adding momentum to the downward spiral.

How did things get so out of hand? Yokonawa wondered, sipping tea to calm his churning stomach, knowing the answer all too well. He remembered the old days, when Japan had wrested the technological lead from a dormant United States. Labor had been cheap in Japan back then. The general population, still recovering from World War II, was willing to work and produce for minimum wages while the United States exported its manufacturing overseas. By the late seventies Japan had seized the world's technological reins, steering global markets in its own direction, taking the best ideas from America and turning them into manufacturing successes, slowly improving a product over time until it became nearly perfect. But then Japan's success became its own demise. Soon the standard of living grew to a level much higher than its neighbors. Soon the average Japanese worker had a college degree and demanded higher wages, bonus plans, medical benefits, and stock options. Soon Japan found that manufacturing products inside Japan made them too costly to be competitive, and it too began to export its manufacturing to other countries, like China, South Korea, Taiwan, and even the United States. Soon after that America had finally awakened from its long sleep and companies like Intel, Compaq, Lucent Technologies, AMD, and Microsoft became world leaders in high technology, leaving Japan eating their silicon dust.

As his eyes landed on the present-day Imperial Palace building, completed in 1968, Minister Fuji Yokonawa silently swore to succeed in restoring Japan to its rightful place as leader of the world's high-tech industry. To accomplish such an ambitious goal he had to make certain that the FBI investigation never got past him, regardless of the consequences. As leader of the Yamato Ichizotu, he too was prepared to die to protect the honor of Japan, the honor of his ancestors.

30

VIDEO CONFERENCING

Erika Conklin sat behind MacClaine's desk fingering the soft pad of her laptop, browsing through the directory labels of the archive disk in the external Zip drive connected to a PCMCIA port in her laptop. Using one of her system's utilities, Erika copied one directory at a time into a secured partition of her disk drive, protected by her virus shield to make certain that any viruses in Matsubara's files would remain contained. She had already gone through the purchasing records of the second Zip disk and done the comparisons between the components purchased by Sakata Electronics in 2003, 2004, and 2005. The results had been four integrated circuits, two manufactured by Dallas Semiconductor, one by AMD, and the last one by IBM. She had E-mailed the information to Charlie Chang, who would alert those corporations immediately so that they could, in turn, verify the integrity of the designs. With some luck, maybe some of those ICs would show signs of sabotage and get pulled out of the market before they shut down in the field, like the recent airline disaster in West Virginia, which already smelled like another sabotaged computer chip.

"This had better be worth it," protested Brent MacClaine, sitting across the desk while holding an ice pack to his forehead. "Haven't felt this bad in a while."

Erika glanced up, regarding him over the rim of the screen. The purplish lump had, as serious as it looked, still could not compare to the beating she had endured the day before. Although the blood in her urine had decreased, her torso still hurt, especially when sitting down or getting up. But she accepted the pain in the same resigned manner that she had learned to accept her forced tour of duty with the FBI, an experience she couldn't wait to put behind her.

Erika shrugged, her eyes still on MacClaine's new beauty mark. "And I thought FBI agents were tough hombres."

MacClaine sighed. "Please, don't get me started."

She smiled, returning her attention to the screen, once again inspecting Matsubara's E-mail directory, going through yesterday's messages, which looked just as benign as the ones she had read earlier, shortly after MacClaine had powered up Matsubara's system at Sakata Electronics.

Nothing interesting here.

She erased the E-mail directory from her drive and downloaded the video-conferencing software. She tapped her fingers on the desk while the external Zip drive hummed away, transferring the requested directory into her hard drive. A window popped up in the middle of her screen. The system informed her that the transfer would take forty-five seconds, and a digital timer appeared on the corner of the window counting down from forty-five.

"You're doing great, Erika," MacClaine said, eyes sill closed.

Erika regarded him warmly. Brent MacClaine could be a bit charming on occasion, if one was willing to overlook his crudeness. He had certainly moved up a few notches on her scale by flying her father up here.

"Especially for a skirt," he added.

She frowned. "That's part of your problem, Brent."

"Huh?"

"You can be such a chauvinist."

"What did *I* say?"

"Never mind." She shook her head and looked at the

screen. A new window appeared, informing her that the data transfer had been successful.

Erika launched the video-conferencing software. It had a menu along its top, which showed options like Dial, Options, Address Book, Settings, and Help. Within the window, a smaller window warned her that the video-conferencing software had detected no camera installation on her system. It gave her two options: Ignore or Cancel.

Erika chose to ignore the warning.

The small window vanished and another warning window replaced it, informing her that the lack of a camera on her side meant that the party at the other end would not be able to see her. At the Continue Y/N? prompt, she selected Y.

She pulled down Address Book, and a new window gave her nine different options:

LOCATION	SPEED DIAL#
MATSUBARA SENDAI	*01
JDA 050 TOKYO	*02
SAKATA TOKYO CONF A	*03
SAKATA TOKYO CONF B	*04
SAKATA OSAKA CONF A	*05
AKITA AMERICA CONF A	*06
AKITA AMERICA CONF B	*07
MITSUBISHI OSAKA A	*08
MITSUBISHI OSAKA B	*09

She leaned back, pouting.

"What are you looking for anyway?" he asked.

"I'm not sure, but I think I'm getting closer to something."

"Whatever you find will be better than what we got from Matsubara. Can't believe he jumped."

Erika shook her head. "Strange people."

"Quite screwy, actually. Never know what to expect from them."

Erika clicked the mouse a few times, and said, "I've just found a video number for the JDA."

"Video number?"

She nodded. "My PC can call this number using the video-conferencing software and a window should appear on my screen showing the view from the camera at the other end of the call."

MacClaine stood and walked around the desk, leaning down to take a look at the screen. Erika tapped a short fingernail against the plasma screen, pointing to the JDA address.

"What good is it?" he asked.

"Well, it all depends on how it's used."

MacClaine put the ice pack down. "I'm afraid I don't understand."

"How long has it been since Matsubara was abducted?"

MacClaine checked his watch. "Three hours."

"And you're certain that no one knows that he's dead?"

He nodded. "My people reacted quickly, taking his body away before a crowd could even gather around him. The local police are helping us stall a few reporters who have called in."

"All right. And where did he go from the episode in the warehouse to the moment your people brought him in?"

He reached for a blue folder on his desk and opened it in between them, running a finger down the surveillance log. "From the warehouse to his home in Mountain View, where he spent the night. Thanks to Freddie Kojata we knew exactly what kind of message to leave Matsubara at his home to make him believe that nothing had gone wrong at the warehouse. The following morning—this morning— he drove to Carmel and played eighteen holes at Pebble Beach, then he went to San Francisco, where he had an early dinner at the Cypress Club in Jackson Square. We grabbed him shortly after that, right before I broke into Sakata Electronics."

"And then he killed himself."

"Are you going somewhere with this?"

"So the JDA probably doesn't know that something has gone wrong, right?"

He checked his watch. "Probably. Although I'm certain they'll get quite suspicious when so many agents fail to report. Matsubara has been out of contact for . . . What's your point?"

She pointed at the screen. "I have a number for the JDA in Tokyo. Now, remember what Freddie told us about Matsubara holding late-evening video conferences a few times a week with Konichi Tanaka at the other end?"

"Yes?"

"Do you know the exact days and times of the video conferences?"

He shrugged. "I'm sure we can get that information from Freddie, but why is it important?"

"Don't you get it? If it's true that the JDA doesn't know that something has gone wrong, then perhaps we can reinforce that belief by making them think that Matsubara is still holding video conferences. We can feed them misinformation, perhaps even make certain that Tanaka will be at his beach house at the specific time of the SEAL strike. Who knows, maybe we'll get lucky and get information on the sabotaged ICs themselves." Erika and MacClaine had gotten word of the imminent SEAL strike just an hour ago, after it became evident that no additional intelligence would come from the recent abductions.

MacClaine looked confused. "How are you going to make the JDA believe that Matsubara is holding a conference call with them if he's dead?"

"Have you been to the movies lately, Brent?"

"Can't say that I have."

"Well, go rent an action flick. They're packed with special effects."

"I'm not following—"

"And most special effects are done with these." She patted the side of her system. "If computers can make us believe that movie scenes are real, then I can certainly make the JDA believe that Oruku Matsubara is at the other end of a video-conference call. All I need is some digitized footage of him, a few clips of his voice, preferably in Japanese, since I presume that's the language he would be speaking in, and of course, a translator. I don't speak Japanese. With that I can create a virtual Oruku Matsubara."

"And what are you going to tell Tanaka?"

Erika raised her palms at the federal agent. "I'm not the spook, Brent. I'm just the engineer providing the communications channel. I'll expect the American intelligence community will figure out what the message should be."

31

FIGHTING FIRE WITH FIRE

"So, Roman. What's your recommendation?" President Lester Williams asked, clutching the football while standing in the colonnade near the French doors leading to the Oval Office. It was a beautiful night and the president wanted some fresh air while getting an update from Palenski, who stood next to Donald Bane.

The director of the FBI ran both thumbs beneath his gray suspenders while glancing at the Rose Garden. "My people were able to penetrate Sakata Electronics, Mr. President. We are preparing to make contact with Tanaka."

The president turned to him. "Contact? How?"

Palenski told him.

"Sounds risky. Have you bought into this, Don?"

Bane nodded. "Yesterday my confidence level that Tanaka would be at his beach house in Cape Muroto this weekend was sixty percent. Palenski's plan would raise that to the ninety percent level."

The president gazed at the stars. "Vuono tells me that his SEAL team is in position awaiting the order to go in. I would like to maximize their chances of success. You yourself have told me that Tanaka presents our best chance of getting our hands on the list of sabotaged chips. I would hate for those SEALs to go in just to find an empty house."

"Then we need to proceed with the FBI's plan, sir," Bane replied.

Keeping his gaze fixed on the night sky over Washington, the president said, "Good luck, gentlemen."

Palenski and Bane left the president staring at the stars. Williams wondered how many other American presidents had admired the constellation from this very spot. Williams thought of Lincoln, Wilson, Roosevelt, Truman, Johnson, Reagan, and both George Bush and George W. Bush, presidents given the difficult task of leading the nation in time of war. He pondered on the many instances they must have struggled with decisions that would shape the future of the nation, even the future of the world itself. He tried putting himself in Lincoln's shoes, facing a divided nation, making the decision to preserve the union, sending brother against brother in the bloodiest war this nation has ever experienced. Then he thought of Roosevelt, the master strategist who coordinated the forces of the world to defeat Hitler. And Truman, the president who had made the difficult decision to drop bombs of mass destruction on a Japan that refused to surrender.

Williams stepped back in the Oval office, stopping in the center, staring at the presidential seal woven into the light blue carpet. A rogue group within the Japanese government was attacking America, triggering some of the worst accidents in its history. Only he knew they were no accidents. They were deliberate acts of cyberterrorism, targeted at crippling his country's high-tech industry, jeopardizing America's future, rapidly pushing the nation into an economic recession as the stock market dropped every day, as corporations struggled to survive in the wake of a disaster.

President Williams grabbed his lucky football, clutching it with both hands, digging his fingers in the pigskin, remembering his Naval Academy days, his commitment to serve this country, to protect it, to make its people prosper. He also recalled the oath he'd taken at the steps of the Capitol Building, the promise he'd made to this nation, which was now under attack, under siege by a ruthless enemy.

Hands behind his back, the American president turned to face the flag next to his desk, whispering his affirmation, silently swearing to uphold his oath and do what his country needed him to do.

And God help any men who gets in my way.

32

ILLUSIONS

Erika Conklin clicked her way through the most recent version of the DreamWorks' DigiSoft video-editing software package. An astonished Brent MacClaine looked over her shoulders as she transposed the facial features of Oruku Matsubara, digitized from an SJPD video clip taken during his questioning, onto the face of Kenny Tozai, a trustworthy FBI special agent from the San Francisco office. Tozai stood in front of a digital camera mounted atop a tripod next to MacClaine. Video and audio cables connected the camera to Erika's laptop.

Erika double clicked on Matsubara's mouth, turning it light gray in color. She then selected an image-link feature on the menu bar. The command slaved the lips of the top image to the one below. She did the same with Matsubara's eyes, linking their movement to the image beneath it, Tozai's own eyes.

"Now," she said, clicking a button under the window displaying Tozai's altered image, switching it back to live mode while keeping Matsubara's head locked over Tozai's. "Say something, Kenny."

The FBI agent scratched his head. "I've always wanted to be in the movies?"

Her old software performed just as Erika had expected, Matsubara's lip movement followed Tozai's. The eyes also responded as programmed, blinking when Tozai blinked. The effect, however, was far from complete. While Matsubara's lips moved, the rest of his jaw did not. In addition, Matsubara's face was narrow and long, in contrast with Tozai's square face. The agent's sideburns and ears protruded beyond Matsubara's slim face, looking monstrous.

Erika used the zoom feature of the software package to magnify the lower portion of the face, highlighting the left side, starting right below the cheek and continuing down to the chin. The software automatically offered her up to fifteen contact points within the selected facial region, an area roughly three square inches. She placed four contact points around the periphery and three more at an imaginary facial line separating the jaw from the cheek. The points linked the facial images at those specific locations. She repeated the procedure on the left side of the face, zoomed back out, and said, "All right, Kenny. Try it again."

"I've never wanted to be in the movies."

This time Matsubara's jaw moved along with the lips. The effect looked quite realistic, but she still had to deal with the two sets of ears from the mismatched head shapes.

Again, she used the zoom feature to blow up the right side of the image. Selecting a fine eraser, she carefully removed the excess skin of Tozai, repeating the virtual surgery on the other side. She looked up from the screen. "Again."

"I'm tired of being in the movies."

Erika grinned. Brent MacClaine patted her on the shoulder. "I'll be damned." The effect was near perfect.

"Now for the final touch," she said, selecting a paintbrush feature that allowed her to blend in the skin coloring of Matsubara's face with Tozai's neck. "There. One more time, Kenny. This time move your head as you normally would when talking."

He did, and the result was as perfect as any special effect in a recent movie. Her software, which had digitized every square millimeter of Matsubara's face, automatically distorted the face according to the movements dictated by the live image below as transmitted by the strategically placed contact points.

"How about the voice?" asked MacClaine, now sitting on the desk facing Erika.

"That was trickier to match, but I got close enough that the party at the other end won't notice. I could also make it sound like a bad audio connection, which would further distort the voice."

Bane pointed to his watch. "Freddie indicated that Matsubara is supposed to initiate the video call in another hour. Do you think we'll be ready?"

"I'm ready with virtual Matsubara now. I've also digitized the picture of the San Jose skyline as background."

Matsubara's video camera had faced large windows overlooking the parking lot and the city in the distance. "That's what I remember," said MacClaine.

"Then the channel is ready. Do you know what you want to say?"

MacClaine nodded.

33

DAI ROKKAN

Konichi Tanaka checked his watch as the live video image of Matsubara appeared on the screen. His subordinate was dressed in one of his usual suits and sat back in his office at Sakata Electronics. The image seemed a bit grainy.

"*Konban wa*, Matsubara-san."

"Good evening, Tanaka-san," replied Matsubara after a few seconds, almost as if there were a delay in the line. His associate also sounded different, his voice seemed raspier. He appeared to be moving a bit slower than the usually agitated Matsubara.

"Are you sick, my friend?"

"I haven't been myself in the last day or so. I think I picked up a flu virus."

"Then you must rest, regain your energy."

The acknowledgment in the form of a slight nod came after a three-second delay. "It seems we don't have a good connection. Should I hang up and try to dial back in again?"

"That won't be necessary. I cannot stay long. What news do you bring?"

"Nothing has changed since the last report from Hashimoto. He is very busy handling our problem."

"At all three locations?"

Matsubara nodded. "I spoke with him briefly today. He

told me to tell you that the fish that got away the first time is almost caught."

Everything appeared to be working according to plan. Yet Tanaka couldn't help to feel uneasy. His *dai rokkan*—his sixth sense—told him something was not right. "Has the extra help arrived?"

The on-line translator, a linguistic expert from the Los Angeles office, translated.

"Extra help?" asked MacClaine, who wore headphones and a lapel microphone that kept him in direct communication with the translator. MacClaine could also communicate directly with Special Agent Tozai via a flesh-colored ear piece. "What extra help?"

"Calm down, Brent," Erika said, sitting next to him working the keyboard and the mouse. She wore a similar set of headphones and a lapel mike, which she used to coach Tozai, whose digitized image was fed into her system, where DigiSoft updated the linked image of Matsubara's face to Tozai's facial movements. The altered image was then transposed on a background that resembled San Jose at night, just as MacClaine had described it. The software mutation of Tozai's original image added a three-second delay to the transmission, which Erika had hoped would not make Tanaka suspicious. So far it looked as if they were getting away with it. But they had to be careful how they answered his questions. Fortunately, Tozai had been well briefed by everyone working the case.

"Please repeat that, Tanaka-san. You're breaking up," the translator said over the headphones immediately following Tozai's fast-spoken Japanese.

That was the prearranged signal for Erika to inject some noise into the line to buy them time on difficult questions. She clicked on a sidebar menu. The screen became grainy and static momentarily clouded the transmission.

* * *

Tanaka frowned when the screen flickered and the audio hissed. As soon as Japan regained the high-tech crown, one of the first directives for the JDA's industrial partners would be higher-fidelity video/audio semi-conductors for improved satellite communications.

He leaned forward, placing both elbows on his desk. "Can you hear me now?"

He got a nod after a small delay. "Now I can. Please repeat your last sentence."

"I sent additional men, my friend. They should have arrived a few hours ago to assist in the fishing expedition."

After a delay, Matsubara nodded. "I received confirmation before this call. The help made it to the boats."

MacClaine removed his headphones and lapel mike as he jumped up from his chair and ran to an adjacent office to call his men covering Matsubara's residence and the warehouse, warning them about the imminent arrival of additional JDA agents. He ordered his men to arrest the Japanese cyberterrorists on the spot.

MacClaine returned to the office, where the conversation continued. He put the headphones back on. ". . . FBI attempted to contact any other corporations?"

Tozai shook his head. "No one has reported anything unusual, except for a break-in last night in this building. One of the guards told me that someone illegally entered the building and made it to the executive suite before security teams found the intruder, who managed to get away."

Erika and MacClaine exchanged glances the moment the translation came through. They had struggled with that one for a while before the call, wondering if they should inform Tanaka of the incident. In the end they had opted to do so, figuring that Matsubara, as liaison between the Japanese companies and the JDA, would have been informed of the break-in, especially since he was supposed to be making this call from his office at Sakata Electronics. If he didn't mention it and somehow Tanaka had already gotten word through another channel, the JDA chief would certainly suspect something was wrong—exactly what the FBI was trying to prevent to keep him from altering his scheduled trip to Cape Muroto.

"Anything *yukuefumei?*"

"Sakata security is still checking. Nothing so far appears to have been taken from the executive suites."

"Do you feel this might be related to the *gaijin* getting away?"

"I'm not sure what to make of it. Security violations are not uncommon in Silicon Valley. Intellectual property is highly coveted these days. I'm waiting to hear the outcome of the ongoing investigation."

Tanaka nodded, apparently satisfied with the explanation.

"I have nothing else to report at this moment but would like to update you right away if there is a problem. Where should I reach you between now and our next phone call?"

According to Freddie Kojata, Matsubara's next scheduled call was on Monday. Erika had thought of this last question during the premeeting briefing with Agent Tozai to get Tanaka to confirm his whereabouts during the upcoming weekend."

"I'll be spending the weekend at my beach house, as usual. Use the direct line only in an emergency. Otherwise contact me on Monday, as scheduled."

MacClaine looked at Erika and leaned over. "Remind me to give you a hug when this is over."

"I'll settle for a handshake, thanks," she replied, smiling.

"*Arigato*, Tanaka-san. I will be in touch," said Tozai.

"*Sayonara*," replied the JDA chief.

The video froze as the line was disconnected. Erika gave Tozai a thumbs-up while MacClaine reached for the phone. As Erika closed the video link and the version of DigiSoft running in the background, MacClaine called Palenski to report.

Tozai and the translator left. Erika grabbed a soda from

MacClaine's small refrigerator and sat back on his desk chair sipping it while contemplating the agents' cluttered office. The place was a shambles. Papers were stacked all over the place.

MacClaine hung up and gave her a mischievous look. "Guess what?"

"I don't think I want to know."

"You're right. You don't. We've been ordered to go to Japan."

She opened her mouth but nothing came out.

He continued. "Palenski wants us to search Tanaka's residence for any relevant software or hardware. They also want us on site when the CIA interrogates him after his capture. They don't want to wait another minute before getting our hands on the list."

"But—but—but that wasn't the arrangement that . . . Palenski never said anything about—"

"I know, I know. New orders. Palenski's sending a bu-bird to pick us up in the morning," MacClaine said, referring to a Bureau plane. "It'll be waiting for us at Moffet Field, that's a nearby naval—"

"I know where that is. I'm from this area, remember?" An edge quickly developed in her voice. "I also know that I don't have much of a choice in the matter, do I?"

"You actually do, but it's not a pretty choice. Palenski asked me to remind you of your recent agreement with him."

She sat back and crossed her arms. "Great."

"What was he talking about . . . if you don't mind my asking?"

She sighed while pouting. "The remainder of my FBI time will be automatically canceled if I cooperate one hundred percent on this case."

"I'm really sorry, Erika. Sounds like they've got you by the . . . well, you know what I mean."

"Yes, they do. And there isn't a damned thing I can do about it."

"Look at it this way," MacClaine said, sitting at the edge

of the desk. "In another week tops you'll be free to do as you please."

"And until then I'm Palenski's slave."

"But at least it's for a noble cause."

She nodded. "That's the only reason I don't tell him to shove that agreement where the sun doesn't shine. We have to put a stop to the cyberterrorist attacks." She paused, interlacing the fingers of both hands and placing them under her chin, as if she were praying. "So, what's the whole plan?"

He told her, taking a minute to describe the Navy strike and how they would be flown aboard the helicopter that would pick up the SEALs and Tanaka after the mission. The plan allowed Erika fifteen minutes in Tanaka's mansion to retrieve anything that might help them find the list of sabotaged components. CIA intelligence had already verified that two high-speed data lines fed into the JDA chief's beach house, which MacClaine described as more like a fortress than a vacation home. The information confirmed the existence of computer hardware and software at the site.

"Great," she said. "To the front lines again . . . like I didn't get enough of it last time." She touched a bruise on her cheek. In the past twenty-four hours, since her beating, the left corner of her lower lip had swollen and turned purple. The bruises on her right cheek and under her left eye had also darkened.

"I think you could use a drink," he said, smiling. "How about dinner and a couple of cocktails . . . on the Bureau, of course."

She shook her head. "Sorry. I don't socialize with feds. . . . Nothing personal."

He grinned. "Fine by me, but I still think you could use a good stiff drink and a good meal. We have a long and boring flight ahead of us tomorrow. There's no catering on bubirds. And I can't let you go out alone . . . so, you're basically stuck with me, or you can try the vending machines down the hallway. I guess we can always order a pizza."

She considered her options for a moment and nodded. "All right, Brent, but I'm warning you. Don't try anything."

"I'm a gentleman." He grinned.

"I've noticed."

34

A GENTLEMAN

They walked into the Fish Market on El Camino Real Boulevard at nine o'clock in the evening. Erika had changed into a pair of clean jeans and a starched, long-sleeved white shirt. She had also put on a little makeup to hide the bruises, specially the one under her eye. Her bangs partially covered the cut on her forehead. The wait at the popular seafood restaurant ran a half hour, so they headed for the bar until their name was announced on the PA system.

MacClaine leaned over the bar and whispered something to the bartender, who nodded, walked over to a waitress, told her something, and she took off.

"What was that all about?" Erika asked.

"A surprise. Have a seat."

They sat at the bar. MacClaine grabbed a few pretzels from a bowl the bartender placed in between them.

"Are we ordering drinks?" she asked.

"We did . . . actually, I did . . . for you, that is."

She shook her head. "I have no idea what—"

The waitress returned, carrying a chilled bottle of Sauvignon Blanc from Vista Wineries on her tray.

"Brent . . . this is so thoughtful of you. First you fly my daddy over, and then this. . . . Thank you so much." Erika leaned over and gave MacClaine a kiss on the cheek.

He shrugged. "It's the least the Bureau can do after all the crap we've put you through. Think of it as a precelebration dinner for all your help on this case. Without you we would still be trying to track down the families of the engineers that carried out the sabotage without a clue that Japanese cyberterrorists were behind it from the beginning."

The bartender placed a wineglass in front of Erika and opened the bottle, giving her the cork, which she smelled while closing her eyes.

MacClaine did the honors, pouring a couple of fingers into Erika's glass. She picked it up and swirled it like a pro, the wine sliding up the walls of the glass without spilling it over the rim. Then she sipped it. "The hell with the meal," she said, narrowing her eyes, regarding MacClaine with a warm stare. "This is just what I needed tonight."

The bartender set a wineglass in front of the agent, but he politely pushed it back. "Just club soda for me, thanks."

"What are you trying to do, Brent? Get me drunk?" She elbowed him lightly.

MacClaine reached for the pretzels. "That newspaper article was right. I'm an alcoholic, or I should say a *recovering* alcoholic. I've been on the wagon for several months now."

She set her glass on the counter and put a hand on his forearm, giving it a gentle squeeze. "Oh, God, Brent . . . I'm sorry. I—I didn't realize that—"

"That's all right," he said, patting her hand. "I'm hoping someday I'll learn how to drink just one or two, and stop. Right now, though, if I start I can't stop until I'm totally plastered. Not a pretty sight."

She pushed her drink away.

"No, no, no. You go ahead, please. It really doesn't bother me," he said.

She hesitated.

MacClaine leaned over and whispered in her ear, "Look. In case you haven't noticed, everyone else is drinking around me. Go ahead. Enjoy it. You certainly deserve it after what you've been through, particularly the beating the other night and then that damned article in the papers."

"All right." She reached for her glass, finishing it in a few minutes. MacClaine poured her a second one.

"You know," she said, sipping it. "In a way I'm glad the article was published. It forced me to face my dad about the lie I've been living for the past four years. It felt like a weight was lifted off my shoulders. Thanks, Brent." She lifted her glass. "Thanks for flying him down here."

By the time his name was announced on the PA system, Erika was working on her third glass, her eyes losing focus. The maître 'd sat them at a small corner table and provided them with menus. Candlelight cast an irresistible glow on her. MacClaine regarded her across the tablecloth, wine bottle, silverware, and glasses. She flashed a mischievous grin at him before she slowly inspected the crowded restaurant.

"Nice place. Food any good?"

He nodded. "The best."

"Good," she said, handing him her menu. "Order for me."

He did, ordering a dozen oysters on the half shell and a large platter of grilled seafood for two.

"What is it about you feds, anyway?" she asked, her eyes dancing while she spoke.

He placed both elbows on the table, leaning forward, smelling her perfume. "What do you mean?"

"Why do you do what you do? Why risk your life the way you do? For a paycheck?"

He raised an eyebrow. "This might sound corny, but I do it because it has to be done, because no one else is signing up to do it."

"Cheers to you," she said, raising her glass and downing it. "Me? I'll never forgive the Bureau for screwing me the way it did. I'm helping out because I might be able to make the accidents stop, but when this is over, it's *adios muchachos* and *hola* big bucks. These last few years I've felt as if I'm on welfare. And I didn't particularly enjoy being called a hooker in the papers. And an affair with Palenski? *Pleeease.* Have you seen what he looks like? And he's always chewing on those cigars. Yecch!"

MacClaine felt a bit amused at her comments, which Erika spouted out because of the alcohol. But they reflected just how she felt. Drunks were not good liars. Brent MacClaine knew that better than anyone else, and Erika Conklin was calling it just as she saw it, without the self-restraint of sobriety.

"Don't you get tired of it, though?" She continued, pouring herself more wine, missing the glass, spilling some on the tablecloth.

"You should wait until the meal arrives before drinking more."

She stared at him, her eyes focusing in and out. "Is the Bureau now going to tell me how much to drink and when?"

"No, I was just making a recommendation. You're a grown-up. You can decide for your own."

Placing both elbows on the table, Erika leaned forward and whispered, "Good, because I'm tired, Brent. I'm *fucking* tired of so much Bureau bullshit running my life. I mean, what is it with you people? Why can't you just leave me alone, let me be? Instead, I'm forced to work in a crime-ridden city for slave wages and live in a roach-infested apartment when I could be making serious bucks at a high-tech firm. I've been beaten, humiliated by the papers, and now I'm being forced to risk my life again by going to the front lines with the SEALs. So, if I want to drink this whole damned bottle, which reminds me so much of the life I've left behind, I will do so, and right in front of you."

"You broke the rules, Erika. You committed a felony. Consider yourself lucky that you're not in a federal prison at the moment, getting molested every night by lesbian guards and fellow inmates."

She sat back, crossing her arms, tears welling in her

eyes. "Save that speech for real criminals, Brent. My password-snatching virus did no harm to anyone. Absolutely . . . absolutely *no* harm, but the Bureau still wanted to make an example out of me. The FBI wanted to send a message to every hacker out there, and they used me as their advertising billboard." She took another sip. "I'm hungry. Where's the food anyway?"

MacClaine was already regretting buying her the bottle of wine, but on the other hand, he couldn't help but feel sorry for her. Six years was a hell of a price to pay for something that apparently had not even created a problem for anyone.

The waitress arrived with the oysters. Erika dug in, squirting lemon juice on half of them. She picked one with a tiny fork, dipped it in horseradish and cocktail sauce, and ate it.

"How is it?"

"Awesome," she said, getting a second one ready. "I'm starving."

They consumed the appetizer in a few minutes. MacClaine ordered a second dozen before their meal arrived. Erika finished off the bottle while eating shrimp stuffed with crabmeat.

"So, Brent," she said, her speech slurring. "Do you ever get tired . . . of your job?"

"Got tired of it a long time ago. My wife left me because of the job. She wanted kids. I was too busy saving the world."

"And you still are. . . . Can I have something else to drink?"

"What would you like?"

"A beer."

MacClaine smiled while waving over their waitress and ordering her a Corona and himself another club soda. They drank them in silence before Erika said, "Thank you . . . for flying my . . . my dad." She stood and leaned down to kiss his cheek but fell on her side instead.

Nearby patrons gazed down disapprovingly.

MacClaine left enough bills on the table to cover the meal and tip, and quickly left the restaurant, holding her up by running an arm around her shoulders while walking side by side.

Outside, she collapsed in his arms, giggling. He cradled her, amazed at how little she weighed.

"God, you sure are soooo strooong," she said, her head landing on his chest, her eyes closing.

He laid her down in the passenger seat and strapped her in. He drove off. His apartment complex was located at the intersection of Lawrence and 101. He got on the phone to check if the new cyberterrorists had surfaced. His men covering Matsubara's placed told him they had not seen anyone yet.

"You know you were mean . . . to me when we first met. But then you were sooooo nice . . . sooooo nice. But that's toooo baaad . . . because I . . . don't date . . . feds."

MacClaine glanced over to her. She had her eyes closed and her head resting against the side window. He ignored her, concentrating on the heavy traffic as El Camino reached Lawrence. He headed north on Lawrence.

"Mean . . . mean, mean," she whispered.

He drove past his complex and decided to keep going, stopping at a Residence Inn just off Lawrence, before reaching 101. With cyberterrorists on the loose he didn't want to risk going to his apartment. Instead, he got a suite for the night and drove up to their unit, located in the rear of the complex of brown buildings.

He carried her up to a second-floor suite, struggling to unlock the front door while trying not to drop her.

The moment he opened the door, Erika jumped off his arms, looking around her, glassy-eyed, confused with the unfamiliar surroundings.

"I think the bedroom's straight ahead," he commented, closing and locking the door.

She didn't acknowledge him but began to undress while walking toward the bedroom, her back to him while she took off her shirt and blue jeans, leaving a trail down the short hallway. She had no bra and wore the cutest black panties, along with a nasty bruise covering most of her left torso. She also had buffed legs, the muscles of which pumped beneath her creamy skin as she reached the bedroom. Once more, MacClaine felt a demon awakening inside of him, but he couldn't bring himself to try to make a move when she was so hopelessly bombed. As a former alcoholic he knew that Erika would remember very little of this evening. He also knew that the FBI analyst would have the headache of a lifetime in the morning.

MacClaine turned on the hallway lights and followed her into the bedroom to make sure she didn't accidentally hurt herself. Erika had already collapsed on the bed, curled on her side like an infant, a hand tucked under her chin, the other resting on her thigh. He watched her in the moonlight glowing through the windows. Her breasts, quite full for her size, sported small pinkish nipples. She had a mole on one of them.

"Cold . . ." she whispered, bracing herself.

MacClaine leaned down and ran an arm under her side, gently lifting her midsection to move the covers out from under her, then lifted them over her, tucking her in.

She opened her eyes.

"Brent?"

"Just tucking you in," he said.

"Where . . . where . . ."

"In a hotel room. You're safe. Sleep. We have a long flight tomorrow."

She squirmed under the blanket. "Okay," she said before closing her eyes. Her breathing became steady in seconds.

MacClaine began to take off his clothes but decided it would be best if at least one of them remained fully dressed. He opted for snatching one of the pillows and going to the living room, closing the bedroom door behind him.

He settled down on the couch, shoved the Beretta under the pillow, and closed his eyes, forcing himself to relax, to forget about computer chips, violent accidents, Japanese cyberterrorists, and SEAL teams. He remembered Erika's words, which oddly enough had also been spoken by Jessica long ago. *Why risk your life for a paycheck?* Was she right? Was MacClaine really making a difference? Was his job really worth all of the personal sacrifice. MacClaine thought of the stiff price he had paid—and continued to pay—to live the life of a federal agent. His marriage had failed miserably, mostly because of him, because of his lack of support, because of his failure to understand Jessica's desire to start a family, to live a normal life, to spend time with him.

I didn't marry a paycheck, Brent. I didn't marry a paycheck.

In the twilight of the room, Jessica's words echoed inside his mind. She had urged him many times to reconsider his assignments, to use his seniority to get a desk job and spend more time at home instead of going undercover for weeks at a time. But Brent MacClaine wouldn't hear any of it. The Bureau was his life. He thrived during his missions and couldn't wait to get back out there after completing each one. One day he had come home to an empty house.

MacClaine suddenly got a craving for a beer. He wanted one so badly that he suddenly found himself getting up and heading for the door.

Where are you going, Brent? You can't handle one beer. You can't stop once you get started. The Bureau needs you to stay sober.

The hell with the FBI. They're the reason why my life's so fucked up! I want a beer and I want it now!

He was about to turn the knob and go outside when Erika screamed.

MacClaine didn't know he could still move so fast. He rushed down the hallway, burst through the door, and found her lying on her side hugging herself while moaning.

"What's wrong? Are you okay?"

"No . . . please . . . no . . . stop . . ."

She was crying and moaning.

"Erika? Are you all right?"

"Help . . . please, help me. . . ."

He sat at the edge of the bed and realized that she was having a nightmare. She was also sweating profusely and had pulled down the sheets to her waist.

MacClaine turned on the ceiling fan on his way to the bathroom and wetted a hand towel, which he used to wipe her forehead.

"Calm down," he whispered in her ear while kneeling by the bed and slowly rubbing her face and neck. "You're safe with me, Erika. You're safe."

She relaxed, her left arm reaching for him, pulling him down. She kissed him on the lips, smiled, and went limp. A moment later she shuddered.

MacClaine was pleasantly surprised but then realized that she was still very drunk and dreaming. He slowly moved her arm off his neck and straightened back up, spending a few more minutes wiping her forehead until her breathing steadied. Once again he tucked her in. This time he couldn't help himself and gave her a kiss on her temple. She stirred and moaned lightly.

He watched her sleep for a few minutes, fighting the urge to crawl in bed and just hug her. He'd slept alone for longer than he'd care to remember.

But that's the life you chose for yourself. You can't handle a personal relationship. You won't be able to give her time.

But I'm getting older. I'm slowing down. Maybe it's time for a change.

Don't make it personal, MacClaine. You can't afford it. Besides, you're fifteen years her senior. She hasn't lived her life. You've already screwed up yours. Go to Japan. Finish this thing. She'll go back to her world and you to yours. In a couple of months you will have forgotten about Erika Conklin.

MacClaine set the wet towel on the nightstand, ran a hand through his hair, gave Erika a last glance, and went back to the living room, once more settling down on the sofa, his urge for a drink gone. He silently thanked Erika as he closed his eyes, again trying to shove away all thoughts of his current mission, slowly falling asleep.

In his dreams he saw himself running away from Hashimoto and his guns, running as fast as his legs would go, turning into an alley, rushing past rusted garbage bins, facing a brick wall at the end of the narrow corridor. He reached for his weapon but his hand slapped an empty holster. He turned around to face Hashimoto but instead saw a man with the head of a rat blocking the alley. MacClaine looked up and spotted Jessica embracing another man in a balcony. He screamed for help. She waved back and went inside with her companion. He turned toward the monster blocking the alley. It lunged. He felt a powerful blow delivered to the side of his face as the mutant struck. MacClaine put up his hands to block a second strike, but the monster got through his defenses, striking him again, and again. *Stop!* MacClaine pleaded. *Stop!* But Ratman did not, hitting him again while screeching out loud. But the monster's voice was that of a female. MacClaine recognized it immediately. It was the voice of Erika Conklin!

"You dirty bastard! You filthy, slimy son of a bitch!"

Erika's face replaced the rat's. MacClaine tried to jump off the couch but missed a step. Instead, he fell next to the sofa, hitting his shoulder against the cocktail table.

"Aghh, damn!"

Erika jumped on top of him, armed with a shoe, whacking him across the head. She was wearing her jeans and an unbuttoned shirt, through which he could see her breasts swinging wildly as she brought her weapon down on him again, hammering his forehead.

"Stop it, would ya? Dammit!" MacClaine staggered back, managing to get to his feet, trying to get his bearings. It was still dark outside.

"You sick pig!" She struck again. This time the fed grabbed the shoe and yanked it off her hand.

"How could you, Brent? How could you do such a

thing!" She pounded his chest with both fists. MacClaine gripped her wrists, holding her back.

"Do what? What is it that you think I've done?"

She raised her eyes, wet with anger. "You raped me, you bastard! You got me drunk and then raped me! That's why you got me that damned wine! It was date rape! Date rape!"

"No, I didn't touch you! You got yourself drunk, remember? I brought you here, to a safe place, to make sure you didn't have another encounter with your Japanese fan club. You were totally out of it but managed to find the bedroom and undress yourself. I just tucked you in, closed the door, and slept right there." He let go of her hands and pointed at the couch.

"What about the wet towel by my bed? You thought you could just wipe it off and I wouldn't know? I—I just can't believe this happened to me! I should have known better."

"I did wipe you with a wet towel!" he said, trying to control his temper, quickly toning down his voice. "But *only* your forehead. You had a nightmare," he added calmly. "You were screaming and sweating, Erika, so I put a wet towel to your face and neck."

She looked confused, her eyes softening, closing halfway, a finger rubbing her left temple. "So . . . so you didn't? . . ."

He shook his head emphatically. "And believe me, you gave me *plenty* of opportunity, but that isn't my style. I think you're gorgeous, but I wouldn't use a cheap trick like that."

"But the wine, and—"

"There was no trick there, Erika. I felt you deserved that small token of appreciation from the FBI after all that you've gone through, which is the same reason I flew your father down here."

"When I woke up and noticed that I was naked, and then I saw the wet towel by the bed . . . all I could think was that—"

"I was just like the feds you've dated back in D.C.?"

She nodded, sitting down, holding her temples between her fingertips. "I'm sorry, Brent. I'm terribly sorry I re-acted that way. I just don't remember much after the bar. Now I have this terrible . . . *horrible* headache," she said. "Oh, God, why do I feel so bad?"

"It's called a hangover," MacClaine said, sitting next to her and buttoning up her shirt.

She looked at him but didn't stop him. Instead, she gave him an apologetic smile. "I've just attacked you because I thought you raped me and here you are actually dressing me. Brent, oh, God, I'm so sorry. I—"

"Don't," he said. "Under the circumstances, I probably would have reacted the same way."

"And look at what I did to you," she said. "I'm truly sorry."

MacClaine finished the last button and put a hand to her cheek. She tilted her head toward it and put one of hers over his. "Don't sweat it. This ain't nothing compared to what I've been through."

She went back to rubbing her temples.

He stood and headed for the door.

"Where are you going?"

"To get you some aspirin across the street. Then I'm putting you back in bed. We still have a few hours to sleep before we head off to Moffet. We have a long flight ahead of us."

"I'll be right here waiting for you." She sat there, smil-ing up at him, her messy hair covering her forehead, falling right above narrowed hazel eyes.

It took all of his self-control not to return to that sofa.

Don't make it personal, MacClaine. You won't be able to give her the time, the companionship. You'll ignore her just as you did Jessica.

His professional side pushed him out the door. Outside, MacClaine took a deep breath, shook his head, and headed for his car.

35

DEVILS WITH GREEN FACES

The ritual was one too familiar for Commander Ray. He stood in front of a set of bunk beds in the aft torpedo room staring at the array of gear spread over a thin mattress.

Wearing a set of jungle camouflage fatigues with multiple pockets, boots with socks turned down over the laces to prevent them from snagging, his reliable and rugged G-shock watch, camouflage cream on his face and neck, and a holstered side arm—a Sig Sauer 9-mm pistol—Ray leaned down and gathered the rest of his first-line equipment, his absolute survival essentials. He shoved in the pockets of his cammies a map of the region, two hundred dollars and thirty-thousand yen, a small compass, a condom for waterproofing, and twenty-five feet of parachute suspension line. Next he reached for a couple of commercial Power bars, a small flashlight, a small roll of wire saw, and a recognition panel for signaling aircraft. The final item in his first-line equipment was a first-aid kit, which included codeine, morphine, a battle dressing, and an Ace bandage.

Ray closed his eyes, moving his hands from pocket to pocket, verifying that even in total darkness he could still reach every item of his basic survival gear, which he placed in the exact same spot in the cammies every time. He placed a Motorola MX300 radio inside a pouch on the left side of his chest and plugged two coiled wires into the unit. One connected to an earpiece, which Ray firmly secured to his right ear, the second to a throat mike, which he wrapped around his neck with a Velcro strip. Lastly, he donned a deflated personal flotation device, which he would inflate on demand during the wet portion of the mission to keep from drowning while hauling so much gear.

Satisfied, he put on an H-harness combat vest, already loaded with six thirty-round magazines for his silenced Heckler & Koch MP5 submachine gun, four fifteen-round clips for his Sig Sauer pistol, three grenades, a pair of handcuffs, insect repellent, a 500-ml bag of Ringer's lactate for IVs, one MRE (Meal, Ready to Eat), a second battle dressing, a knife, a water canteen and water purification tablets, a strobe light, one M-18 smoke grenade, and a second medical kit. This second-line equipment added a total of seventeen pounds, mostly from the ammunition. The H-harness also made a great handle for someone to grab if Ray got wounded and needed help to get out of Dodge, just as Norma Mendez had done when she had pulled him out of Noriega's hangar in Panama after Ray fell unconscious from the multiple head wounds.

Ray jumped and listened, making adjustments to the gear when hearing a rattling sound. He repeated the procedure a half dozen times, until all of his gear remained silent during motion.

The rucksack contained Ray's third-line equipment, including a PRC-90 rescue radio, extra batteries for the PRC and for the MX300, three additional magazines for the MP5, two more MREs, a poncho, water bladders, a small machete, six square feet of camouflage net, a set of night-vision goggles, an assortment of demolition material—mostly C4 charges and fuses—and three Claymore anti-personnel mines, each holding inside its plastic case a slab of C4 behind seven hundred steel balls. He donned the rucksack, feeling the familiar sixty pounds of life-saving equipment, silently giving thanks to God and his instructors at Coronado for the grueling physical conditioning that he had maintained since his graduation, an exercise program that gave him the strength to haul his gear for many miles across any terrain.

Ray grabbed his MP5, fixed a condom over the muzzle of the silencer, and secured it to the H-harness under his left arm with two Velcro straps.

"What's the word from the recon team, Sting?"

Ray turned around. The powerful Bishop walked toward him in full battle dress. He hauled the ammunition for the powerful M-60 machine gun strapped to his left side in two links of one hundred rounds each, carefully packed in the upper portion of his battle vest. Each pack provided a feed tray to guide the rounds into the M-60 during a mission. Ray also knew that Bishop hauled three additional packs in the extralarge rucksack hanging from his shoulders. Bishop's side arm was equally impressive, a huge Smith & Wesson model 67 pistol with an extracapacity magazine of twenty .45 caliber rounds. In his sidearm alone Bishop carried more firepower than an M-16 rifle.

Ray stared at the 250-pound warrior hauling eighty pounds of gear and was silently grateful that Bishop was on his side. The oversized soldier was one of a handful of SEALs strong enough to operate an M-60 with little effort, as if it were an Uzi. In addition, Bishop was the squad's medic, hauling twenty pounds of first-aid gear.

Behind him, nearly hidden by Bishop's bulk, walked Norma Mendez, her small frame in sharp contrast with Ray's right-hand man. Norma carried a silenced Uzi submachine gun, light but reliable and durable. Its simplistic design lent itself to SEAL use. Like Ray, she favored the small and proven Sig Sauer 9-mm pistol, the rounds of which were compatible with the Uzi.

The commander of SEAL Team Five checked his watch. The most recent intelligence report indicated that Tanaka should be home by now. The final green light for the infiltration had arrived less than two hours ago. "The LZ is clean," he said, referring to the report from the security team, which had left the *Polk* four hours before aboard the minisub and had called in to report twenty minutes ago.

Bishop nodded and pointed an index finger at the ceiling. "The squad's locked and loaded by the escape hatch, Sting."

Ray stared at his two finest warriors, each wearing camouflage cream and full battle gear. They were ready. He was ready, just as he'd been ready in Panama, Desert Storm, and Afghanistan, just as previous generations of SEALs had been ready when their country had called upon them. And today the United States of America had called upon SEAL Team Five to live up to a tradition of courage and loyalty that dated back to 1943, when the U.S. Navy had formed a secret force to clear beach obstacles for the amphibious invasion of Sicily. The Naval Combat Demolition Unit soon evolved into the Underwater Demolition Teams responsible for clearing and charting beaches throughout the Pacific during World War II. From Kwajalein to Saipan, from Leyte to Okinawa, UDT warriors, operating with face masks, snorkels, and swim fins—and the ability of the swimmer to hold his breath underwater for a long time—prepared the beaches for their marine brothers. Then came Korea, where the UDT carried out multiple secret missions at the request of the newly formed Central Intelligence Agency. The SEALs had been formally commissioned by the time the Vietnam War started, and they fought with utmost courage and honor, earning hundreds of Bronze Stars, Navy Commendation Medals, and Purple Hearts.

Ray's stare gravitated from his subordinates to the array of pipes and ducts running above the bunk beds, the quiet hum of the vessel's engines filling the silence in the room.

Vietnam.

Ray put a hand right over his sternum, sliding a finger between secured gear, its tip brushing against the Purple Heart he wore along with his dog tags under his cammies. He touched it for luck. It had been one of many posthumous awards presented to the families of SEALs killed in Vietnam.

Ray wore it with pride.

It belonged to his father.

36

HANGOVER

Erika Conklin swore never to drink again as she leaned forward in her seat while holding an airsick bag to her mouth. She felt another spasm coming and didn't fight it, vomiting bile into the bag.

Her eyes filled as every muscle in her body tensed before relaxing again. She sat back, wiping her mouth with a tissue before shoving it in the bag and closing it.

"Oh, God . . . I'm never eating an oyster again," she cried, taking a deep breath, the turbulence adding to her nausea.

Brent MacClaine, who sat next to her aboard a Gulfstream jet as it cruised past a mild storm, handed her another tissue. "You shouldn't have mixed beer with wine. Pretty deadly combination."

"I feel like I'm going to die," she said, grabbing a pack of sugar-free gum, unwrapping a stick, and popping it in her mouth, rubbing her abdomen. Her stomach had rebelled from the moment they took off eight hours ago.

MacClaine smiled. "You'll survive. Trust me. I'm an authority in the field . . . unfortunately."

"I thought that these private jets were more comfortable," she said, shifting her weight as the craft banked to the left and then dropped, forcing more bile up her throat. She clenched her teeth, forcing it back down. "These seats are worse than economy class on commercial flights, and there's no in-flight beverages."

"The FBI owns two jets. This one's the old bubird modified a few years back to accommodate more seats. The new one's being used only by the HBOs," said MacClaine. "That one's really nice, with big comfy seats, a minibar, in-flight movies, and all kinds of other amenities."

She shook her head. "Tax dollars at work."

He nodded. "HBOs get the Cadillac. Bottom-dwellers get the econobox."

"Great."

"Hey, at least the bathroom works."

"Thank God for *that*." She had almost lived in the lavatory for the first two hours of the flight, when her hangover had really kicked into high gear, making her empty everything in her stomach. The experience had exhausted her to the point that she had collapsed on her seat. The storm had woken her up just thirty minutes ago.

The plane stopped jerking. Erika looked out of the oval window. Clouds parted, giving way to a moonless, star-filled sky.

MacClaine handed her a glass of water in a plastic cup, which she sipped for a couple of minutes, breathing deeply. Her focus slowly returned.

"How much longer do we have?"

He checked his watch. "About six more hours. We're being dropped in Seoul, where a helicopter's going to take us to a Navy vessel sailing near Japan. Then we wait until it's time to go in."

Erika had gone through the routine a few times in her mind, and every time her heart began to hammer her chest. "I'm *definitely* not cut out for this."

"Relax," MacClaine said. "You've done great so far."

"Yeah, *right*. If getting the crap beat out of you is your definition of doing great, I'd hate to screw up."

"You don't want to screw up in this business, Erika. I've seen it and it ain't pretty."

"That's comforting to hear."

MacClaine put a hand over hers and squeezed it gently. Erika relaxed at his touch and turned to face him.

"Don't worry about a thing," he said, his prizefighter face turning serious. "There's going to be plenty of navy SEALs securing the area, and I'll be by your side the entire time. Nothing's going to happen to you. I swear to you that I'll protect you with my own life."

She inspected this stranger, who just forty-eight hours ago had come across as another chauvinist pig FBI agent, but who since had exposed a tender side that Erika Conklin found quite appealing.

"But remember to be quick once we get in there," he added. "You won't have much time."

She nodded. "Fifteen minutes max, right?"

"That's it. And then we're out of there."

She reached for the laptop carrying case under her seat and pulled out a T9000 personal communicator out of a side pocket. The handheld unit combined the functionality of a cellular phone with that of a palmtop computer.

"Nice phone," MacClaine said.

Erika smiled and opened the cover, revealing a small screen and a miniature keyboard. She powered it up and waited while the system booted up.

"Just how small can they get?"

"This is it," she said. "The smallest computer on the planet, and it's wireless too. It's got a microprocessor which is three generations old, but for this form factor that's plenty of computing power. I can access the Internet and send E-mail to anyone I want from anywhere on the planet. With this puppy I'm never disconnected."

"You sure need little fingers to work it, though," he commented. "What are you going to do?"

"Check on the folks back home," she said. "Make sure that the data link's ready to receive the moment I begin to dump on them." In addition to capturing Tanaka, the FBI's plan called for Erika to direct the SEALs to seize anything that she felt could contain information pertinent to the sabotaged integrated circuits, including diskettes, magnetic tapes, disk drives, Zip disks, and even entire computer systems. Erika then planned to transmit as many files as she could via a dedicated satellite link to Charlie Chang back in Washington so that her team, with the assistance of linguistic experts, could get a head start on translating the information into English and searching for the coveted list of sabotaged computer chips before she returned to Washington. In the meantime, Erika, with the handy assistance of two CIA officers trained in the art of chemical interrogation, would attempt to extract intelligence from a reluctant Tanaka.

"Dump on them? I don't understand."

She explained.

"On that little thing?"

"No, no. For that kind of work I brought that." She pointed to her laptop computer carrying case and other hardware."

"Oh. So what are you going to do with this little toy?"

"I'll show you."

The T9000 completed its boot-up sequence, giving her a number of options across the left side of the screen. She selected the mail menu. Instantly, the wireless communicator established a link with one of many satellites in geosynchronous orbit around the earth, going through a coded handshake protocol, and relaying the connection to a second satellite, and then a third, which covered the eastern United States. It downloaded her signal to a receiver in the systems lab of the J. Edgar Hoover Building in Washington, D.C., where Charlie Chang and a team of ten other programmers were getting ready for the massive data dump.

The entire sequence took less than five seconds. The message Connection Established appeared on her screen, along with two options, one for standard E-mail and the second for real-time communication. Erika chose the latter, waiting a few moments while the system at the other end alerted the user of her call.

Chang: Boss! Did you get there?

"Now, that's really cool," MacClaine said, leaning over to get a better look. "You're really talking to them over a wireless link through that little computer?"

She nodded. "Watch." Using her two index fingers, she began to peck the keyboard.

Erika: Nope. Still en route. How are you doing?

Chang: Will be ready in another couple of hours. Everybody's pretty tense over here. Palenski usually visits the lab once or twice a year. He's been here three times today. He's like wanting to make sure that I'm getting all the help I need.

Erika: Pretty big stakes, Charlie. How's everything else?

Chang: Good news on the list of companies you got from that Zip at Sataka. Intel found a version of an embedded microprocessor sabotaged. It's used heavily in control systems, both industrial and military. We think it could be tied to the chemical plant in Pasadena and also the malfunctioning air force jet over Vegas. There is a massive recall in progress. Hundreds of plants and military equipment are being reworked by field personnel. We're talking anything from oil refineries to army tanks. The FAA still has all commercial jetliners grounded until we find all of the sabotaged components.

Erika looked at MacClaine. He put a hand on her shoulder and rubbed it. "Damn it," she said. "If we would have found that purchasing list just forty-eight hours before, we could have prevented those disasters."

MacClaine said, "You're doing the best you can. Think of all of the accidents you've prevented."

She nodded and continued to peck.

Erika: How's everything else going?

Chang: Still working on your version of the Detroit virus, and still no known cure for the little demon. The workstations are going nuts and still can't break the sequence I've extracted from the petri dish. It keeps coming back claiming it's a true random sequence. Is it?

Erika: Nope.

Chang: But why can't I find a formula that matches the mutation sequence?

Erika: That's because of the multiple nesting, which is next to impossible to resolve unless the system knows the mutation sequence formula, which I solely posess.

Chang: So, you knew all this time that it couldn't be broken? Why make me sweat it out for three days?

Erika: I seem to remember you were the one who wanted to try to break it. I just wanted you to store it and forget about it. I don't believe it can be broken without the key.

Chang: And guess what? Neither do I, so, could I get this key from you?"

Erika: I'll attach it to an E-mail. Verify that it works, and then archive the virus and the antidote in the electronic vault, along with the other toxic viruses. With some luck this virus will never see the light of day again. I'll check in the moment we get to the Navy vessel.

Chang: You got a name for this vessel?

Erika: It's called the *Blue Ridge*. I'll check in later. 'Bye.

Chang: Later, boss.

Erika terminated the transmission and leaned back. "Everything's ready, or will be ready shortly, on my end."

MacClaine also rested his head against the back of the seat and wondered how the SEAL operation was progressing. The elite force's success was paramount to their mission.

37

OWNERS OF THE NIGHT

SOUTHERN JAPAN

The Zodiac's dark shape blended with the night, cruising across calm waters, the light droning of its outboard masked by the whistling wind. Waves slapped its rubber sides in a rhythm that matched Commander Derek Ray's increasing heartbeat. It didn't matter how many times the SEAL commander had done a wet insertion. The sheer reality of entering enemy territory to carry out a covert operation always had a way of challenging Ray's steel nerves. That plus the cold. Ray was soaked and thoroughly chilled. His squad had to leave the lock-in-lock-out chamber of the *Polk* as it cruised at three knots at a depth of thirty feet, make it up the ascent line to the Zodiac without any breathing apparatus, and pull themselves and their gear aboard. To make matters worse, the submarine crew had a minor depth excursion during the transfer process, taking the SEAL boat and its crew of eight down for a memorable thirty-second ride under the sea.

Ray shook his head. At least the motor had started after a few tries, unlike his last insertion, when sea water had managed to leak through a defective seal, forcing the SEALs to paddle for a mile to reach shore.

Ray glanced at the stars while taking a deep breath, the wet cammies sticking to his skin, chilling him. He ignored the cold and gazed at the rocky cliffs outlining the ocean front before dropping his eyes to the nearing shoreline, already secured by his recon team, who had worn Draeger underwater rebreathers to survey the beach from the safety of the sea before giving the insertion team the green light. That was one advantage his father had not had in Vietnam. Ray wouldn't consider a wet insertion aboard a rubber boat unless a security team had inspected the beach first. His father, who'd led dozens of ambushes along the many canals feeding the Bassac River in the Lower Mekong Delta, had not had that luxury.

Ray briefly closed his eyes. Vietnam. June 17, 1969. Lieutenant James Thomas Ray led a squad of SEALs aboard a SEAL team assault boat (STAB) to set up yet another ambush along the riverbank of the Bassac River. His team had set up many such ambushes in this region, normally controlled by the Vietcong and used as a main avenue to supply troops and equipment from the north to the Saigon area. Ray's SEALs had been routinely creating havoc among the VC by attacking their sampans—shallow boats with small outboards—from the safety of the riverbank as the VC used them to maneuver along the canals in the region. But that night's mission proved anything but routine. Word had reached the SEALs from an army intelligence officer about a large deployment of Vietcong gear a mile inland from the shores of the Bassac. Ray and his squad had immediately jumped at the opportunity of hitting the VC and headed that way. It had been an ambush. The VC had spotted their approach to the riverbank and waited until the STAB and its 50-caliber machine gun had gotten well out of sight and the SEAL team had advanced a few hundred feet inland before opening fire on the SEALs. Lieutenant Thomas Ray had immediately ordered his squad to "leapfrog" away from the trap. The technique called for the soldier closest to the enemy to fire his weapon until going dry. He would then race to the other end of the patrol and the next man would fire, and so on. The SEALs quickly broke contact and raced back to the riverbank, but the VC went after them. The STAB approached the shore at full speed while putting out cover fire with the 50-caliber machine gun. But there were too many VC. The SEALs ran the risk of being overrun by the wave of Vietcong and their AK-47s. Thomas Ray remained a dozen feet from the shore with his Stoner model 63 light machine gun and five hundred rounds of ammunition, keeping the enemy at bay while his team made it to the STAB. He took multiple rounds in the face and chest as he crawled back to the boat while his team covered his escape. Sting's father had sacrificed himself to save his men. For inner strength, Ray always invoked the memory of the brave father he never knew, the war hero whose legend had intrigued him throughout his childhood, inspiring him to join the elite American fighting force in an effort to get to know him better by following in his footsteps, by becoming a U.S. Navy SEAL.

Derek Ray sat at the rear of the Zodiac, also known as the combat rubber raiding craft (CRRC), next to the coxswain, who kept his left hand on the silent outboard's throttle and his eyes glued on the shoreline. A rookie sat across from Ray, eyes closed, lips moving. Ray sighed, also feeling like praying. Bishop lay in the front of the rubber duck, his elbows planted on the inflatable edge, hands gripping the powerful M60 machine gun aimed straight ahead, a huge sheath knife strapped to his right lower leg. Taped to the sheath was a pull-ring signal flare. One end was red smoke, the other a red flare. Norma Mendez, lying next to Bishop, also had a similar knife-flare combo taped to her left leg. Her Uzi covered the starboard side of the CRRC. A rookie covered the port side, and two more sat in the middle, one staring at his boots, the other at the stars. The latter one was Petty Officer Second Class George Yokosaka, a second-generation Japanese, handpicked by Ray at Coronado to double as interpreter.

Ray took a deep breath, their combined firepower and training momentarily relaxing him. But another realization quickly brushed aside the brief feeling of confidence, the elite fighting force at the army base located just a few miles from Tanaka's estate. One false move and it would be bad news for his squad. The sheer magnitude of the enemy would crush them if his team were spotted. Even all of his training and experience could not compensate for so many soldiers hunting them down. As in all his previous missions, secrecy would be his finest weapon.

His eyes landed on the kid sitting on the other side of the coxswain. Ray joined him in a short prayer.

As the coxswain throttled down the outboard, Norma Mendez glanced over her left shoulder, catching Ray with his eyes closed. Wet and cold, she turned her attention back to the starboard section of the vessel, her Uzi pointed at the darkness, listening to the waves and the nearing surf, sounds that brought back memories of her escape from Cuba—and a night in the Gulf of Mexico. Norma Mendez remembered the fear, the cold, the shivering of her toddler as the water and the wind stripped him of his body heat. Norma had held him tight, had tried to radiate her heat onto him, but the child had stopped responding, had stopped moving, his purple lips no longer trembling, his eyes without focus. Then she had screamed, had cursed those who had forced her to take such desperate measures. But her cries had gone unheard in the night, which continued to rob her of her heat, of her sanity, of her life as she drifted at the mercy of the currents. She remembered the coppery smell of her own blood as it dripped down her legs and into the water, attracting the dorsal fins that reflected the moonlight while circling the inner tube. Clutching her dead son, no longer afraid of losing him, Norma had shouted at the nearing beasts, had pushed them away with the broken oar, had fought bravely against staggering odds. But then she had grown tired. The relentless sea, the wind, the night, the cold, the incessant battle all took their toll on her. Norma had momentarily lost track of her son's body while she struggled to fend off a large hammerhead, missing the attack of another predator from behind, who would have struck her side had her dead son not been shoved in between the inner tube and her torso. In a moment her baby was gone. In the night, Norma Mendez had cried out as the sharks lost themselves in a frenzy while tearing at the small body just a dozen feet from her.

A tear escaped her left eye, leaving a narrow track down her camouflaged face. Under her floppy hat, her brown eyes narrowed at the waves, the shiny fins disappearing from her mind as the Japanese shore came into view under the minute starlight.

"You okay, Loca?" Bishop whispered in the dark.

"Just an eyelash," she whispered. "And keep your eyes on your target. Not on me. We're on a mission, not at your place."

"Loca, you're just too tough. Imagine the kind of children we could make."

That brought a smile to her face. "I'm too much of a woman for you. You ran out of steam on me the other night, remember?"

Bishop frowned. "Cut me some slack, would ya? I'd spent the entire day with the rookies on the beach."

"Guess I'm just gonna have to get me a virile Cuban. They can go on and on and on."

"Nothing can replace this two hundred and fifty pounds of pure Colorado beef."

Norma turned to him, grinned, and elbowed him. The nights she had spent in Bishop's arms had indeed been quite memorable, helping her forget her past. And recently she had even developed feelings for this giant man, who seemed genuinely interested in pursuing a relationship with her.

"All clear," came Ray's voice through her earpiece. "The security team has given us the green light. We're going in."

The coxswain cut the engine and grabbed an oar to use it as a rudder while four other SEALs also picked up oars and began to row through the surf, keeping the Zodiac straight. Bishop, Mendez, Ray, and a rookie kept their weapons trained on the incoming shoreline.

The SEALs jumped off a dozen feet from shore. Bishop, Mendez, and Ray moved ahead of the boat while the rest of the men hauled it ashore.

Wearing a set of night-vision goggles, Ray left the surf and inspected the small deserted beach surrounded by rocky cliffs.

A figure appeared from behind a sand dune wearing a black neoprene wet suit. His face mask hung loose from his neck, swim fins secured to lanyards, his Draeger rebreather strapped to his chest. Unlike conventional scuba gear used by sports divers, which emits noise and bubbles, the Draeger recycled the diver's air, removing carbon dioxide by passing it through a canister of baralyme and injecting oxygen from a small cylinder before returning the mixture back to the regulator. That eliminated bubbles or noise, providing the SEAL with a stealthy approach to the target.

"All clear, Sting," said Petty Officer First Class Dave Fox, a SEAL who Ray had trained at Coronado. Fox had an innate ability to navigate underwater at night. He had driven the minisub and the two swim pairs, which made up the security team, in total darkness to this location. Leaving the SDV parked twenty feet underwater, Fox had led his team to the beach, where they had surveyed the area for an hour before going ashore. "There's a few nice dunes back there to hide the rubber duck," he said, extending a thumb over his left shoulder toward the darkness behind him.

Ray brought a hand to his throat mike and pressed it against his larynx. "Take the duck to the dunes in back and cover it."

There was no reply, but George Yokosaka and three other SEALs hauled the CRRC ashore while following another security team member in a wet suit.

"We're out of here," said the frogman while reaching for his fins, sporting the number 945, Fox's Basic Underwater Demolition/SEAL student number. It had been almost seven years since Fox survived the grueling BUD/S training, but the number would follow him for life. "Don't have too much fun up there, and just worry about footprints beyond those dunes over there. The high tide will cover everything else in a few hours."

Ray grinned. "See ya."

In a few minutes the security team had disappeared beneath the waves, heading back to the SDV and then on to the *Polk*.

Ray removed his NVGs and used his night-vision binoculars to inspect the cliffs. After several seconds he said, "There's someone up there." He handed the binoculars to Bishop, who looked in the direction Ray pointed.

"Yep. Looks like a man. What do you think, Loca?"

Mendez took the binoculars and inspected the lone figure atop a cliff roughly a mile to their right. "It's a man all right, clutching a weapon." She handed the binoculars to Ray, who inspected the cliff once again. "It's a sentry. Do you think he saw us?"

"Should I take him out?" asked Bishop, pointing to a nearby rookie, whose weapon was a silenced Heckler & Koch PSG-1 sniper rifle. "The way he's standing on that overhang, I can hit him on the side and make him fall over the edge."

"That might be inside Tanaka's property, Chief. There could be other guards nearby," Ray said, kneeling on the sand and checking his Global Positioning System unit. He compared the longitude and latitude readings of the GPS unit with the laminated map he had extracted from a pouch on his cammies. "He's definitely inside Tanaka's estate. We'll leave him alone for now." Standing and putting away the binoculars, the map, and the GPS unit, he added, "Chief, Loca, let's make sure the duck's secured and covered. Also get one of the rookies to wipe away our footprints."

The trio walked to the sand dunes, where the rest of the

squad shoveled sand over the plastic sheet covering the boat.

"Loca, you're point. We have two hours to reach the target, eliminate the sentries without tipping Tanaka, capture the JDA chief, and secure the area. Then the chopper arrives with the feds, who will search the place for no more than fifteen minutes for high-tech stuff. Then we all get the hell out of Dodge aboard the chopper."

Mendez and Bishop had heard this in far more detail during the past twelve hours. They nodded.

Ray ran a hand through the hairless track up the side of his head. "All right, then. Everybody lock and load. Let's get moving."

The team reached a vertical section of the cliff, which ran almost two hundred feet straight up, leading them to a spot roughly a mile south of the target. Mendez removed one of two coiled 10-mm ropes from her rucksack, each a hundred twenty feet in length. As point, she also donned a padded sling and slid in a few key climbing tools. The metallic utensils rattled as she secured the sling and approached the wall.

"Need a lift?" Bishop asked as she put on a set of night-vision goggles.

She nodded while pointing to a crack four feet above her. Bishop lifted her slender frame from behind. Mendez jammed her right hand in the crack with the thumb up and outside the crack, also lifting her left leg, bent at the knee, pressing the ball of the boot against the rock surface, pulling herself up while her left hand grabbed a small boulder. In ten minutes she had climbed halfway up, keeping her upper body leaning away from the rock, forcing her feet into it.

Norma Mendez was no longer cold as she reached for a ten-foot-wide ledge protruding above her. She swung herself onto it and rested on her back, shaking each limb, perspiration soaking her cammies. She took a sip from her water bladder before reaching for the climbing tools hanging loose from the sling, selecting a titanium hex with a two-foot Kevlar attachment. She ran the hex down a crack that narrowed at the bottom, firmly wedging the titanium piece three inches inside the rock before removing one of the nylon ropes and tying the standing end to the Kevlar runner.

Pressing against her throat mike, she said "Rope," and threw the rope into the night. It uncoiled itself as it fell.

Ray caught the rope after it slapped a clump of boulders by the foot of the wall. He gave it two hard tugs, verifying that Mendez had secured it to a substantial anchor. Still, he would not risk more than one man going up at a time. He pointed to a rookie, and the SEAL immediately started climbing.

Ray removed his NVGs and used the binoculars to inspect Mendez's progress, catching her greenish silhouette already climbing the last stretch of rock.

Spiderwoman, he thought.

He shifted his attention to the sentry still standing at the top of the cliff overlooking the ocean, before scanning the rest of the beach and the sea, finally putting the binoculars away as the next SEAL went up the rope.

Ray was last, reaching the top of the cliff a bit out of breath. He frowned in disappointment. Ten years ago he would have scaled this wall without flinching. Now his lungs burned.

"You're getting old, buddy."

Drenched in sweat, he gave the rope a final tug, pulling himself up, placing his knees on the rocky ledge and rolling away from the edge. He stood and inspected his surroundings. Dense woods outlined the half-moon-shaped clearing. SEALs covered the treeline. He gathered the rope Mendez had tied to a large rock and coiled it. Slung around his left shoulder was Mendez's second rope, which Ray had also coiled after completing the first half of the climb.

He walked up to Bishop, who stood on the left side of the clearing with Norma Mendez inspecting the laminated map. Like Ray, they wore night-vision goggles, which, combined with their dark cammies, floppy hats, face paint,

and the assortment of gear, made them look like some kind
of futuristic warriors. Ray handed Mendez her nylon ropes
and pulled out his handheld GPS, switching it on. The unit
beeped twice and came alive, providing Ray with instant
longitude and latitude information.

"Perimeter secured, Sting," said Mendez.

Ray nodded and eyed the GPS display while pointing
to a spot on the map. He then inspected the luminous dial
of his small compass. "That way," he finally said.

Mendez, glistening with perspiration from the heat and
the climb, moved toward the woods. Ray followed her,
and the rest of the team fell behind him, single file, ten
feet spread. Bishop covered the rear.

Ray moved with ease, Mendez's slim silhouette, light
green in color, contrasting sharply against the dark green
jungle as she twisted her body to conform with the bends
in the heavy foliage.

His silenced MP5 leading the way, Ray wearily inspected his surroundings. Insects clicked. Branches rustled
as the breeze swept across the canopy overhead. Mosquitoes buzzed in his ears, even with the floppy hat. He felt
two lumps on the back of his neck. As he walked, he slung
the MP5, reached for the insect repellant tube, and squirted
a half inch on his palm, applying it generously to his neck
and face as the team moved steadily in a northwesterly
course.

So far this operation had progressed uneventfully. He
checked his watch and determined that they were slightly
ahead of schedule. If they did this right, the Japanese
would not know what had hit them.

If we do it right.

Ray rubbed a finger across his father's Purple Heart and
followed the point up an inclined trail layered with moss-
slick boulders and lush ferns. The mosquitoes continued
to hover but did not settle on him.

He carefully balanced himself on the slippery rocks,
keeping his knees bent, the rubber soles of his boots providing enough friction to propel himself up and forward,

the smell of mold and rotting wood mixing with the sweet-smelling resin of trees.

They continued at the same pace for twenty minutes, reaching the road that lead to Tanaka's estate, where the plan called for Ray and his team to set up a trip wire meant to delay enemy forces from the nearby base after the SEAL strike had begun.

Suddenly, Norma stopped, lifting her left fist.

Halt.

Ray did likewise, passing the signal down.

She followed it by bringing an index and middle fingers up to her eyes, like a snake's tongue.

Enemy in sight.

She stretched her index finger.

Just one.

Ray passed on the warning and also extended his hand toward the leaf-littered ground, palm facing down.

Take cover.

His squad vanished behind moss-draped trees, overgrown ferns, and a fallen log. He approached Norma, frozen in a crouch by a line of bushes overlooking a winding and unpaved road leading to the estate.

He parted the shrubbery slowly with his MP5. A shiny Toyota Land Cruiser blocked the gravel road. An Asian wearing dark trousers and a gray windbreaker stood in front of the utility vehicle clutching a machine gun, confirming Tanaka's presence in the mansion.

They waited for five minutes, verifying that the sentry was alone. Then the SEAL commander grabbed his hunting knife by the blade, raised it over his shoulder, and threw it at the guard with all his might. The black shape streaked across the night, stabbing the sentry in the neck. The guard dropped the weapon and fell to his knees, hands on his bleeding neck.

Ray and Norma jumped out of the bush and reached the Asian just as he collapsed, mouth wide open in a silent scream. The SEAL commander dragged him by his feet back into the woods while Norma picked up the machine gun, an old Uzi. Blood jetted from the Asian's neck wound as his wide-open eyes slowly lost focus before they became fixed on the trees. As he undressed him, Ray took a deep breath. He had not killed a man since Afghanistan.

The SEAL commander tossed the windbreaker and trousers to one of the rookies and pointed at the road. The young SEAL put them on and also grabbed the dead Asian's gun, taking up his temporary post by the Land Cruiser while the demolition team set up trip wires and C4 charges on the truck and nearby trees to slow down any reinforcements. The entire squad then continued on toward the clearing, spreading their forces around the target. Ray and Norma formed one of four rifle teams. Ray now led. Norma followed ten feet behind. Bishop and a rookie had gone to the edge of the cliff to disable the sentry they had spotted earlier.

Walking on tiptoes while remaining in a crouch, using the silenced MP5 to part the underbrush, Ray moved as fast as he could, realizing that he didn't have much time before someone tried to make contact with the dead Asian.

Slowly, with caution, Ray remained roughly thirty feet from the edge of the clearing, close enough to pick up any movement near the treeline, yet far enough to blend in with the surrounding vegetation.

Flies droned in the dark, some landing on his neck and forehead. Ray ignored them, his concentration focused on a shadow that had just detached itself from a tree two dozen feet ahead: the silhouette of a man backlit by the mansion's floodlights holding a rifle aimed at the clearing.

Ray stopped, briefly turned around to verify Norma's position, made a couple of hand signals, and turned toward the sentry while scanning the surroundings, searching for other shadows, finding none. His narrowed gaze landed once more on his target, a rifle hanging from the sentry's left shoulder.

Insects continued to buzz around him. He inspected his prey once more, a powerful man with a crew cut and bulging muscles stretching civilian clothing similar to that worn by the man he had killed up the road.

Moss-furred rocks bordered a downed log, half covered with sword ferns. Ray hid behind the rotting log, peeking through the ferns at the still figure just a dozen feet away. He thought about simply using the silenced MP5, but the force from the 9-mm rounds could push him into the clearing, telegraphing Ray's presence.

The Navy warrior put down the weapon and reached for his knife, which he clutched in his right hand, the steel edge protruding upward from the fist. Then slowly, with the stealth of a snake, he slid over the log and the slippery rocks, the noise from the whistling wind masking his own, the long branches of the sword ferns projecting over him, shielding him.

Beads of sweat now rolled down his forehead and accumulated over his brows as Sting Ray closed the gap to six feet before surging from under the cape of vegetation as the startled sentry began to turn around, but not before the blade, driven at an angle into the base of the neck, severed the spinal cord.

The soldier fell, dark splashes of blood streaming down his back. Ray replaced the knife in his ankle holster and dragged the body behind the fallen log, where Norma hid it beneath the ferns.

He moved with caution into the jungle beyond, the MP5 once more clasped in front of him. Searching for his next victim, feeling certain that he would find him down the edge of the clearing just like the first, the SEAL commander remained in a crouch while holding a course parallel to the treeline, predatory eyes scanning for shadows breaking the natural pattern of the thicket.

Ray paused by the decaying stump of the fallen tree. A primordial-looking fern, its leaves wider than the rest of the ferns in the area, grew out of its center and cascaded over the leaf-covered terrain. Beyond it extended a well-defined trail that looked like a tunnel in the tangled brush. At the entrance to this tunnel, flanked by a pencil-thin trunk from which palm leaves projected at an angle, stood another man, also facing the clearing, his weapon hanging loosely from his left shoulder.

Ray liked patterns, for they removed the uncertainty of his hunt. Tanaka had spaced his men around the perimeter of the clearing to obtain multiple vantage points over any intruder breaking into the estate. In the process, however, they opened themselves for an attack from the forest, which Ray once again prepared to mount.

Stealthily dragging himself past the stump, across the leaf-littered floor, Ray approached his new prey. He crawled next to a bush full of large flowers. The clicking of insects intensified, mixing with the humming of mosquitoes hovering near the flowers.

Eight feet.

The sentry remained immobile, like a dark statue attached to the side of the tunnel, next to a cloud of gnats dancing around a narrow beam from the estate's floodlights that had pierced through the branches of a cypress.

Ray inched forward, pressing his boots against the rotting tree stump—

Snap!

Ray froze. The toe of his boot had noisily dislodged a slice of bark off the stump.

The sentry pivoted on his right foot and began to turn around, hands reaching for his automatic weapon. The SEAL commander slowly released his breath as he squeezed the trigger once. A light mechanical sound, like the latch of a door, mixed with the forest's natural noises, followed by the subsonic bullet impacting flesh. The sentry fell to the ground holding his neck, collapsing on his side.

Ray listened, making certain no one had heard him. Over the next minute he received reports from his other rifle teams, informing him that the perimeter had been secured. The only remaining security force was inside the mansion, beyond the manicured lawns of the estate. The first phase of the operation had been completed. He checked his watch. One hour and forty minutes had elapsed since arriving at the beach. They had twenty more minutes to capture Tanaka and secure the area before sending the signal to the chopper, which would be already en route from the USS *Blue Ridge*.

He glanced at Norma Mendez crouched next to him in the bush encircling the estate. The two-story structure looked more like a temple than a residence, with vine-laced columns supporting the sloping roof. A cobblestone walkway connected the stone steps at the front of the house to a small stone shack on the west side and what appeared to be a heated pool beyond the shack. Hissing steam rose from the water, outlined by accent lights evenly spaced around the edge.

He spotted two guards on the far side, near the pool. Three others a hundred feet away smoked cigarettes by the columns flanking the stone steps. Suddenly, the two guards by the pool collapsed, falling to the ground without making a sound.

Ray glanced at the three guards still smoking, their weapons hanging loosely from their shoulders. He pointed at the two on the left and then pointed at himself. Next he pointed at the third guard and then at Norma Mendez, who nodded. Ray lined up his first target in the center of the MP5's forward sight. He fired in single-shot mode, feeling the weapon's light recoil as the bulky silencer absorbed the detonation of the subsonic bullet, which struck the closest guard in the chest. Before he fell, Ray already had the second guard in his sights. He fired at the same time as Norma. The remaining guards also fell.

"Northern perimeter secured. Three dead back here," came the voice from Bishop.

"Two dead by the pool. West perimeter. Area's clean," came another voice.

"One dead on the east perimeter."

"Move in," Ray ordered, before rushing across the lawn, scrambling up the steps, and reaching the heavy front door, which was unlocked. He pressed his left shoulder against it, inching it open just enough for Mendez and himself to get through.

Slate floors covered a large foyer, illuminated by round paper lamps. Stone statues of ancient warriors lined the walls. Ray slowly scanned them with the MP5 to make certain a guard was not hiding disguised as one. Satisfied, they proceeded down the long hallway, reaching the rooms in the center of the mansion, mostly officelike areas with computer equipment scattered on desks.

They continued searching, encountering minimal resistance. Mendez disabled a man in the kitchen with karate chops to the neck. Ray disabled a second man drinking hot tea in the dining room. They reached the bedrooms a minute later, swinging their weapons toward a large figure emerging from a room near the back of the mansion.

"Easy. It's me, Sting. Look at what I've found in here. The horniest guy in town."

Ray lowered the MP5 and exhaled in relief. It was Bishop. Inside the room he found Konichi Tanaka in the company of three Asian women, all covering their bare chests with their arms.

"Cyanide pills," Ray said in a brief moment of panic. He had been briefed regarding the suicidal tendencies of the Japanese cyberterrorists. There was a strong possibility that Tanaka might also try to kill himself if captured, to protect the secrecy of the operation.

Bishop grinned and held a small plastic bag with two pills. "No suicides on my watch."

Ray briefly eyed the JDA chief, who remained quiet, standing by the bed wearing only his underpants while the women sobbed and braced themselves. He checked his watch. They were two minutes ahead of schedule. So far the operation had been textbook. He turned to a rookie and said, "Send the signal and then go find George. I have a few questions for Mr. Tanaka."

*   *   *

Konichi Tanaka remained quiet, avoiding glancing at his watch as the intruders led him away from the bedroom and into his office. He had pressed a silent alarm button underneath his bed the moment the first intruder had burst inside the room. The intelligence officer had used the screaming of his whores as a distraction to alert the Yamato clan. Now all he had to do was bide his time until the rescue force arrived.

38

COMPLICATIONS

Minister Yokonawa woke up when the cellular phone rang. He stood, picking up the small unit next to his bed while his wife stirred under the covers.

"*Moshi-moshi?*" he said, half-asleep, glancing at the alarm clock. It was the middle of the night. This had better be good.

"Yokonawa-san?"

"*Hai,*" he replied, recognizing the voice of his chief of security, also a member of the Yamato clan.

"I'm afraid we may have a problem in Cape Muroto. We just received an alarm from Tanaka-san. We're sending scouts from Joshi's base to investigate now."

Fully awakened by the news, Yokonawa bolted out of bed, the phone pressed against his left ear, fearing the worst. "Send our men along with the scouts and report your observations to me directly."

"*Hai,* Yokonawa-san."

Yokonawa leaned back and closed his eyes, his mind racing through the possible scenarios, wondering if Tanaka may have been compromised by the Americans. His right-hand man in the Yamato Ichizotu may have been taken hostage, possibly facing a chemical interrogation. Yokonawa knew that he could not let Tanaka be taken prisoner. If the JDA chief had failed to crack his cyanide capsule, then it fell on the elder minister to break the investigative chain by eliminating his subordinate. Tanaka represented another line of defense, just like Matsubara and the American engineers. Each buffer zone had been designed to hold back the enemy, to keep it from reaching the core, run by Yokonawa himself.

Yokonawa checked his watch, exhaling in disappointment. He dreaded the thought of the FBI getting past Tanaka and converging on him, exposing him, shaming his family name, his country. The deceitful Americans could also try to turn the situation into an opportunity, forcing Tanaka and Yokonawa to work for them, to become their agents.

The minister closed his eyes. If that happened, Yokonawa would be forced to share national secrets with the Americans or risk exposure.

I will kill myself before I let them do that to me!

Careful not to wake up his wife, Yokonawa stood, grabbed his cellular phone, and put on a kimono before sliding the shoji screen aside and walking across the living room and into the kitchen.

He grabbed a beer from the minibar and drank it while staring at the night sky over Tokyo.

39

MURPHY'S LAW

Erika Conklin's heart pounded her chest with an intensity that matched the deafening rotor of the Navy transport helicopter as it left the deck of the LCC-class vessel and headed into the darkness. The craft suddenly dropped so low that she could see the waves a few feet below her. When she made the observation to Brent MacClaine, who sat next to her on the metallic floor in the spacious rear compartment, he told her that the helicopter was avoiding detection by Japanese coastal radar systems, especially in light of the large army base north of the target.

MacClaine handed her an object that resembled an electric shaver. "A stun gun. Just point and press this trigger. It shoots two probes up to thirty feet away."

"Why would I be needing this? I thought you said that the SEALs have secured the area."

"They have, but it never hurts to be extra careful, just in case. It's also far more effective than a shoe." He touched the bruise on his forehead.

She punched him lightly on the shoulder before inspecting the object, which had a belt strap, like her T9000 Internet communicator. "What's this?" She pointed to an attachment on the back.

"That's a reload. After you shoot the first set, snap off the spent cartridge and reload by attaching the new one.

Then point and shoot a second time. Try not to shoot yourself."

Erika made a face while inspecting the weapon one more time before strapping it next to her T9000.

MacClaine leaned down and grabbed two dark vests, handing one to Erika. "They're made out of Kevlar. Bulletproof. Put it on, just in case."

Erika was liking this less and less. "Just in case of *what*, Brent?"

MacClaine smirked while setting his vest aside. "Just in case. Don't want anything to happen to that pretty little face."

Erika ignored him, feeling the light-weight vest. She put it on over her shirt, securing it across the front with heavy-duty snaps. She had seen agents wear them before, and at the time had also felt sorry for them, risking their lives for a paycheck. Erika frowned, the thought making her want to reconsider her decision to put her life on the line again.

A little too late for that, honey.

As she gazed out of a side window, seeing nothing but stars, darkness, and the surf created by the rotor's downwash, she wondered if the reason why she had chosen to go on had anything to do with the deal she had made with Palenski or with the realization that she alone possessed the right combination of skills to put an end to the cyberterrorism strikes plaguing her nation. She decided that it was a little of both. Palenski's deal had gotten her started, and now she felt carried by the whitewater rapids of a mission in its final stage. She only hoped that the final stage led to a peaceful lake, not Niagara Falls.

She began to sweat almost right away. It felt like a furnace inside the vest. She started to take it off. "I'll put it on right before we get there."

"We *are* there," MacClaine replied as he donned his vest.

The helicopter came in from the southwest, without navigation lights, skimming the water, its pilot and copilot wearing the night-vision goggles that kept them from crashing into the sea. Land suddenly began to rise in the horizon, a mere sliver of light at first, before the yellowish glow atop the rocky cliffs slowly separated from the beach. The craft cruised over the waves breaking by the shore, maintaining altitude as it hovered over the sand, coming dangerously close to the vertical wall. Only then did the helicopter gain altitude, as it climbed vertically the two hundred feet separating it from the estate.

Erika Conklin watched the activity on the ground. Men in dark outfits used hand signals to guide the craft, which landed on a grassy field between a large mausoleumlike building and the jungle. The men approached the helicopter as it touched down. Erika could not make out their faces, which seemed to blend in with the night. Even as they walked toward the craft she had a hard time following them. They seemed to appear and disappear from her field of view, like . . .

"Ghosts," she said.

MacClaine turned to her. "What did you say?"

"Those guys outside." She pointed at the dark silhouettes. "They look like ghosts."

He patted her leg. "SEALs. Be glad they're on our side. Let's go."

She left her laptop inside the helicopter and followed MacClaine out of the decelerating craft. Two of the ghostly men waited for them. One was huge, with bulging muscles everywhere and holding a ridiculously large machine gun. His companion was . . .

A woman!

Erika thought she had seen it all, but she faced a petite woman with features hidden by heavy camouflage cream. She held a small machine gun and inspected Erika, sneering ever so slightly at her Kevlar vest.

MacClaine shouted, "I'm Special Agent MacClaine! This is Technical Analyst Conklin!"

The overgrown SEAL nodded. "Come this way," he said in a deep voice before walking away from them. The female SEAL gave them an indifferent look and also turned around. Erika and MacClaine exchanged a brief glance before following them to the front steps of a Japanese temple. Wooden columns surrounded the large structure, supporting a sloping roof.

"Did you find Tanaka?" MacClaine asked.

Neither SEAL replied. They just kept walking, leading the feds up the steps and into the front room, a spacious foyer lined with eerie, life-size statues of Japanese warriors. The dim gleam from overhead round paper lamps outlined the camouflaged, hard-edged features on a third SEAL, this one of average built but with a hairless track over his left temple and scar tissue covering his square chin. The facial scars, combined with his angular features, the camouflage cream, and the dark uniform and gear, conveyed a sense of confidence that the man knew how to handle this kind of situation. The face also looked vaguely familiar but she couldn't place it.

"I'll take it from here," the last SEAL said. The husky one and the woman went back outside. "I'm Commander Derek Ray." He turned to Erika and extended a gloved hand.

Erika shook it, suddenly remembering where she had seen that face. "Derek Ray? Aren't you the—"

"President's stepson, yes." He leaned closer and added, "but don't bother looking for the Secret Service. They didn't want to get their silk suits wet."

Erika smiled. "I'm Erika Conklin, FBI analyst. This is Special Agent Brent MacClaine. It's a pleasure meeting you."

MacClaine and Ray shook hands.

"Did you find Tanaka?" MacClaine asked.

Ray nodded. "Got him in a room back there." He headed in that direction as he continued. "Won't talk, though. One of my men speaks fluent Japanese, but he can't get him to say one word."

"You don't need a translator," said MacClaine as they stepped into a wide hallway flanked by large screens of landscapes, ducks, butterflies, and colorful flowers and birds. "Tanaka speaks over five languages, including English."

"Hope you guys have better luck. The offices are also back here. There's some computer gear in each. We left everything as we found it. Would you like to see the hardware first or the prisoner?"

"We can talk to Tanaka later," said Erika. "Right now I want to get my hands on the stuff."

Ray looked at MacClaine, who said, "It's her case."

They went into the first office area, just to the left of the hallway. Erika spotted six computers sharing two disk servers. The systems were on. She promptly turned them off and began to unhook the cables networking them. "I need these taken to the helicopter."

"Everything?" Ray asked.

"Except for the monitors and keyboards."

While Ray pressed his throat and began to speak, Erika rummaged through the cabinets and drawers, finding a number of diskettes and Zip disks labeled in Japanese. She began to hand them to MacClaine, who shoved them all in a nylon bag. By the time they were finished, three SEALs, different from the two who had greeted them at the improvised helipad, were already busy hauling gear out of the mansion.

The SEAL commander led them through two additional rooms, also containing computer hardware, but not as much as the first room. Erika was finished in less than ten minutes, collecting over two dozen Zip disks and nearly a hundred diskettes. Ray's team had secured the computer hardware in the cargo section between seats.

Erika now sat in the rear of the helicopter, next to George Yokosaka, the SEAL fluent in Japanese. MacClaine and Ray chatted with the pilot.

Suddenly, an explosion beyond the trees shook the helicopter. MacClaine came rushing back from the front and sat next to her. "We have company! Ray says that's the trip wire down the access road. Japanese troops must be heading this way!"

The SEAL team abruptly emerged from several locations at once. Three from the jungle, three more from behind columns, and the large warrior and his female companion from somewhere else. They rushed into the helicopter, sitting around the edges of the cargo section. Two SEALs flanked Tanaka, who wore a pair of slacks and undershirt. The JDA chief kept his gaze on the metallic floor. The extralarge SEAL manned one of the machine guns mounted on the left side of the craft while the female SEAL handled the right one. Both kept looking out of their small windows, weapons pointed at the access road.

Erika focused on her work. She had to get going with the wireless data dump. She pulled out her laptop and connected it to an external Zip drive. She enabled her high-speed wireless modem and hooked up via satellite to the systems lab at the J. Edgar Hoover Building in Washington. Even before the last SEAL had settled inside the craft and the rotor had begun to accelerate, the FBI analyst had already started to transfer the files from the first Zip disk, labeled JDA Confidential Files #1, as translated by Yokosaka, who browsed through the contents of the nylon bag. The transfer went quite rapidly, almost at the rate of one megabyte of information every two seconds, taking nearly a minute to complete the first thirty megabytes of data.

The helicopter left the ground and hovered for a moment before turning toward the ocean.

Erika took her eyes off the screen for one second to glance at the ground fifteen feet below, catching the glimpse of a dark figure racing across the lawn. She waved at the large SEAL behind the machine-gun mount but he was looking the wrong way. She turned to MacClaine.

"Brent, did we leave some of the SEALs behind?"

The large agent shook his head. "Shouldn't have. Why?"

"Because I think I just saw—"

Machine-gun fire erupted from multiple locations on the ground, striking the underside of the craft, punching holes through the metallic floor. Three SEALs clutched their chests as rounds ripped through them. One of them was George Yokosaka. In the same instant, Erika felt a powerful force pushing her back, shoving her against the side of the craft with animal strength.

She landed on the floor, dazed, her mind as cloudy as her vision, agonizing screams mixing with the rattling guns below. Then she felt a strong pair of hands lifting her back up.

"I've got you!" MacClaine shouted over the ear-piercing noise shaking the craft as the side gunners returned the fire, the multiple reports deafening inside the crowded compartment as they sprayed the ground with explosive rounds.

"What . . . what happ—"

"You got shot, but the vest took it! Relax! I've got you!" He placed his body in between her and the floor while hugging her.

"We're under attack!" shouted Ray into his headgear as smoke began to fill the compartment. The muzzle flashes from the side guns created a stroboscopic effect through the haze. Spent cartridges flew through the air, ejected out of the side of the weapons. "Get us out of here! Now, dammit!"

Two more SEALs fell to the floor, blood spurting from their chests. Tanaka also collapsed, his abdomen torn open by the rapid fire, spilling his smoking intestines on the floor. The smell of burnt flesh mixed with that of gunpowder.

The helicopter trembled but began to move away from the line of fire, flying over the jungle north of the mansion. The gunners jerked their weapons in many directions while firing, creating enough of a distraction that the ground activity momentarily ceased.

Trees scraped the helicopter's underside as the pilot struggled to gain altitude, but the single turbine responded by spewing inky smoke.

"Hold on!" shouted Derek Ray, his features barely visible through the murky cloud enveloping the disabled craft. "We're going down!"

The helicopter sank in the forest, turning on its side as it bounced against tree trunks, shuddering when the rotors cut into the upper branches, pruning the treetops before breaking up.

"Brent!" Erika screamed as the helicopter fell through the heavy canopy, snapping branches, tearing vines, stopping halfway down to the leaf-littered terrain.

MacClaine embraced her tightly, using his body to cushion her as wood cracked and the craft once more dropped, abruptly hooking to a lower branch, which gave a moment later with a loud snapping sound. They fell a third time, stopping just a few feet from the ground, the smell of gunpowder mixing with that of spilled fuel.

Then a fist of flames turned the night into day.

40

BAD NEWS

"Damned wireless links!" complained Charlie Chang while glancing at the bar on the side of the screen, which informed him that only 30 percent of the transfer had completed successfully. "They're too unreliable!"

Roman Palenski gnawed impatiently on an unlit cigar. "How long before you can reconnect?"

Chang stood and shook his head. He wore a white lab coat over a pair of shorts and a shirt. His pale legs beneath the knee-length coat gave the impression that he wore nothing underneath. "Don't know, sir. It's up to her. I can't do anything from this end except receive data."

Palenski rubbed his bald head. "Can you do something with what you have so far?"

Chang eyed the screen and nodded. "I've got, like, almost a hundred meg of data in there." He patted the side of the desktop PC. "We'll get busy translating. See what we find." He waved two FBI agents over. Both were fluent in Japanese.

Palenski stepped aside as the trio huddled around the system. Chang led the show, typing and clicking the mouse while windows popped up on the screen, each filled with Kanji characters.

"Well?" Palenski said after a couple of minutes, hands in his pockets now while shifting his weight anxiously from leg to leg, nibbling the end of the cigar. "What are you finding?"

"It's going to be a while, sir," said Chang, pointing to a window on the screen. "Looks like we got lots of files but no directory that tells us how they're organized. That portion of the data must have gotten lost when the transmission was terminated."

"Great," Palenski mumbled. "Just fucking great. Let's see what else goes wrong tonight."

The door to the lab swung open and one of his aides ran inside the cavernous room, a blond in her midtwenties with shapely legs and a skirt too tight for running. She held a mobile phone in her left hand.

"What now?" he asked.

She handed him the phone. "The Pentagon, sir. Something's gone terribly wrong."

Palenski winced, feeling acid squirting in his stomach as he pressed the small unit against his left ear. "Yeah?"

"Roman, Vuono here. We're really screwed. The *Ridge* got a brief emergency transmission from the team. They think the chopper got shot down outside Tanaka's place."

Palenski closed his eyes and bit hard into the cigar.

41

MODERN HEROES

SOUTHERN JAPAN

"Move! Let's go! *Now!*" shouted Derek Ray as he helped Erika Conklin out of the burning craft. Erika caught a glimpse of the nylon bag holding the disks and she snatched it just as she left the cabin, clutching it tightly to her chest.

Her eyes stung from the smoke, which also burned her throat. She felt carried by multiple sets of hands down to the ground, where someone dropped her next to a large rock.

She sat up, confused, dazed, rubbing her eyes, coughing to clear her airway, feeling the intense heat as the fire spread throughout the craft. She watched Brent jumping out of the wreck, landing on his side, rolling away from the inferno.

"It's gonna blow!" shouted Norma Mendez, who along with Bishop and Ray had been the only ones to survive the attack. The rest of the team had either been killed by the ground fire or were being consumed by the spreading flames.

Bishop was about to run back inside the burning chopper to pull out his teammates but both Ray and Mendez held him back.

"They're gone!" shouted Ray. "There's nothing you can do!"

"Come!" Mendez screamed, a hand pulling on his gear vest. "Come. Let's go!"

"Move out! Now! Loca, you're point!" said Ray. "You." He pointed at MacClaine, who stood by Erika. "Know how to use this?" Ray held out an automatic weapon he had pulled out of the fire.

"You bet," MacClaine said, reaching for it.

"Good. Now you two follow her." He pointed at Norma Mendez. "We'll cover the rear."

"We have company, Sting!" said Bishop, pointing toward the estate.

Erika looked to her left as she ran behind MacClaine, who clutched the weapon in both hands. Men in camouflage gear moved toward them in swarms, dark figures backlit by the pulsating flames, their automatic weapons crackling like popcorn in the night.

A few hundred feet from the burning wreck the jungle became pitch-black. Then she heard Ray screaming.

"Loca, Bishop, NVGs!" Ray shouted over the machine-gun fire, using his free hand to put on the night-vision goggles hanging from his neck. "Bishop, take the woman. Loca, guide MacClaine. Move it! Fall back to the first checkpoint."

The night turned light green, just in time for Ray to leap over a fallen tree and other debris, the MP5 clutched in his right hand. He set the fire selector to full automatic fire and emptied the magazine on the incoming men, forcing them to hit the ground. He followed that with two grenades before scrambling after his team.

They continued running for five minutes, dashing past heavy foliage, reaching a cluster of moss-draped trees leading to a trail that veered around to the same side of the jungle that they had used on the way up.

"We're too hot," Norma Mendez said over the squad channel. "Coming up to the first checkpoint."

Derek Ray reached a curtain of tangled vines by the

cluster of trees. Beams of light forked through the foliage, searching for him. He inserted a fresh magazine in the MP5, aimed it at the incoming lights, and fired. The suppressed weapon vibrated in his hands as silenced rounds found their marks while he swept the jungle at waist level before throwing two grenades at the incoming men.

Ray turned away from the flashes to avoid getting blinded by the NVGs.

The blasts tore through the bush, followed by screams.

He continued, across a foggy meadow, disappearing in the jungle at the other end, reaching the first checkpoint. Mendez, MacClaine, Bishop, and the FBI woman waited for him.

Lights in the woods across the meadow made him narrow his eyes in anger. The Japanese were coming in large numbers. His decimated team could not survive such head-on confrontation. He had to discourage the soldiers from continuing their pursuit.

"Move it, Chief. You're point. Norma, you stay with me. You two follow the chief to the second checkpoint."

As the SEAL vanished in the foliage with the feds in tow, Ray and Mendez reached for their rucksacks and removed four M-18 Claymore mines, quickly setting each shaped charge twenty feet apart across the edge of the meadow, facing the incoming enemy. In less than a minute they had them wired to four M57 firing devices, or clackers, hand detonators in the shape of small staple guns.

Lying side by side behind a tree stump, they waited while the first soldiers emerged out of the woods and cautiously walked in the starlit meadow. Others followed when their compatriots didn't get shot at. Within thirty seconds over twenty men appeared, moving straight for the SEAL trap.

Ray waited until the enemy force was within a dozen feet, and nodded. He held two clackers. Mendez held the other two. They pressed them in unison.

The antipersonnel mines, each packing seven hundred steel balls behind a charge of C4 explosives, went off with flesh-ripping force, fusillading the enemy with the energy equivalent to two dozen shotguns being fired at once.

Erika Conklin felt a bit out of breath but strong enough to keep up with Bishop and MacClaine. She shuddered when a powerful blast tore through the night, followed by the agonizing screams of many men.

"What . . . what was that?" she asked MacClaine, running in front of her.

"Bad news . . . for the Japs," he said, rushing through a short meadow before entering another strip of forest.

They kept the pace for a nearly unbearable ten minutes, covering what Erika estimated to be at least a half mile before reaching a small clearing.

"Hold it," Bishop said, inspecting the path they had just taken. He put a hand to his throat. "Reached second checkpoint and holding." Then he pressed a finger against his left ear, nodded, and said, "Got it." He turned to them. "We wait here."

Still clutching the nylon bag, Erika sat down, panting, breathing in short sobbing gasps, swallowing hard, and breathing heavily again, feeling she was asphyxiating.

MacClaine sat next to her, putting a hand on her shoulder. "Easy, there. Take it easy and breath slowly or you'll hyperventilate. Do as I do."

Erika nodded, her face inches from his as she followed MacClaine's breathing pattern, inhaling deeply through her nostrils, holding it, and exhaling through her mouth. It took her just a couple of minutes before her breathing became normal.

"There," he said, tousling her hair while smiling. "You did all right. We lost Tanaka, but at least you were smart enough to grab the files."

She sat up, rubbing her aching chest, where the vest had stopped a round from ripping her open. "My chest feels like it's on fire."

Bishop knelt next to them. "Keep it low," he whispered. "Sound travels far in the woods."

Erika nodded. "Sorry," she replied. "All of this is a bit new for me."

"You're doing fine," Bishop said, a grin breaking his stolid face. "We managed to delay the enemy for a while. They're going to be pretty busy picking up the pieces."

"How are we getting out of here?" asked Erika. "Are they going to send another helicopter?"

Bishop shook his head. "Afraid not. Looks like we're going out the same way we came in."

"Don't tell me," MacClaine said. "In the drink?"

Bishop nodded. "We got a boat hidden in the sand."

"How do we get down from the cliffs to the beach?"

Bishop told them.

A boat? A sub? A little climb down to the beach? Erika closed her eyes, refusing to believe that all of this was actually happening to her, and all because she had written that damned password-snatching virus four years ago. Her body was a mess. Muscles that she didn't know existed protested the physical abuse she had endured in the past few days with an intensity that matched the pounding in her temples, making her wish that she had never agreed to assist Palenski in this capacity. Maybe she should have just stuck to completing her time at the Bureau instead of taking Palenski's shortcut, which had seemed quite attractive at the time. Little did she know that the contract included bodily injury and the possibility of violent death.

Violent death.

She pressed her lips together, chastising herself for feeling so selfish. Many innocent people had died violent deaths because of the sabotaged integrated circuits, because of the lust for global dominance by some extreme faction in Japan. Trains had derailed, buildings had burned to the ground, planes had fallen from the sky, entire cities had turned into battle zones following power blackouts. Men, women, and children had been killed, maimed, burned. People had lost spouses. Parents had lost their children. Children had been orphaned. Death and destruction reigned in the land of the free.

How dare you complain about sore muscles and a few bruised ribs?

"You okay?" asked MacClaine.

Erika opened her eyes, gazing into his blackened face. "I'm fine," she said in a low voice while standing. "Just fine, but our country isn't, and today we failed—"

"Shhh," Bishop said, motioning her to get down while shifting his huge machine gun to his left flank.

Erika complied, crouching next to MacClaine, who picked up his weapon and aimed it in the same direction as Bishop.

Ray and Mendez reached their position, kneeling next to Bishop. Ray held up four fingers and pointed to the trees behind him and then to the foliage in front of him. Bishop and Norma nodded and then rushed toward the other side of the clearing, waving Erika and MacClaine over.

They followed the two warriors. "There's a search party right behind us," Bishop whispered.

MacClaine noticed that Ray remained hiding behind a large fern.

The foursome crossed a wall of tangled vines and lost themselves in the forest. Norma led, followed by MacClaine and Erika. Bishop covered the rear.

Commander Derek Ray watched them leave and waited patiently, slinging the MP5, reaching for his knife when hearing hastening footsteps over leaves and dry branches coming from the direction of Tanaka's estate. He had seen them running single file a few minutes ago, and Mendez and he had made enough noise to lead them this way.

The warrior frowned under the camouflage cream as the first soldier went by, a dark figure in fatigues clutching a rifle.

The SEAL commander curled the fingers of his left hand over the rubber handle of his black, double-edge steel knife.

A second figure rushed past his position, roughly ten

feet behind the first. Ray watched him disappear, followed by a third soldier.

Sting Ray rose to a deep crouch, wondering if he should use the silenced MP5 instead of the blade, but the disciplined warrior in him forced him to stick to the most silent weapon of all, clutching it until his knuckles turned white.

The last soldier neared. Ray heard no one behind him. A tall, corpulent man holding a light machine gun rushed across the tangle underbrush with powerful strides. Ray waited, his cammies blending him with the green and brown hues of his surroundings. Predatory eyes watched from behind thin vines and lush ferns at the unsuspecting prey hurrying down the trail.

The attack was sudden. Ray lunged, expertly maneuvering himself behind the running silhouette, close enough to maximize his advantage, yet far away to avoid telegraphing his presence.

He used his free hand to latch on to the soldier's neck from behind. As expected, the forward momentum of the bulky figure, almost twice the size of the slender Derek Ray, nearly lifted the SEAL off his feet. But he had anticipated that and already had his left hand coming down and around, the razor-sharp blade finding its intended target, slicing through skin and cartilage, severing the larynx.

Then Ray let go of him and watched him drop the weapon, veer off course, and crash against a tree off to the left of the path, a sharp branch impaling his abdomen, holding him up while blood jetted from the inch-deep gash carved by the knife Ray still clutched.

Ray hurried after the other soldiers. The woods rushed past him as he sprinted with the energy of a wild cat, his leg muscles protesting the effort, his nostrils flaring as he took in lungfuls of warm, humid air. He spotted the next figure fifteen feet ahead, a dark green silhouette partly obscured by the dense vegetation and by the tears filming his bloodshot eyes.

Ray closed the gap, vines and branches scratching him as he decided that the soldiers made enough noise to mask the light mechanical sounds of his suppressed MP5.

Ten feet.

Ray pressed on with a hunter's determination, the silencer of his Heckler & Koch MP5 piercing the thick undergrowth as he closed the gap to eight feet, index finger fixed around the trigger, his left hand under the silencer, dark eyes on the back of a soldier who had made the cardinal mistake of not checking his rear.

The noise of his quarry masking his own, Ray fired once, twice, both rounds finding their marks on the back of the soldier, who collapsed over some boulders, limbs twisted at unnatural angles.

Ray didn't bother to stop, leaping over him and going after the next soldier, who continued to follow the leader, totally unaware of the missing men.

Ray fired again, this time from a distance of fifteen feet. The soldier went down with a scream, another figure sprawled in the bush.

One more.

Ray jumped over his latest victim and searched for the remaining one as he continued running, quickly realizing his mistake. There was no one in front of him anymore. The lead soldier must have heard his comrade scream and—

Before he could stop and hide, Ray saw an elbow appear from behind a tree, and he trembled from the powerful blow delivered to his nose.

Crimson spots flashed in front of his eyes as his legs gave and he fell on his side, only to catch a glimpse of a swinging boot striking his solar plexus. The powerful kick sent him rolling over the leaves. He had barely stopped moving when a second kick shoved him in the opposite direction. A third kick to his groin left him praying for death. He felt his bladder muscles weaken and fought for control as the man shouted Japanese phrases while poking him with the muzzle of his weapon.

Derek Ray could barely hear the soldier, his abdomen and groin blazing like fire, tears bursting from his eyes, mixing with the blood channeling out of his nostrils. Curled in a fetal position, gasping for the air he couldn't breathe fast enough, stifled sobs rattling in his gorge, Ray tried to focus in spite of the excruciating pain.

The man hissed more foreign phrases, the alien sounds blending with the distant shouts of men.

The soldier's rapid Japanese came accompanied by a second kick to the groin. The savage pain streaking up his burning testicles ate him from the inside, scourging him, raking his intestines like a sizzling iron claw.

Ray heard the man's voice rattling, but it seemed distant, far away from the pain-maddened reality of his predicament. Even if he had been fluent in Japanese, he could not have answered. The demon clamping his throat prevented him from uttering the most primitive of sounds.

But he could still see the shape of the enemy looming over him, a hand on the knife, the other on the firearm, a boot shoved against Ray's throat, pinning him down.

Then Ray heard a scream, and for a moment he thought it was his own. The soldier fell to his knees, a hand on his neck as he frantically looked in both directions before vanishing from his field of view. Silence followed. Then something scampered noisily behind him.

"Hey, Sting."

Ray heard the voice of Norma Mendez, also distant but welcomed, for it meant that he would live to fight another day.

"Boy, that guy sure did you good."

Ray, albeit dazed, did manage to murmur, "No . . . shit. Th—thanks, Loca."

"Anytime."

Slowly, with the help of Norma Mendez, Ray managed to stand, the pain from his groin and abdomen still arresting. His eyes continued to tear, forcing him to blink rapidly.

"Good thing I decided to double back and check up on you. Better get out of here, though. I hear choppers."

Focus slowly returned to Ray, and with it the realization

that she was right. He remembered the high-altitude photos of the base, recalled those transport helicopters. "Let's go," he said, mustering strength.

Erika looked at MacClaine in sheer disbelief as they reached the edge of the abyss, the sea breeze whipping her face, the whistling noise mixing with helicopters in the distance. Dan Bishop put away the small radio he had been using to try to make contact with a nearby submarine.

"Did you reach anybody?"

He shook his head and uncoiled the ropes Norma Mendez had given him, tying one to a nearby tree, the other end to the second rope, and throwing both into the night.

"Great," she said.

"Don't worry," said Bishop, walking up to them. "You'll be down on the beach in no time."

"And then what?" asked Erika.

"We get on the boat and head out. Hopefully somebody will pick us up before daylight."

Shouts and gunfire echoed in the woods.

Bishop extended a thumb toward the trees and added, "But our odds are surely much better than staying here. We better get moving. You ever done this before?" Bishop asked MacClaine.

The fed nodded. "I was in the reserves for a few years back in the seventies."

"And you?"

"Grew up on a ranch. I can handle it." She tied the nylon bag to the side of her blue jeans.

The firing intensified. Bishop pressed a hand against his throat mike. "Where are you, Sting?" He listened for a moment and then pointed at MacClaine. "They're very hot. Choppers just dropped fresh troops in the bush. We need to be down in a few minutes to make way for Sting and Loca. You go down first and hold the rope for her. I'll go third."

MacClaine used Bishop's knife to cut off the bottom of

his pants, draping the cloth over his hands while walking over to the edge. He looked down at the sandy beach, and shrugged. "Just like in the old days at Fort Hood."

"Careful, Brent," Erika said, touching him in the arm.

"I'll manage."

"Avoid lateral motion while descending to minimize the strain on the rope," said Bishop. "Also unbuckle your belt and loop it over the rope for stability."

MacClaine complied. Holding the rope with both hands, he stood at the edge. "Pretty dark down there."

Bishop nodded, handing him a penlight. "There's a rubber boat covered with sand and debris nearby. Use this to find it."

MacClaine pocketed the small light and was gone. Erika crossed her arms and took a deep breath. It was then that she realized that she had the T9000 personal communicator with her, shoved in the pocket of her jeans underneath the bulletproof vest.

Erika inspected the unit to make sure it had not been damaged. Bishop walked over, his large hulk towering over her.

"What's that?"

She told him.

"Can you call somebody with it?"

"If it's not busted I should be able to reach Washington."

Ray dashed through the jungle, following the slim silhouette of Norma Mendez as the two SEALs attempted to outrun a group of soldiers that had rappelled into the bush from a hovering helicopter.

His lungs burning, as well as his legs, Ray said, "Hold."

Norma halted, swinging around, weapon ready. Ray veered to her left and knelt on the cushion of leaves layering the ground.

"Let's shed some gear," he said, removing his backpack, which contained his third-line equipment, the gear that he needed the least to survive. Norma did likewise, removing the C4 charges and her last Claymore mine. Ray had none left. The SEALs transferred the ammunition clips from the backpack into empty pockets of their gear vest, which contained their second-line equipment.

"Set the C4," Ray said, taking the backpacks and the Claymore and moving twenty feet down the trail. "I'll take care of this baby."

Norma molded a half pound of C4 against a rock. She ran a trip wire across the path, connecting it to the safety pin of a grenade, which she pressed against the plastic explosive. She completed the operation in less than one minute. When she joined Ray, the SEAL commander had the deadly Claymore ready, facing the incoming enemy.

The two warriors moved thirty feet away and waited, listening intently for the rustling of leaves and the scraping of cloth against vines and tree bark.

The first blast illuminated the jungle with a bright flash, followed by the cries of the wounded and the angry shouts of their comrades, some of whom continued down the trail.

Ray and Norma dropped behind a wide tree as the remaining soldiers approached the Claymore. Ray pressed the clacker but nothing happened. The soldiers ran past it, getting dangerously close to the SEALs.

"Shit!" Ray hissed. "It didn't go off."

The soldiers were right on top of them. The SEALs swung their weapons in their direction and fired.

The first two figures fell back, collapsing against the men following behind. Muzzle flashes came alive in the night, the multiple reports slicing through the forest just as the sound of a near miss buzzed in Ray's left ear. Additional gunfire broke out from their left flank. A sinking feeling descended on the SEAL commander when realizing that the enemy was spreading across the area to try to sandwich them in a deadly cross-fire. Two rounds exploded on the tree next to him. Clouds of bark stung his side.

Norma swung her weapon to the new target, firing the

remaining rounds and reloading the Uzi. Ray grabbed her by the shoulder and pulled her back just as her chest burst with blood.

"Sting!" She fell to her side, clutching the right side of her chest, her wide-open mouth gasping for air.

"Bastards!" he shouted over the deafening gunfire, uncontrolled anger swelling inside of him. He grabbed her Uzi, firing it with his left hand and the MP5 with his right, sweeping the jungle at waist level until both weapons ran dry. He dropped the Uzi, and reloaded the MP5, noticing that he only had two magazines left, and swung Norma's light frame over his right shoulder.

"My legs," she moaned. "I can't . . . feel them."

Tears welling in his eyes, the SEAL commander raced down the trail toward the clearing. He had to get her out of there immediately.

"You better put your phone away," said Bishop the moment an explosion and gunfire rattled the woods nearby. He put on his night-vision goggles and looked down the cliff. "MacClaine's almost through. Get ready to go." He handed Erika two pieces of terry cloth. "Drape this over your hands to keep the rope from burning them."

Erika turned off the T9000 and strapped it on her belt. She had dialed Palenski but the call had failed to go through even though the signal strength was halfway up the scale. "We'll have to try later." She tied the cloth to her hands before grabbing the taut nylon rope, looping two of the straps of her bulletproof vest over the rope for security.

Bishop stood at the edge, a hand on the rope as he gazed down the vertical wall with the NVGs.

"He's finished. Go, go, go!"

Heart pounding, mouth dry, Erika began her descent, keeping her feet against the rock while climbing down slowly, working her hands one at a time. She didn't glance up or down, not that it would have done her any good. In the moonless night she could barely see the rocky wall in front of her.

And so she continued, foot after agonizing foot, clutching the rope firmly with one hand while lowering the other beneath the first, and repeating the process over and over. She nearly lost her footing once but quickly regained it without losing her grip.

"I see you," a familiar voice said below, over the sound of breaking waves and the whistling wind. "Just another twenty feet."

Erika listened to MacClaine, feeling a surge of energy as she continued her descent, ignoring her burning muscles until she felt a pair of strong arms catching her, setting her on the sand.

"I'm glad you've made it," he said. "For a moment there I thought—"

There was a large commotion at the top. Gunfire followed by shouts and more gunfire.

"Come, follow me." MacClaine led the way using the penlight. "I've found the boat. We need to get it ready. From the sounds of it I don't think we'll have much time to do that after the SEALs get down here."

"That's an order, dammit!" Ray shouted while facing the jungle after setting Norma Mendez on the ground next to Bishop. "Field-dress the wound and then get her to the beach while I hold them back!"

"I'm not leaving without my commanding officer!" Bishop replied, slicing open Norma's shirt, exposing a bullet wound just above her right breast. Bishop gave her two shots of morphine and expertly applied a field dressing, taking just under two minutes to do so.

"Cold . . . I'm . . . so . . . my legs . . ." Norma mumbled, eyes closed while turning her head from side to side.

"She needs help! Get her on that rubber duck to the clinic on the *Polk* or the *Ridge*! But get her out of here! Now move it! I'll handle these bastards."

"Here!" Bishop said, dropping his M60 machine gun by Ray's feet, along with two boxes of rounds, two Claymore mines, and his last two grenades from his rucksack. He clasped Ray's left shoulder. "I'll see you in hell, Sting."

Ray put a hand over Bishop's. "Lock and load, my friend."

Bishop nodded. "Lock and load."

"I'm taking a lot of them with me. Just get her out of here."

Ray set the Claymores facing the jungle while Bishop clipped Norma's H-harness to his own and disappeared down the cliff.

The SEAL commander heard noises in several directions at once. He pocketed the grenades, grabbed the huge M60 machine gun and ammunition boxes, and ran the wires from the Claymores while retreating behind a fallen tree at the edge of the clearing, wedging himself between the rotting trunk and a huge cypress, which Bishop had used to secure the nylon rope for their hasty getaway.

He set the M60 in front of him, opened one of the ammo boxes, and ran the belt into the feeder on the side of the weapon. He set Bishop's grenades by his feet, attached clackers to the wires and waited.

Touching his father's Purple Heart, Commander Derek Sting Ray bravely faced the incoming shapes head on, swinging the M60 in their direction and firing in full automatic mode. He would protect this cliff with his life.

The large weapon began spitting rounds at the rate of five-hundred-and-fifty per minute, its muzzle flashes illuminating the bush like sheet lightning.

MacClaine began tugging on the Zodiac, roughly twelve feet long and six across. The sand and debris fell to the sides as he pulled on a rope attached to the front of the vessel and began dragging it toward the water. Erika joined in, her sneakers sinking in the sand, her arms, already exhausted from the steep descent, throbbing every time she yanked on the rope. Sweat dripped from her forehead and into her eyes, stinging them. The bulletproof vest was cooking her insides, but she chose to keep it on. It had already saved her life once.

She wiped the side of her face against her shoulder while keeping the pressure on the rope, towing the raft toward the shore. The multiple reports from the cliff, combined with the stroboscopic flashes intensified their hauling effort.

Derek Ray kept his index finger on the trigger while the M60 rattled in his hands. The Japanese, being efficient at almost everything, including guerrilla warfare, converged their troops on this rocky cliff, making his job harder by the minute. A helicopter loomed over the clearing. Ray turned the M60 in its direction, using tracers to adjust his fire, pounding the side of the hovering craft until smoke and flames burst from the single turbine. The craft trembled and backed away, getting out of the line of fire.

Ray returned his attention to the dark silhouettes crossing his field of view, some of them trying to reach the nylon rope. He held them back with his cover fire, which he knew he would be unable to maintain indefinitely. He had already consumed one of the two ammunition boxes for the M60, and the MP5 only had one magazine left.

But he pressed on while facing a far more powerful enemy, refusing to give up, willing to give up his life to buy his subordinates, the FBI agents, and their coveted cargo of computer disks the precious minutes they needed to get on the raft and disappear in the dark ocean.

And so he continued to fire, continued to pound trees, turning them into mulch, continued to cut down branches and vines, forcing the enemy to remain hidden, to stay out of sight, to hold back their attack. Then the M60 ran dry and moments later the dark shapes of armed men loomed across the defoliated forest. Kicking Bishop's weapon aside, Ray waited until several figures ventured into the clearing.

Hiding behind the log, he pressed both clackers. The deafening sound rumbled the cliff top, followed by moaning and screaming. Picking up the MP5, Ray set it in single-shot mode to conserve ammunition and waited, surveying his killing ground.

More figures left the woods. Ray fired. One dropped. The others returned the fire. Several rounds struck the cypress, resulting in multiple bursts of bark and the whipping sound of the nylon rope snapping.

"Bastards!" he shouted as he watched the end of the rope dash across the clearing and go over the edge.

Bishop used his own body to cushion Norma's fall as the rope gave way and he fell several feet into the sandy beach. Norma moaned. Bishop grunted from the impact but recovered quickly, getting to his feet, unclipping Norma's vest, checking that the field dressing was still secured to her chest, and cradling her while looking for the feds. He spotted them halfway to the water, dragging the rubber duck.

He rushed toward them.

Ray threw the empty MP5 to the side and dove beneath the fallen log while grabbing the Sig Sauer. The incoming figures pounded the log. Ray rolled away from it, grabbed the two grenades by his feet, and threw them at a group of men thirty feet away.

The blasts came seconds later, powerful, bright, followed by moaning and shouts and more gunfire from a different direction. The woods around him began to collapse under the heavy fire as the SEAL commander crawled to the edge of the abyss while remaining close to the tree line, hoping to have lost his pursuers.

He put on the night-vision goggles for a moment and

glanced down at the beach, exhaling in relief when spotting Bishop and Norma joining the feds by the shore. He started to back away silently in the night.

Soldiers raced into the clearing but didn't go after him, confirming his suspicion that they had lost him. Instead they began to fire their weapons at the beach.

Ray removed the NVGs, feeling anger swelling inside of him. The several hundred feet separating the Japanese soldiers from his escaping team was not far enough to guarantee their survival.

Touching his father's Purple Heart with his left hand, Sting Ray lifted his right arm, seeing no choice but to give away his position. He aimed the weapon at the dark figures twenty feet away and fired. Three of them fell over the edge while screaming. Two dove for cover. The rest returned the fire.

As Ray grabbed his last grenade and pulled on the safety pin, he felt a stabbing pain on his left leg, followed by others on his right shoulder, chest, and abdomen.

Lids twitching as he lay there bleeding, numb, Ray glanced at the stars. Figures converged on him. Ray had always wondered how his father felt before his death. Now he knew. His father had been angry, just as Ray was now enraged. He despised these men for taking away from him the pleasure of seeing his son being born, growing up, becoming a man, like his father and his grandfather before him. He hated them for robbing his son of his father, for making him wonder for an entire lifetime who Derek Ray had really been, the man behind the decorated hero in the picture on the mantle.

As his vision tunneled, Ray, able to feel the pear-shaped object still clutched in his right hand, released it.

The Japanese squad gathering around the fallen warrior was puzzled at the grin on the man's face as he expired. A moment later they learned why.

*   *   *

"Get on the boat!" shouted MacClaine as another blast at the top of the cliff rocked the night.

They had reached the shore, waves lapping his knees. Bishop had already placed Norma inside the boat and was helping Erika get on while he and MacClaine pushed it through the surf.

The fusillade from above, which had started moments ago and abruptly stopped, picked up again. Sand exploded behind them as the two men pushed hard, forcing the boat into deeper waters, before also climbing on and beginning to row. Erika joined in while Bishop started the engine, which purred to life. He floored it and the boat gathered speed.

"Take this!" Bishop shouted at MacClaine while pointing at the outboard. "I have to look after her! And you, see if you can reach somebody on that phone!"

MacClaine became the coxswain, keeping the vessel's nose pointed at the dark horizon while Erika began to fiddle with the T9000. Bishop knelt by Norma and changed the field dressing, already soaked in blood. He removed the 500-ml bag of Ringer's lactate from his vest and applied the IV to her left forearm just as he had been taught at Coronado, just as he had done multiple times to other wounded SEALs in Grenada, Desert Storm and Afghanistan.

"Stay with me, Loca!"

"I . . . cold . . . Bishop . . . Dan?"

"I'm here. I'm here with you."

"Sting?"

Bishop shook his head. "He's the reason we were able to make it to the boat."

"*Ca-cabrónes* . . . I hope . . . rot in hell." She turned her head and began to cough.

Bishop turned an angered face to the cracking of machine-gun fire. Rounds continued to fall around them. Two of them struck the boat just as it cleared the waves, multiple hissing sounds making Erika clench her teeth while trying to dial Washington but the call didn't go through.

"Dammit!" shouted Bishop, reaching for a large plastic bag secured to the corner of the boat with Velcro straps.

"What's that?" asked MacClaine as he kept the deflating boat facing the ocean.

"Small raft!"

The SEAL unwrapped it and waited for a couple of minutes until MacClaine got the deflating Zodiac a half mile away from shore, out of the range of the guns, whose distant cracking no longer posed a danger for them. Pulling a cord on the small canister of compressed air attached to the raft, Bishop threw it overboard while holding on to a rope. A dark green flat raft roughly seven feet square inflated in seconds.

While Bishop held on to a nylon rope that ran through dozens of metallic loop holes around the raft, Erika and MacClaine transferred Norma onto it and then climbed aboard themselves. Erika kept the diskettes in the nylon bag from touching the water.

As the Zodiac tipped backward because of the weight of the outboard and fuel tank, Bishop jumped over, sea water running over the top of the raft, which was meant to carry only three passengers. At least it kept them afloat and the South Pacific waters were not cold this time of the year.

They watched the boat sink. While Bishop tended Norma's wound, Erika tried to reach Washington again. This time she used the communicator's E-mail system, while she tried to keep it dry as waves lapped the sides of the raft, white foam running across it's surface, wetting her jeans.

The T9000 followed its boot-up sequence. She launched the software and waited as the system established a wireless satellite link.

Bishop pointed at two helicopters hovering over the beach, obviously searching for them. "Whatever you're going to do, you'd better do it quick."

42

NEW CONNECTION

"Stop the presses!" shouted Charlie Chang the moment a window popped up on his system. "Get Palenski over here right away!" Two men raced out of the systems lab while he read the words on the screen

Erika:	You there, Charlie?
Chang:	Boss! Where are you? Are you okay?
Erika:	We're floating on a raft just off the coast of Japan! We need help and quick!
Chang:	Do you have coordinates?

43

PREDATORS

SOUTHERN JAPAN

"Coordinates," Erika said to Bishop, who leaned over in the raft while she pecked away on the tiny keyboard.

He glanced at the handheld GPS and gave them to her in longitude and latitude. She typed them in.

Chang:	Palenski's right here. The coordinates are being sent to the Pentagon to get you guys help. Hang in there.
Erika:	Thanks. We have a wounded SEAL with us. Please also get some paramedics ready.
Chang:	Got it. Palenski wants to know what happened to the rest of the team.

Erika spent a couple of minutes providing details of the mission, including the brave stand by Commander Derek Ray to hold back the enemy until they could escape.

Chang:	The boss tells me that a rescue helicopter from the *Blue Ridge* is on its way, as well as two F-16s from our forces in South Korea to keep the enemy away until the helicopter gets there. Flight surgeon and emergency equipment is on board. Hang in there. ETA thirty minutes for the helicopter. Less than five for the air force jets, which already have the enemy choppers on missile lock as a warning to leave the area.

Erika: Great. By the way, were you able to download any of the data I
            sent before we got shot down?
Chang: About 100 meg. We're still deciphering. Nothing so far.
Erika: I managed to salvage all of the Zip disks and many diskettes.
            As soon as I get to a computer I'll send them over.
Chang: Awesome! Say, Palenski wants you sign off to conserve your
            battery. Check back with us in 30 if the chopper's not there.
Erika: All right. Thanks.
Chang: Glad you're all right.

"How is she doing?" Erika asked after terminating the
transmission and powering down the unit. Enemy helicopters hovered near the spot where they had boarded the
Zodiac. Then they moved back inland, obviously having
detected the American jets' missile lock warning.

Bishop shook his head. "Doesn't look like the bullet
damaged anything vital, but I can't seem to stop the hemorrhage. How long before help gets here?"

She told him.

Bishop checked the IV and frowned. "I'm pumping her
with fluids but she's losing them faster than I can replenish
them." He looked at Norma Mendez, who had her eyes
closed but kept shaking her head from side to side while
mumbling that she was cold. "I don't think she can hold
out much longer without real medical help."

MacClaine pushed Erika toward the center of the raft
while pointing to a dark shape cutting through a wave a
few feet from the raft. "Looks like the Japanese choppers
won't be bothering us, but we've got new problems,
folks."

Erika covered her mouth. "Was that a—"

"Shark," said MacClaine. "We're in the Pacific. Warm
waters. Plenty of them. There goes another."

"The blood," said Bishop, pointing at the sheet of water
sweeping over the surface of the raft. "The salt water's
stained with her blood. It's attracting them."

"Shoot one of them. Maybe that'll distract them," offered MacClaine.

Bishop did, firing his pistol at the closest shark, but the blood from the wounded shark only added to the commotion.

"What can we do?" asked Erika.

"We pray that the rescue chopper gets here fast enough," said MacClaine. "Otherwise all they're going to find's a deflated raft drifting among the waves."

"Maybe this will help." She handed Bishop her stun gun. "Hurt them without making them bleed."

The SEAL zapped a nearby shark, which immediately went into a frenzy, splashing away from the boat in a hurry.

"Bad news for that shark," said MacClaine. "But doesn't look like the others give a damn."

Norma Mendez had her eyes closed but heard the words that brought her back to another time, to another part of the world. She remembered the blood, the inner tube, the screams of her baby boy, soaked in sea water as they drifted in the Gulf of Mexico. Norma saw the sharks, felt the jabbing pain as one lunged, snatching her son away, tearing him apart.

The female warrior opened her eyes and saw the waves pounding the sides of the small raft, running over it, touching her, receding back, taking with them traces of her blood, which continued to flow from her wound in spite of Bishop's best efforts. She felt the stabbing pain in her chest every time she breathed, like a white-hot claw raking her from the inside, slowly eroding her life.

Norma heard their shouts as they tried to keep the sharks at bay. She felt death nearing, just like the circling predators, closing in on the tiny raft, aroused by her blood. Life rapidly escaped her, even with the IV. Her vision grew cloudier, her breathing difficult, but perhaps her death could bring life to others, just as Ray had done on that clearing, sacrificing himself to buy the rest of the team enough time to escape.

Norma thought once more of her lost child. Using the last of her strength, she forced her broken body into a roll.

"Oh, my God!" Erika gasped when Norma went overboard.

Bishop and MacClaine tried to reach for her but two large fins converged on her body, dragging it under. MacClaine had to hold the large SEAL back to keep him from jumping after her.

"Loca! Oh, God! *No!*" Bishop shouted, stretching his arms at the dark sea.

"She's gone!" MacClaine shouted. "There's nothing you can do for her."

"Dammit, Loca!" Bishop said. "Why? Why did you do that?"

"For us," said Erika, wiping her cheeks.

"Those damned Japs," MacClaine cursed. "We should just nuke them again. Bastards never learned their lesson in '45."

Bishop sat back, burying his face in his hands.

The three of them huddled in the middle of the raft, floating a bit higher now, the water no longer running across its surface. The fins slowly disappeared, until they saw nothing but waves. Moments later they heard the distant sounds of jet engines.

Bishop pulled out a small radio and struggled to direct the rescue party, his voice choked with emotion. One of the Japanese helicopters turned toward the rescue attempt, but quickly doubled back to the beach when one of the F-16s fired warning shots.

44

THE VIRUS MASTER

In the privacy of a visiting officer's stateroom Erika Conklin sat behind a small desk wearing a pair of dark blue shorts and a white shirt. Her hair was still wet from the shower she had taken in the executive officer's bathroom, while Brent MacClaine kept watch to make certain that the seamen who had shot hungry looks at the beautiful FBI analyst shortly after their arrival would not be trying to get an even better look, particularly when considering that the *Ridge* had been at sea for almost three months.

While MacClaine looked over her shoulder, Erika worked with a laptop computer that belonged to the vessel's commanding officer. She had first backed up the contents of the hard drive into a Zip drive before configuring the system to resemble the computer that she had lost during the helicopter crash. Then she worked with Charlie Chang to download her software through a satellite link, re-creating her old directories.

Erika now went through each diskette, copying the files to the laptop's hard drive before also forwarding the information to Chang in Washington. Unfortunately, there were no Zip drives aboard the Ridge, preventing her from downloading the hundreds of megabytes of data in the Zip disks. The *Ridge*'s skipper had already contacted the American embassy in Tokyo and a diplomatic helicopter was already on the way with two Zip drives purchased locally. In the meantime, Erika had to settle for the data in the hundreds of diskettes, each holding just 1.44 megabytes.

She completed the electronic transmission of all diskettes within two hours. The analysis phase of that data rested on Chang and the Japanese translators at the FBI headquarters. She would transmit again when the drives arrived from Tokyo. Now she proceeded to explore an idea that had come to her after hearing MacClaine's comments about nuking Japan. In addition to her old software, Chang had also sent her a copy of Snatcher, her password-snatching virus, safely contained in a software capsule. The program had been written in assembly code and then compiled, which turned it into machine code, the ones and zeroes that all computers understood, regardless of their country of origin. All systems had an operating system at the machine-language level that directly controlled the hardware and interfaced it with applications like word-processing software and spreadsheets, and of course, games. Her machine-language password-snatching virus penetrated the operating system, embedding itself deep within the lowest levels of the computer as it operated normally. Snatcher monitored all activities, waiting for a user to attempt to log in, detecting the event, and immediately making a copy of the password the user entered to gain access to the particular system or network.

Erika released Snatcher into the Internet service providers for Tokyo, Osaka, Sendai, Kyoto, Nagasaki, Kobe, Sapporo, and several other major cities. Then she sat back and sipped a soda.

"Palenski knows you're doing this?" asked MacClaine, pulling up a chair and sitting next to her.

"I sent him an E-mail."

"When?"

"Oh . . . about thirty minutes ago."

He frowned. "We could get in trouble for this, you know?"

She laughed.

"Guess you got a point. So what happens now?" MacClaine asked.

"Now we wait until the passwords start to show up."

"How long does that take?"

She shrugged. "Depends. Most corporations and industries have links to at least one of the backbones that I'm monitoring. I'll give it no more than ten minutes before the first one arrives."

"How many do we need?"

Before she could answer there was a knock on the door. It was Bishop. Erika smiled. "Hi, Dan."

Without the gear, floppy hat, and camouflage cream, Dan Bishop looked like an overgrown small-town boy. He smiled briefly. "The skipper says there's a call for you from Washington. Says it's very important. You can take it there." He pointed at a wall phone.

Erika nodded and picked it up. Bishop left, closing the door behind him. MacClaine leaned close to listen.

"Hello?"

"Conklin! Palenski here. How are you doing, kid?"

"Fine, sir. Thanks."

"I'm calling for a couple of reasons. First of all to say thanks from all here in Washington. We're not out of the woods yet, but you have definitely done your country a great service. Chang and the rest of your team are busy going through the data you sent them. With some luck something will show."

"That's what I'm afraid of, sir," Erika replied. "I think we will need to make our own luck. I doubt that Tanaka would have kept something as sensitive as the list of components in just any diskette. I get the feeling that the information is probably locked away in some basement in the JDA. When we lost Tanaka we also lost the ability to get the list."

There was a long silence, followed by a heavy sigh. "Yeah . . . I read your E-mail. Are you doing that now?"

"It's happening as we speak."

"Will they know?"

"No, sir. I've learned my lesson the hard way about making sure the password-snatching virus is totally transparent and untraceable this time."

Palenski grunted. "You're really something else, Conklin."

She didn't reply.

"We're going to miss you around here."

A sinking feeling descended on Erika Conklin when hearing those words. She expected to be glad to finally leave the Bureau and get on with her life. Now she wasn't so certain.

"Well, I haven't left yet, sir." She made a face after saying those words. MacClaine gave her a strange look.

"In any case," continued Palenski. "Keep me posted on your progress with that virus. I'm in agreement with you on the extent of the strike . . . for now. I will brief the president accordingly and get back to you."

She hung up the phone and took a deep breath, exhaling through her mouth while extending her lower lip, ruffling her bangs. "I guess he's bought in."

"Sounded like it."

She turned to face the screen.

"Any passwords yet?"

She shook her head. "The system will beep at us when they come in. But I do have a new E-mail message from Charlie." She clicked away for a few seconds, and said, "It's Detroit II, safely encapsulated in a software caplet."

"That's the nasty virus you were telling me about?"

She nodded while moving the file to her petri dish for safekeeping until launch time. "But first we need the roots in order to get it past the defense layers of their networks."

"How many root passwords do we need?"

"I guess it all depends on how much damage we want to do. But they all have to be from networks that control businesses like banks and investment firms, or maybe telecommunications. As I explained to Palenski in my E-mail, I'm not touching anything that has to do with transportation, hospitals, or power because that could kill innocent people."

MacClaine nodded. "That's the deal and the Bureau will stick to it. No loss of innocent lives."

She took another sip of soda as she regarded his bruised face with curiosity. "How do *you* feel about it?"

"I want to stop the attack on our country. Period. If your approach gets us there, I'm in. If it doesn't and we need to take harsher measures, then we just have to take harsher measures."

"As long as those harsher measures don't involve killing civilians. Remember, Brent, two wrongs don't make a right. Innocent people are innocent people, regardless of nationality. Let's not let ourselves get dragged down to the standards of criminals. We value life. These cyberterrorists in Japan obviously do not. I will not let anyone unleash Detroit II on anything but my carefully contained scenario."

MacClaine grinned. "You're such a crusader. I guess that's why I like you."

She continued to regard him while drinking the soda. "Is that why you didn't take advantage of me the other night, Brent? Because you *like* me?"

"Let me tell you something about that night, little lady. You pulled me down in bed with you and actually kissed me."

Her hazel eyes grew in size. "I *kissed* you?"

"Don't sound so disgusted."

She leaned forward and put a hand to her mouth. "Oh, God, no. I didn't mean it that way. Did I really kiss you?"

He brought his extended fingers to his right temple in a mock salute. "Scout's honor."

"How come you didn't tell me that before?"

"At the time you were armed and dangerous."

"And what else did you let me do to you?"

"That was enough, and believe me, it took all of my self-control not to crawl in bed with you. But I just tucked you in and left the room."

She leaned over and kissed him on the lips.

"What was that for?" he asked.

"Something I've been meaning to give you since that moment, for having been so decent. Most guys I know would have taken advantage of the moment."

"I'm not like most of the guys you know."

They laughed and kissed again, this time more intensely, the moment interrupted by a double beep from the laptop.

She pulled away, running a finger over his lips before turning to the screen. "Looks like we got something."

He leaned toward her. "What?"

"Got a password for the Kyoto National Museum. Not bad." She turned to him and they kissed again, this time while embracing. Erika felt a little dizzy and wasn't certain if it was from lack of sleep combined with the excitement of the past day or because of the deep sense of comfort while in MacClaine's arms. Another double beep brought them back to the reality of the moment.

"The root password for the Tokyo Medical and Surgical Clinic. I could do some serious damage there, but can't touch it."

Two more double beeps; the Industrial Bank of Japan and Kansai International Airport near Osaka and Kobe.

Over the next two hours the passwords arrived for many businesses, industries, banks, insurance and investment corporations, hotels, hospitals, airports, train stations, government agencies, and others.

Erika carefully screened the list, selecting the passwords and respective Web sites of those that complied with her moral guidelines, and moving them to a separate directory. She sent copies of every snatched password to Charlie Chang for safekeeping in Washington. After two hours of grabbing passwords, which resulted in over four hundred of them, she decided it was time to do the real damage. By then MacClaine had left twice to contact Palenski. He returned with a couple of turkey sandwiches and chips, and also the Zip drives from Tokyo.

"Here. Compliments of the crew."

"Great," she said, munching on half a sandwich while hooking up the drive to the laptop and loading the first Zip disk. While she performed the first download into her hard drive, she also launched her E-mail software to advise Charlie Chang that more data was on the way.

Erika:	Hi, there.
Chang:	Hello. Boss. Got the list of passwords.
Erika:	Remember there's two of them. I intend to use the one labeled "Touchables."
Chang:	Got it. Did you receive the copy of Detroit II that I sent a couple of hours ago?
Erika:	It's safe in my drive.
Chang:	Good. Was pretty nervous about sending that thing over the network. Sounds like the software capsule kept it caged.
Erika:	Viruses are just like explosives, Charlie. No one gets hurt as long as you know how to handle them, and as long as they don't fall into the wrong hands.
Chang:	You're right.
Erika:	The reason I called is because I just got the Zip drive. Stand by for first major data dump.
Chang:	Ready when you are.
Erika:	Found anything yet on the other stuff I sent over?
Chang:	No list of chips but we've come across lots of interesting E-mails from KT to his pals in Tokyo.
Erika:	Hmm . . . anybody I know?
Chang:	Can't talk about it. I've been told not to discuss names with anyone but Palenski. Sorry, boss. Need-to-know, I guess.

Erika frowned and turned to MacClaine. *"Need-to-know?* You'd figure that after coming up with the damned theories and risking my life the way I have that I should have a need, or right, to know."

"Don't take it personally," MacClaine said, a hand patting her thigh. "We actually don't have a need to know at the moment."

She didn't like it. "What bothers me is that this whole thing's nothing but a one-way street. There is no sense of a team. As long as I'm needed I have the Bureau behind me, but the moment I'm not—or at least perceived that I have nothing else to contribute—I'm immediately shut out."

MacClaine couldn't help a smile.

"It's not funny, Brent. It's actually pretty sad that after everything I've done they won't trust me enough to keep me on the inside of the investigation."

"Welcome to the world of intelligence. Need-to-know isn't just a policy created by our leaders to keep the little people—that's us—in the dark. It's a way to safeguard information, to keep it from falling in the wrong hands. After all, even under chemical interrogations you can only confess to what you know. We use need-to-know as standard operating practice. Other intelligence networks use different methods to protect their information, including suicide pills. Now, given the choice, I'd take need-to-know any day over Cyanide." He pointed at the screen. "You left your man hanging in there."

Chang: Boss, you still there?
Erika: Yep. What's the word from Palenski on releasing Detroit II?
Chang: He's with the president now. Will let you know.

She terminated the transmission and leaned back, running slim fingers through her auburn hair. "Of course. Don't call us, we'll call you. Always on the outside."

MacClaine remained silent while Erika just stared at the screen. A moment later, she began to pound the keys and work the pointer. "Well, might as well get ready to rumble."

"What are you doing?"

"Getting Detroit II ready for deployment," she replied.

"How are you doing that?"

She pointed at the screen. "See that?"

0   01011010.10101010.01011001.01110100.10111010.01000110.11010101
1   01000010.00000111.01011111.10100000.1000010.011010100.00000101

2 01111010.11111010.01011101.01110100.10101010.00000010.10101001

3 00001010.01010010.01111101.01110100.11010010.01111110.11110001

He leaned forward and stared at the strings of ones and zeroes. "Yeah. What's that?"

"Detroit II, say hello to Brent MacClaine. Brent, this is Detroit II, in machine language. Ones and zeroes."

MacClaine smiled. "Hmm . . . how come I also see a number two and a number three?"

"Oh, those are just the row numbers of the string. It starts at row zero and continues in row one and so forth."

"How many rows are there?"

"About a thousand. But this is the critical part." She browsed down many screens.

127 01011010.10101010.01011001.01110100.10111010.01000110.11010101

128 00000000.00000000.10001101.01010100.10010111.01011001.11001000

129 01011010.10101010.01011001.01110100.10111010.01000110.11010101

130 01011010.10101010.01011001.01110100.10111010.01000110.11010101

"Looks the same to me," he said.

"Row one hundred twenty-seven contains the actual mutation sequence. That's the string of seven bytes that—"

"Slow down. What's a byte?"

"A byte is made of eight bits. Each one or zero represents a single bit. So anyway, in these seven bytes is the signature of this particular mutation of Detroit II. According to the mutation key that I programmed, this section will change every time the virus replicates itself. The next two bytes, starting in row one hundred twenty-eight, hold the encoded Web address of the network the virus will attack.

"But those two bytes only have zeroes."

"That's the default setting, which tells the virus to attack everything and anything, regardless of its network address. So we're going to force it to attack only specific addresses. Here is the first one." She opened another window and clicked on a file.

TOUCHABLE ADDRESSES

LOCATION	CODED ADDRESS
MINISTRY OF JUSTICE	11000111.11110011
FUJI BANK, LTD., TOKYO	11000111.11000000
SUMITOMO BANK, LTD., OSAKA	11000111.11001100
BANK OF TOKYO, LTD.	11000111.11000001
MITSUBISHI ELECTRONICS, LTD.	11000111.01010011
MINISTRY OF DEFENSE	11000111.11110100
TOKYO UNIVERSITY	11000111.10001100
MINISTRY OF EDUCATION	11000111.11110110

The list went on, totaling almost four hundred independent institutions.

"Touchable addresses?"

She shrugged. "Couldn't think of a better name. I also have the untouchable list."

"Well, that list sure's going to do some damage," MacClaine observed.

"That's the idea. Pain without loss of life. Accounts can get restored and files can get reloaded from archives, but the loss of life is forever."

"I'm with you. What's next?"

"See the first byte of every address?"

"Yeah . . . it looks the same for all addresses."

"That first byte defines the country of origin. The second byte is the specific address of the network. But there are also some commonalities on the second byte. All government institutions, for example, begin with four ones. The last four bits of the second byte refer to the code of that specific government institution, like the Ministry of Education or Defense."

"That makes sense."

"Everything is very logical in computer code. To the uneducated eye those strings look like a bunch of ones and zeroes, but a trained programmer can read them like a language. See, just a one-minute explanation and some of those bits begin to make sense, right."

"Yep. So what happens next?"

"We create multiple copies of Detroit II and give each a unique address. Then we'll be ready."

45

RETALIATION

"Will this really work the way you're describing it, Roman?" asked President Lester Williams while walking in the Rose Garden side by side with the FBI director. The secretaries of defense and state followed them.

The commander in chief stopped to smell a yellow rose, trying in vain to improve his mood this morning. His bloodshot eyes reflected the many tears he had shed at the loss of his courageous stepson, not to mention the heavy burden of also having to console the First Lady, who was still knocked out from the sedative given to her by the president's physician moments after the news of the death of Commander Derek Ray reached the White House.

"My technical analyst assures me that it will, sir. So far she has been pretty much on the money with her assessments."

"Are there any other options?"

"We must retaliate in the same manner in which we were attacked, sir," added Palenski.

"The Japanese are masters of attacking without being confrontational, sir," said Secretary of State Christopher Milley in his aristocratic voice. "They like to be indirect when they attack, like what they're doing right now, killing us with this sabotage scheme while also claiming that we're being racist against them when the FBI tries to work the case. We can't respond with open threats. We must be indirect, subtle in our counterattack while at the same time delivering a decisive blow, and Miss Conklin's proposal is exactly what we need to put an end to this."

President Williams listened in silence, considering his options. His country simply could not go on like this. The Japanese had attacked America without warning, without remorse, for the mere purpose of dislodging it from its hard-earned first place in the computer industry.

"Are we ready to do it?" Williams asked, stopping to observe an American Beauty, its deep crimson hue reminding the president of the blood that had been shed by his countrymen at the hand of these Japanese cyberterrorists.

"My people are standing by, Mr. President."

"How long will it be before we see the effects?"

"Around twelve hours, sir, maybe a little less."

"And the loss of life will be minimal?"

"That's the only way Miss Conklin agreed to help. We're hitting them where it hurts the most, in their pocketbook."

"What if that doesn't work?" asked the president, remembering just how obstinate Japan had been toward the end of World War II, forcing Truman to use his biggest hammer to force them to surrender. "What would you gentlemen suggest then?"

"Then we take the next step, Mr. President," Vuono replied. "We cut this virus loose across their land, targeting transportation systems and power. The effect will be quite devastating. It will take Japan a long time to recover from such strike, and the casualty rate is expected to be high. It will be the equivalent of a Hiroshima and Nagasaki during World War Two, sir. They will have no choice but to surrender the list to us."

Lester Williams stared at the scarlet petals, feeling its texture with his thumb and index finger. "Very well," he said. "Give the order for the first phase, and let's pray we don't have to go any further."

46

DIGITAL OVERFLOW

"I hope I don't live to regret this," Erika said after hanging up with Palenski, who had called her from the White House.

MacClaine put a hand to her shoulder and squeezed it gently. "I'm right behind you."

With a single click of the mouse Erika Conklin released dozens of copies of her unbreakable version of the Detroit virus, each safely contained inside a custom software capsule and capped with a stolen root password. Each virus also contained a unique address to keep it from being able to survive outside of its programmed host environment. If a virus attached itself to an E-mail message and managed to jump to another network, it would perish because the address of that new network was not compatible with its embedded address.

Within minutes the capsules reached their destinations, got past the security points by issuing the stolen passwords, and penetrated the inner cores of the operating systems of many businesses and government institutions across several Japanese cities. Inside each system, the software pellets broke up, releasing an electronic homing missile that searched for the directory containing the resident antivirus software and deleted every instance that remotely resembled its own code. Future antivirus checks would not detect Detroit II, which in reality was not a virus, but a virus-*making* factory, or a virus master.

The virus master released an electronic worm, which crawled through every directory in the host systems and left behind a slightly different strain of the virus, following the nested key that Erika had created to make it's sequence impossible to break with today's computers.

As Erika finished her fourth soda, the worms had completed their infection cycle. Detroit II had dug its electronic teeth into the systems and was ready to start devouring files, which it did at a rapacious rate, corrupting everything in its path. In a matter of hours the computer systems and records of hundreds of Japanese corporations and government agencies had vanished. In many cases, the infected systems of a corporation with networked systems across other cities than the one infected would also result in the infection of the branches if they shared the same Web address, bringing down entire networks.

"Damage is high," Erika said while reviewing the information on her system, which provided her with a real-time update of the destruction. "The mutation key is also working as I expected."

"The mutation key?"

"The key is a formula that controls the mutation sequence of the virus, modifying the seven-byte signature in a preprogrammed fashion. I designed it such that the sequence could not be broken with today's computers because the number of permutations exceed the capability of our systems. The key also makes certain that the modification of the seven-byte signature doesn't overflow, which could be very bad news."

"Overflow?"

"Yeah, spill over into adjacent bytes, also altering them. It could, for example, alter the target address in which the virus is allowed to operate. That would essentially give the virus random addresses. It would turn my controlled fire into a wildfire. But we won't have to worry about that because the design of the key will keep it bound to the seven-byte signature field only."

She sent an E-mail to Washington to confirm the completion of her mission.

MacClaine stood behind her and rubbed her shoulders as they watched the screen for another fifteen minutes. Then he rubbed his eyes. Erika yawned.

"Why don't we get some rest?" he asked. "It's almost four in the morning. A chopper will pick us up at three this afternoon to take us back to Seoul. This time we take a commercial flight back."

She nodded. "I think I could sleep for three days straight."

"Same here."

They faced the bunk beds on the side of the small stateroom.

"You like being on top?" he asked.

Erika laughed. "As a matter of fact I do, but right now I'm too tired to even think about that."

MacClaine helped her up to the top bunk. "That's all right," he said. "Gives me something to look forward to."

She kissed him good night and rolled over. MacClaine settled himself in the lower bunk and closed his eyes, falling asleep moments later.

47

RESISTANCE

Fuji Yokonawa, Japan's minister of industry and commerce, watched the sunrise from his corner office while sipping tea to calm his upset stomach. Joggers made their way around the Imperial Palace and tourists snapped pictures, oblivious of the businessmen panicking in the adjacent financial district, where a mysterious computer virus had corrupted millions of accounts, erasing the transactions of billions of yen that had occurred yesterday before they could be backed up to tape. The early reports on his desk indicated that most banking firms were in the process of retrieving data two days old and downloading it into their servers while at the same time dealing with the mess of lost deposits, withdrawals, transfers, and loans from personal, corporate, and government accounts. But the virus had not been limited to Tokyo's financial district. Reports were already flowing in from Osaka, Kobe, Nagasaki, and Kyoto of missing files and corrupted software systems. He feared that other sections of the country had also experienced such high-tech attacks but communications were down between Tokyo and those areas owing to malfunctioning systems. The elderly minister also feared that those systems had also fallen victim to this mysterious virus, which somehow had managed to get past the security points installed in all networked systems, wiping out their electronic backbone overnight. Fortunately transportation, hospitals, the military, and power-distribution systems had apparently not been affected by the attack. He had no reports of accidents or loss of lives. But over 70 percent of the phones were down, as well as networks servicing universities, high schools, homes, insurance agencies, and even many government agencies. The Nikkei had not opened this morning because many transactions from yesterday were lost and the corrupted software had shut down the network.

Yokonawa had already been on the phone twice this morning with the prime minister, who could not understand how Japan's computer network could be so vulnerable. Implied in the message was the statement that unless things returned to normal immediately the minister of industry and commerce must resign for having failed at his task of protecting the Japanese industry from such attacks. Minister Yokonawa had also received a private message from the American ambassador in Tokyo, who relayed a fax from the secretary of state in Washington, expressing his regrets about the virus that had attacked so many of Japan's systems. The American government was willing to assist its ally in the eradication and destruction of the virus before it migrated into the transportation and power distribution systems in the next twenty-four hours, which would certainly endanger the general population. In return, the American government needed for the prime minister to provide Japan's technical expertise in the identification of the American semiconductor devices that may have been altered prior to production. A private fax number had been provided.

How did they know I was next in line? My people told me that Tanaka was killed in the attack. Did he talk before that?

Yokonawa's hands trembled, and he almost spilled his tea. He set the cup down on his desk and picked up a report from the head of the technical services department within his ministry, who assured Yokonawa that the virus had been isolated and a team of programmers were in the process of breaking it. The estimate was within the next twelve to twenty-four hours.

The minister wondered if the Americans were serious about their threat to take this virus to the next level and strike at the general population. The United States always had been soft when it came to the loss of civilian life. They simply did not have the stomach.

Deciding that his operation could still be salvaged, especially if his lead programmers could find a cure for the virus, eliminating America's ability to pressure him, Yokonawa buzzed his secretary to dictate a letter to the American ambassador in Tokyo.

48

EXTREME MEASURES

President Lester Williams struggled to remain logical and in control. His nation needed him to stay focused. He had locked himself inside the Oval Office for the past three hours, mourning the loss of Derek. And with Elizabeth sedated, he found himself having to gut it out alone. But now he had a decision to make. In his left hand he held a copy of the fax that had arrived an hour ago from the ambassador in Tokyo.

Williams crumpled it in his fist while looking up at the midnight sky over Washington. This powerful faction within the Japanese government was resisting, pushing back, calling America's bluff, continuing to underestimate the power of the United States. They had drawn first blood and now simply watched as his country slowly bled to death. These cyberterrorists had struck without warning, just as bin Laden's soldiers had attacked America in 2001. And the cyberterrorists now expected to get away with it.

Over my dead body.

President Lester Williams understood how George W. Bush had felt on the eve of giving the order to attack those responsible for the September 11th strikes. He understood his anger, his frustration, his utter incredulity that a terrorist organization could be so bold, so deceitful, so downright arrogant as to think that it could strike against the United States and get away with it.

Tonight President Lester Williams prepared himself to retaliate in kind. He needed that list of sabotaged components, of the millions of ticking time bombs sprinkled across the nation, across the world itself, waiting to go off with the metal-ripping force of Pasadena, Florida, Nevada, Denver, and West Virginia.

And he was willing to go to any extreme measure to acquire it.

49

DIFFICULT DECISIONS

FBI Headquarters, Washington, D.C.

Roman Palenski walked into the systems lab and grabbed a chair next to Charlie Chang, who immediately stopped his work on a computer and pushed his glasses up the bridge of his nose. "Yes, sir?"

"Charlie, how would you like to become the new section head for this area?"

Chang leaned back, his wide eyes studying the large FBI director.

"But—but, like, that's Erika's job. What about—"

"Erika's on her way out, and I'm looking for a suitable replacement. I've been keeping my eye on you, son. I think you're a team player and know how to get things done without asking needless questions. Am I right?"

Chang quickly nodded. "I'm your man, sir. Like, I'll do what it takes, you know. Questions? No questions. Just do my job."

"Great," Palenski said. "Because there is a *very* special job I need you to do for me now."

Ten minutes later, Palenski left the systems lab not necessarily feeling good about himself, but he was out of choices. The president had just handed him a very difficult and sensitive task, leaving Palenski out of options and out of time. He went to his office and asked his secretary to raise the *Blue Ridge*. He had to speak to Brent MacClaine immediately.

50

PLAYING HARDBALL

Brent MacClaine was awakened by a young sailor. The fed checked his watch, realizing that he had been asleep for nearly eight hours. It was just before noon, local time. Erika was still asleep in the top bunk. A Navy transport helicopter was due to arrive at three in the afternoon to take them to Seoul, Korea, where they would catch a commercial flight back home.

"Yeah?" he said in a low voice to avoid waking up Erika, who he felt stirring overhead.

"Call from Washington, sir. Line two." The sailor pointed at the phone on the wall behind the desk, where the laptop continued to display the status of the controlled damage done by Detroit II.

MacClaine stood, aching all over, thanking the sailor as he left the stateroom, staggering across the vinyl floor barefoot. Heavy eyed, half-asleep, he grabbed the black unit.

"MacClaine."

"MacClaine, this is Roman Palenski."

The federal agent became fully awake in the next millisecond. "Yes, sir?"

"Bad news, I'm afraid. An hour ago we received a message from the Japanese government through our ambassador in Tokyo. Bottom line's that Japan refuses to release the list. They want to play hardball, and so must we."

MacClaine sighed, fearing that it might come to that. "What do you need me to do, sir?"

"I have a concern that Miss Conklin might be against taking this next step, and frankly I can't risk the safety of the nation on her naïveté."

MacClaine didn't like what he was hearing. "What do you have in mind, sir?"

"I understand from one of her subordinates that she is currently monitoring the activities of the virus on her system."

MacClaine glanced down at the small unit. Information scrolled across two windows, displaying combinations of ones and zeroes and Japanese characters. "Looks that way, sir."

"We're about to commence the second phase. I need you to keep her away from that monitor for the next couple of hours to give us time to do what we have to do."

MacClaine remained silent, considering his options.

"You still there?"

"Yes, sir."

"This is a matter of national security, MacClaine. Our people are being killed. You yourself were nearly killed. Those SEALs gave their lives for this mission. You get my point?"

"Yes, sir."

"We can't stand by and let the cyberterrorists get away with this. Do you also understand that?"

"I do, sir."

"Difficult times call for difficult decisions, MacClaine. Our commander in chief has given the order to strike without any rules, without any level of containment. That virus is getting released in minutes across Osaka. Then we give them ten hours to release the list or we strike Kyoto. Next will be Tokyo. And we keep going until somebody comes to their senses over there and complies."

MacClaine closed his eyes, remembering Erika's words.

Two wrongs don't make a right. Don't drop down to their level. There has to be another way.

But was there? History told him there was but one way to fight terrorism.

He who has the bigger hammer wins.

Period.

"And I'm not going to beat around the bush on this one, MacClaine. So before I go, I want to remind you of one more thing, on the outside chance that any strange thoughts may cross your mind."

"Sir?"

"You're a career fed, MacClaine. She *isn't*. She's essentially out. Her debt to the Bureau has been cancelled because of her contributions to this case. She will be returning to the private sector starting next week. That was the deal I made with her and I'm honoring it. Her record will be cleared and she'll also get a phenomenal letter of recommendation. But you're in a different situation. You've put in over twenty years with the Bureau. In a few more you get full pension. Keep that in mind."

MacClaine frowned. *Message received.*

"Yes, sir."

He hung up the phone and just sat there, in the dark, watching Erika sleep, the only illumination coming from the sunlight filtering through the small porthole above the desk and the glow from the laptop's screen. His mind raced through his options, struggling for the right thing to do. On one side he understood his superior's position. Japan had to be dealt with swiftly, decisively. But Erika also had a very valid position. Was killing more innocent civilians the right way to handle this problem?

"Damn," he whispered. "What should I do?"

Erika sat up in her bunk. "Brent? Are you on the phone?" She rubbed her eyes and yawned.

He shook his head. "No . . . just thinking out loud."

"Oh, okay." She jumped off the bed and stretched again. "God, that felt good. How long was I asleep?"

"About eight and a half hours."

"Now I'm starving."

MacClaine stepped in front of her, blocking her view of the computer on the desk. Abruptly, he embraced her and kissed her. She was taken momentarily aback, then responded.

"Hmm . . ." she said, leaning back. "To what do I owe this pleasant surprise?"

He tried to be as charming as he could without overdoing it. "Let's just say that I got plenty of rest."

She made a face. "*Here?* In a Navy ship in the middle of the Pacific?"

He shrugged and reached over to lock the stateroom's door. "I can think of worse places."

She gave him a flirtatious smile. "I guess I can wait a little before eating."

He picked up her light frame with ease and slowly set her down on the bed. She slapped him on the butt. "You're a bad boy, Brent MacClaine. You know that? A *really* bad boy."

"You have *no* idea," he said, sitting at the edge of the bed, leaning down, kissing her again, raising her T-shirt, embracing her. She hugged him back, kissing his neck, unbuttoning his shirt, kissing his chest. He closed his eyes, not having felt this way with anyone since Jessica, before the Bureau ruined his life, before . . .

MacClaine jumped away, hands on his forehead as guilt overwhelmed him. "I can't, Erika. I can't do this. I . . . care about you too much."

She slowly stood, lowering the T-shirt, putting a hand to his cheek, dropping it to his chest and rubbing it. "I care about you too a great deal, Brent. And I want this. I really want us to have this moment."

He cupped her face. "God, you're so lovely. But you don't understand. I want it too, but not under these circumstances. I don't want to screw up this relationship."

"I don't understand."

He turned around and crossed his arms. "The hell with my pension. Those bastards can keep it."

"*Pension?* What are you talking about?"

He faced her again and told her about his conversation with Palenski.

"So he asked you to distract me?" Her hazel eyes turned into high-power laser beams, cutting right through him.

He nodded.

"And is that why you—"

"No, no. I really wanted to—"

"That bastard! I can't believe this! And you . . . I'm dealing with *you* later, mister!" She pushed him aside and sat behind the laptop.

"Erika, I—"

"Save it! I hope I'm not too late! How long since he called you?"

MacClaine felt like the biggest jerk in the world. He had just kissed off his career at the FBI and had also angered the woman he slowly realized he loved as much as he had once loved Jessica MacClaine.

"Brent! How long?"

"Ah . . . about twenty minutes ago."

"Damn! They don't know what they're doing!"

51

NEED-TO-KNOW POLICY

Roman Palenski stood behind Charlie Chang as the young analyst monitored the status of the virus penetration into the primary artery of Osaka's local backbone.

"Oh, oh," Chang said, pointing to a window on his computer. "I think Erika just figured out what we're doing."

Erika:	Charlie! What in the hell are you doing?
Chang:	Following orders.
Erika:	The key, Charlie. Did you modify it in any way?

Chang looked at Palenski, who nodded. "It's too late now. It doesn't matter that she knows."

Chang:	Yes. It was the only way to make sure you couldn't interfere. Palenski's right beside me. He's reminding you that this is a matter of national security. Do not try to interfere.
Erika:	Dammit, Charlie. What part of the mutating equation did you change?
Chang:	Sorry, Need-to-know only.
Erika:	Well, you tell Palenski that unless I fucking know what the key modification was, there is a very, very, very good chance that the virus will not only attack your target addresses but other places as well, including the United States!!! Now, do I have a need to know or not???

Palenski shouted to an aide to get the *Blue Ridge* on the phone immediately.

Chang: I don't understand. What do you mean? I sent the virus just like you did, except to the other list of addresses and with a new nesting key to make sure you couldn't interfere before we forced Japan to yield the list.

Erika: Charlie! Charlie! You're a very smart kid, but you're no hacker. You think in conventional ways. Hackers do not. Do you remember how long the signature length of the original Detroit virus was?

Chang: Yes. Seven bytes long.

Erika: And the sequence of mutations is what defines each virus, right?

Chang: Right.

Erika: The mutation is accomplished by using the seven-byte code of the existing mutation as the input of the equation that computes the new mutation. You with me so far?

Chang: Yes.

Erika: The key that I designed to nest the mutation sequences keeps the mutation within the seven-byte field, avoiding an overflow into adjacent bytes. Any changes to the mutation equation will alter that. Do you know what would happen then?

Chang: Oh, shit. I think I know. The addresses!

Erika: Correct. The two bytes right after the seven-byte signature define the target address. An overflow will alter the information of those two bytes, creating random addresses for the virus.

Palenski noticed that Charlie Chang was no longer moving. The young programmer stared at the screen while mumbling something Palenski couldn't make out. Just then one of his aides told him to pick up the phone.

52

DAMAGE CONTROL

"I know I should have gone through you for this, but we are where we are, and now I need you to correct it."

Erika was fuming. She held the phone next to her ear while MacClaine leaned over to listen. "And why should I help again? I did what you've asked me to do. I'm out, remember? I no longer have a need to know."

Silence.

"Erika, listen to me," Palenski said, his voice now softer. "If what you say is true, then innocent lives could be at stake at other places."

"Innocent lives *are* at stake, in Osaka! Or is the price of life in Osaka lower than somewhere else?"

More silence.

She added, "I'll help you again, but it's going to cost you."

"We're not prepared to—"

"Then get one of your hot-shot programmers over there to help you."

"All right, all right, but I'm going to have to clear it with—"

She told him her price and hung up without waiting for an answer.

53

DIGITAL MELTDOWN

OSAKA, JAPAN

At exactly 4:15 P.M., Detroit II reached the core of Osaka's computerized subway system, the heart of the logic managing the mind-numbing task of keeping dozens of trains arriving and departing multiple stations at specific times. The system also controlled the critical ventilation systems, lighting, automatic doors, and computerized ticket tellers. In a large underground control room that looked like mission control in Houston, Texas, dozens of technicians sat behind large screens and control panels while monitoring the status of the entire system. The floor was divided into sections, according to their area of responsibility. Lighting systems occupied a corner; ventilation another. The real-time position of each subway train was displayed on an overhead projector, constantly scrutinized by a group of technicians in the center of the room.

The ventilation section experienced the first shutdown at 4:30 P.M. It came abruptly, without warning. The monitors went blank and the system would not reboot. The experienced crew immediately brought up a backup system, but it, too, failed to respond. The section head then switched to manual, which was as good as no control. The complexity of the control system monitoring and directing the flow of cool air throughout the underground city, plus the delicate extraction of toxic fumes from all of the operating equipment rivaled that of an oil refinery. By 4:41 P.M. the carbon monoxide levels began to climb, as well as the ambient temperature. Just as the section head picked up the red emergency phone next to his station to call for immediate assistance, the lines went down. In the same instant, the lights went out across the subterranean complex. Emergency lights came on, but the panicking crowd found itself trapped because the automatic doors had defaulted to their locked position during a power failure. At a crowded station, a train remained at the ramp, unable to move because the power for that grid had gone down. A second train approaching the station five minutes later began to slow down, but not in time to keep it from crashing against the stationary train. The resulting explosion sent a shockwave down corridors packed with people, followed by blistering smoke. Hundreds perished in the first few minutes following the explosion. Many more suffocated as they failed to pry open the automatic doors.

Just as the underground blast rumbled across the streets at 4:47 P.M., the traffic-light system began to malfunction, creating hundreds of accidents in minutes, turning the city into havoc, preventing emergency rescue crews from reaching the crash sites. But even if they had, it would had done the victims little good. By 4:50 P.M. the power outage had also shut down the hospitals across Osaka.

And Erika Conklin got to see all of the reports on her 13-inch screen, as the field results from the original release of Detroit II now incorporated data from this most recent infection.

"Bastards," she mumbled, trembling, watching the data flashing on her screen, reading the machine code, absorbing the magnitude of the attack. "They really did it. They really released it on innocent people."

MacClaine, who had remained silent, stepped behind her and put his hands on her shoulders. "How bad is it?"

Erika shook him off. "Don't touch me. And it's bad. Really fucking bad. People are dying, Brent. Innocent people. And you let them do it. You sat on that chair and felt sorry for yourself instead of waking me up so that I could have done something about it. You're just like the rest of them. I can't believe I trusted you."

"Look, I'm sorry. I . . . I have nothing to say to my defense. I was wrong."

"Yes, you were," she said pointing at the screen. "All of you were. Look."

MUTATION	TIME	ADDRESS STRING	COUNTRY DECODE
000000000	1615	10000111.11000011	OSAKA, JAPAN ** ORIGINAL **
000123980	1618	10000110.11110011	NEW ZEALAND
000436271	1621	10100111.11000011	PAKISTAN
001625918	1645	11000011.00110011	IRELAND
003811774	1700	00000101.11110011	SOUTH KOREA
006026020	1713	11100111.11110011	U.S.A.

"These are the mutation sequences from the original virus released in Osaka that affected the address strings because Charlie used the wrong mutation key. The original mutation, the one with all zeroes, attacked Osaka a quarter after four, about an hour ago. Three minutes later, mutation number one hundred twenty-three thousand nine hundred eighty modified the address string, firing a copy of Detroit II to New Zealand."

"Where in New Zealand?"

"Don't know that. I don't have the coding file for the rest of the string, just for the country segment. Anyway, as you can see, in just under an hour, Detroit II mutated over six million times and modified the address string five times."

She began to work the keyboard and several windows flashed on her screen, each filled with binary code.

"What are you doing now?"

"Sending potions to those addresses. With some luck the five bastard children from the Osaka virus will not make any new babies with different addresses before I can eradicate them."

MacClaine's jaw dropped. "You mean that each of those new viruses can create *new* addresses?"

She nodded, breathing heavily while popping up a new window on the screen. "I've just written a script to go through the mutations of the virus strain fired at New Zealand at four-eighteen this afternoon. Let's see the damage done."

MUTATION#	TIME	ADDRESS STRING	COUNTRY DECODE
000000000	1618	10000110.11110011	NEW ZEALAND
000803024	1625	11100101.10001100	SCOTLAND
001900021	1656	10110111.10011001	VENEZUELA
002005002	1710	10000110.11100100	NEW ZEALAND

Erika shook her head. "The last virus mutation triggered a second virus at a new address within New Zealand."

"What are you going to do?" He pulled up a chair and sat next to her in the stateroom.

"I'll show you."

Erika prepared hundreds of copies of Sentinel, a virus-like program with embedded instructions to seek out and eliminate any mutations of Detroit II as dictated by the new key. She released them at the outer edges of the Osaka network, where the sentinels would patrol the virtual space around Osaka and catch any viruses that mutation sequences had altered their target addresses. Then she did the same to those five countries infected so far, sending hundreds of copies of Sentinel to attack the locations being infected by Detroit II. At the same time, she had Charlie Chang use the Hewlett-Packard workstations to predict the future countries that the multiple offsprings of Detroit II would try to attack. She did this to stay ahead of the virus and clamp it from spreading any further while the Sentinels came in from behind and killed the unintended international versions of Detroit II.

After thirty minutes monitoring activities, Erika stood and stretched.

"So far so good," she said, sitting back down.

"What is?"

"The Sentinels appear to have contained the international mutations."

MacClaine rubbed his chin. "Was there any damage done before they were contained?"

"We won't know for sure for another hour or so, but so far I have received reports of isolated incidents in each country. I can't tell what has been damaged or exactly where within the country, just that Detroit II was successful in killing files before the Sentinels arrived."

"What about everything inside Osaka?"

She turned around and burned him with her stare. "The people in Osaka are screwed, Brent. Royally screwed, but that's what you all wanted, right? Well, guess what? Mission accomplished. You managed to turned a perfectly peaceful city into a killing zone."

The phone rang before he could reply.

She stood and picked it up. "Yes?"

"Conklin?"

"Yes?" Erika said, recognizing Palenski's voice.

"Miss Conklin?"

Erika stopped. There was someone with Palenski. They had her on a speaker box. The voice sounded familiar but she couldn't place it. "Yes?"

"This is President Lester Williams. Do you recognize my voice?"

Erika's legs gave and she collapsed on the chair. "Yes—yes, sir. I do."

MacClaine whispered, "Who is it?"

She put a hand over the phone. "The president!"

He leaned down to listen.

"Miss Conklin, I am the commander in chief of the United States, and as such, I'm chartered with the protection of the way of life in our country. The people of this country elected me to protect them from all harm, foreign or domestic. We are now in a time of war, a quite unconventional war, but nevertheless a war. Cyberterrorists from an extreme faction within the Japanese government have attacked our nation, causing great pain among my people. I, as leader of this great nation, must retaliate in—"

"But, sir, I—"

"Do *not* interrupt me again."

Erika nodded. "Yes, sir. Sorry, sir." She swallowed a lump and clutched the phone to her ear.

"As I was saying, it falls on me to make very difficult decisions that in the end come down to my judgment, after I have gotten the opportunity to discuss the issue with my closest advisors. That's how decisions are made at the national level, Miss Conklin. You are not responsible for the fate of the country. I am. And the decision that I made to deal with the country harboring these ruthless cyberterrorists was one of a measured response. First we struck their financial and government institutions. When that failed to motivate them, I had to take the next prudent step to ensure the release of the list of sabotaged computer chips. Now, I don't expect you to either understand or agree with that decision, but I do expect you to abide by it and not undermine it. Do you understand that?"

"Yes, sir."

"Now, I gave the order to strike Osaka with your computer virus. I also understand that there was a problem with the way that was technically carried out and that there might be a risk of exposure outside of the intended target area. Could you please provide me with a damage assessment?"

"Yes—sure—yes, sir."

"Pace yourself," MacClaine whispered. "Calm down."

She nodded and took a deep breath, taking five minutes to brief the president on the multiple offsprings of Detroit II spreading to other countries. She also explained her current plan to contain the international infection cycle.

"How long before we know if this unintentional infection has been fixed?"

She checked her watch. "So far it appears to be contained to about twenty isolated Web sites around the world.

I'm estimating that it will be completely eradicated within the hour. By morning I should have a list of the specific businesses or institutions affected around the world, in case we choose to make financial reparations."

"Very well," the president said. "You have done your nation a great service, Miss Conklin, and for that I thank you. Is there anything I can do for you?"

Erika couldn't help herself. "I have two questions, Mr. President."

"Go ahead."

"What about the list, sir?"

"All right. Our embassy in Tokyo just received from the prime minister a fax containing the list of sabotaged components, which has already been sent to all relevant companies. We also received a letter expressing his regret for the poor behavior exhibited by several members of his administration. He assured me that an internal investigation will be carried out. In the meantime, the prime minister has offered to make financial reparations in return for a cure for the computer virus that has struck his country. I have told the prime minister that the cure would be released as soon as certain funds are transferred to the Department of Treasury, which my administration will then use to assist in the recovery process."

Erika didn't know what to say. Perhaps the president was right after all. Perhaps the only way to defeat evil was by becoming worse than evil.

"Is there anything else you wish to know, Miss Conklin?"

"Yes, sir." Erika asked about her deal with Palenski for financial compensation.

There was silence, followed by, "My administration will do the right thing, Miss Conklin."

"Thank you, sir."

"Very well, then. Again, thank you for your support on this project. With some luck we will be able to recall all faulty components before one triggers another disaster. Good-bye, Miss Conklin."

"Good-bye, Mr. President."

She stared at the phone for a moment after the line went dead. Then she hung it up on the wall. "I guess it's over."

MacClaine nodded. "Ready to go home?"

54

FAREWELLS

SOUTH KOREA

A helicopter took them to Kimp'o International Airport in Seoul. Erika slept most of the way there. MacClaine gazed out the window, contemplating the vast expanse of blue ocean as well as his future, not certain what to do next.

The Bureau made up his mind for him shortly after they arrived at the crowded airport. Two FBI agents waited for them. They gave Erika a first-class ticket to Washington, D.C. Her plane left in less than an hour. MacClaine had different instructions. Palenski wanted him to stay a week in Seoul and then also spend a few days in Taiwan and Hong Kong, visiting the regional FBI offices to get familiar with the foreign operations division. The FBI director felt that the experience would be good for MacClaine in his new role as head of the office of international affairs. He had been promoted, which also meant a transfer to Washington, D.C.

"What are you going to do?" Erika asked him after congratulating MacClaine while the agents waited across the crowded concourse.

He shrugged. "I need to think about this. Lately I've been seeing myself as moving *out* of the Bureau, not *up* the Bureau. What about you?"

"Pack up and head back to the West Coast. I'm going

to spend some time at the ranch, rest a while, and then decide what I'm going to do."

He nodded, followed by several seconds of uncomfortable silence.

"Will I ever see you again?" he asked.

She nodded. "You know where I'll be." She kissed him just as they began boarding her flight. "I have to go now."

"Take care of yourself, Erika."

"You too, Brent. And thanks for everything."

He studied her eyes, her lips, the short auburn hair framing her narrow face. Then she was gone.

Brent MacClaine just stood there, long after the plane had pulled out of the gate. Then he turned around and followed the agents out of the airport.

EPILOGUE

Erika Conklin stepped out of the house and into another clear and cool morning. She stood on the front porch wearing a pair of faded jeans, a flannel shirt, and boots. Two of her brothers stood by the stables with buckets of feed while her father and younger brother inspected the vineyards.

She breathed in the clean air and stretched, nodding approvingly at the relaxing sight and also at the cable running down to the house from a nearby telephone pole. Her new high-speed line to access the Internet.

The past two months had been quite busy ones for the computer engineer. After using some of the Bureau's money to get her family's ranch solvent, something that would have made her grandmother proud, Erika had invested in three powerful PCs and two disk servers. She had decided to go into business by herself as a computer consultant. Her first project had been expected. The folks at DreamWorks were desperate for a new and improved version of DigiSoft and were willing to pay her a hefty consulting fee to get it. She had signed a contract with them two weeks ago. Word of her work at the FBI had reached several banks in northern California, which wanted to hire her services to develop protection shields against hackers. She had signed that contract four days ago. And just yesterday two software companies had called her regarding the implementation of virus shields for upcoming software releases. Best of all, she could do all of that from her small office at the house and still have time to host a couple of one-hour tours a day of her family's winery.

She smiled, deciding that life had certainly taken a turn for the best since leaving the FBI, something that now seemed like eons ago.

The smile, however, turned into a frown. She had not heard from Brent MacClaine since their hasty good-bye in Seoul. Perhaps it wasn't meant to be. Perhaps she was better off. MacClaine might have reminded her of a life she was trying to forget.

Or was she?

During the past weeks she had reflected on her FBI experience, on the lessons she had learned, on the people she had met, including a group of very courageous soldiers who had given their life for their country. Erika remembered the military funeral at Arlington, shortly before she'd left Washington for good. The government of Japan had returned the mortal remains of the fallen SEALs. Erika remembered a nation in mourning, the president standing by the First Lady, who sat next to an expectant mother. Erika had remained in the back, next to Palenski. MacClaine had not been able to make it back from Hong Kong in time, and by the time he'd reached Washington, Erika had already left for California.

Perhaps it wasn't meant to be.

But it had certainly been the experience of a lifetime. A semiconductor recall of unprecedented proportions had followed the delivery of the list from Japan. Many corporations, from auto manufacturers to construction firms, had been down for weeks as their systems were updated with fixed versions of the semiconductors. The same had happened at many locations around the world. High-tech companies across the country had put in a courageous effort to bring the country back on-line, working around the clock to manufacture replacement ICs for shipment to hundreds of thousands of field sites in need of upgrades. But the crisis soon passed. Systems came back on-line and America once more grew confident of its high-tech industry, as reflected by their rising stocks. The accidental spread of Detroit II had caused minimal damage overseas. An import-export company in New Zealand lost some accounts, as well as a financial firm in Ireland. Ironically, the worst collateral damage had occurred in the United States, where an offspring of the Detroit II virus released in Osaka had attacked the offices of the Internal Revenue Service in Austin, Texas. Overnight, the federal agency had lost the ability to pursue many audits across several states, resulting in the loss of millions of potential dollars in unpaid taxes. Two words always came to mind whenever she thought of the IRS fiasco: poetic justice.

Erika pressed her lips together. In the end she had done the right thing. She had helped her nation during its time of need, and in the process she had also helped herself and her family's business. The president had certainly exceeded her expectations. The financial compensation more than made up for her years in Washington and her dangerous journey to find the list.

Her eyes gravitated to a lonely vehicle cruising up the winding road snaking its way up from the Sonoma Valley. She followed the dark sedan as it cruised by the bend in the gravel road leading up to the ranch, a cloud of dust trailing it.

Erika checked her watch. The first tour didn't start for another hour.

The sedan drove up to the side of the winery, parking in the recently finished lot by the side of the processing building. A well-built man in a business suit got out and did a three-sixty, inspecting the area. Her father and brother in the vineyards looked toward him and then to Erika, who raised her hand. "I got it!" she shouted.

As they returned to their work, Erika walked down the

steps from the front porch and approached the stranger. "May I help you?"

The man turned around. "Hi, stranger."

She was momentarily at a loss for words. Then she said, "Brent?"

He smiled. He looked as though he had lost—

"Thirty pounds," he said. "Jog every morning and bicycle every evening."

She smiled. They hugged. His arms felt good wrapped around her. She ran a hand through his hair and took a deep breath.

"You look great," she said, regarding him with affection.

"And so do you. How have you been?"

"Fine. But—but, what happened to you? I never heard from you again. I tried calling the Bureau but they could never connect me to you. Did you get my messages?"

"Every one of them."

"And why didn't you call me back?"

"Because," he said, rubbing his chin while looking away. The lost pounds had thinned his once-sagging face, making him look younger and ruggedly handsome. "Bureau rules while on a mission. Remember?"

She nodded. "Barely. It all seems like some kind of distant dream now."

"I wanted to see you again," he said, caressing her cheek with a finger.

"What brings you to this part of the world? I thought you were now a big shot in Washington."

He frowned. "I'm not sure about a big shot, but I am in Washington."

She gazed into his brown eyes. "Still trying to save the world?"

He nodded. "I still feel I'm making a difference."

"What about *your* life, Brent?" *And what about us?*

He took her hands in his. "I'm in the middle of a very important international case, probably the biggest of my career. I came by to see you and also to say good-bye for a little while. I'll be living in Taiwan for the next year.

We're getting close to cracking a cyberterrorist ring that's costing the region billions in damages every year. Pretty big incentive to eliminate it. When that case is over I've been thinking about leaving, maybe find me some nice country girl and settle down."

She slowly shook her head and smiled. "You won't, Brent. You can't. It's in your blood."

He shook his head. "I don't plan to do this forever, Erika."

She sighed. "When will I see you again?"

He smiled, reaching into his coat pocket and handing her an envelope. It contained a round-trip ticket to Taiwan.

"I hear Taipei is lovely in the fall. Perhaps I'll see you in a couple of months?"

She smiled and hugged him. "Perhaps," she replied.

"I have to go now," he said, checking his watch. "Nobody knows I drove up here."

Brent kissed her, hugging her tight. Erika didn't resist, surrendering herself to his touch, his embrace.

Then he winked. "See you in a little while."

The taste of him still on her lips, Erika Conklin watched him leave, until all that remained of his brief visit was a thinning cloud of dust curling up in the northern California skies.